THE RED
BRANCH TALES

BOOKS BY RANDY LEE EICKHOFF

THE ULSTER CYCLE
The Raid
The Feast
The Sorrows
The Destruction of the Inn
He Stands Alone
The Red Branch Tales

The Odyssey: A Modern Translation of Homer's Classic Tale

NOVELS
The Fourth Horseman
Bowie (with Leonard C. Lewis)
A Hand to Execute
The Gombeen Man
Fallon's Wake
Return to Ithaca
Then Came Christmas

NONFICTION
Exiled

THE RED BRANCH TALES

Randy Lee Eickhoff

A TOM DOHERTY ASSOCIATES BOOK

NEW YORK

THE RED BRANCH TALES

Copyright © 2003 by Randy Lee Eickhoff

This book is printed on acid-free paper.

A Forge Book
Published by Tom Doherty Associates, LLC
175 Fifth Avenue
New York, NY 10010

www.tor.com

Forge® is a registered trademark of Tom Doherty Associates, LLC.

ISBN 0-312-87019-1

First Edition: March 2003

Printed in the United States of America

0 9 8 7 6 5 4 3 2 1

For Dianne

Acknowledgments

I would like to thank Trinity College Library, Dublin, for allowing me access to the Ancient Manuscripts Department and Early Published Books Department.

Contents

Introduction

Four books—*The Book of Leinster, The Yellow Book of Lecan, The Book of the Dun Cow,* and *The Book of Invasions*—remain that provide an account of Ancient Irish literature, although a broad explication certainly exists with Seamus Deane's *Field Day Anthology*, which consists of samples from various Irish periods. Very little, however, explores the large corpus of the Ulster Cycle, sometimes called the Red Branch Cycle, which was primarily responsible for establishing the cultural identity of today's Ireland.

The last attempt at analyzing the Ulster Cycle was by Rudolf Thurneysen in his *Die irische Helden- und Königsage* (Halle, 1921). This work established certain critical parameters, but in it the stories themselves were sketchy and, in some cases, incomplete. T. F. O'Rahilly examined critically many of the sagas in his *Early Irish History and Mythology* (Dublin, 1946), and his scholarship helped to bring a sense of order to the sprawling mythology. Yet he still did little to examine and explain the Ulster Cycle.

Part of the problem with the Ulster Cycle is in the linguistics and language. Ancient Irish is far more complicated than Middle Irish, which, in turn, is far more complicated than Modern Irish. A rough comparison for the English-speaking reader would be the evolution from Anglo-Saxon to Modern English. Yet even with that comparison the knotty problems faced by translators of Ancient Irish are scarcely revealed. Language is not a pure or static entity, since it reflects and is shaped by the ever-changing customs and religious beliefs of a society. Much of what is commonplace disappears as a society evolves, and what is taken for general knowledge at the time becomes an obscurity three or four hundred years later.

Problems exist as well with double entendres, regional humor, superstitions, and the complexities of myth and religion. Spelling can be irritating because what has become static in modern language was a hodgepodge affair centuries before. Indeed, some words even alter definitions through time. This alteration is very apparent in the Irish language.

Perhaps the hardest task in trying to preserve a culture is piecing together what has been lost. The Ulster Cycle is a prime example of this difficulty, since many of the stories that once existed in an oral tradition were lost or fragmented in transcription. Unfortunately, we cannot even be certain if any single story is the "correct" version, because a scribe may have "corrupted" a text either accidentally or deliberately. The ancient bards also created a problem when they transmitted many of the stories orally to students in a type of shorthand that provided an outline of the story with instruction on how the "tale-teller" might embellish to accommodate the necessity of the moment.

Three manuscripts are of special interest to today's scholar, although they are by no means the sole sources of the stories that constitute the Ulster Cycle. *The Book of the Dun Cow (Lebor Na hUidre)*, written before 1106 and now in the Royal Irish Academy in Dublin, contains many of the heroic sagas. *The Book of Leinster (Lebor Laigan)*, written before 1160, contains history, genealogy, saga, and poetry; it is now in Trinity College Library, Dublin. Rawlinson B 502 contains twelve leaves, written in the eleventh century, in which the *Annals of Tigernach* are recorded and seventy leaves written in the twelfth century that are concerned with historical matter, law tracts, the *Dinnshenchas,* and *Saltair na Rann.* Rawlinson B is in the Bodleian Library at Oxford, England.

These are not the only materials, however. Four vellums written in the late fourteenth or early fifteenth century in the west of Ireland are *The Yellow Book of Lecan, The Great Book of Lecan, The Book of Hy Many,* and *The Book of Ballynote. The Yellow Book of Lecan* is especially important because it contains the earliest extant copy of *Táin Bó Cuailngé—The Cattle-Raid of Cooley*—which is not only the central saga of the Ulster Cycle but the story that defines the cultural identity of today's Ireland. *The Yellow Book of Lecan* may be found in Trinity Library, while the other three are in the Royal Irish Academy.

It is surprising that not all of the ancient stories have been translated, and for many of those that have been translated there exist one or two versions only. Some, as well, were altered by translators to fit the social conventions of their day. Lady Gregory freely admitted in a letter to a friend that she deliberately altered her story of Cúchulainn to "avoid offending the sensibilities" of her readers. This translation, however, follows as closely as possible the original.

Ancient Irish stories are categorized as Destructions, Cattle-raids, Courtships, Battles, Cave Stories, Voyages, Tragedies, Adventures, Banquets, Sieges, Plunderings, Elopements, Eruptions, Visions, Love Stories, Hastings, and Invasions. Most of the stories in the Ulster Cycle concern heroes of the Ulaid, a people in northeastern Ireland. They were led by their king Conchobor, whose main residence was at Emain Macha, near modern-day Armagh. Yet the stories also concern people from Connacht, led by Maeve and Ailill, who were the traditional enemies of the

Ulaid. The daughter of Maeve and Ailill is Findabair or Guenivere. Most of the stories are written in a combination of prose and poetry. Narration is usually in prose, while mood and atmosphere are established primarily through poetry. Magic is still a necessary ingredient, and the gods are fond of dabbling in the affairs of men.

The stories are extremely important because they provide the only glimpse we have into that ancient culture. They reflect the customs of that pre-Christian era when warriors fought from chariots, took heads as trophies and, to assume the power of their enemies, were heavily influenced by the Druids, who provided them with mystical answers about the universe and believed strongly in magic. Many mythological elements in the stories suggest the influence of nature. For example, the alphabet (Oghams) is an eclectic mix of trees, birds, and other natural phenomena.

Strangely enough, although these tales have slipped away from scholastic use, other stories that have borrowed elements from the Irish stories still are in common use. For example, *Fled Bricrend (Bricriu's Feast)* is seldom regarded by scholars today, but its principal element, a beheading game, became the major element of *Sir Gawain and the Green Knight*.

Thomas Cahill has demonstrated how the Irish influence on world literature was accomplished in his work *How the Irish Saved Civilization* with the suggestion that Ireland was a repository of knowledge and literature during the oft-referred to "Dark Ages." We know, for example, that the monk Columcille was responsible for an armed outbreak for refusing to return a book he had borrowed.

Columcille was a prince of the Clan O'Donnell, a great-great-grandson of Niall of the Nine Hostages. He studied under St. Finnian at the monastery of Moville. From there, he went to Leinster to study under the bard Gemman before entering the monastery of Clonard.

The events in the story of what happened to cause Columcille to migrate to Scotland are murky. Bede simply reports, "Venit de Hibernia . . . praedicaturus verbum Dei," while Adarman says, "Pro Christo perigrinar: volens enavigavit." The romantic version, however, maintains that he talked Clan Neill into rising up against King Diarmait at Cooldrevny in A.D. 561, citing the following reasons: (1) the king's violation of sanctuary when Columcille sought it on the occasion of the murder of Prince Curnan, a relative of Columcille; and (2) Diarmait's judgment against Columcille for secretly making a copy of St. Finnian's psalter.

Columcille confessed his involvement in the subsequent battle when Diarmait was defeated after losing three thousand men, and St. Molaise, Columcille's confessor, ordered Columcille to leave Ireland and preach the Gospel to as many individuals as had been killed.

Columcille was forty-four when he sailed from Ireland in a *currach* made of wicker and covered with hides. He landed at Iona, where he founded a monastery and a community of holy men and scholars. He spent the next thirty years preaching to the inhabitants of Northern Scotland. According to legend, he never spent an hour without study, prayer, and contemplation. He allegedly wrote three hundred books. From Northern Scotland, his scholarship spread south, across the English Channel, and into Europe.

Although we cannot credit Columcille for single-handedly educating the known world, he did influence the Irish monks to become passionate scribes not only of the scriptures but of other classical texts that might have been lost after the fall of the Roman Empire. It does not require a large leap of the imagination to see how stories and the elements of stories were carried from Ireland to the rest of the world.

For those wishing a more complete reference to Early Irish

literature, I heartily recommend *Studies in Irish Literature and History* by James Carney (Dublin, 1979) and *Early Irish Literature* by Myles Dillon (Chicago, 1948).

The language of these tales varies considerably, and the meanings of some terms are subjects of scholastic debate. Some of the tales go back to A.D. 8, but we have very few of these manuscripts because the coast of Ireland was raided constantly at this time by the Vikings. Very few of the manuscripts predating the year 1000 have survived. Those that have are generally fragmented and corrupt, thanks to a few zealous interpolators over the years. Among the missing is *The Book of Druimm Snechtai,* which contained several stories that might have allowed historians, linguists, and translators an opportunity to correct some of the glaring errors in existing works.

What remains, however, provides a rich look into a culture that remained uncorrupted for years until priests found their way to the island and managed to change the Irish civilization into a Christian civilization that created social victims in a society that had been governed fairly by the Brehon Laws for hundreds of years. In the following stories, I have tried to give readers a taste of the ancient world and leave judgment to them.

Author's Note

The reader will discover discrepancies, in some instances, in the spelling of names from tale to tale. I would like to remind the reader that these stories were not the work of a single individual but have been gleaned from a variety of sources. In addition, I would like to remind the reader once again that an ideogrammatic approach was used by the ancient writers to spell words, including most proper nouns. Old Irish does not, for example, have a letter *v* in its vocabulary, and as a result Maeve appears as Medb, Mab, Meadbh, Medbh, and in a variety of other ways in these stories. Perhaps I should have selected one spelling and stayed with it throughout all the tales. I thought about that, then discarded it, as I wished the reader to be thoroughly aware of the disparate spellings that very from tale to tale. There are, in some instances, many variants, and we cannot be certain if two separate characters share a similar name. Ideally, this would not exist, but we are dealing with an ancient world here, and we must also take into consideration those dialectical differences that must have existed from province to province. I have tried to indicate those places where I think there is a distinct possibility that two different characters might share similar sounding names. But a translator, working in a nearly forgotten language where no definitive dictionary exists, must rely on connotation as well as on definition, and it is impossible to be absolutely certain in some instances. For this, I beg the reader's indulgence.

The Beginning of Emain Macha

This tale is found in *The Book of Leinster* (c. 1160) and is only one of the stories that explain how the Red Branch was established. Another version of the naming of Emain Macha is related in *The Pangs of Ulster.*

ONCE THREE KINGS, ALL FROM Ulster, ruled equally over Ireland. They were Díthorba, the son of Diman from Uisnech in Meath; Áed Ruad, the son of Bádurn, son of Argatmar, from Tír Áedha; and Cimbáeth, son of Fintan, son of Argatmar, from Finnabair on the Plain of Inis.

Now these three decided that it would be better by far if they took turns ruling over Ireland, and so they made arrangements by which each would rule for seven years before giving way to the other two. They had twenty-one rules written to ensure that each king would hand over the right to rule at the end of his seven years. This would, they thought, be good enough to ensure that each king's reign would be free from interference by the other two kings. As a result, each year there would be a great harvest of fruit and every color dyed into garments would hold fast and true and not fade or shade, and no woman would die again in childbearing.

These rules were hard-held and strict with accounting. First, seven Druids would be made available to chant those spells that would sear the flesh of the false one. Second, seven poets would sing satirical songs shaming the scandalous one. Then seven champions would be named to inflict harsh wounds upon the flesh of the arrogant one who failed in his promised obligations.

But the rules did not need to be enacted, for each of the three kings ruled wisely and carefully attended to the pact that had been drawn up among them. Each of them ruled three times as king for a total of sixty-three years.

One day Áed Ruad rode out along the place called Eas Ruaid,[1] guiding his dappled horse carefully in the swift waters. But a fish jumped after a mayfly and startled the dappled horse, who reared and unseated his rider, pitching him into the swift current, where he drowned. For three days the others searched for his body and, when they found it, they buried him at Sídhe Ruaid, the Mound of the Red Man. He left one child as heir, a daughter named Macha Mong-Ruad,[2] who demanded that her father's rightful place in the succession of rule be granted to her. But the other two kings, Cimbáeth and Díthorba, refused to surrender her father's seventh to her as she was a woman.[3]

Furious at her treatment, Macha brought together a huge army and destroyed the forces of the other two in battle but took only what she regarded as her seventh. She ruled for seven years as Ireland's queen before the death of Díthorba, who fell in battle at the Corann.[4] Five stalwart sons stood staunchly at his burial, and then in turn each—Báeth, Bras, Betach, Úallach, and Borbchas—demanded that Macha defer to the accord authored by their father and the other two. But Macha refused and said, "Why should I surrender what I won on the field of battle? The pact drawn between your father and mine and Cimbáeth no longer applies, for none of you would listen to reason when it was offered."

Incensed, the five sons raised an army and came to unseat Macha from her throne, but the terrible rage of Macha rose up, and she led her army into battle. Oh, the wanton slaughter that rose to feed the ravens that day! Many heads were taken by Macha's blade, and the rest of the army fled in terror into the wilds of Connacht.

But Macha was weary with war after this, and she married Cimbáeth (and a wise choice he made to keep his own head!) and merged his army into hers to regain the strength that she had lost during the last war with the five sons. Then, knowing full well that the five sons stubbornly refused to agree to her might, she cleverly disguised herself as a leper by rubbing herself with rye dough and red dye until it seemed suppurating sores leaked yellow pus from her skin.

She entered the wild forests of Connacht and soon found them in Bairinn, where they were roasting a wild boar slain by Bras over a red fire.

"What's this?" Báeth said, when Macha came up to them, whining about her hunger and begging for a morsel from the roasting pig. "What foulness do we find here?"

"Please," she whimpered, holding forth a hand that seemed more a claw than one with flesh and fingers. "Just a bite or two for a poor old hag."[5]

"Well, now," said Betach. "Let's let the old gal have a bite or two if she has any news about that bitch Macha."

"Don't encourage her," grumbled Borbchas.

"You'd begrudge her a mouthful or two from that big carcass?" Báeth asked, pointing at the pig roasting on the spit over the crackling fire made from beech trees. "Even with your gut we won't eat the whole thing."

So they all sat down and listened to the stories Macha made up on the spot as she ate the sliver of roasted meat the five sons gave to her for news of herself.

Then Bras brought out a skin of mead and they took to swilling it from their own cups, and soon they began to see Macha in a different light. It was Báeth who first noticed her eyes and, squinting his own against the smoke and drink befuddling him at the time, said, "You know, this hag has won—won—beaut—pretty eyes." He pursed his lips, sucking in his cheeks as he contemplated her. "What say we fuck her?"[6]

"Ah, don't be that way here," Borbchas said. "We don't need to be watching your shortcomings."

"And I don't want to be shaming you," Báeth said, rising. He grabbed her and took her off into the woods to the roaring laughter of his brothers.

"Now then," he said, placing her on her feet. "Let's see what you have, old girl."

He reached for the neckline of her dress, but when he pulled it free, he saw Macha's young breasts and frowned, shaking his head against his fuddled vision.

"What—" he began, but then squawked as Macha overpowered him and tied him to a tree with strips of cloth torn from his own clothes. She gagged him to keep him from yelling a warning to his brothers, then made her way back to the fire, pretending to be weary from lovemaking.

"Where is our brother?" the others asked when she stumbled out of the woods and stood warming herself next to the fire.

"Ah, the drink left him and then the shame came upon him after he saw that he had slept with a leper," she said.

The others roared with laughter at this, and Bras leaped to

his feet, seizing her and throwing her over his shoulder. "Well, lass, there's no shame in that. We decided that each of us was going to give you a tickle or two when we heard Báeth bawling with pleasure. There must be a knowing way in those legs of yours when you lock them around the waist of a man."

And so it was that each of them took her into the dark of the wood away from the fire and each found himself tied with strips of his own clothing. Then Macha tied them together and marched them meekly to Ulster, where she brought them to the judgment of her warriors.

"Ah, let's kill them and be done with it," growled one. He jabbed a dirty finger at the rafters, where the heads of others lined the beams.

"No," Macha said. "I don't think that would be wise. My rule would become suspect if I let that happen. Instead, let us make them slaves and have them build a mighty fortress around me that will become the Great Hall of the new ruling city of Ulster forever."

And with that, she took a golden brooch out of her cloak and marked out the lines the buildings were to follow in what came to be known as Emain Macha.[7]

The Pangs
of the Ulaid

This story was apparently sung to give meaning to the time when Maeve elects to invade Ulster and Cúchulainn is forced to stand alone before her mighty armies. It is the second of two stories intended to provide the origin of Emain Macha. *Noinden Ulad* is similar to other tales that appear in the *Dinnsenchas* to give imaginative reasons for the merging of the Otherworld with this world in a story about love between a fairy creature and a mortal.

IN THE WILDERNESS ON THE heights of mountains[1] lived one Crunniuc Mac Agnoan, whose wealth was numbered in the cows he kept upon the mountain meadows. His four sons lived with him for a time, but his wife had died, and a man without a wife is a lonely man indeed. So it was with Crunniuc, who spent each evening alone on his couch, staring at the sun as it set on another lonely day.

One day while he lay alone on his couch, staring through

the open door at the sun setting redly in the west, he chanced to see a beautiful woman, richly garbed, coming toward him. Without saying a word, she entered the house and cooked for him, kneading bread and milking the cow herself, and cleaned for him, and ordered the servants to their tasks. She took a seat next to Crunniuc at the table. When evening came, she was the last to leave her couch and smoor the fire. Then she turned right[2] and laid herself down beside him, placing her hand upon his thigh.

For a long time, she stayed with Crunniuc, who was dizzy with his good fortune, which continued to increase with the woman's presence in his house. But she was happy as well with the choice she had made, for Crunniuc was a handsome man with silver and black hair that curled gently at the nape of his neck and a fine wide forehead above blue eyes that sparkled like gems in the sunlight.

Now it was known that the men of Ulster held great feasts and festivals, and all the men and women worked hard to attend these. So it was that Crunniuc, pleased with his success and the beauty of his new wife, thought they should attend the assembly. Yet, for some strange reason, his wife was reluctant to go.

One day Crunniuc, perplexed by her evasion of his questions, said, "Listen, now. There's a good time to be had at this festival. Everyone will be there, and I want us to go and have a good time as well."

His wife sat still by the fire, staring into the coals, then shook her head and said, "This would not be a good thing."

"But why?" he asked.

For a moment, he thought she would not answer him, but then she sighed and said, "If we go, 'tis certain that you will speak about me in the gathering. That would bring an end to our life together, for we cannot stay together if you tell others about us."

THE RED BRANCH TALES 25

"I won't say a word," Crunniuc promised, sensing her wavering.

"I don't know," she said doubtfully.

But Crunniuc wheedled and begged, and reluctantly she gave in to his whim. So it came that Crunniuc, dressed in his best garb, made his way with his silent and apprehensive new wife to the great fair being held at the king's land. When they arrived, Crunniuc was immediately taken with the great splashes of color in the costumes that seemed richly to express the stations of all who were there. And there were games aplenty to challenge the men and gatherings for the women, who shared new secrets of sewing and spinning and ways to cook pork. Eventually, Crunniuc relaxed as the honey-rich mead found its way down his throat with increasing regularity. Even his wife relaxed somewhat as she engaged the other wives in talk and gossip.

In the ninth hour of the fair, the royal chariot was brought forth and challenges were made and races held around the fort. But the king's horses, a pair of matched black whose hooves struck sparks from the ground, could not be beaten by any there. The people were ecstatic about this, for as the king triumphs, so does the land, and the bards made ready to praise the king,[3] and the poets and Druids of his household cried, "Never have such swift horses been seen as these! In all of Erin there can be none to stand against them!"

"Stuff and nonsense," said Crunniuc thickly (for he had been sampling greatly the rich mead). He looked around blearily, eyeing the rippling muscles of the great blacks. He shook his head. "Pips and pipes, I say!"

A poet nearby heard Crunniuc's loud declaration and said loftily, "I suppose a man like you would have horses that are their match?"

Crunniuc belched and wiped his mouth and said, "Horses? Aye, I have horses! But I wouldn't dust their hooves in such a race. My wife can run as fast as those blacks. Take note!"

The poet eyed Crunniuc with displeasure. "I will do that," he said. Crunniuc nodded and glanced at the cup in his hand and, seeing that it was empty, lurched away to find more mead. "I'll certainly take note of that," the poet muttered and took himself away to the king, where he related the drunken ramblings of Crunniuc.

"He said that?" the king asked, annoyed.

"He did," the poet said.

"Bring the braggart to me," the king demanded. "Then find his wife and bring her forth so we can end this tongue wagging before it gets out."

Guards were immediately dispatched to find Crunniuc, who wasn't hard to discover beside the mead keg. He protested the rough treatment of the guards, who unceremoniously bundled him up to the king, but his protest was more for the spilled mead left soaking into the ground than for the hands the guards laid upon him.

His wife now was found in the company of other women, where she was learning a new way of embossing red thread through white. She looked up at the messengers waiting respectfully before her. "Yes?" she said pleasantly. "Is there something I can do for you?"

The messenger hemmed and hawed and shuffled his feet across the greensward and finally blurted out, "We have come to bring you before the king to answer for your husband's words."

"My husband? What words?" she asked, her gray eyes narrowing suspiciously.

"He claims your foot is faster than the hooves of the king's horses," he said. "Now he's the prisoner of the king."

She shook her head sadly. "Ah, but my husband chose his words badly. As you can see, I am about to be delivered of a child." And she stood so all there could see her round belly beneath her gown. "It would be foolish to expect me to run a race in such a condition."

The messenger started to dig a dirty finger into his nose, then thought better of it and shook his head. "That may be, lady, but you still must come before the king and give him the word."

Shaking her head sadly, Crunniuc's wife followed the messenger to where the king waited impatiently.

"There you are!" he said rudely. He waved a hand at Crunniuc, standing sheepishly at the side, swaying slightly from the drink taken. "This—this—'man' claims that you are faster than my blacks, which have withstood all challenges today. Is there truth to his words?"

Word had spread throughout the crowd of Crunniuc's rash boast, and now many crowded around to see the manner of woman that had brought the insulting words forth.

"This is not right," she said, annoyed at the gaping japes around her. "No woman should be subjected to such ridicule while she is in this condition. I am near my time."

The king glanced at her swollen belly and shrugged. "Nevertheless, your man has made the boast, and I cannot have doubt lingering over my horses. You see how it is," he said, spreading his royal hands in dismissal. "You'll have to run the race."

She pulled her shoulders back and gazed sternly at him, but his eyes did not flinch. Then she turned to all surrounding them and said, "I am close to my time. Help me, here. Please. In the name of the mothers who bore each of you!"

But cruel laughter met her words, and then the king said to his guards, "Enough. Take your swords and strike that man's head from his shoulders for the insult he has given me!"

Obediently, the men turned away, drawing their swords, but she cried out, "Shame upon all here who have ignored my plea. I curse all here for failing to help a woman in her distress." She spat upon the ground, and the crowd murmured uneasily. "Very well. I'll run your race. But this is only the beginning of the bad times you have drawn upon your people."

"What is your name?" the king asked.

"My name and the names of my children shall cling to this ground forever. I am Macha, the daughter of Sainrith Mac Imbath,[4] and whatever happens this day shall be on your heads forever! Bring up your chariot, great king!"

Flushing at the mockery she made of him, the king ordered his chariot and the great blacks to be brought forth. At the signal, the driver slapped the reins smartly across the backs of the horses, and they leaped forward, but they were not faster than the woman whose white feet seemed barely to touch the grass as she ran away from the horses. Strain as they would, those mighty steeds could not close the gap upon the fleeing woman, and she easily crossed the finish line ahead of them, only to collapse in great pain as her water broke.

She gave a great scream and was immediately delivered of twins, a son and a daughter, and to this day that place is called Emain Macha, "Twins of Macha," in their honor.

But all men who heard that terrible scream suddenly felt a weakness in their bellies as the woman raised herself up on her elbows and glared around the assembly. "From this hour forth, all here down through the ninth generation of the ninth generation, all men will suffer as I have suffered for five days and four nights whenever a great need of your warrior skills comes. In the time of greatest emergency, you shall be helpless in this land that will never know peace."

And so it was from the days of Crunniuc to the days of Fergus Mac Donnell or until the time of Forc Mac Dallan Mac Mainech Mac Lugaid. Only three classes of people escaped the curse: women, children, and the great champion Cúchulainn, because he was not descended from Ulster. None also who lived beyond the borders of Ulster met with that debility.

And this is the cause of *Noinden Ulad*.

Finit.

The Capture of
the Fairy Hill

De Gabáil in t-Sídhe is one of the first of the tales leading up to
the *Táin Bó Cuailngé (The Cattle-Raid of Cooley)*. As far as I can
tell, only two manuscripts have a version of this tale, one in MS.
D.4.2 in the Royal Irish Academy and the other in *The Book of
Leinster,* from roughly the middle of the twelfth century. This
translation was taken from *The Book of Leinster.*

ONCE A FAMOUS KING RULED over the *Tuatha Dé Danann*
in Erin and his name was The Dagda. His power was great
even though it belonged to the Mac Míled after they had conquered the country. The *Tuatha* had led raids against their
crops, destroying the corn and souring the milk from the Mac
Míled cows until the Mac Míled sought a truce from The
Dagda. After that, he lifted the curse that had been placed upon
the corn and milk.

Now, at first, his strength was great, and he gave out the

command of various fairy mounds to men of the *Tuatha*. Lug Mac Ethnend received Sídhe Rodrubán, Ogma received Sídhe Aircelltrai, but The Dagda held back four fairy mounds: Sídhe Leithet Lachtmaige, Oí Asídhe, Cnocc Báine, and Brú Ruair. These he had decided to keep for himself. But, then, he had had Sídhe In Broga as well from the very beginning.

Then Mac Oac came to The Dagda and petitioned for land as he had received none when it was distributed. He was a fosterling to Midir of Bri Léith and to Nindid the Seer.

"Sorry, but I don't have any left for you," The Dagda said. "I have already apportioned that out which I do not mean to keep for myself."

"Well," Mac Oac said, scratching his head, "at least let me be given a day and a night in your own house."

This The Dagda granted. And after a day and a night was up, The Dagda said, "It is time for you to leave since the time I have given you has passed."

"Unfortunately," said Mac Oac, "you fail to understand that a day and a night make up the time of the world and that is what you have given to me."

Disgruntled, The Dagda nevertheless had to admit that Mac Oac had outsmarted him and left and Mac Oac remained in the Sídhe.

That was the most wonderful of all the land given, for three trees are always with fruit there and a pig always alive and a roasted swine and a vat filled with mead and never does the fruitfulness of that fairy mound cease.

The Story of
Baili Binnbérlaig

Scél Baili Binnbérlaig is to be found in H.3.18, p. 47, and in the
British Museum MS. Harl. 5280, fol. 48a. Irish poetry shares the
use of kennings—a language game—with that of Iceland, to a
degree. These are similar to those used by Cúchulainn and Emer
on their first meeting in *Tochmarc Emire* so that their conversation would not be understood by Emer's friends, who were standing nearby. A regular training in the use of such expressions
formed part of the curriculum of the aspiring *fili* or bard, and
these various modes were found under the name *bérla na filed*
(the language or dialect of the poets). The young *fili*, at the time
called *anroth*, was required to master these in the sixth year of
his apprenticeship. The story begins in fragments that are a bit
confusing to the reader. I believe these were names so well-
known at the time that the speaker would work their definitions
automatically into his narration.

Baile, the Sweetspoken, Mac Buan. Now Caba Mac Cing Mac Ross Mac Rugraide had three grandsons: Monach and Buan and Fercorb, but Buan's only son was Baile. He was the special love of Aillinn, the daughter of Lugaid Mac Fergus of the sea or of the daughter of Eogan Mac Dathi, and he was the special love of all who saw him or heard about him. Both men and women were enamored of him when they heard the tales about him. He and Aillinn fell in love and agreed to meet secretly at Ross Na Ríg at the house of Maelduib on the brink of the river Boyne in Breg.

Baile came from the north to meet her, from Emain Macha, across Sliab Fuaid, over Murthemne to Tráig Baili. There they unyoked their chariots and set the horses to graze in the pasture. Then they settled in to much merrymaking.

As they were enjoying themselves, suddenly they saw a horrible figure coming toward them from the south. His approach seemed harsh, yet he sped over the earth like a darting hawk from a cliff or the wind from the green sea. He kept his left side toward the land.

"Quickly!" said Baile. "Ask him where he goes and from where he has come and why he is in such a hurry!"

"To Tuaig-Inber," the man said harshly. "I am going back north now from Mount Leinster, and I have no news to tell you but that the daughter of Lugaid Mac Fergus has given her love to Baile Mac Buan and was going to meet him when the Leinster warriors overtook her and slew her. Such is as it should be, though; the Druids and prophets predicted that they would never meet in their lives but would come together after death and then never part." He shrugged. "Well, 'tisn't much I can say but warm arms are not snuggly in that case. But that is my news and enough of it to have for you, I'm thinking."

With that, he hastened away and would not stop although they tried to ask him to explain himself further.

When Baile heard that, his heart burst within him, and he fell dead on the spot. They raised his tomb over him and set his headstone there. Then the warriors of Ulster held their funeral games to celebrate the life that had been his. A yew grew up through his grave, and on top of it one could see the form and shape of Baile's head. That is why it is called Tráig Baili today.

Then the same man went south to where the maiden Aillinn waited and entered the leafy house where she waited patiently for her lover to come. When she saw the man hurrying toward her, she said, "Where are you going and from where have you come?"

"From the north of Erin, from Tuaig-Inber, and past this place to Leinster," the man replied irritably.

"I see," the maiden said, then eagerly asked, "Do you have any news?"

The man shook his head impatiently. "None that would please you. By the side of Tráig Baili, I saw the Ulster men playing at funeral games and digging a tomb and placing a stone upon it. Written on the stone was the name of Baile Mac Buan, the royal heir of Ulster, who was apparently getting ready to meet his love but"—he shrugged—"it was not their fate to meet while alive, only after death."

With that he sped away, chuckling with glee to himself over his evil tale while Aillinn fell dead and her grave was readied over her. An apple tree grew through her grave and at the end of the seventh year became a very large tree, and one who looked closely at it could see the shape of her head on its top.

At the end of seven years, the princes and prophets cut down the yew over the grave of Baile and made a poet's board out of it. The visions of loves and feasts are written upon it. In

Leinster, the same was made of the apple tree out of Ailinn's grave.

Then came All-Hallows, and Cormac Mac Art made a great feast as was the custom then, and the poets brought their boards with them to the feast. When Cormac saw them, he asked to hold them, and they were brought to him and placed in his hands. Much to the astonishment of all, the two boards leaped together with a thunderous clap and twined together as the woodbine runs over the branch, and it was impossible to part them again.

They were kept and treasured greatly at Tara until Dunlang Mac Enna burnt them when he slew the maidens. It is because of this the poet said:

> "Great was the love of Ailinn
> For Baile that not even the din
> Of war could stem nor could
> The making of them from wood."

And to this answered Cormaic ui Quinn:

> "It is from Aluime that
> We find Traig Baile but
> This cannot be the way
> For love to grow by day."

And was answered by Fland Mac Lonain:

> "It is the way of Cormac that we found
> The secret of their love that is sound
> To all here and we must forget
> What happened to Ailinn and Baile that
>
> It will not happen anymore
> Here upon this sandy shore.

We can see how the yew tree
Has found its mate in the apple tree."

And Cormac said:

[text missing]

The Birth of Conchobor the King

The story of Conchobor is incredibly complex. At times, we see him as a cruel and unjust king who is ruled by his passions, as when he tries to force Deirdre to marry him, only to be ultimately responsible for the deaths of her husband, Naisi, and his two brothers and the splitting apart of the Red Branch when some, led by Fergus Mac Róich, leave after burning down the Great Hall because they cannot follow a leader without honor. Yet he is generally regarded by history as a brave warrior and a just ruler, and it is, indeed, history that records Conchobor as having been born on the same day as Christ and dying in a rage after hearing the details of Christ's death. The story of Conchobor's birth exists in two versions, the oldest having been composed in the early eighth century. This story claims that Conchobor was the son of Nessa, a princess of Ulster, and Cathbad, the Druid of the Ulster court.

Now some say Conchobor Mac Nessa was the son of Cathbad the Druid, while others claim his father was Fachtna Fathach, the king of Ulster. And well he might have been, for stranger tales are told of the birth of heroes and wise men. Conchobor was a wise and great king and, if the truth be told, why shouldn't he have been so? He was born in the same hour as the birth of Christ in Palestine. For seven years, the prophets and Druids had been reading the signs, and all were in agreement that when Christ was born a notable chief, a great warrior-leader, would be born in Erin. And on the night that he slipped into this world, Cathbad chanted a prophecy to his wife, Nessa:

> "Ah, Nessa! Great danger lies ahead for you!
> Now, let all rise to their feet at the moment you
> Give birth! Bold beautiful is your hand color,
> Eochaid Yellowheel's daughter!
> But do not wail senseless tears, my wife,
> For your son will lead many in his life,
> And the whole world will know his deeds
> By the type of life he continues to lead.
> At the same hour when the great king
> Of the world is born, so you will bring
> Your son into the world and all will
> Praise him even to Doomsday. Still
> Heroes will not defy him and never
> Will he be a hostage taken. Never!
> Not him nor Christ the King
> Who will bear death's sting
> Together yet apart many land miles
> And sea miles. So linger awhile,
> My wife, and on Inis's plain bear

Him proudly beneath the stars
Upon the gray flagstone in the meadow.
Glorious will be his story even in shadowed
Fear, for he will be the king of grace
And the Hound of Ulster for a space
Of time and many kings will pledge
Themselves to him until his pledge
Is broken and then great will be
His fall and the world will see
His disgrace and curse the same.
Conchobor will be the name
By which he will be called.
And I tell you that this is all foretold
By the stars, and I know his
Weapons will be red and his
Courage never failing. Great routs
Will be fought by him. No doubt
About that. He will find his death
When he avenges the great death
Of the suffering God. He will hew
A great path over the slanting plain
Of Laim with his sword unstained."

Strange, though, Conchobor did not bear his father's name
but was called Mac Nessa after his mother. Her name had once
been Assa, the gentle one, and she was the daughter of Eochaid
Yellowheel, the king of Ulster, who demanded that she be
taught by twelve tutors, to whom she would always be docile
and ready to learn her lessons well.

But one night all her tutors were slaughtered by Cathbad
the Druid, who came from the south of Ulster with twenty-
seven men on a great raid. Cathbad not only was a man of great
knowledge and skilled in the ways of the Druid but also had
the strength of giants in his arms.

When the gentle girl saw the bloodied bodies of her tutors sprawled upon the green, she became filled with a great rage, and although she did not know who had killed her teachers, she gathered men to her and set out to wreak revenge upon all. She led her warriors on raids throughout all of Erin, and so terrible was her rage that her name was changed to Niassa because of her strength and warrior-wiles.

Then came the time when she wandered into a wilderness while her people readied the meal. She happened upon a quiet forest pool and stayed to bathe. She took her clothes off and placed them on the sweet-smelling bushes. Her breasts were firm and rosy-tipped and her hips wide, and generous hair grew between her legs. She stepped into the pool, and by happenstance, along came Cathbad the Druid, who saw her naked in the water.

Immediately, Cathbad drew his sword and held it over her head as he stood between her and her clothes and weapons.

"Mercy!" Nessa cried, trying to cover herself with her hands.

But Cathbad shook his head and replied, "You must grant three wishes to me."

For a moment Nessa studied him intently (he was a handsome man with dark curly hair) and at last agreed, saying, "Very well. Ask them."

"First, you must be loyal to me. Second, you must grant your friendship to me. And third, you must remain as my one and only wife for as long as I live," he said.[1]

"Those are strange wishes," she said, "but better to grant them than to lose my head. Besides, my weapon is gone."[2]

Then she came out of the pool, and Cathbad's breath caught in his throat at her naked loveliness, and they and their people became united in that place in the wilderness.

Later, Cathbad found a favorable time when they could go into Ulster and meet with Nessa's father, who was pleased at her choice of husband and gave them land in celebration of their marriage. This land became Rath Cathbad, and it lies in the Picts country near the river Conchobor in Crith Rois. There, Nessa bore Cathbad his son.

Cathbad took his child and held him to his heart and gave thanks for him. Then he prophesied to him and spoke this lay:

> "Welcome, little one who has come
> Here as has been predicted by some
> Who have said you will be a great lord,
> My son, the son of gentle Cathbad
> And of my wife in this fortress
> Of Brig na m-Brat, where Nessa
> Lays with my son and grandson.
> Here I give you my word you will be
> The rare gem of the world and will be
> The King of Rath Line, a poet
> And generous as the great
> Leader of warriors beyond the sea,
> My little bird from Brug, see
> My little lamb, all. Welcome!"

The Tidings of Conchobor Mac Nessa

This tale not only accounts for Conchobor becoming King of the Red Branch through the manipulations of his mother, but identifies many of the warriors who had formed an alliance with Conchobor. This is one of the few tales that provides today's reader with a glimpse of the lifestyle of the times.

A MARVELOUS AND PRINCELY MAN was Conchobor Mac Nessa, the king of Ulster. He was named for his mother, namely Nessa, the daughter of Eochaid Yellowheel, king of Ulster.[1] Before she became known as Nessa the Harsh-one she was known as Assa, for she was a mild-mannered young lady who was easily taught and seldom challenged the twelve tutors or foster-fathers[2] that her father, Eochaid, decreed she should have [in Munster].[3] She was a pleasant student and quick of mind, and her tutors loved her.

Now at this time there was a fierce champion in Erin

named Cathbad Mac Rossa. He was not only a skilled warrior but a wizard as well, and this made him extremely dangerous when he raided into the districts of Munster.[4] On one dark night, he led his warriors to the home of the foster-fathers of Eochaid's daughter, and when they stubbornly resisted, he slaughtered them, leaving no witnesses behind so Nessa had no knowledge of who had been the blood red man who had raided the house she loved. The night rang with the clash of swords on shields and the cries of pain from the wounded and slain. But when bright moonlight streamed in through the doors and windows of the house, black pools of blood covered the floor around the headless bodies.

When Nessa came out from the hiding place where her foster-fathers had unceremoniously stuffed her at the first alarm, she walked wide-eyed around the house, seeing the savaged bodies of the men she had loved for their kind and gentle ways. A fierce anger began to smolder in her, and she felt the bloodlust tremble in her arms and breast and thighs. She bent slowly and picked up a sword and shield, hefted the sword, testing its balance and weight in her strong hand, and felt the warrior's revenge surge through her.

She gathered men around her, warriors who at first resented being led by a young woman, then swallowed their contemptuous words when they saw how skillfully she used her sword in battle. When she took her first heads, they wondered quietly among themselves what type of woman this should be who had such skill with arms despite her youth. The warriors soon took pride in being led by such a strong woman. Three *eneads*(?)[5] of warriors followed her throughout Erin as she searched for those who had killed her foster-fathers and tutors. She left a great path of carnage in her wake, ruthlessly slaughtering those who came in her path, for she had no way of knowing if any of them had taken part in the great slaughter in the house of her foster-fathers.

"Ah, now," one grizzled warrior said wearily around the fire one night. "This is no easy woman we're following, now but a woman with a heart of stone. 'Tis certain I am that I would not want to be bedding one like her when the bloodlust is upon her. 'Tis no Assa she is, but Nessa."

"Then," said another, "she should be called Nessa from now on."

And so the legend of Nessa was born as the greenswards ran red with blood wherever she placed her bare foot.

Soon, however, she left Munster and made her way into the province of Ulster,[6] where she led quick and brilliant raids against some of the outlying landowners.

One day while her warriors were preparing the evening meal, Nessa went to a small pond deep in the middle of the forest to bathe away the dust of travel. She had stripped herself naked and stepped gratefully into the cool waters of the shadowed pool and was enjoying herself fully when suddenly Cathbad appeared on the bank, staring at her. She started toward her weapons, her sword and spears, which she had left carelessly on the bank, thinking herself safe, but the wizard stepped between her and the weapons and would not move until she came out of the water and joined him in lovemaking on the soft green grass beneath the branches of a great oak. She became his beloved wife and bore him a son. This son was Conchobor Mac Cathbad.

Ah, but great was the dignity within the youth when he was born, and why not? He was born in the same hour as Christ, and seven years before his birth great seers had been foretelling his coming, claiming that upon Christ's nativity a wondrous birth would occur upon the flat stone in the field and this birth would bring a greatness to the land of Erin and the boy's name would ring forever down through the centuries from that land.[7]

By the time the youth was seven years old, his fame had

already spread across the land, and it was at this age that his mother decided she would work her womanly magic to make Conchobor the king of Ulster.

Now at this time, Nessa, the daughter of Eochaid, was not married[8] and had caught the wandering eye of Fergus Mac Roich. One day when she passed him, switching her hips tantalizingly near his great paw, he reached out and grabbed her and tried to pull her upon his lap. Laughing, she slipped away from him and danced out of his reach. She watched the hunger in his eyes grow as he contemplated her rich hips and heavy breasts.

"Ah, lass," he growled, beckoning. "Bring yourself here and I'll show you a step or two of dancing."

She laughed and shook her head, wagging her finger playfully at him. "No, no. Not until I receive a *guerdon*[9] from you."

"What is it you want?" Fergus said thickly, feeling lust swell through his *bod*.[10]

"Well," she teased, "step down from your role as king for a year and let my son rule in your place so that his son may be called the son of a king and entitled to those rights."

Fergus shook his mammoth head at this, and Nessa came tantalizingly close to him, bending forward playfully so he could see the deep valley between her breasts. "Think about what all you could have with this. And, it's only for a year."

Still, Fergus stubbornly refused to step down from his reign. But every time Nessa came within his eye, he would watch her and become frustrated and irritated, and the servants quickly learned that it was better not to be in the way of his great fists when the heat came upon him.

At last, however, the warriors had had enough of Fergus's frustrations and said, "Grant her boon. What have you got to lose but a year of worries and headaches from listening to the whining and posturing of fools? You'll still be the king, although he will be the year's king."

"I don't know," Fergus said, clawing his callused fingers through his red, curly beard.

Then the day came when he chanced to see Nessa naked for her bath and the lust swelled so strongly within him that he thought he would burst, and that night Nessa entered his bed and her son sat in Fergus's chair in the Great Hall as king of the Red Branch.

Such was Nessa's skill in lovemaking that Fergus never became aware how she began to work with her son and those who had promised to be foster-fathers to him and the servants of his household. She suggested that Conchobor seize the wealth of every second man and give that wealth to another who would swear allegiance to him. She dipped into her own coffers and cheerfully handed out gold and silver to those who swore to support Conchobor, and when her own riches ran low, she took the great treasury of Ulster and redistributed it as well to the champions of Ulster, for the best warriors of Ulster would be needed at the year's end, when Fergus tried to reclaim his throne.

So it came that when the year ended and Fergus came to reclaim his pledge, the Ulster warriors had become used to the new riches that came their way from the successful raids Conchobor led them upon and refused to let Fergus sit again upon the throne of the Red Branch.

"Buckles and hogwash!" Fergus snapped. "I don't care how rich you've become. A deal is a deal and a pledge is a pledge and now's the time when the piper pays for the dancing he's done."

"What was that?" one asked, frowning at Fergus. "You don't make any sense."

"I was king and now I reclaim it," he said. "It's my right."

"Right is what we makes it," a veteran growled.

Blood glowed in Fergus's eyes at that, and others hastily

stepped between them, waving their hands. "Now let's have a talk about this," they said.

So they held an assembly in the Great Hall, but this time they refused to remember what they had counseled Fergus upon and blamed him for giving up the throne of Ulster to Nessa as a bride-price. The truth was, not a one there wanted to see the tightfisted Fergus come back upon the throne, for they remembered the great gifts of Conchobor to them. Speeches flew back and forth like winged swallows that day in the Great Hall, and at last a consensus was reached and delivered to the satisfaction of all but Fergus: "What Fergus sold, let it be taken from him; what Conchobor bought, let him keep."

So it was that Fergus stepped down from the throne of Ulster and that Conchobor became the *Ard Rí*, the High King of a fifth of Erin.[11]

So greatly did the Ulster warriors honor Conchobor that when any of the warriors married, his wife slept the first night in Conchobor's bed so that he would be her first husband.[12]

No wiser king has ever ruled, for Conchobor never delivered a judgment when it was not proper for him to pass his ruling. This practice kept the land from becoming barren and his crops the worse for all of that. Instead, his crops flourished and, as he flourished, so did the warriors of the Red Branch and all of Ulster flourish, and great riches came from the land to enrich the granaries of the Red Branch.

Never has there been a mightier champion, yet never was he allowed to go first into battle, for the Red Branch warriors were afraid of losing him to the sudden sword of one of their foes. Many tried and true war veterans and valiant heroes kept stubbornly in front of him so no danger might happen to him.

Wherever Conchobor traveled in Ulster, his host's wife cheerfully spent the night in his bed to honor him. (Of course, Conchobor was an extremely handsome man and, the truth be told, a far better lover than most of the husbands at the time, so the wives eagerly looked forward to his visits with their husbands.)

Conchobor kept three hundred sixty-five people in his household so that each day of the year had a different man in charge of feeding the lot of them. The first man to begin on a day would also be the last, and this was no small task of feasting, as each man had a pig and a deer and a vat of mead set aside for him. Yet there were some, like Fergus Mac Róich, for whom this was only a slight tasting and not a meal.

Fergus was a truly noble man. Seven feet stood between his ear and his lips and seven fists[13] between his eyes. There were seven fists in his nose and seven fists in his lips. His hair was so thick that when he washed it a full bushel of water would be wrung from it. But it was his *bód* that drew healthy gasps of pleasure from any woman who entered his bed, for he had seven fists in it as well and his bag hung like a bushel bag between his legs. Such was his stamina in bed that seven women would exhaust themselves before he was sated—unless Flidais, the lusty woodland goddess, came with them. And his appetite took seven pigs and seven vats and seven deer to be sated. He had the strength of seven hundred in him, so Fergus had to feed the entire Red Branch for a full week to be equal to the duty of the rest of the men of the Red Branch.

Now Conchobor was no piker when it came to providing a heavy board for his men. Each Samhain he took for his own, as this was a special time of the year when the men and women of the *Sídhes* were out and about and if a man lost his senses somewhere other than the safety of Emain Macha, the next day would find him in his grave or barrow and a place marked for the setting of his headstone. So Conchobor had a great chore in front of him, and never did he shirk from its practice. For three days before and three days after All-Hallows, great feasting would be held in Conchobor's house, which was beautiful indeed in comparison to the rest of the houses of the Red Branch.

Three houses were owned by him: the *Cróeb-ruad*,[14] the *Téite Brecc*,[15] and the Red Branch.[16] In the Red Branch was the Great Hall, where the heads and trophies and spoils of war were kept and divided. The kings lived in the *Cróeb-ruad* (guesthouse) while in the *Téite Brecc* the spears and the shields and the swords were carefully kept and guarded, and a visitor to this house would stare dumbfounded at the light sparkling from the golden hilts of the swords and the blue sheen of the spear blades and the collars and coils of gold and silver and the silver and golden rings around the shields and the many cups and horns and goblets that were kept here for feasting days.

This was a safe house and sorely needed, for whenever a rude remark came during the feasting, the battle-blood would boil through the warriors' veins and they would rise up against each other, trying to smite heads and shields with swords. So Conchobor wisely held that weapons would be stored in the *Téite Brecc* along with the great shields:

> The *Ochoin* of Conchobor, with its rims of gold, whose
>   voice would roar if the king was sorely pressed
> Cúchulainn's great black shield Fubán
> Conall Cernach's Lámthapad
> Flidais's Ochnech
> the Orderg of Furbaide
> the Cosrach of Causcrad
> the Echtach of Amairgin
> the Ir of Chondere
> the Chaindel of Nuada
> the Leochain of Fergusand
> the Uthach of Dubthach
> the Lettach of Errge
> the Ratach of Mend
> the Luithech of Naisi
> the Nithch of Loegaire

the Croda of Cormac
the Ciatharlan of Sencid
the Comla Chatha of Celtchar.

But more than the shields of these great warriors were there, far more shields than can be numbered were kept there for the others who might need one and for the time when members of the boy-troop would take their arms.

Dignity and delight and fame were evident in Conchobor's house, and no hero was greater than Fergus Mac Róig, who in the fight of Gárech on the great Cattle-Raid of Cooley cut off the tops of the three Formaela of Meath with three quick blows of his great sword *In Caladbolg*,[17] and those three flat-topped hills stand there still as a mark to his power.

No one was there as brave as Conall Cernach, the son of Amergen the Dark-Haired, who, from the first time he picked up his sword and spear, never went a day without killing a Connacht warrior in battle or burning down their houses on great and quick raids across the border into the Connacht territory. So terrible was his rage and beautiful his bravery that he slept each night with the head of a Connacht warrior beneath his knees.[18] No cattle owner in all of Erin had not been visited at least once by Conall in one of his raging raids, and no land had not felt the fury of his slaughter. This was the great warrior who divided Mac Da Thó's pig as a trophy of valor in front of the champions of the men of Erin. And the man who avenged any Ulster warrior against the rest of Erin and will until the Day of Doom. Wherever he went, he took a spear in his hand and never returned it until he had the head of a Connacht warrior in his fist.

But the most famous was a young boy around whom all the men of Erin carefully drove their chariots lest they give him offense: Cúchulainn son of Sualtam son of Beccaltach son of Móraltach son of Umendruad out of the *Sídhe* and Dolb son of

Beccaltach's brother and Ethne Ingubai, wife of Elemaire out of the *Sídhe*, his sister and Dechtaine, Cathbad's daughter, Cúchulainn's mother.

Cúchulainn's deeds were very cutting and very keen.[19] A great "warp-spasm" would come upon him when he was angry, and he would spin around inside his skin so his feet would be behind him. His ankles were as swift as the wind, and each hair in his head would become as sharp as the thorn of a haw tree and stand out from his head, and a drop of blood would glisten on the end of each hair. One eye would sink to the size of a needle eye within his head and the other bulge out to the size of a fist. When this fury was upon him, he would not recognize either friend or foe, and he would slay any who stood in front of him. He was the only one who had earned all the great feats of Scáthach Buanann, the daughter of Ardgeimm in Letha:

>   the feat of Catt
>   the feat of Cuar
>   the apple feat
>   the edge feat
>   the supine feat
>   the little dart feat
>   the rope feat
>   the body feat
>   the champion's leap
>   the casting of the rod
>   the shield-leap
>   the folding[20] of a noble champion
>   the gapped spear[21]
>   the *bai*[22] of quickness
>   the wheel feat
>   the edge feat

the feat on breaths
the champion's cry
the stroke with power
the side stroke
the run against a spear[23]
the straightening of the body on its point
the binding of a hero.

Each room of Conchobor's house had one hundred fifty rooms in it, and three couples were in each of the rooms. A bright wainscot of red yew ran around the house and into each of the rooms. Yet as brilliant as were these rooms, far better was Conchobor's room. Bronze pillars stood in front of the door, and each pillar had rings of silver wrapped around the top with friezes of golden birds with precious gems as their eyes. A rod of silver topped with three golden apples stood by Conchobor's hand, and when he shook it, the rest of the house would fall silent so his voice could be heard, and if a needle fell upon the floor, it would ring out and disturb that silence, such was the respect in which Conchobor was held by the Red Branch warriors.

Olf Guala, Gerg's great vat, which was brought out of Glen Ceirg after Conchobor slew its owner, was never empty and was always before the warriors upon the floor of the Feasting Hall.

The house was overseen by Bricriu Mac Carbaid, and nine sons of Carbaid the Great were always there—Glaine and Gormainech, Maine Minscoth and Ailill, Duress and Ret and Bricriu.

Now Bricriu was known for his foul and bitter tongue, which always seemed to lash out with words barbed like venom. If he tried to hold his thoughts back from the others, a purple boil would grow out of his forehead as large as a man's fist.[24]

When that happened, he would turn to Conchobor with a wicked gleam in his eye and say, "Well, I think tonight it will burst."

Truly many wondrous persons were in Conchobor's house. . . .

The Tale of the Pig-Keepers

This story is one of the tales that is a precursor to *Táin Bó Cuailngé*.

WHAT CAUSED THE PIG-KEEPERS to quarrel? Not hard to tell.

There was bad blood between Ochall Ochne, king of the Sídhe Cruachan in Connacht, and Bodb, king of the Sídhe of Femen Plain in Munster. They had two pig-keepers: Friuch, who served Bodb, and Rucht, who served Ochall.[1] Both were highly skilled magicians gifted with shape-shifting like Mongán Mac Fiachna.

Now these two were once very good friends, and each would trade feeding grounds if one had better feed than the other. But, as all good things are, some people began to cause trouble between them. Connacht men said that Rucht was the better pig-keeper, while Munster men said that Friuch was the better.

One year Munster had the better feed for pigs, and Rucht brought his pigs down from the North to visit his friend. Friuch greeted him as a longtime friend, and that night while they were having a dram around the fire, Friuch said, "Do you know that some people say your power is greater than mine?"

"Stuff and nonsense," Rucht said. He belched. "It's certainly no less than yours."

"Hmm," Friuch said. "Well, I don't know about that. Let's test it. I'll cast a spell upon your pigs—with your leave, of course," he added hastily, "so that no matter how much they eat, they'll remain lean while mine fatten."

Rucht belched again, then casually waved his hand in agreement. And so it was left at that. But when Rucht took his pigs home, they were so lean and poorly fed that they barely survived the trip. When the Connacht men saw the sorry state of the pigs, they laughed at Rucht and said rudely, " 'Twas a bad day when you went to Munster. Sure it is that your friend's power is far greater than yours."

"Well, now," Rucht said, fuming. "We'll see about that. The next time the acorn mast is greater here, I'll play the same trick upon him and leave his pigs looking the thin side of bacon."

So the next year, the mast came heavier in Connacht, and Friuch came with his pigs to visit his friend. But without telling Friuch what he was going to do, Rucht cast a spell upon his pigs so that they kept getting skinnier and skinnier until they nearly caught up with their shadows. The Connacht men were forced to agree that the pig-keepers were equal in magic. But when Friuch returned home with his lean pigs, Bodb took one look at them and refused to let Friuch remain as the pig-keeper for the Munster men. And, to make matters worse, Ochall decided that it would be best if the two friends played their games apart from the swine and dismissed Rucht as the head pig-keeper for the Connacht men.

Friendship fell by the wayside then, and the two began battling, changing shape whimsically, each in hopes of gaining an advantage over the other. The first two years they spent in the shape of hawks and vultures, first in the stronghold of Cruachan and then on the Femen Plain.

One day the Munster men complained loudly, saying, "Those damned birds make a racket that would raise the dead. For the entire year, they've sat there, squawking at each other."

At that time, Fuidell Mac Fiadmire, Ochall's steward, came over the hill, and they made him welcome. The birds squawked loudly, and Fuidell frowned, saying, "Those two raucous birds seem to be the same as the two we had up north last year. For an entire year, we could hardly hear ourselves think!"

Suddenly, the two birds faded away and the two pig-keepers stood there. The Munster men made them welcome, but the two pig-keepers looked at them sullenly.

"Stuff your welcome," Friuch said rudely. "We bring you war-wailing and a chomping at the corpses of your friends."

"What have you been doing?" Bodb asked.

"Making trouble from the day we left until today. For two years, we shaped into birds, and you saw what we did, leaving our droppings at will. We did the same at Cruachan for a full year and another at the fairy mound on Femen Plain. Now, since all of you have seen how powerful we are, we are going to become creatures in the sea and live there for two years. And your nets will remain empty."

One went into the river Shannon while the other patrolled the river Siuir, and for two years they tangled with each other underwater. The first year they were glimpsed chewing at each other madly in the Siuir, the next in the Shannon.

Then they became two stags and raided the females of each other and wrecked the homeland of each other.

Then, furious because neither had gained an edge, they became two warriors, slashing and stabbing furiously at each other, and then two phantoms that screamed eerily at each other. After that, they became two dragons, first crisping each other's fields, then pouring freezing snow down on the land.

And then they dropped down out of the air as two maggots. One fell into the spring of the river Cronn in Cooley, and the cow of Dáire Mac Fiachna slurped it up. The other fell into the spring-fed well of Garad in Connacht, and one of Maeve's cows lapped it up. From this were born the two great bulls— Finnbennach on the Plain of Ai and Donn on Cooley's pastures.[2]

Their names were Rucht and Friuch when they were pig-keepers; Ingen and Eitte when they were birds of prey;[3] Bled and Blod when they were in the sea;[4] Rinn and Faebur as warriors;[5] Scáth and Sciath as phantoms;[6] and Crunniuc and Tuinniuc when they were maggots.[7]

When they became the bulls, they were the White-horned One of Aí and the Brown Bull of Cooley. The Brown Bull was huge, dark, haughty, ferocious, and intelligent. Thirty grown boys could fit on his back, and he led his herd with reckless bravery. Whitehorn had a white head and white feet, and his body was blood red.

Athirne
and Amergin

This is a compilation of two stories that come from two texts: *Bretha Nemed* and *The Book of Leinster*.

WHY WAS ATHIRNE KNOWN AS Athirne the Fierce? Not hard to tell. It's because of a poem he sang when in his mother's womb.

When Athirne's mother was pregnant, the fire in her house went out, so she went to fetch fire from where a feast was being prepared. It was to be an enormous feast for many warriors, and much eating and drinking would be done. The vats had already been filled with mead, and when the mead smell reached her nose, the baby inside her leaped up fiercely as if demanding a dram for himself and knocked her pins over needles out the door.

To satisfy her thirst and the thirst of the child, the woman asked the brewer three times for a taste of the mead, but the brewer refused, claiming that it wasn't ready.

"But my child," she began, only to be rudely interrupted by the brewer.

"I don't care if your thirst puts sand in your throat and the babe comes out your side," he said rudely. "The mead cannot be disturbed now, and you'll have to wait until you give birth."

"That may be a while yet," she said. She winced and placed her hands over her belly, where the baby was kicking violently.

"Then it's a while you'll wait," he said, shrugging. "It matters nothing to me if you wait or go elsewhere."

Now the tops of the barrels had been covered until the arrival of the king, for whom the mead was being made. When the king came into the house, they heard a soft voice chanting, and as they listened, they realized the child in the woman's womb was chanting a poem about the mead. Suddenly the hoops of all the unopened barrels snapped apart and a flood of mead washed through the house, tumbling the feast-makers this way and that. Women shrieked as the foaming mess went up their dresses, and men cursed as they tumbled head over heels in the flood, banging their noggins against the thick beams of the house.

The woman held her hands into the flood three times and drank from her palms before she left the house. The child in her womb, Athirne he would be called, was sated by the taste of the mead and belched and was happy from it.

Now here is a lesson for any who has been wise enough to hear it, and that is, if a poet who has been refused a drink chants a proper poem, the barrels will explode and none there will have a taste of that which has been denied the poet. It is a wise man who realizes this and learns his lesson well.

Now Athirne Ailgesach Mac Ferchertne became the most miserly man in all Erin. Once he went to the house of Midir of Brí Léith and fasted against him and came away with the three cranes of refusal and misery, which he set beside his house to dissuade any of Erin's men from coming to his house after hospitality.[1]

"Don't come, don't come," said the first crane.

"Go away, go away," said the second crane.

"Pass by, pass by," said the third crane.

Such was Athirne's greed that he would never eat his fill where anyone could see him for fear that he might be made to share it with others. Once he went off with a fine pig and a bottle of mead and stuffed himself alone. But just then he saw a man approaching.

"Are you going to eat that all yourself?" asked the man. And when Athirne didn't answer, the man took the pig and bottle of mead from him.

"Who are you?" said Athirne, annoyed at the man's effrontery.

"My name is not well known," the man replied. "It is Sethor Ethor Othor Dele Dreng Gerce Mec Gerce Gér Gér Dír Dír."[2]

Athirne couldn't make a satire on that name, so he lost the pig. The man was probably sent by God to take the pig, because from then on Athirne was just as hospitable as anyone else.

In Ulster, there lived a famous blacksmith named Eccet Salach the Smith. Some people, however, called him Echen. He was a master of every craft, and there has never been a better blacksmith before or since. A son was born to him, who was named Amergin.

For the first fourteen years of his life, Amergin remained silent and was the cause of much despair to his parents, for his skin was black, his teeth were white, and his face turned black and blue at times. Snot dribbled down his nose and into his mouth, and his cheeks looked like a squirrel's cheeks stuffed with acorns. His eyes were always red and sunken deep into his face and seemed to burn with special thought. His bushy eyebrows grew like ropes over his eyes, and his hair stood straight out from his head like prickly thorns. His calves and thighs were like the spouts on the blacksmith's bellows, and his toes were crooked and his ankles large. His belly ballooned to the size of a huge house and became gray whale. His back was knobbly and scabby with boils. The proper use of a toilet was unknown to him, and his buttocks were caked with crap.

His favorite treats were boiled curds, sea salt, red blackberries,[3] white berries, burnt ears of grain, bunches of garlic, and one-eyed nuts,[4] which he used to play with on the floor, drawing a circle and shooting one after the other out of the circle with his thumb and forefinger.

Once Athirne sent his servant Greth to Eccet Salach to order an ax, and Greth saw the hideous boy sitting on the floor of the house, drooling. He made a noise, and the boy stared up at him with anger deep within his eyes. Eccet's daughter then heard the boy chant:

"Does Greth eat curds?
Does Greth eat curds?
Does Greth eat curds?
A fair bush, a foul bush
A fair bush, a foul bush,
Bunches of garlic, hollow of pine,
Apples and curds mellowed by thyme.
I ask again: Does Greth eat curds?"

Frightened, Greth ran out of the house and sprinted across the fields, falling in mud, until he finally made it back to Athirne, who gave him a look of astonishment as he staggered into the house.

"What's the matter with you?" demanded Athirne. "You look terrible. Have you been fighting?"

"I might as well have," Greth gasped, mopping sweat from his brow. "I met a boy today who hasn't spoken for fourteen years, and if you don't take care, why that boy will end up in your seat in your house."

"What's this?" Athirne said suspiciously. "What did you hear?"

"That's easy," Greth said, and repeated the chant he had heard from the boy.

Shortly after this, Eccet returned to his house, and his daughter told him that his boy had spoken to Athirne's servant, who had come by to ask Eccet to make an ax for him.

"What did he say?" said Eccet. His daughter told him.

"I think I know what will come of this," said Eccet, rubbing his callused hands over his face. " 'Tis certain I am that Athirne will come and kill the boy so he won't get the better of him, for the boy who said that has great wisdom."

The next day the girl left the house and took the boy with her when she went south to take care of the cattle pasturing on Sliab Mis.

After they had gone, Eccet made a clay image of the boy, baked it in his forge to firm it, then dressed it in nice clothes and placed it where it looked like the boy sleeping.

It wasn't long before Athirne and Greth arrived and thought they saw the boy asleep. They noticed that their ax was ready, and Athirne took it by the handle and brought it down hard upon the head of the clay boy. Then he and Greth fled as a large cry of alarm was raised.

They were chased back to their household, where Athirne had gathered all of his property, his cattle and sheep and goats, inside the walls of his fortress and barred the gate.

The Ulster warriors arrived and besieged him until a treaty was made. Eccet was given the price of seven slaves for the insult and attempted murder by Athirne, and Athirne was forced to take the boy as his foster-son and teach him the skills of a poet.

And that is how Athirne lost his place as the chief poet of Ulster and Amergin took his place. *Finit.*

The Guesting
of Athirne

Incipit Aigidecht Aithirni can be found in *The Book of Leinster,*
p. 118a, and Harleian 5280 (H), fol. 77a. Both texts must be used
to correct defects in each. I estimate that this was probably tran-
scribed in the early eleventh century. In the early Middle Irish
language, the poems on the seasons are written in heptasyllabic
meter with trisyllabic endings, the end of the stanza marked by
a shorter line of five syllables with monosyllabic endings. The
other five poems are written in various meters. I have not tried
to follow that scheme in this translation, electing instead to work
in a looser structure more native to this day while giving the
flavor of the original. A third copy of this text can be found in
MS. 23.N.10, pp. 15–16, in the Royal Irish Academy.

ONCE UPON A TIME ATHIRNE Ailgessach[1] came to the
house of Amirgen, his foster-son, and stayed a night. As he was
about to depart the next day, Amirgen detained him by saying,

"It is good for one to stay at home
When the leaves turn to gold in autumn
As there is much work for everyone
To do through the all-too-short days.
This is the time of the speckled fawns
To whom the red stalks of the bracken
Offer safe shelter while stags run
From the many fair mounds
To the chorus of bellowing hinds.
In the long-leafed woods we find
The acorns and bring in the corn
From the fields over the brown
Earth. By the place of the near
Ruined Fort, spiked thorn bushes tear
At the flesh when we walk
Through them. The thick stalks
Bear a heavy harvest that bows
Them near to the ground and in rows
Of great trees, hazelnuts fall
Near the great fort's wall."

So Athirne stayed through the autumn to help his foster-son with the harvest and the gathering. When winter came, he again made ready to leave, but Amirgen said,

"Ah, this is the time of dark deep
Winter when heavy seas roll and sleep
Comes over the nether region of the world.
The meadow birds sing sorrow boldly
All except the darkly red blood ravens
Whose song seems extremely craven
When fierce winter winds wail
And the sky becomes a black gale.
Insolent hounds lay by the fire

Cracking bones while upon the fire
The iron vessel bubbles throughout
The dark black day without redoubt."

And again Athirne stayed, contented to sit by the fire while winter winds raged outside the door. In the spring he again tried to leave, but Amirgen said,

"The day is chilly and raw
And still we must use haw
Lanterns in the dark. Icy
Spring makes walking dicey
While the cold leaps into
One's face. The ducks seem to
Shiver in the pool-water and cry
While harsh-shrieking cranes lie
Up a blasphemous chorus and
From the wilderness wolf bands
Scent the early morning air.
The birds seem to be scared
Of the many wild beasts that
Chase them as they dart
Through the woods and out
Of the green grass gouts."

Once more in the summer Athirne tried to depart, but Amirgen said,

"Summer is a good season to see
The peace found in a tall forest tree.
The whistling wind does not tear
At the leaves nor does it wear
The tree down. Rivers flow gently
Now and in the fire turf burns slowly."

So it was now that he was allowed to depart. When he began to leave, Amirgen's foster-sons asked if Athirne would recite some of his poetry so they might know something of his craft. So Amirgen ordered a bull to be brought into the house to be slaughtered. But Athirne spoke against this, saying,

"This mighty bull is strong-tailed
With large horns and shaggy, wild
Hair. He is a stout-necked one
Who obviously is not done
Yet with the cows of your herd."

Then Amirgen sent the bull back to the herd and had a calf brought in to be killed in place of the bull, but Athirne said,

"The calf is wild-eyed with wonder
At what lies before him. His shoulder
Shows the strength yet to come
But it is not covered yet with meat
Enough for all who will seat
Themselves at your table.
Better take him back to the stable."

Then a sheep was brought in to be killed. Athirne looked at it carefully and said,

"This lambkin with its crooked horns
Has had its fleece carefully shorn.
Still, there is much to be desired
Before the lamb's flesh is fired."

At last, a pig was brought into the house, and Athirne nodded his head and said,

"Welcome the pig to the fire
Built warmly within this shire.
A large fire is indeed needed
Before the pig's flesh is treated
To the carver's knife. I say
We eat its flesh this day."

And after the pig had been feasted, Athirne went home, having finished his visit with Amirgen in this manner. *Finis*.

The Battle
of Etair

This story may be found in *The Book of Leinster*, p. 114b. It is titled *Incipit Talland Etair* and apparently dates from the tenth or eleventh century. It provides a reason for the making of the "brain ball" that eventually brings about the death of Conchobor.

ONCE IN ERIN THERE LIVED a coldhearted, merciless man, Athirne Ailgesach of Ulster. So miserly was he that he would ask a one-eyed man to give him his only eye and demand a woman sleep with him when she was in the midst of childbirth. If this was not done, then he would threaten to cast a satire—a poem to ridicule—against them until he got his way. He caused so much ill-feeling among the Red Branch warriors that Conchobor Mac Nessa ordered him to make a circuit of Erin, singing his tales as he went.

At first, he went to the left around Connacht. Then he went between two fords belonging to Eochaid Mac Luchta, the king of Meath, south of Connacht. But Eochaid would not let him stay and took him south across the Shannon to the men of Munster.

"We don't want you to be ungrateful to us, Athirne," said Eochaid worriedly. "If we have any jewels or treasures you like, take them."

Athirne smiled a yellowed, snaggle-toothed smile and said, "The one thing I would like is the single eye in your head."

"I won't refuse you even that," Eochaid said, and put his finger under his eye, tore it out of its socket, and dropped it in Athirne's hand. Blind now, he told his servant to take him to water so that he could wash the blood from his face.

As Eochaid poured water three times over his face, he asked the servant, "Has the eye been torn out of my head?"[1]

To which the servant suddenly cried out, "The lake is red with blood from where your eye has been!"

"Then," Eochaid said grimly, "Dergderc[2] shall be its name forever."

And because the king had shown such selfless care for the sake of his people, God[3] miraculously restored both eyes in his head.

After that, Athirne went to Tigernach Tétbuillech, the king of Munster. But he took nothing from Tigernach except to ask for a night with the queen in his bed. When Tigernach hesitated, Athirne said that if the king did not grant his request, he would make a satire upon the entire country and all of the Munster warriors would lose their honor forever. So the queen was brought to his bed and slept with him to save the honor of her husband and the men of Munster.

Then Athirne left for Leinster and stopped in Ard Brestine south of Moyfea to rest. The Leinster warriors heard that he was coming to their lands and went immediately to where he rested and offered him jewels and gold to stay away from Leinster, fearing that he might leave satires upon them. Anyone who didn't give Athirne a gift would lose everything he had, and no one killed by him was entitled to recompense. For that reason, any man would give him anything he wanted: the eyes from his head or whatever treasure he wanted, even the services of his wife in Athirne's bed.

But Athirne saw that he was really not welcome in Leinster and decided to leave satires upon the men of Leinster, knowing full well that, if the warriors killed him, then the Red Branch warriors would never be finished avenging his death. He was quite pleased with this requirement placed upon the home of a murdered poet, for it gave him great power, and he wielded it whenever and wherever he could.

So he told the men of Leinster in Brestine that unless they gave him the greatest jewel on the hill, he would leave a satire upon them so black that they would never be able to hold their heads up in Erin again.

The men looked at each other in bewilderment. "But what is the greatest jewel on the hill?" they asked, and argued bitterly among themselves, each having a different value upon his belongings, yet ready to sacrifice anything to keep Athirne away from their lands and the warriors' honor with them.

The men of Leinster at last decided to ask the Lord of the Elements to help them avoid the outrage threatened to be done to them. They waited for an answer, but none of them saw a horseman training his horse on the hill above them. He turned his horse toward them and leaped from the hillside. The horse's great hooves ripped up a large chunk of sod, which struck the king, Fergus Fairge, in the chest.

In the clayey side of the sod, Fergus saw a brooch made with eighty ounces of red gold and touched it wonderingly. "What's this on my chest?" he asked.

Athirne laughed delightedly, chanting:

"A brooch there is in Ard Brestine:
From a horse's hooves it has been given.
Over it a great judgment has been passed,
In the mantle of Mane son of Durthacht."

"That's the jewel that I sought," he said. "My father's brother buried it there after the Ulster warriors suffered their terrible defeat in the Battle of Brestine."

Without another word, Fergus plucked the brooch from his chest and handed it to Athirne. "Now, will you leave us in peace?" he asked anxiously.

Smiling secretly to himself, Athirne went to Mes Gegra, the king of Leinster, who had a brother called Mes Róida. Their parents had both been deaf and dumb. Mes Gegra flinched inwardly when he saw Athirne but still gave him a great welcome. Then Athirne demanded that the king's wife spend the night making love in Athirne's bed.

Annoyed, Mes Gegra said, "Why should I give you my wife?"

"For the sake of your honor," snapped Athirne. "Otherwise, kill me, if you dare, and the shame that will be brought upon the men of Leinster shall be so great that the men of Ulster will never be finished slaying you."

Mes Gegra's eyes narrowed, and he said, "I will not give you my wife for the sake of any man of Ulster save yourself. She will sleep with you, but know this: there is no man of Ulster who could take her unless I give her to him willingly."

"What's this? You would refuse me?"

"You, no, but any other man from Ulster, yes," the king replied.

Furious, Athirne said, "Then I will not rest until a man from Ulster carries off both your head and your wife."

"That's up to you." The king shrugged. "I'll make you welcome for the sake of hospitality, but only you."

Buan, Mes Gegra's wife, slept with Athirne that night. But Athirne was still irritated at Mes Gegra's refusal of the men from Ulster and traveled throughout Leinster for a whole year, demanding the wives of the kings and princes and nobles of Leinster. When the year was up, he took one hundred and fifty wives with him to his own country.

To his chariot driver, Athirne said, "Go and tell the men of Ulster to come and meet me, for I think the men of Leinster will be coming after me for the sake of their honor."

The men of Leinster went to the Tolka to bid farewell to Athirne, hoping that he would lift his satire from them. But Athirne ignored them and left, taking no blessing with him either. As the Leinster men thought about what Athirne had done and what they had given him but received nothing in return for their pains save a satire to dishonor them, they became furious and went after him to retrieve their wives. They caught him at Ainech Lagen, but at the same time the men of Ulster came, and battle immediately broke out between Leinster and Ulster.

The men of Leinster were so furious that they routed the men of Ulster, who retreated east to the sea until they reached the safety of Dún Etair, where they stayed for nine days without food or drink, having only seawater and mud there. Athirne, of course, had plenty: seven hundred cattle he kept in the middle of the stronghold, but not one of the Ulster men tasted so much as a drop of their milk. Athirne had it all thrown over the cliff so that no one would have a morsel from him. When wounded men were brought to him, he refused them everything and they bled to death.

Finally the Ulster leaders came to him, begging him at least to let Conchobor drink, but he refused even the king of the Red Branch. All Conchobor had to eat was what the girl Leborcham could fetch him upon her back from Emain Macha.

Now Leborcham was the daughter of a slave and slave-girl

from Conchobor's house. Few had ever seen anyone as ugly as she. Her feet and knees were back-turned, and her heels and calves front-turned, yet she could travel the length and breadth of Erin in one day. At the end of each day, she returned to the Red Branch and reported to Conchobor what she had seen in her travels. When she returned, she brought sixty cakes from the ovens in Emain Macha to the warriors in Dún Etair, carrying Conchobor's share upon her back.

The fighting continued day and night around the fortress as the men of Leinster claimed that they had built Dún Etair. Cúchulainn's Gap is there, and everyone wanted Cúchulainn to build a bridge over it, but he refused, preferring to bridge it himself with a hail of spears. Conchobor advised Cúchulainn that he not use all of his power until more men arrived from Emain Macha as he had sent Leborcham to bring more warriors to help the Red Branch.

Mess-Dead, son of Amergin, Cúchulainn's seven-year-old foster-son, was placed to guard the gate of the fortress, and every hour of the day he killed nine men who came to try to carry off Ulster hostages three times a day. He was so powerful that the Leinster men decided that they would avoid the rules of war and when reinforcements came for the men of Leinster at Benn Etair, they sent seven hundred champions to the gate to kill them. As they cut off the head of Mess-Dead, he defied them by giving his war cry.

When Cúchulainn heard the cry, he said, "Either the sky is falling upon us or the sea is crashing upon us or my foster-son cries in rage at unequal combat coming against him."

Cúchulainn then raged away, cutting the armies of Leinster in two behind him. Fighting was terrible, dust rising in clouds, swords harsh against swords, shields clashing, men screaming.

Three lines of battle were joined from midmorning to midafternoon, and the men of Leinster were routed. They quickly raised a red wall between them and the Ulster warriors, for they knew there was a *geis*[4] upon the men of Ulster forbidding them to cross over a red wall.

Many Ulster men fell in that battle. Mess-Dead, son of Amergin, was the first. Brianan Brethach, Condla, Beothach, Conaed Mac Morna, and many others also fell.

[text missing]

Conall Cernach went off alone in pursuit of the fleeing Leinster men, to avenge his brothers, Mess-Dead and Láegaire, who had fallen in the battle. He passed Drummainech, through Uib Gabla, into Forcathain, by Uachtar Aird, past Naas, to Clane.

When the Leinster men reached their own territory, they dispersed, each to his own lands. But Mes Gegra, the king, stayed behind the hosts, alone with his charioteer on the Path of Clane.

His charioteer said, "If you like, I'll sleep first, then you."

Mes Gegra agreed to this, and while his charioteer slept, he saw a wonderful nut, far bigger than a man's head, floating down the river toward him. He waded out into the water and brought it to shore and cut it in two with his knife, leaving half for his chariot driver.

But when he looked around, he saw the charioteer suddenly lifted up from the ground in his sleep, and then he awoke. Mes Gegra frowned and said, "What's wrong?"

"I had a bad dream," the charioteer said. "Have you eaten the nut?"

"Now, how did you—never mind. Yes, I have," Mes Gegra said.

"Did you leave half for me?"

"I did that. A little, anyway."

"The man who would eat a little when I wasn't looking would certainly eat a lot," the charioteer said hotly.

The king shrugged and held out his hand, but the charioteer quickly drew his sword and cut off the king's hand.

"That was uncalled for," the king said, gripping his wound. "Open my fist and see what I was giving you. You will find your share of the nut in that."

The charioteer pried open the king's fist, and when he saw that the king had not lied, he fell upon his sword. It went through his belly and out his back, pointing west.

Mes Gegra bound his wound and awkwardly yoked the chariot himself. Then, gathering his severed hand, he set off and came to the western bank of a ford. Conall Cernach was on the eastern bank.

"What is it you want?" Mes Gegra said.

"Your life," Conall said. "You killed my brothers and now I will avenge their deaths."

Mes Gegra shook his head. "Look for yourself. Do you see their heads upon my belt or upon my chariot rail?"

It was then that Conall noticed Mes Gegra's severed hand. Yet he drew his sword and banged it hard against his shield.

Mes Gegra looked at him scornfully. "There's no valor in fighting a one-handed man," he said.

"Then I'll tie one hand to my side," Conall replied, and lashed his left hand to his side with three ropes. Satisfied, Mes Gegra drew his own sword, and they entered the ford and fought over the water, delivering such wounds to each other that the waters ran red with blood.

But Conall was far stronger than Mes Gegra and delivered a terrible blow to the king's chest. Mes Gegra fell backward and said, "Take my head, Conall, and add my glory to your own."

So Conall cut off Mes Gegra's head and took it to a flagstone on the edge of the ford. A drop of blood fell from the neck and went straight through the stone into the earth. He put the head down on the stone, and the head went through the stone onto the earth and fell into the river.

Until then Conall had been known as Conall Clóenbráigtech.[5] This was one of the Ulster warriors' three blemishes: Conall of the Crooked Neck, Cúchulainn Goll,[6] and Cúscraid Mend.[7] The women of Ulster were divided into three groups, each group loving one of these three men. The ones that loved Cúchulainn squinted when they spoke to him; the ones that loved Conall crooked their necks; and the ones that loved Cúscraid stammered when they spoke to him.

So Conall lifted the head out of the river onto his shoulder, and from then on he was straight-necked. Conall got into his chariot alone, and his charioteer took Mes Gegra's chariot. They traveled as far as Uachtar Fine, where they encountered fifty women, namely Mes Gegra's wife, Buan, and her maidens, coming south from the border.

"Whose woman are you?" asked Conall.

"I am the wife of Mes Gegra, the king," she replied haughtily.

"Then you must come with me."

"And what warrior would tell me to do that?" she said.

"Your husband," Conall answered.

"Do you have any proof of this?"

Conall jerked a broad thumb over his shoulder. "There are his chariot and horses."

"That means nothing," Buan said. "He gives many such treasures."

"Then," Conall shouted, "here is his head!"

He threw it in the dirt between them, and as Buan mourned her loss, the head turned red, then white.

"What's the matter with the head?" asked Conall suspiciously.

"There was a dispute between my husband and Athirne," Buan explained. "My husband declared that no Ulster man would carry me away. What ails the head is the breaking of his word."

Conall shrugged. "Well, be that as it may. Come away with me, now."

She asked for some time to mourn her husband, but Conall refused her. Then she lifted up such a cry of lamentation that it could be heard as far as Tara and Allen. Then she fell backward, dead. Her grave is on that road. It is named Coll Buana, after the hazel (*coll*) that grew through her grave.

Conall shrugged and looked at his charioteer. "Gather the head now, and let's be off."

His charioteer spat and said, "Rather you didn't tell me to do that. I got a bad feeling about this all."

"Then cut out the brain and take it with you. Mix it with lime and make a ball out of it. The head can stay here with the woman."

When they returned to Emain Macha, the Ulster warriors rejoiced at Conall's slaying of Leinster's king. This, then, was the great circuit Athirne made of Erin and the slaying of Mes Gegra by Conall Cernach, and the Battle of Etair sometimes called the Battle of Howth was finished. *Finit.*

The Battle
of Cumar

Although one can argue about whether this story rightfully belongs in the Ulster Cycle, I believe it to be if not a *remscela* then most certainly a tale from the pre-*Táin* period. Only one copy of it is known, and that is the paper manuscript 23.K.37 in the Royal Irish Academy. This copy apparently was finished in 1717 but by two authors, with the first four pages being in a neat, almost traditional hand, while the remaining pages are more carelessly written. The syntax is quite modern, but a bit flamboyant in places and representative of a far older style. The main incidents seem to come from the *Dincenchus* of *Druim Criaich* in *The Book of Leinster,* but they have gone through many variations over the years. Consequently, I believe the text has been corrupted.

ONCE THERE LIVED A GREAT and famous king of Erin, notably Eochaid Feidlioch Mac Finn Mac Finnlogh. During his reign, Erin became quite prosperous and little strife was seen as the provinces agreed upon their territorial boundaries. The chiefs were not alarmed at the behavior of their men in the various feasts and festivals, and popular sedition was, for the most part, ignored. The farmers and the innkeepers had an abundance of food and mead, and the unmarried women did not make journeys around the countryside from the rocky white-foam and tempest-tossed harbor of Cliodna's Wave to the rocky rough Wave in the North or from the Peak of Edar with its fine grassy swards and rich fishing in the east to gloomy, mist-wrapped Dub Carrgach in the west of Connacht, only because they feared a scandal might be attached to their names.[1]

The cattle grazed peacefully in their pastures and gave freely of their milk, and Erin's groves were melodic with the songs of cuckoos merging with soughing winds moving through elms. The plains were level and softly grassed and yielded every crop that was planted, while forest trees grew straight and smooth with heavy foliage and her ponds and backwaters were calm and full of fish. The mountains were peaceful and untroubled, tranquil; streams stood clear like running glass, and the forests were filled with game for the determined hunter. The harbors were beautifully strong, and her strands were dry with dunes sloping gently to the sea.[2]

The people rested easily, then, as rents were kept low by the chiefs, who had no need of more money than they already had. The roar of the forests was not heard under the screaming of wind or showers of cleansing rain. The dew came heavily and stayed on the plains until the noonday sun took it away. The planets were in accord, and perhaps this was because the second adopted son of Augustus[3] ruled wisely and carefully. This was the beginning of the third year[4] of Eochaid Feidlioch's reign that received God's light generously from the Creator who made the universe and the gentle Son born of the Hebrew virgin without the loss of her virginity that graced its presence. It was in the third year of Conaire's reign that He was crucified.[5]

The reign of Eochaid Feidlioch lasted twelve years from the time the royal prince, venomous Fachtna Fathach, fell in the Battle of Leithruidhe Ruidhe on the slopes of Conachail in the Corann[6] south. Tara was held in fair rule at that time by that strong soldier[7] who kept the peasants safe from raids by the warriors and nobles yet granted freedom to the poets without limitations.

Now Eochaid had a lovely and high-breasted wife of gentle ways called Cloithfionn,[8] who was the bright-skinned daughter of Airtidh Uchtleathaiin [Broad-Chest] Mac Fergus Mac Ailill Aidneach. She was the mother of the warrior's children, his three brave sons and six beautiful daughters. The poet said:

> Maeve and Mumain of delicate form,
> Eile and comely Deirdre were born,
> And Cloithrionn and Ethne made six
> And none could be said to be beauty-sick.

And this was followed by three sons, who were the three Fionna of Emain:

> Vigorous bragging arrogant Bres
> Venomous strong-formed Nar
> Heroic abundant rash Lothar.

They were called the Fionna of Emain because they were brought up at Emain Macha and Eochaid Salbuidhi [Yellow-heel] Mac Lodun, who was the father of Conchobor's mother, Nessa, educated all equally, showing preference to none. Their father gave each of them much land that included the rough land of the Gamanraidhe, the royal Cascade of Ruadh (where Aodh Ruadh Mac Badarn drowned), and the sharp-cragged and

rough-cliffed island known as Corca Baisginn where Cúchulainn made his famous combat leap. All of this was the estate of
the Fionna of Emain of the Ulaid.[9] The poem that was sung:

> The three sons Eochaidh Feidlioch the Fair
> Included the rambunctious Bres whose bare
> Speech caused many problems and comely
> Nar whose servants were dutiful and wonderfully
> Loyal and well-shaped Lothar who was seen
> Romping around Emain Macha's green.
> Here were the bold three greatly valued.
> The famous fair Fionna who shared
> A gentle raising by Eochaid Yellowheel
> Who was a constant tutor who well-
> Knew how to guard his foster lads.
> Around them the Ulster lads
> Were placed as guards, noble boys
> Who planned to treachery and whose toys
> Included weapons to protect the three.
> Eochaid Feidlioch gave lands to the three
> That ran from the royal Cascade of Ruadh deep
> To the chasm gallant Cúchulainn leaped.
> All of this territory once was Gamanraidh
> In Connacht where the poets rough.

Eochaid Feidlioch was the *Ard-Rí*[10] at Tara, and this was
the time when no slaughter of the peasants took place and nobles did not plot to overthrow the king and no province felt the
need to revolt.

One day the king was at home in Tara with only four
fighting men: himself, Cet Mac Maga,[11] Conall Cernach Mac
Amergen, and Glunchenn the Druid. The day was lazily warm,
and bees buzzed heavily around the fragrant vines. Glunchenn
said at last, "This is a day meant for little but pleasure. Let's

go to the House of the Ladies, where we might be able to scare up a game of *fidchell*."[12]

The others were in agreement with this fine idea (besides, it was cooler where the ladies lived), and they went off to the high-arched, solid and comfortable, high-windowed and elegant, sheltered, pillared, spacious, festive, thickly doored, white-painted, rush-strewn, and lamp-lit room where the queen held court.[13] She sat in a carefully carved chair watching the ladies around her cutting lace. Mes Buachalla[14] sat in the other chair. She was the daughter of Eochaid Airemun, and her beauty ensured that she would be properly and highly courted.

"Well," said the lady, "what is it that brings you here?" Her beautiful lips spread in a generous smile.

"We thought a game might be appropriate," Eochaid said. The board was brought to them, and Glunchenn the Druid coached Cet and Conall against the king, but Eochaid still beat them.

"Well," the queen said, "who gets to claim the victory of that game?"

"If it was me," Glunchenn said gallantly, "I would give it to you."

Eochaid laughed and said, "Well, I would want more lasting treasure than that. Why, I wouldn't take it from my niece, and what I have she doesn't want."[15]

The lady's eyes flashed hard, and she raised her eyes, saying, "Well, I tell you that if you want to play roosters and hens, you can do it in your own bed tonight."

Eochaid rose indignantly and said, "I also give you my word that I will not give it to her tonight, but I will not give it to you either from this night forever." He turned to the others, white-faced with fury. "Stop that handiwork!" he bawled.

The others looked up at him, startled.

He turned around slowly in the room, his eyes snapping sparks like fireflies. "Order the men to catch up your horses and yoke them to your chariots. Have your beds and linens gathered and placed in carts. Whatever flocks and herds you have, gather them as well and take everything with you. Cet and Conall Cernach, I charge you to bind over the marriage property of that . . . that . . . 'lady' and take her to the Ulster men tonight. Make certain that she has a fighting champion to travel with her, however, for her safety."

The lady rose, eyes snapping wrathfully. "Take your own property, as we have no way of remaining here, and since you obviously have no intention of dividing the kingdom with us, we will leave and separate from our friends and companions."

At once the king said, "Depart quickly then! Promptly so that visitors and travelers coming to Tara will not see your cattle landless or your followers disgraced and taunted by young girls. I want no crowds in your house, no scholars making pap poems preaching purity of yourself, no harp-players plucking strings tenderly in your bedchamber. You have brought dishonor upon yourself in a place meant to give you honor."

Then the lady flew into such a passionate rage that speech slipped away from her lips and her tongue cleaved hard in her mouth. Her face blazed red with shame, and harsh tears fell from her feverish eyes to soak the front of her purple gown. Then she found her tongue again and demanded that the servants hurry to fetch her property so they could leave immediately.

The servants ran to the grassy desolate slopes where the horses had been left and ordered the guards to bring them to the gate to be harnessed. The guards rose from their tiny, gray-roofed, wide-doored huts and went out to catch the sleek and well-fed horses. They brought the horses to Tara and harnessed them by the gate.

The queen bade her gentle farewell to the people at Tara and stepped into her chariot. Then she raised her hands and begged the gods to treat her well on this journey and not to keep her from getting her revenge for the dishonor done to her name by the evil within Eochaid. Then she ordered her horses to be galloped furiously northward from Tara. When Glunchenn the Druid saw this, he said:

"This is not a good thing our king has done
To treat a woman so. For this insult Clofinn's
Children will wreak great havoc. To Rath Cruachan
They will march, for they loved the friend of Clothrann.
Their sister has made many false appearances that
Will cause the rise of a huge army and that
Will bring about the Battle of Cumar, where much
Blood and gore and heads will fall and things like such
On the bodies of great heroes like Cet and Conall.
The bodies of the Red Branch heroes will be mangled
And noble Eochaid will die when they fight
With their good father for this my sight
Has given me. The Fionna by Eochaid will fall
And Clothrann's great heart will come to a boil.
This will be the fall of the family.
Woe! Woe! For this is the evil wrath of the family."

Disdaining a detachment of soldiers to accompany her, that white-robed beautifully dressed queen went on to Duba An Banguba, the fine grassed mountain of Modarn. From the hard sleep those ladies had that night Druim Banguba has its name.[16]

From there they went to the Druid's Lawn, to Emain, and when the women there saw their approach, Leabharcam sprang forward to meet them. With her horsey mouth she whinnied a welcome when she saw the weight of the lady's gift and went back to the Red Branch and told the heroes there what she had seen. That is when Conchobor went forward to greet the lady and welcome her to Emain.

They asked her why she had left her husband at Tara, and

the woman told them that it was Eochaid who, in a fit of anger, had thrown her out of his stronghold. It was then that Conchobor spoke:

> "Then why did you come to my house,
> Queen of Eochaid Feidlech's house?
> Is it a great quarrel or is it your anger
> That brings you here, a stranger?"

Well did she answer that one! And when he had heard her, Conchobor was taken with great pity and gave her the most fertile land he held with its herds and vast dwellings that were shaded by shaking aspen, and long, downy beds made from hazel were readied for the lady.[17]

Other stately houses were readied for the rest, and sunny rooms were made for the ladies to do their sewing of fringes to cloth and the fine needlework on head coverings. There they could comb and weave wool. But for this night, they were served a great feast at Emain, and the grateful lady sent messages to her sons, for she knew how anxious they would be.

Her sons came, then, and asked her what had been the great quarrel that had resulted in her being driven from the house.

"I really don't know," she said. "Other than that he fears you will come against him and drive him from Tara."

"This is far from our minds," her sons said. "We have not plotted against him with our great army."

"Well, then, I would suggest you pay heed to Conchobor's plan to avenge my honor," she said. "Bring your great champions here and take every piece of land you can and throw Eochaid from his throne and give his lands to those who help you."

Her sons looked with disbelief at each other, then said, "This is a most evil plan! It is foul indeed for a sovereign's family to stir up anger against him in his age when any other foe was afraid to attack him in his youth. The rest of Erin would treat us with contempt if we do that."

"Enough of this jousting of words," Conchobor said. "I know what you are thinking and that is even if you drive Eochaid from his throne the rest of the warriors in the land will still think of Tara as belonging to him. But this is not so. It doesn't matter the man if he is driven from his lands for three days. After that, they belong to the one who drove him from them. Yet this dishonor upon your mother and your failure to avenge her loss will diminish you in the eyes of others and you will never be admitted to your royal rank again. Nor your sons or their sons after them. All will be lost."

This logic was perverse, but they accepted it on their mother's advice, and the malicious and warring Ulster men and the lying and torturous venomous counsels of Conchobor convinced them to bring their army together and drive their father from his lands. They asked Conchobor what help he was willing to give them, for they knew that they would have to battle all of Erin in the coming war.

"I will give you three thousand soldiers and the Red Branch heroes to help you," he said. "But I advise you to send bands of warriors to hold the others in Erin within their houses by siege and keep the provincial kings in their own provinces. Then muster your army and attack as quickly as you can." And he recited:

> "Arise the Fionna of Emain
> For ambition drives such men
> To fair Tara there to do war
> And slay Eochaid in that war.
> The younger thorn is sharper
> By far and this is not a harper's
> Tale I'm telling you. Your father consumes
> Much in his age that would seem to some

That greed has become his stay.

Now I say you must be on your way

And slay Erin's High King this day."

Quickly the sons did as Conchobor bade them and assembled their armies at Emain. They groomed their swift and muzzled horses, braced their chariots and honed their weapons, and marked their armor well so they would all be known in battle and none would mistake friend for foe. They sent fast runners with messages to Nuada Necht Mac Sedna Sithbac, the haughty and rich prince of the Galian; to swift-striking Lugh Mac Lugaid Whitehand of smooth Munster; to Daire Redface Mac Dega, the red-sworded high king from whom Eochad Mac Lachtna takes his title, promising them lands and cattle if they would not come against them in battle.

The next day, the three sons of Eochaid Feidlech rose and marched southwest out of Emain to Boromhe Road[18] and then to Betha Mountain and past the head of fair Loch Frobal and over the green Plain of Ith to the heather-ruled Glen of River Finn, to Great Bernus and Minor Bernus and to the Estuary of the Two Salmon, where they stayed the night. The next day they marched swiftly over the Plain of Eine that was corn-rich and over fast-flowing Drobais and Buibe and over the bright Plain of Cedne through fruitful Cairbre and over the Stream of the Clear Well, over the Cascade of Dara, where Dara the Fomorian Druid drowned, to beautiful Ces Couruin, to the Mountain of Segais, to the Plain of the Dagda's Track, to the Plain of Ae Mac Allguba, to the Valley of the Road, to Cruachan, where Maeve waited for them, and there was no one save sunny-haired Clothrann to divide their tribute to the Cruachan company. The Fionna of Emain went in a chariot to speak with their Cruachan sister, and when she heard her brothers and the senseless babble of the others, she became disgusted and set about to delay their travel.

Then Ruad and Loch, the two Druids who were sons of Rochedul, approached them and tried to abort their expedition. Ruad said, "This is not a wise thing you do this year. Your army cannot protect you in the battlefield, for they will face a braver force by far.

> Great is the army of Eochaid
> That will keep your army instead
> Of allowing it to rule the battle
> And drive off Tara's cattle.
> You may have friends from Emain
> To help you but I say again
> That you will be defeated this day
> If you carry to Tara this armed fray."

Then Loch tried to stop them by saying,

> "Oh great warriors, for this deed
> You need a king who will lead
> You to victory. But no one
> Here has seen or ever done
> This deed before. There will be bitter
> Cries of woe this year, this winter,
> Over those who will die.
> I say let this mischief lie."

After the Druids had left them, the Fionna became very angry over the bad prophecy that suggested they would die fast if they continued on the way they had chosen. They sent fast warriors after them who slew the Druids on the account of that prophecy and this is why the "Druid's Mound" takes its name north of Cruachan this day. They went that night to their camp, and Clothrann came up the green-peaked hill to Cruachan. They sat and saw a noble pair dressed in pure white robes sitting opposite them. One was a handmaid who was attractive and white and gray-eyed and rosy-cheeked and bright-haired and red-lipped and sprightly and smooth-handed and white-throated with an elegant and deep bosom that drew the eye daringly, and white-toothed and eyebrow brown. The lady wore a pure white tunic and soft silken mantle that had thin red borders, and over her shoulders was a smooth cloak held by a crooked pin with a crystal set within it. That brooch was hard to look at, for it seemed to change colors if one studied it too closely. Her hair seemed purple, and she wore soft shoes upon her feet. No lady seemed to excell her in looks. She was there, then she was not, and Bres, the oldest of Eochaid's sons, saw her crossing the plain as he went to inspect the troops.

"Who are you?" he asked. "Why are you alone?"

"I come to speak with those who are death-doomed," she said.

"What's this?" he said scornfully. "No one is death-doomed. A mere fantasy that. Death is a coincidence; not long-fated."

"They are doomed," she said firmly. "If they want for longer life, then they need to come to terms with Erin's king."

"We are determined not to do that," Bres said. "We are the ones who should rule Erin; not he."

"That is an evil plan," she said.

By now, Bres's blood had boiled, and he felt himself standing to as he studied the deep cleft of her white breasts. He reached out and ripped her clothes from her and threw her naked on the ground and raped her again and again.

At last he rose, dripping with sweat, and took her white garments to wipe his dripping *bod*. When she could speak again, she said, "Shame and sorrow will come down upon you for this sin and wickedness you have committed."

"Is that right?" Bres sneered. "And who are the likes of you to be bringing down curses upon another?"

"I am Clothrinn, the daughter of Eochaid Feidlech,"[19] she

said. "I came to halt the destruction and to keep you from having right on your side when you go to war against our father."

Bres recoiled from her as he realized what she had done. He began to shake violently and said, "The curse and shame should fall on you, for you knew who you were, and I did not."

And he went away from her, but the others found her there and raped her as well and she said the same thing to them and that is how Glen of the Sin got its name at Cruachan to the south. From this union the lady became pregnant and bore a son who became known as Lugaid Redstripe.[20] The poet said,

> "Clothrinn the White bore a son that night
> Sired by her three brothers in light
> Of the moon. In Glen Sanbh his name
> Was Cian. But Lugaid was his real name.
> A thousand hostages Lugaid's son
> Would gather before his deeds were done.
> This was Criomthann of the White Sea
> Whose sin caused that crime to be
> Begun and Clothrann was his mother.
> It wasn't any other."

Still, they rose early the next day and went to Athlone and halted and camped at the hill now called Cealt. Erin's High King did not know they were there, and they put up their highly colorful tents, giving that place the name the Rath of the Tents. Then and only then did they send messengers to their father, telling him of their plans and advising him to vacate Tara. When they entered Eochaid's house and he asked them why they had come, they said, "We have come to tell you to leave this land and Tara to your sons and surrender the throne."

All there sat up in amazement at their brashness, and Conall Cernach,[21] who was sitting at the king's right hand as an honored guest, rose and drew his sword, meaning to behead the messengers. They looked murderous death in the eye as he stepped down, but Eochaid stopped him. But when Cet Mac Maga heard about the message, he tried to behead them and Eochaid had to restrain him as well.

"Where is Gluinchenn the Druid?" Eochaid demanded.

"Here," said the Druid.

"Use your magic and see if these rogues have spoken the truth," Eochaid said. "And see if my sons and I should go separate ways or what."

And then Eochaid said,

> "Tell me no lies, great Gluinchenn
> And me truly what to do. Then
> Tell me what will be concerning the three
> Fionna of Emain who came from my tree.
> What wanton destruction will they make
> Upon Tara for their greed's sake?"

> Gluinchenn: Against you I see the shade
> Of death coming to you, Eochaid,
> To take from you the kingdom and
> Army that you might have. This band
> Of men is here to destroy prosperity.

> Eochaid: Then what will come of it? Tell me
> This with your prophecy. What will happen
> With this planned destruction?

The wise Druid shook his hoary head and said, "I suggest you bring your army together, for your three sons come to you with well-marshaled strength: three battalions each with three thousand men following each of them."

Eochaid heaved a sigh and rose and went to gather his

army. He had only one night to put his army together to fight his sons, but he still managed to gather three thousand veteran warriors. These were those who stayed around him as his retainers. Then his chief warrior, Cet Mac Maga, gathered them and Conall Cernach Mac Amergin managed to bring young mercenaries to help him, and these numbered two thousand. Then came the chiefs of Bregh and Meath and Raon Mac Rochedul, the red king of the Ulster men, and grim Colamain of Tara with two thousand men. Now Eochaid's army numbered six thousand, and they left and marched to Cumar Ford, where they camped that night.

"Where is Gluinchenn the Druid?" Eochaid asked.

"I am here," said the Druid.

"Go to my sons and offer them terms," Eochaid said.

"What terms should I offer?" the Druid said.

"Two-thirds of Erin shall be theirs while I retain Tara and one-third for myself."

The Druid went to where the sons were encamped and entered their tent.

"You are welcome, wise Druid," they said.

"Until today, I would have welcomed that honor," said the Druid.

"It is still an honor," they said.

"I come from Eochaid to offer terms," he said, ignoring them.

"What are they?" the sons asked.

"Two-thirds of Erin for you to divide among yourselves. The other third remains with Eochaid along with Tara."

Lothar laughed. "Well, I say he should simply give it up to keep it from being taken from him."

The Druid frowned and said, "Why will you not accept his terms? A wise prince is the one who accepts terms freely offered. And it would be better for you if you did accept them, for only twenty-seven of you will be able to travel across the

Shannon tomorrow regardless how large your army is. The ridge to be traveled is called Anúar Ridge now but will be known as Ridge of Gore tomorrow after the blood of your bodies has been spilled. This well will be known as the Well of the Heads." And he recited,

> "Alas, that you went where you went,
> Fionna of Emain, to Emain, where you sent
> Word out to those to follow you on
> This course which you think you've won.
> But you are rebelling against the king
> And Clothfionn herself brought the sting
> Of a curse upon you. You have been
> Destroyed by her actions. Do you ken
> What I'm saying? At Comar Ford
> You will come against brave Eochaid."

And the Druid went back to Eochaid and told him what had happened since he went until he returned to the presence of Eochaid.

> Gluinchenn: Rise now, Tara's king,
> For your sons bring the sting
> Of their vile deed that drives them
> To seek their own death, it seems.

> Eochaid: This bothers me the slaying
> Of my sons who come to me staying
> True to their evil conspire
> To overthrow the king, their sire.
> If they are not slain, death's rattle
> I'll hear tomorrow in battle.

Gluinchenn: Do not despair for you
Will still be Tara's king. But you
Must tomorrow be battle-brave
If your throne you will save.

Eochaid: How do those three come
To Cumar Ford? What is the sum
Of men who come with them to
Bring battle to me to gain their due?

Gluinchenn: Bres has come from the south
Where he fought against Colamain. Lothar
Brings mercenaries for his deed
Against you. He's the worst seed!

Eochaid: Then Lothar will be slain by me
As we make ready to cross that bloody sea
Of battle. And as for Bres, well, I say,
'Tis by another he'll fall that day.

After speaking with his Druid, Eochaid fasted that night at
Cumar to the northeast. There they remained until morning,
when the three battalions across the river rose and began to
make themselves ready for battle. Eochaid rose and called for
his fighting ware. He took a heavy, hard-hitting sword and
belted it around his waist. It was an old sword and had served
him well in much combat, being worn smooth and hard and
polished from haft to point. He took two long spears with a
clever twist worked into their heads with clever charms and
riveted well to their shafts. He lifted his great warrior's shield,
so large a three-year-old boar could lay across it. Then he took
his crested helmet arranged with glittering stones along its band.
Then his great war-soul rose up within him, and he felt the
rage of lions and the frenzy of a furious bear and ordered his

men into three hard regiments, the mercenaries in one, Colamain in another, and two thousand veterans around himself.
Then he said,

> "Alas, the blood in my heart rages
> Against all the advice that my sages
> Can give to me. I know what this day
> Will bring: If I am not dead this day,
> I will not live. I will not live. I will not die
> For upon this day a plague must lie
> Brought by the war goddess. My sons
> Will die before this bloody day is done.
> The body of my body will fall,
> Those once at my knee will fall,
> And vomit bloody streams
> In place of their jealous dreams."

Then his mercenaries and warriors came to him and said,
"Our king, leave to us the youngest of your children and we
pledge that, although we are few, our shield-straps are held by
heroes." Conall laughed and recited,

> "I say that you should leave your youngest son
> To us, Eochaid. I promise you before we are done
> This day I will meet him face to face
> In battle at Crithech Ridge where he will face
> My wrath along with that of many men
> Who carry heroes' weapons. Not then
> Will he escape our slaughter unless we
> Are all dead in his place. But that won't be
> Coming for some time now. He will fall
> To our swords like many scythes fell
> Sheaves of wheat. He won't escape this field
> Until dark death upon him is dealt."

Sadly, Eochaid gave them permission to attack Nar and his battalions, which was a serious charge for the mercenaries. The veterans then came around Eochaid and said, "Why should we not draw the best of the lot? Let us take Lothar to task. He is the wisest in all of Erin and the most valorous. When you slew Factna Fathac Mac Ros Róich, we held your kingdom together for you for many years. When you slew Eochaid Broadchest in the Battle of Clarach in Coruinn, we were the band of heroes who held the field for you that day. Now we will fight for you again this day until we drive those battalions to dust.

> "Leave Lothar to us so that we
> Can return the hurt to him. See
> That we mean business. Gray hair
> May fleck our crowns but there
> Are many here who remember
> How he took our young members
> From our families. We won't retreat
> From this field. Please, we entreat
> You to let us carry the battle to him
> And let Lothar fall to his whim."

At that moment, the mercenaries took the battle to Bres, and the others took up their positions on the battlefield, marking out the areas they would defend. They charged forward, and when the sons saw that, they sent deadly troops against them and made three battalions of equal size to attack in a hard charge like a single man. They raised their flowing leopard standards high, and their awful bows of battle, and thundered down upon the men. When the mercenaries and stout Colamain and the two thousand veterans saw that, they came together in three close battle-formations. Then the battalions met with the bosses of their shining shields clashing and stabbing with gray spears that soon ran red with gore. They gave fierce battle-drinks to each other until they gained the advantage with their wide-hopped lances and clanging dagger-sharp heavy spears. They reached into the hollow of their shields and drew their short swords and came together fiercely, slashing and stabbing, until many mangled men lay upon the gore-dripped ground with shrunken lips stretched in battle screams and torsos gashed wide with wounds. Each slope was heavy with battle bones, and yet the battle still raged.

Then Bres saw Eochaid and the Colamain coming westward and attacked them with his battalions, boldly, proudly, hastily, like a roaring rip-tide wave that rolled up from the depths of the ocean to rage across the land, falling in swift streams down the ravines of mountains. Grimly the battalions dealt death to each other with stout spears and slashing swords and poisoned darts and swift shafts.

Now Bres came east over the great stream to attack the Colamain, and Cet Mac Maga came west over the stream to attack Nar. Many sons and seniors of noble families fell with red streams streaming from war-wounds, and many lay in pools of blood and gore poured like a raging river across the land. Many waved shorn red stumps in defiance, swinging swords with other hands; others lay in death-agony. Then Bres raged a terrible charge in a warlike wrathful onset at the hosts of the Colamain. But the brave warrior Raon Mac Rochedul saw that and said, "I have advice to give to you. Get your men and weapons together and leave this field, for we have sworn ourselves to the prince of Erin. Now here is my plan, let us pretend to flee over this hill, and when his men follow and stretch themselves out, we will turn and give them rout."

They all quickly agreed to this, and when Bres saw the Colamain running away, he gleefully order the army to pursue them.

"Chase them down before they reach their homes so you

can gather their lands to yourselves!" bawled a captain, rushing fiercely after them.

When Raon Mac Rochedul and the Colamain heard that, they spun about and faced west, standing so close together that their spears bristled like black thorns, making a shield-guarded fortress of themselves against the horde chasing them.

Then Raon Mac Rochedul, the red king, attacked in a martial fury, slaying a hundred in his path, and raged again among them killing another hundred in his fierce rush until he had hacked a path to Bres. Then he stood before him and taunted him with rough words. The blushing Bres brandished his sword, and they brought brisk bloody battle upon each other, swinging swords over shields, banging bosses, strokes falling that could open the doors of death. Bres received fifty hard wounds in that battle, and Raon, raising his shining smooth-pointed hard-edged sword, struck savagely a stroke against Bres's face. Frantic, Bres raised his sword to guard the blow and watched it fall in two pieces from his hand.

"Give me leave to go and get another sword," panted Bres, eyes glaring wildly.

"All right," Raon said. "As long as it's to me you return to battle."

Then the battle of the battalions surged around them.

Nar's battalion and the mercenaries came west over the stream toward the battle. Hearts steeled themselves against the onslaught and champions grimly gripped their swords and then, even though sorely wounded, they pressed on hard against the bellies of the others, slicing them open so their entrails came out in great streams of blood and a large din that ached against the ears rose from that savage attack and fainting men and feeble folk fell faintly in the battle and clots of brown blood and lumps of gore flew around the plain and hill. The mercenaries held against Nar, however, and Nar, with a hundred and fifty heroes at his command, fell under the savage counterattack of the mercenaries.

Meanwhile, Eochaid came with his two thousand veterans, who arranged a brown-red battle shield around him, leveling sharp spears through the gaps between the shields to defend themselves from the blue weapons of those who followed Lothar. The two thousand battle-hardened veterans stood in front of their king to protect him from the swords and spears. Then came Cet with his Connacht men and Conall Cernach with his Ulster men, who came with red-weaponed slaughter down upon Lothar's army in the middle of the field. And then came a proud strong hasty fight and darting strife as terrible blows hacked gobs of flesh from bodies and warriors screamed in fury and pain and fell upon the blood-soaked ground and closer and closer the warriors came to each other. Not one of Lothar's men came without a gray lance or shining shield or hero's hand-stone, save in the hollow of his curved shield.

They met fiercely, fiercely hacking, fiercely stabbing, and the fallen wailed ululating wails of wounded pride and the shrill screams of battle sounded starkly as lips went dead and faces blanched and eyes were torn out and brainpans lopped off and arms and legs hacked away. The crows and ravens were merry feasting that day, and the sprites and goblins and madmen of the plains and demons screamed from every corner of battle.

Lothar went to the brink of the ford where he had seen his father and found him in the middle of the ford with Conall on his right and Cet on his left, and every one had brought his stone with him, as had Lothar. Then Lothar raised his hand and skillfully and swiftly struck, his whole strength stepped into his forearm and his forearm into his fist and the strength of his fist into his stone and made a straight shot at his father at the rear of the battle. The thick stone spun like a wheel, and Cet and Conall raised their shields against it. But the stone was too sharply thrown and sped through the two shields and struck the broad chest and noble bosom of the High King so that he fell crosswise to the stream with his royal shield and hero's armor in the swampy pools of Cumar Ford. A great gout of black blood burst from his lips and the king raised himself and spat bloody foam into the waters. He saw the stone buried in the ford and put one foot on it so that only a third stayed aboveground and he kept his foot on that stone as long as the battle raged. It lies there to this day and still the mark of his foot is on it.[22]

But when the two kingly soldiers in strength and manhood, when the two hard-hitting war hounds, the two battle-brave men, the two fierce lions, the two bears of mighty deeds, the two red tidal waves, the two flood-bursts, the two venomous snakes, the two hounds Conall and Cet saw that shot, they seized their weapons, and the two thousand experienced veterans spent their force and fury on the hosts so that bodies were mangled and trunks gashed wide and eyes blinded with blood bursts and many feet were by necks and necks by feet and Lothar's army defeated and beheaded in that combat.

Cet and Conall went grimly into battle like two hammers on a rough iron anvil, and a great slaughter then hewed through the warriors. In vain the battalions came together, and Cet and Conall savaged them and slew them and mutilated them and gore and blood dripped from their shields and armor and swords. A hundred fell by each man that day, and then Cet and Lothar met and there was no talk or parley offered. They hurled themselves at each other, each swinging his sword harshly against the other's shield. When Conall Cernach saw that, he charged into Lothar and knocked him sprawling. Then he hacked and hewed at him, and Lothar rolled to his feet and paid back Conall while keeping his battle raging against Cet. But no one was ever in greater need than Lothar caught between those two champions. Others came to aid Lothar but were beaten back by Cet and Conall, and they left Lothar lying alone in his wounds on the battlefield. When the other two battalions saw that, they turned their faces to the west and abandoned their families and lands.

Then nine of the Ulster princes who were foster-brothers of Lothar charged and lifted him out of the battle and put a bier of wattles under him on the shoulders of champions. Yet the rout was so great that the slaughter increased, and they retreated slowly with weary worn warriors. Eochaid followed them to the western side, and then the slaughter rose again with stabbing and spearing from the campground to the Celt. The men rallied to Eochaid's battle-cry, and from that to the Shannon, a thousand warriors fell so that nine of them escaped with each of the sons over the river.

Nine of them went over Snamh-da-en and nine over Ath Liag and the third nine over Athlone round Bres. Raon Mac Rochedul charged after them over Athlone, and although others held back, he did not and grimly chased them to the Plain of Ai, where he slew three of each party and came himself to western Connacht. There Bres held his fort, but none of his men survived to cover his retreat except his son Da Thi, who stayed to fight with Raon. But Raon beheaded him and came after Bres fiercely and boldly until he caught him. Then they made a powerful assault on each other. The warriors in the fort of Bres saw this and opened the gates of the fort. When Raon saw that, he seized a spear as thick as his wrist and, taking careful aim, threw it at the royal warrior. It struck him in the middle of the chest and came out equally balanced on both sides. Then Raon beheaded him in front of his own fort and returned with the two heads upon the boss of his shield.

Lothar sped across Snamh-da-en over the Shannon with nine others with him. They followed him until he reached his own fort in western Connacht at Cera. But when he got there, he found Cet, and Cet took the heads of his nine men and made a cairn over them. Lothar's Tomb at the White Lake of Cera is called after him.

Nar went with his people over the West Ford, and the mercenaries followed, led grimly by Conall. None of them knew Lothar was dead, and they beheaded Nar and his nine followers at the Land of Slaughter in the western districts of Umall and returned victorious over the Shannon.

The heroes brought the heads of the three sons and laid them at the feet of Eochaid. When he saw them, he exclaimed, "I am saddened to see these heads."

Then he wept bitterly and said,

> "Dress these three heads
> And cover the bloody red
> Edges of their wounds. Clean
> Their faces so they will seem
> As royal as they were.
> Alas that they were
> So marked with desire
> That they took battle to their sire
> And fell in this raging battle.
> I did not hear their death-rattle
> But I say to you to place
> Two heads to my right, place
> The other to my left, and mine
> In the middle. The world is nothing
> To me now. I shall now take
> Them back to Tara for their sake."

After those words, he took the heads back with him to Tara, and when he arrived there, he said, weeping, " 'Tis a pity I did not die before you. My share of the throne is now a drink of death." And with every movement he made, a clot of blood fell from his mouth. He spoke,

"We fought the battle of Cumar
And drank a deadly draft there.
We overthrew a hostile host
And took the lie from their boast
That my sons would rule over me
But see, there they are on the Dead Sea."

Then a great shivering came over the king and he felt chilled and went seven days without food or drink. Death and dissolution came upon him, and he ordered his people to carry him to the land of Connacht to Cruachan Ai, where they would build his tomb and pile heavy sod over him and place the heads of his three sons on one side and their three bodies on the other. The heads were brought to him, and he looked at the head of Bres and said, "Dear was he who had this head. It was not this head that hid from guests or companies or armies."

And he said,

"Many were welcomed to the fort of Bres
And never did any go without rest.
He was a good host and welcomed strangers
Despite whatever they brought in danger.
Nar was the youngest of the men
And was pursued to the sea and then
Slain there while Lothar—no deed
Was foolish to him—did not heed
The gray beards who pursued him
To Cera and to Cle-na-con then
Slew him there. No one should speak
Ill of them for all their bad feats.
Raon dashed after Bres and slew
Da Thi while Bres still flew
Toward his fort. There he fell
With a spear that was well-

Cast yet I cannot say that he
Deserved to die before me."

After he recited that poem Eochaid said, "I feel death's breath upon my face. Carry me to where my sons were beheaded so I might see their wounds and scars."

This they did, lifting him up and carrying him along, and a hundred and fifty men were assigned to each of them, to each of Eochaid and his three sons. They carried him to Tara, and the king said, "This is a dear inheritance and state from which I am parted. I hope that no future king of Erin is not succeeded by his son without another king between them."

This is why there is a *geis* upon a son rebelling against his father for Erin's rule.

Then Eochaid said farewell to Erin, Tara, and his people with the following:

"Farewell to you, my Tara around
Whom many kings fought sound
Battle. Your throne is empty tonight
With no king or heir in your sight.
Many shields clashed and battled
And many a throat gave up death's rattle
To seize or keep your great throne.
But to such things men are borne
And I honored you, I, Eochaid
To whom I feel the coming shade
Of death. Great pleasure I had
Here and little displeasure I had.
But now, your colors will change
And armies will for you exchange
Great battle blows. I regret well
That I must not bid you farewell."

Then Eochaid fell silent and with dimming eyes contemplated the royal fortress. A great sorrow broke in his chest, and he heaved one final despairing sigh as his great heart broke in his chest and he died. He was taken by the route that he commanded, and the men and women went weary with wailing for him. He was taken to Cruachan Ai and buried there with the bodies of his three sons, and heavy sods of earth were heaped over them at Cruachan.

That is the Battle of Cumar and the tragical death of Eochaid Feidlech's three sons and of Eochaid Feidlech himself so far.

Finit um 22 la da mí Nobembear, 1717.

The House of the King and High King

Lánellach Tigi Rích 7 Ruirech is a very short text in Old Irish that seems to have been used to establish the seating requirements according to rank. The reference to Conchobor appears to intend Conchobor Mac Nessa, although he is not referred to by this name.

HERE BELOW IS THE FULL listing of the house of the king and High King:

1. Conchobor sat in the chief seat.
2. Goibne [a smith] sat by his knee.
3. Foride [a Druid] sat beside him.
4. Tot Mac Eogain Orbrecht [a judge] sat in front.
5. Augune sat behind the king.
6. The spearman sat by the houseposts.

7. The sureties [the ones who made the covenants for rightful claims] sat before the king.

8. Búamond [the ruling woman] sat in the level rush-strewn place.

9. The hospitallers sat by the king's forearms [to serve him].

10. The [text missing] and leeches sat with the drink-measure beside the cupbearers. [I take this to mean next to the hospitallers.]

11. The leather-bottle makers and brewers sat on the great threshing-floor.

12. The jesters sat between the two candles on the front floor of the house.

13. Other *daernemed* [satirists and magicians] sat by the doorposts.

14. The horn-blowers, charioteers, and flute-players sat in the front.

15. The attendants sat and stood by the pillars.

16. The hunters, fishermen, catchers [trappers?], and builders sat in a cubicle apart.

The Tale of
Mac Da Thó's
Pig

Every important figure of the Ulster Cycle is present in this story
of feasting and fighting except Cúchulainn, who is not only not
involved in the story but not even mentioned in it. This absence
would seem to indicate that this is one of the oldest stories of
the cycle. There are difficulties with attaching the story as one
of the *remscela* to *Táin Bó Cuailngé*. The pig in question is huge,
so large that forty oxen can be laid across it. This would seem
to suggest that it is either a mythic beast or else intended to be
satirical. As Connacht and Ulster eventually go to war over a
bull, we have the two provinces falling out again over a dog. Mac
Da Thó, it seems, promises this wondrous dog to both provinces,
then pretends innocence on the day they show up to claim it.
During the bragging contest for the right to carve the roasted
pig and deliver the sections to those who deserve them—i.e., the
champion's portion, the subject of *Fled Bricrend*, which I translated as *The Feast,* the heroes are not only shamed but ridiculed
as well. Lóegaire has been speared and chased away from the

border, where he has been guarding one of the passages; the father of Aengus has had his left hand cut off (a possible association with the story of Nuada), Éogan has lost an eye, and Fer Loga becomes a comical figure when he demands that the Ulster women sing "Fer Loga Is My Darling" to him every night. The story appears to come from the ninth or tenth century yet is laid in Leinster instead of Ulster or Connacht.

NOW THERE ONCE WAS A famous king of Lagin, a land-holder in Leinster, if you will, named Mac Da Thó.[1] This man owned a hound called Ailbe[2] that used to protect all of Lagin and could easily run the province in a day without tiring. This is how the Plain of Ailbe gathered its name. People used to say about him,

> Mesroida was Mac Da Thó's name,
> The owner of the pig, the same
> One that feasted Conchobor and Ailill.
> He also owned the cunning hound Ailbe
> From whom comes the Plain of Ailbe.

The hound's fame quickly spread throughout the land, and messengers came from Ailill and Maeve to ask for the hound, for such a hound surely belonged in a royal house and not in the house of a minor king, even a landholder. As fate would have it, messengers arrived at the same time from Conchobor, the king of the Red Branch in Ulster, to ask for the hound as well.

All were made welcome, for Mac Da Thó's hostel was renowned as one of the five chief hostels in all of Erin that always had hot water ready for his guests. The others were Da Derga's hostel in Cúalu and Forgall Manach's beside Lusk and Mac Da Réo's in Bréife and Da Choca's in western Meath. Each hostel had seven doors and seven roads led through it and there were seven hearths and seven caldrons there as well to provide for guests. An ox and a salted pig would be placed in each of the seven caldrons, and as each man passed one of the caldrons, he would stab a fork into it and bring up what he would eat. If he missed the flesh, however, why then there would be only an empty platter left for him, for he would not be given a second try.

This time, however, the messengers were taken to Mac Da Thó's couch, where he had retired for the night, before being led to the caldrons so that they might deliver the requests of their kings.

"We have come from Connacht, where Ailill and his wife, Maeve,[3] rule, to ask for your hound," the leader of the messengers[4] said. "Now, we don't expect you to make a gift of such a wonderful animal without receiving something in return. So to this, you will receive one hundred and sixty milch cows at once and a fine chariot with two horses, each sired from the best in Connacht to pull it. At the end of the year, the same will again be given to you."

Mac Da Thó's mouth gaped wide at this, for these riches would make him among the wealthiest in all of Erin. Yet the Ulster messengers were not to be outdone by their Connacht counterparts, and to this the leader among them spoke up, casting a withering glance at the Connacht speaker as he said, "We come from Conchobor to request the hound. Our king is no tightfisted skinflint to be pandering after something for nothing. He will match those Connacht gifts and add precious stones and the friendship of Ulster to your lands."

Mac Da Thó nodded politely and gestured that the messengers should be taken away and given food and bed. Then he fell into a black silence and for three days and nights went without food or drink or sleep, tossing and turning at night until finally his wife said crossly, "This is long enough for fasting. Food is brought to you, but you nibble at nothing."

Yet he remained silent, and finally she threw her hands up into the air and said:

"Night has fallen but there is no sleep
Within it for Mac Da Thó who thinks deep
Thoughts to himself but shares
Them with no one who cares.

He turns away from his willing wife
To face the wall despite the strife
He has faced in war. Yet night
Brings terrors out of my sight."

"Enough!" said Mac Da Thó
Tiredly. "You batter words so
Much one forgets Crimthann Níad Náir
Who said, "Tell no secret to fair

Women for they cannot keep
The words to themselves. Sleep
Is harmed by their nattering. Slaves
Do not receive jewels and brave

Men do not need to bring worries
To their wives. Such flurries
Would cause men despair
If women committed them to air."

And his wife answered, saying,
"What is this foolish braying
You make to the air? A woman
Is worthy of hearing her man

Speak when things are amiss!
Why do you prattle on with this
Thought and say nothing to me?
Maybe I could help you see

What is possible beyond your means.
But until you speak to me what seems
To be your problem only remains
With you despite what you retain

Within your heart, thinking me
To be only a receptacle for your seed.
Shame! Shame! For thinking like this!
'Tis no wonder things have gone amiss!"

"All right, woman!" said he wearily.
"Enough nattering to make your dreary
Point! It's like this, you see: Conchobor
Has sent word to me that upon his honor

He will befriend my house and pay
Me handsomely for my hound. Stay,
I'm not finished! For into the fray
Comes the word of Ailill and Maeve today

That they too want my hound
And their offer is equally sound!
Now this seems like a good barter
To set them against the other

But this is surely an evil day
For Mac Da Thó, for to say
One deserves a dog over another
Is to insult badly the other!

Ah, woe is me! For I can see
That many brave men will be
Slain for the sake of this hound!
And I cannot see any sound

Way to get out of this fix!
May nettles and thorny sticks
Be pushed into their asses
For all this trouble their molasses

Tongues have wagged my way!
So, woman, you've heard! Now say
Your thoughts and do not bray
Yourself at the moon. I say

That many men will be slain
If I go Maeve's way or deign
To give the hound to Conchobor
For that king's great honor!"

His wife shook her long locks
And mocked his words: "You block
Of wood! The answer is surely simple!
Give the hound to both! Those ample

Fools will fight over it! What difference
Does it make who wins? The inference
Here, if you can't tell, is when done
It's no matter who gets the bone!"

"Well," the man said dubiously,
"I can't say I'm glad. Obviously,
It matters not to me who wins
The hound in the battle-din.

But for every winner a loser marks
The day he came out second-lark.
Mind! I'm not saying that this food
For thought isn't very good,

But I don't see what I can lose
By trying your way. Now, those
Servants can bring back the food.
I'll eat now for a while. Understood?"

And Mac Da Thó rose, his spirits lifted with the hope of an answer to his predicament. He scratched his hairy belly through his robe and bawled, "Here, now! Bring food, damnit! And let my guests know that their host is over his, his—"

"Malediction?" his wife suggested coolly.

"Yes, mal—mal—whatever! Tell them I had a bellyache! Tell them whatever! Bring food and drink and let us make merry!"

And he clapped his hands together, happy for once that the big problem that had filled his belly with gas had gone away with his wife's suggestion. In time, he would convince himself that the idea came to him in sleep, but this would be only after much meat and drink had worked its way down his gullet. For three days and nights, he led the feasting while the messengers from Ulster and Connacht eyed each other suspiciously over the table, each certain that the other had gotten the spoils since Mac Da Thó had not offered the hound to them.

At last, on the eve of the third day of feasting, Mac Da Thó belched and gathered a tankard up in one huge hand and pulled aside the Connacht messengers and said to them, "You've enjoyed yourselves, eh? Good, good! Well, then, enough of the endless yammering, I tell you! I had my doubts about how serious you were when you brought Ailill's offer to me! Oh, now, don't be getting your chins down! It's not your fault if that's all Maeve told you to offer me! The truth of the matter is I've decided to take your offer and give the mutt to Maeve and Ailill and have sent my offer on its way, telling them to come here with a large army to fetch it away. I'll give them a fine feast and fair presents and the hound will be theirs."

Those messengers were delighted with the words of Mac Da Thó and went away from his hostel with a jubilant heart, singing bold songs as they traveled. Mac Da Thó watched their party disappear over the Plain of Ailbe, then turned away, rubbing his hands together with great satisfaction.

"All right," he muttered to himself. "We've got those out of the nest. Now for Conchobor's men."

He wandered through his house until he found the messengers sitting close to the fire from a great chill that had entered the room. They looked up as he came toward them, rubbing his hands together cheerfully.

"There you are," he cried. "I've been looking all around for you. Well, I've come to the decision after a long doubt and have decided that Conchobor can have the hound. But he must come here to claim it," he said, wagging an admonishing finger at the messengers. "I don't want to let the hound go simply in the hands of strangers. You understand," he hastened to add, "I mean nothing by this. One has to be careful in such transactions, you know. After all, he is one of a kind. The hound, I mean. Tell Conchobor to come and collect his prize and to bring the best of the Red Branch with him. We'll have a large feast and there'll be presents and that sort of thing. You know, a special celebration!"

With a glad heart, the messengers rose and thanked Mac Da Thó profusely for his wise decision and left to carry his words back to the Ulster king Conchobor. Mac Da Thó watched them leave, beaming and waving until they passed from view, then slouched against the door beam and drew a deep, ragged breath, grateful that so far his ruse had worked. Not that he cared that much for the hound, which, truth be known, was a bit of a problem now and then, when it became a bit cranky and took a chew out of someone or other. In some way, he would be glad to be rid of it, yet owning such an animal was a marked honor, for there wasn't any like it in all of Erin.

"Still," he muttered, staring out across the plain at the dwindling specks of travelers, "there comes a time when a gift can be a curse."

With a sigh, he turned away from the doorway and went inside to finish making his plans for the Connacht and Ulster kings.

Now the people from Connacht and Ulster were pleased indeed to know that the great hound would be added to their riches and honors. Rapidly, they put together bands of warriors to go with the kings to the home of Mac Da Thó to retrieve the hound. The two provinces could not have timed their arrival better—or for the worse—as they appeared at Mac Da Thó's door at the same time, each eyeing the other suspiciously, certain that bad plans had been made by the others but not certain what they were.

Mac Da Thó went himself to greet his guests and welcome them into his house. "Here! Here! Glad I am that you have arrived together—although I had not expected you to arrive together as one, you are, nevertheless, welcome indeed to my home! Enter! Enter! Ceremony is good but a bit pompous given the circumstances, don't you think?"

Beaming, he stepped aside to let Conchobor and Ailill and Maeve enter ahead of him.[5] One half of the house had been set aside for use by the Connacht men and one half for the Ulster warriors. The house was well made for such a division as it had seven entrances with fifty paces between each door and fifty beds for each door. Such a magnificent hostel was needed for a feast this large, but few friendly faces showed at that feast, for many there had slain others whose relatives now looked across the board at those who had injured them in one way or another. These were ancient enemies, however, for a war had been between Connacht and Ulster for three hundred years before Christ had come into the world, and the memories of the clans were far longer than that.

Mac Da Thó was aware of the enmity bristling among those gathered for the feast and shouted gaily, "Bring forth the pig chosen for this feast!"

Obediently his servants brought in the pig to be slaughtered, and no ordinary pig was led in. This one had been fed by sixty milch cows for seven years, but the milk that had fed that pig surely had venom in it for the number of men that would be slaughtered on its account. But the pig alone would not be enough for such a crowd as this; forty oxen as well were laid across its back for roasting besides other food that had already been readied.

Normally Mac Da Thó would have seated himself with the guest of honor, but this time the host attended to the particulars of the feast himself, beaming as he moved among his guests, saying, "Welcome! Welcome! I hope this meets with your pleasure, but if not, why then let me know and it will be slaughtered for your taste tomorrow. There are plenty of pigs and cattle in Leinster and enough that none should go away wanting!"

Conchobor tore his eyes away from Maeve's budding charms and looked at the feast prepared, saying grudgingly, "There seems to be enough here for all. The pig looks good."

"Indeed," Ailill answered. Then he frowned. "But tell me, Conchobor: how should it be divided among those here?"

"How else," Bricriu Mac Carbaid butted in from his couch. "Where Erin's heroes gather, they always choose the portions by the contest of arms." The poisoned-tongued one laughed maliciously. "Therefore, let each give the other a punch on the nose to settle which is the best."[6]

Ailill nodded with satisfaction and said blandly to Conchobor, "Well, that certainly seems reasonable, don't you think?"

Conchobor's eyes narrowed at Ailill's sudden agreement, for he did not trust the Connacht king more than a squirrel trusts his acorn stash to another in late fall. "All right," he agreed. "That seems fair. We have a number of warriors here who have wandered around the border—as your warriors will remember. Or not, as the case may be," he said, smiling with satisfaction at the sudden flush to Ailill's face.

Senlaech Arad, from Cruachan Conalathe in the West, laughed and said, "Well, you will have need of those warriors tonight, Conchobor. I have left enough of them sitting in the muddy water of Luachar Dedad without the fat cattle that stayed with me."

Munremur Mac Gerrcind laughed scornfully at Senlaech's boast and said, "None of those was fatter than the oxen you left with me as you showed your heels to our lands. You left so fast you even left your own brother, Cruithne Mac Ruailinde, behind. Such is Connacht's boast?"

"That was no worse than Irloth son of Fergus Mac Leit, who was left dead by Echbel Mac Dedad at Tara Luachra," said Cu Roi's son Lugaid, his eyes flaring brightly with his boast.

He was answered by Celtchar Mac Uthecair, who said, "And what sort of man was Congancnes Mac Dedad? I myself cut off his head!"

Then the warriors began shouting across the hall, shaking meaty fists to emphasize their insulting words as they boasted about the reputation of the ones they had killed in single combat or in a raid into the other's lands. Mac Da Thó stood aside and watched as the arguments weaved back and forth with first one side gaining the advantage, only to be beaten by the other, who had slain a man of greater reputation.

At last, however, it came down to one man who had defeated or beaten every one there: Cet Mac Matach of Connacht. He swaggered to where the weapons had been stacked and hung his weapon above all the others and then went to the pig and sat down beside it, taking the carving knife in his hand. He raised his eyebrows and glanced scornfully around the room. "Now, then, find someone to match my deeds in all of Erin or else I shall carve this pig to my liking. Well?"

A great silence fell upon the room as the Connacht men glared in triumph across the room at the Ulster host, for none of the Ulster men there could match Cet in his deeds.

Conchobor looked angrily at Loegaire and said, "All right, Loegaire. Stand up to this man and bring the honor to Ulster, where it belongs."

"As you wish," Loegaire said, rising. He gave a hitch in his belt and stared across the room at Cet sitting arrogantly beside the pig. "Well, Cet, the honor of carving that pig cannot belong to you. Not in front of all here."

"Is that right, Loegaire?" Cet sneered. "Well, then, let me remind you of your own custom that every one of you who takes arms as a youth makes Connacht his first raid, right? Of course, I'm right, and you know where this is going, for you did the same. I met you at the border and sent you scrambling back home with my lance in your side. You left your chariot and fine horses and your charioteer behind as well, didn't you? You shouldn't get the pig for that deed." He laughed.

"Ah me. I was young then," Loegaire said, sighing. "Nevertheless, it is true." And he sat down and covered his head from the shameful reminder of his encounter with Cet.

A tall fair warrior leaped to his feet on the Ulster side of the room and said, "No, Cet. You should not be allowed to carve that pig."

Cet squinted through the dim light of the room at the shadowed warrior. "And who is this beanpole squawking a warrior's words among his betters?"

"A better warrior than you. I am Aengus Mac Lám Gabaid[7] of Ulster."

"Ah," Cet said. He scratched his chin through his beard with a dirty fingernail. "Does anyone know how his father got his name? Speak, Ulster! Do any of you know?"

"Tell us, then," a man from Ulster shouted angrily.

"That I'll do. One day, when I came east into your lands to get cattle, a great alarm was raised among your people. One who answered it was Lám Gabaid, who came recklessly at me in challenge. He threw a large lance at me, but I snatched it out of the air and threw it back at him. It sliced off his hand, which fell to the ground and stayed there while he went away from the field. Now, if his father ran from me, what brings this stripling to challenge my right to the pig?"

Aengus shook his head and sat back down on his couch and lifted his cup of mead, sipping it, eyes averted from all.

"Well?" challenged Cet. "Is that it? Speak up or I'll put the knife to this pig."

Another tall and fair warrior stood up and said, "All right. You don't have the right to carve this pig, Cet."

"Oh?" Cet said, raising his eyebrows. "And who is this would-be warrior?"

"Eogan Mor Mac Durthacht," came the answer. "The king of Fernmag."[8]

"Oh." Cet yawned. "Of course. I've run across him before."

"And where might that have been?" Eogan asked.

"In front of your own house," Cet replied ruthlessly. "I was stealing your cattle when you came in answer to the alarm your people raised, screaming their heads off in fear, I might add. You threw your spear at me. I caught it on the boss of my shield and jerked it out and cast it back at you. It went clean through your head—not much there to stop it—and put out one eye. That's why you stand there looking around the room with only one eye. Is that the great feat of arms you wanted to tell this group?"

Eogan sat down, face flaming in shame.

Cet looked around the room in triumph. "Well?" he challenged. "Continue the contest, or let me carve this pig to my liking."

"No, not yet," said Munremur Mac Gerrcind, rising to his feet. He hooked his thumbs in his belt and glared across at Cet.

"Is that Munremur?" Cet asked, peering through the gloom.

"It is," said the men of Erin.

"I washed my hands in your blood, Munremur," Cet said. "Or have you forgotten the day only three days ago when I carried off three of your warriors' heads along with the head of your oldest son?"

Munremur shook his own head at this and resumed his seat on his couch.

"Continue the contest," said Cet. "Who else?"

"I challenge you," said Mend Mac Salchad.

"Who is this?"

"Mend!" shouted the Ulster warriors.

"What's this? Now the sons of herdsmen want to challenge me? Sit down, pup! I am the one who baptized your father with the blade of my sword. I whacked his heel, and he stumped away with only one foot. What could the son of a one-footed man bring to this gathering to challenge my right?"

Men sat down, and Cet grinned, shouting, "Again! Who challenges my right to this pig?"

"Very well, you shall have it," said a tall, gray-haired warrior who rose to his feet. Not a few there shrank away from his battle-scarred visage, which showed his ferocity in war.

Cet looked at him and said, "And who is this?"

"This is Celtchair Mac Uthecair!" shouted the Ulster side.

"Wait a little, Celtchair, unless you want to exchange blows now," said Cet, frowning. He tapped his fingers against the side of his head, then brightened. "Ah yes. Now I remember! I came to your house and everyone sounded the alarm and rushed toward me. You came yourself, if you think back rightly! I am the one who threw the spear that went through your balls and has left you childless and stinking of urine ever since. And now you think you have the ballocks to challenge me?"

Celtchair flamed with embarrassment and sat down, rolling to one hip as the sudden memory of his loss brought back the pain he had known.

"All right, who's next?" Cet asked mockingly. "Come! Which of you has a challenge for me?"

"A—a—all right," said Cusraid the Stammerer of Macha Mac Conchobor.

"And who are you?"

"This is Cusraid," said another.

Cet eyed the young man boldly. "Well, he has the makings of a king the way he stands with his shoulders back and all."

"And—and no thanks to you, Cet," the young man said furiously.

"You're right about that," Cet answered, laughing. "You came to the border to try your first feat of arms and we met. You left behind a third of your people as you fled with a spear of mine through your neck. That's why you can't say a word without tonguing it twice. That's why you are called the Stammerer."

The youth meekly sat, and Cet made an impatient gesture with his hand. "All of you here from Ulster are pan-fries, would-be sword-bearers!" And with that, he started from his right and moved insultingly to his left, ripping apart each warrior who had failed to meet him in deeds until the entire Ulster contingent was left staring sheepishly at the floor.

"Right, then," he said, taking a fresh hold on the carving knife. "There's none here that can match my deeds, and I claim this pig."

At that moment, the door burst open, and Conall Cernach leaped into the middle of the floor and threw back his magnif-

icent head, staring around the room at all seated there. The
men of Ulster gave a glad shout of welcome to see Conall, and
Conchobor himself rose from his seat of honor and took the
helmet from Conall's head. Conall looked at Cet and frowned.

"And what are you doing with that knife in your hand?"
he demanded.

"That is Cet Mac Matach, who has won the right of carving," the Connacht men shouted gleefully.

"That true, Cet?" Conall said, a broad smile slowly forming
on his face. "You're the one who claims the pig?"

"True enough," said Cet. Then he said:

> "Welcome, Conall, great stone-hearted
> Warrior with the fierce fire glow started
> Behind the glitter of ice in your eyes.
> I know the hero's anger in your breast
> And the wounds you have inflicted
> In the triumph of battles you've conflicted.
> I see you have truly earned the name
> From your father, son of Finnchoem!"

To this Conall answered:

> "Well spoke, Cet Mac Matach, ice-hearted
> Warrior you are, whose strength has started
> Many wars! You're a strong chariot leader
> In battle and have fought many battles as leader
> Of men after strong bulls in others' lands
> At the head of your warrior bands."

"Oh, I like this," Conchobor said, sitting and smiling gleefully. "This promises to be good."

Cet stared at Conall, then raised his eyebrows. "But?"

"The right to cut that pig, though, well, that will have to

be left in our meeting and your parting," Conall said. He clapped his enormous hands together. The thunder made the others wince and probe their ears with questing fingers. "It'll make a good story to be told by the charioteers when they meet with the awl-men who repair harnesses. Ah, I can hear it now, the tale of noble warriors meeting in battle, men who have each performed great battle-deeds." He glanced around the hall, his eyes dancing merrily. "I think a good number of men will step over the bodies of others tonight!" He looked back at Cet. "Get away from that pig, wanting warrior!"

Cet flushed and shook his head. "And what makes you think you are deserving of it?"

"By my right," Conall said. "I'll have you with a sword in single combat if you wish. I swear by whatever my people wish to swear that since I first took arms I have never been a day without the head of a Connacht man swinging from my belt or chariot rim or gone a night without plundering someone's herd. When I sleep, I place the head of a Connacht man beneath my knees."

"True! All true!" shouted the Ulster men, making obscene gestures at the Connacht forces.

"And if you give me the lie, why I'm for you," Conall said, touching the haft of the great sword at his belt.

Cet shook his head, face flaming as he rose. "That may be true, and if it is, why then, you are a better warrior than I. But if my brother Anluan were in this house, he would give the lie back to you in your teeth and match you easily in a contest of swords. But"—he spread his hands as he looked around the room—"as you can see, he isn't here."

"Oh, but he is," Conall said, and reached into a pouch at his belt and took out Anluan's head. The others gasped as he raised the gory trophy for all to see. Conall threw it disdainfully at Cet's chest. When it struck him, a great gout of blood gushed from its lips and spattered over Cet.

Cet rose and silently moved over to the Connacht side, mopping his brother's blood from him.

Conall went to the side of the pig and sat comfortably, then looked around at the Connacht host. "Well, then. Let us continue. Who here can challenge me?"

But not one of the others there stood, for they could see the power of Conall in the head staring with dead eyes at them from Mac Da Thó's floor. Yet they spoke angrily among themselves, and the men of Ulster rose and formed a barrier around Conall with their shields as he picked up the knife and started carving the pig.

There was an evil custom in the house that others would throw stones or goblets or cups or whatever they could lay their hands upon at those across from them, and today was no different as the Connacht men began to throw things at Conall. But the Ulster shield-wall held strongly, and Conall took the end of the pig's tail in his mouth and swiftly divided the pig, sucking on the belly that was big enough to feed nine men.

> A mighty pig that was for one man
> To eat alone for enough meat for a band
> Of men was on the haunch alone
> But Conall tore that from its bone
> And swallowed it in one gulp. He
> Continued to cut and eat until he
> Tired of taunting the Connacht host
> With his feasting and his boast
> Left the others hungry and mad
> While the Ulster host seemed glad.

He ate until the entire pig was gone except for the trotters, which he gave to the Connacht men for their share, and a quarter that he gave to the Ulster men.

Insulted, the Connacht men rose up wrathfully and, drawing their swords, rushed at the Ulster men, who held their ground. Then the brawl broke apart and crowns were rapped, ears shorn off, noses bloodied, and blows fell upon blows until the center of the room seemed a brawling mass of arms and legs punching and kicking and blood ran in rivers to each of the doors. The doors burst open and the brawlers tumbled out, biting and jabbing each other's eyes with forefingers, and a fine brawl it was with each gleefully punching another. Fergus wrenched a huge oak from the ground by its roots and laid about him at will, knocking Connacht men senseless to his left and right.

At last, Mac Da Thó came out, leading the great hound. He unleashed it and told it to choose which side it favored. The hound promptly loped over to the Ulster side and, when a Connacht man tried to turn it, snapped his hand off. The man howled and held his stump aloft, bright blood spurting redly from it, and then the rout was on.

The Ulster men roared and flew into a battle frenzy, the hound howling and leading the attack. Then the hound bit the chariot pole of Ailill and Maeve in half, and the charioteer, Fer Loga, took the moment to swing his sword and cut the hound's head from its body. The Connacht force seized the head and jammed it on a pole. That place where this happened is called Ibar Cinn Chon,[9] and from this Connacht takes its name.

The Connacht men poured out upon the road over Belach Mugna, past Roiru and Ath Midbine in Maistiu, past Kildare, past Raith Imgan into Feeguild, to Ath Mic Lugna, past Druim Da Maige, and over Drochat Cairpri with the Ulster host in full pursuit, whacking off stragglers who stepped too far behind. There, at Ath Cinn Chon in Fir Bili, the hound's head fell from its pole, yet the Connacht men did not stop to seize it. They fled on, all except Fir Loga, Ailill's charioteer, who hid in the tall heather beside the road.

When the Ulster force came by in full pursuit, Fir Loga

leaped from hiding onto the back of Conchobor's chariot and wrapped his arm around the king's head, holding a knife to his throat.

"I think this moment is mine," he said to Conchobor.

Conchobor grimaced and felt the edge of the knife against his throat. "Yes, as you will," he replied.

"I don't want much," Fir Loga said modestly. "Just a chance to pay a visit to your house at Emain Macha. Every night, I want the women and their maiden daughters to come to my door and sing,

> "Fir Loga is my darling,
> None here compares to his daring
> And none can match his way
> Of loving for the entire day!"

"Not a very good rhyme," Conchobor said. "But you shall have it. The choice is not much else for me to make."

And the women of Ulster agreed and came to Fir Loga's room each night to sing the bit of doggerel verse. After a year, Fir Loga left and went back to his own lands, taking with him two horses from Conchobor along with bridles of gold.

And this is how Ulster and Connacht came to blows over Mac Da Thó's hound and pig.

Finit.

The Violent
Deaths of Goll
and Garb

These are two of Cúchulainn's exploits and his dealings with his uncle Conchobor, the king of the Red Branch. The text, *Aided Guill Maic Carbada Ocus Aided Gairb Glinne Rige,* is taken from the oldest copy, which is found in *The Book of Leinster,* pp. 107b–111b.

ℳANY GESSA LAY UPON CÚCHULAINN, the famous boy-warrior of the Red Branch, on the son of Conchobor's sister, on the bright-cloaked one of Magh Line, on the guardian of Bregia. These were forbidden to him: he could not name himself to a single warrior; he could not move a single foot from his chosen path before a fight with one man; he could not refuse a duel; he could not enter a meeting without being given permission; he could not go to a meeting with only one warrior; he could not sleep among women without men beside them. He was forbidden to make love to a woman before he was married, and he had to rise before the sun rose upon Emain Macha.

Once upon a time he rose in Emain Macha before the sun, yawned and stretched, then said to his charioteer, "Well, Laeg!"

"I know what is upon your mind," Laeg grumbled.

"And what is that?" Cúchulainn said.

"Harness the horses and yoke the chariot."

"You're right." Cúchulainn grinned.

"Well, I have anticipated you this time," Laeg said. "Come and see. The horses are harnessed and the chariot yoked."

Cúchulainn went forward and came across Conchobor.

"What are you doing up so early?" Conchobor asked.

"It's been a long time since I patrolled Murthemne," Cúchulainn answered. "I think this would be a very good time to do so."

"Don't stay away too long," cautioned Conchobor. "When you are long gone, nothing seems right here."

Cúchulainn went to his chariot and leaped inside it. Laeg slapped the reins against the horses and steered them toward the road Murthemne.

"Well, Laeg," Cúchulainn shouted. "This height is wonderful."[1]

"Good enough reason for that." Laeg grunted. "We can see that the sea is clear." And then he said the words and made a lay:

> Laeg: Delightful is the height and the town on the Plain of
>   Murthemne
> Which seems to be strong and plentiful on land and clear by sea.

> Cúchulainn: We cannot stay here forever watching Murthemne's
>   plain
> For we must seek out someone to fight before going to Emain.

Laeg: You are right; I have never seen you leave Emain
And return without trophies on your chariot-train.

Cúchulainn: So we must stay here, Laeg Mac Riangabra, and find
A valiant combat and take a bloody trophy to Emain.

Laeg: That does not hurt my feelings, Cúchulainn, more
Than to know what to find and what is in store
For you. The horses have raced far to Cruachan
And many other places. This fair place and plane
Is no different from many others. Fifty heads
Once hung from these rails from the iron head
Of your spear. Therefore I say we find only one
Duel to be fought; you've already a hundred done
For the glory of Emain. That's enough to do
For anyone—even one as strong as you.

"Well," Cúchulainn said, yawning. "Unharness the horses
and unyoke the chariot while I catch a little sleep before we
find someone to fight. You know that I cannot return to Emain
Macha without a trophy. That is forbidden to me."

Without another word, Laeg unharnessed the horses and
let them graze and unyoked the chariot. He placed the skins of
the chariot on the grass where Cúchulainn could lay upon them
and a pillow for his head. Cúchulainn lay down and within
moments was asleep while Laeg kept a watch over him.

Not long after Laeg began his watch, he saw a huge boat
coming toward the shore. The prow of that boat was as large
as a mountain, and the stern seemed to loom even larger. Far
larger than the branch of a straight oak over the forest floor
seemed to be the hero sitting in the front of the boat. He rowed
with two oars of twice molten iron, and when the sea monsters
rose up in wrath around him, he sliced them apart with the
strokes of the oars, lashing them so fiercely that they flew up

to the heavens and fell into the middle of the boat. Then he would laugh mockingly at them, and his mouth gaped so wide that a three-tiered boat with a crew of nine could pass over his maw and liver and [text unreadable] seemed to fly where his gullet and neck joined. One of his two eyes outside his head seemed like the mouth of a wooden goblet, but a crane would hardly get the other eye from the top of his cheek. His sedgelike hair was roughly grown like an ox lead and [text unreadable] rose up on his head with the racing wind.

So Laeg saw and described him with a lay:

"Over a vast and clear sea I see
A boat making for Erin's land. A tree
Is the height of the boat and sitting
Within is a hero who seems more fitting
Than the warriors of the Gaels. He
Slices through the waves of the sea
That seem to spray up to the heavens
And one eye in his head seems shriven
As large as a calf's caldron. The other eye
Would be a match for a crane. I'd die
If I had to carry that great black shield
That four troops of ten men couldn't yield.
I see a claymore by his side—a full thirty
Feet long is its blade. That would deal a dirty
Blow to many men when his wrath is up.
Cúchulainn! Wake up, I say. Wake up!
Let us be away before that man makes
Us fight him! For heaven's sake!"

Cúchulainn: Now I swear strongly upon my pointed shield
Laeg, that I will not leave this field
Until I see if I can make that man yield.

Laeg: If all of Ulster's men were around you, son
Of Dechtine, even then the fight would soon be done.

"Well, Laeg," said Cúchulainn, "go and meet that man and find out where he is from, who are his kinfolk, what is his name, and where he is thinking to travel."

Sighing deeply, Laeg did as he was told. He halted on the bank opposite the great man and said, "Where have you come from?"

But the man didn't answer Laeg.

"I said," Laeg shouted a little louder, "where have you come from?"

Still, he didn't speak.

A third time Laeg shouted, "Where are you from, great one? What is your name? How long has your journey been?"

At last, the man gave Laeg a long, slow, and insulting look before he answered. "I see that you are a charioteer," the man said. "That is the only reason I would bother speaking to you."

"Fair enough," Laeg said quickly. "As long as you speak. That is all I ask."

"I am Goll[2] Mac Carbad, son of the king of northern Germany. We are three brothers: Goll and Cromm and Rig. We cast lots concerning the islands of Britain, Denmark, and Erin. My lot fell first upon Erin."

"I swear by my gods," said Laeg, "that it is a first lot that has all the fruit of a last. This may not be a good thing for you."

"That is a brave answer! You seem to be a good servant!" Goll laughed. "To whom do you belong?"

"To that man on the hill in the middle of the plain in front of you," replied Laeg, a bit annoyed at the rough ease with which the man spoke.

"Who is that up there?" Goll asked, shading his eyes with his broad palm and squinting against the sun.

"That," Laeg said gloomily, yet with a bit of pride, "is Cúchulainn Mac Sualtam, one of Erin's great men."

"I've heard of that wee hero," Goll said contemptuously. "Tell him to come down and accept me as his master, and I will leave him in charge of Erin instead of taking it for myself. Or"—Goll shrugged—"he may simply leave the country. Makes no difference to me."

Sighing, Laeg went to Cúchulainn and shook his head grimly.

"Well?" Cúchulainn asked. "Who is that?"

"Goll Mac Carbad," Laeg said and told Cúchulainn all the man had said. "He said that you could either accept him or leave Erin."

"I see," Cúchulainn answered, grinning broadly. "Well, go down to him and tell him not to set foot upon this land or anywhere in Erin. He is not to come into Ulster's territory as long as I am alive."

"This isn't going to be good," Laeg muttered, but he turned dutifully and went back to deliver his message. "Well, Goll, the hero on the hill has said that you are not to land your boat here or anywhere else on Erin and to stay out of Erin as long as he"—he jerked his thumb over his shoulder—"is still living."

Goll laughed and shoved his boat so that it would go over nine landing-planks onto the land. Laeg sighed and returned to Cúchulainn while the warrior charged down the hill to meet Goll. Each of them began to fight, but Goll moved faster and seized Cúchulainn and wrenched his weapons from him and tossed him over his shoulder toward his boat.

"Well, softy," said Laeg to Cúchulainn. "He's made right sport of you. He's had as easy a time with you as a cow would with a calf. I can see that he has wrenched you, and made you as tired as a woman delivering a child. He has turned you around like ivy climbing a tree and cut you like an ax does an oak. He has smashed you down like a fish upon the sand and poured you out as foam is poured out upon a pool of water. He's made you runny like a little boy's shit. No one this day would count you among Erin's bravest warriors. That's for certain. Get away from me."

Cúchulainn leaped over nine ridges away from Goll, but Goll ignored him. Then Cúchulainn changed direction and leaped and landed as lightly upon Goll's shield as would a bird. But Goll used his elbow to shake his shield and fling Cúchulainn away from him. Again Cúchulainn leaped upon the shield, this time taking *Cruadín Catuchend* from its sheath. The sword was so sharp that it could cut as easily stone, tree, or bone. He swiped at Goll with it and sliced off his head at the neck. Then he swung a second stroke, which cut Goll's body in half, and each half fell to the earth. Again, Cúchulainn delivered a stroke that made another two pieces of him and uttered this lay:

"You see within my hand Goll's head,
Laeg Mac Riangabra! Goll came instead
To seize this land and offered to let me
Govern Erin while he returned to Germany.
But I would have had to accept his rule
And to become a servant would make me rue
The day I was born. I answered this foolish man
With battle upon these bloody sands, then
I cut off his head and let this foolish man
Fall upon the strand. You see his head in my hand."

Cúchulainn sighed and said, "Well, Laeg, harness the horses and put the whip to them."

"Where are we going now?" asked Laeg.

"To Emain Macha," replied Cúchulainn.

"I wish you would stay at Dundalk with Foall's daughter,"[3] said Laeg.

Cúchulainn narrowed his eyes as he looked at Laeg.

"What's with you today, Laeg? Didn't you hear what Concho-bor said as we were leaving?"

"Conchobor cares only when you are fighting on behalf of Ulster," said Laeg. "Otherwise, he wants you to go or stay. The choice makes much little difference to him."

"If that is true, then I will leave Ulster," said Cúchulainn. "I'll stay away for a year and Ulster will not have my services. But if that is a lie, why then you will be banned from me and will be no servant of mine. I don't want to kill a charioteer."

Now we turn away for a while from Cúchulainn and look at Conall Mac Gleo Glas of Cualngé, who was the owner of a large hostel that could handle a hundred. At daybreak, he went to Emain Macha with a hundred and fifty charioteers, some in yellow cloaks, others in red, green, blue, purple, and black cloaks. Conchobor was sitting on a bench on top of the earthen wall outside of Emain, enjoying the sun with his warriors around him.

"Welcome, Conall Mac Gleo Glas!" he shouted.

"That's what we've come for," said Conall.

"Then you shall have it." Conchobor beamed.

"No, no. You misunderstand," said Conall. "I have put together a great banquet for you."

"All right," said Conchobor. "I am honored. How many should I bring?"

"Any of Ulster's men, women, and children you want to ask," Conall answered. "I could maintain all of Ulster's living and dead for a full year at Dún Colptha in Cualngé."

Conchobor laughed and said, "All right. Yoke your horses, men of Ulster."

The horses were harnessed and yoked to the chariots. All of the nobles of Ulster went, a vast crowd: sons of kings and princes, soldiers and young lords, the nimble servants, the youths and curly-headed women, damsels and maidens and young lads, companies and trains, musicians and minstrels, those who sang songs and made them, historians, judges, messengers, jugglers, servants and fools and criers all went out of Emain.

All of Ulster came with Conchobor on the path, and Conall said, "I give you a choice of two paths, Conchobor."

"What are those?" Conchobor asked.

"A path smooth but long or a path short and rough."

"The path short and rough," Conchobor said, looking up and squinting at the sun. "The sun has passed the shoulder of the day."

"Well, there's nothing rough in it except Garb⁴ of Glenn Rige," Conall said.

" 'Tis not into Glenn Rige that we are going," Conchobor said, "but into Sliab Fuait ahead. We never turn aside for Garb of Glenn Rige."

Garb did not see that the Ulster people were passing him until he heard the rumbling of the chariot wheels. Then he roared through the rear guard of Conchobor's army, slaughtering fifty heroes with deadly wounds and fatal death blows.

Conchobor went to the house of Conall Mac Glas in Dún Colptha, where everyone sat according to arts and ranks and laws and nobility, all in the company of rare and rich wines. The houses were uplifted and strewn with fresh reeds and rushes, and downy mattresses had been laid upon the floor for their use. Everything was elegantly served to Ulaid's warriors in the wide-wombed hostel of Conall that night.

"Well, Conchobor, have all arrived? Any been delayed?" asked Conall.

"None has been delayed," Conchobor said, belching and frowning. "But why do you ask that question?"

"I want to let loose this hound, Conbél, which protects this house," Conall said. And the hound was set loose.

The best of food and beer was given to everyone, and then they readied the baths. His May cotton-grass was plucked for each warrior separately. A hero's war-ax was given by Conall to each warrior. The serfs and doorkeepers were set to watch. Inebriating, mirthful mead was dealt out of horns and vessels to the Ulster men.

But it is not our purpose to relate the merrymaking of the Ulster host here.

Now Cúchulainn and Laeg were making ready to leave. "Put Goll's head in the chariot," Cúchulainn said. "Whip up the horses and let's be off to Emain."

The chariot leaped forward, and they sped away, the two great iron wheels of Cúchulainn's chariot churning deep dikes of dirt where it made along the sides of the road. Like flocks of darkling birds did the sod fly from the horses' hooves. Like a flock of swans was the foam flung from their lips over their shoulders. Like smoke from a royal household was the dust and the breath and the dense vapor merging from the rushing horses and chariots expertly guided by Laeg that day.

And so they roared toward Emain. But when they arrived, there was no one to meet them. "Well, Laeg," said Cúchulainn, "I don't think anyone's here."

"Why do you suppose that is?" Laeg asked, scratching his head.

"Because," Cúchulainn said patiently, "I don't hear any calls or cries coming from within. I don't hear the messengers, nor the set-to that usually one hears. I don't hear music or anything. Hold fast to the reins while I go and see if a deadly sickness has fallen upon the city."

Laeg held the horses while Cúchulainn entered Emain and found Suanán Salcenn, Conchobor's seneschal, who never left the city.

"Well, Suanán, where is everyone?" Cúchulainn asked.

"They've gone to the house of Conall Mac Glo Glas in Cualngé," answered Suanán.

"Did Conchobor say anything about me?" Cúchulainn asked.

"I didn't hear anything," Suanán said, shrugging.

"So," Cúchulainn said, miffed. "It would appear that what Laeg said about Conchobor is true. He cares for me only so much as what I can do for Ulster. Well," he said angrily, "I'll not leave Emain as I found it. I shall place a ring of fire around it, and no one will escape it or survive this slaughter!"

Only two things could restrain Cúchulainn when anger such as this fell upon him: the sight of naked women flouncing teasingly toward him and soothing songs sung to him. Women were not handy, so Suanán sang a stave:

> "But take my welcome, great Cúchulainn
> Grandson of red-sworded Cathbad! Again
> I sing to you of gay nights
> And women and pretty sights
> And ask that you be welcomed now
> On behalf of Conchobor! Tell me how
> You have come this dark night
> To Emain Macha's happy site!"

Or words to that effect. It is enough to say that Cúchulainn did not burn Emain Macha that night, but he did leave it and returned to Laeg, who still held the bridles of the horses. "Well, Laeg," Cúchulainn said. "Put a whip to those horses and let us go to the house of Conall Mac Gleo Glas in Cualngé, for that is where everyone and Conchobor have gone."

"If you would do as I wish," Laeg said, "we would not leave Emain tonight. It's the end of the day. The treetops are bowed [text obscure] woods. Deer have gone to nest. The chariot needs washing. Motion is sluggish—I don't think this night is a good one for traveling."

"You're not forbidding me to go, are you?" Cúchulainn queried.

"Oh no, no," Laeg said hastily. He sighed and climbed back into the chariot. "Well, will you go the long and smooth way or the short and rough way?"

"The short and rough one!" Cúchulainn ordered.

"The only thing rough about it is Garb of Glenn Rige," said Laeg.

"I don't turn off my path for anyone," Cúchulainn said.

Cúchulainn's chariot rolled forward on the road until he saw in the glen those Ulster men that Garb had butchered. It was then that Cúchulainn went to Garb and the two began fighting. Each of them struck the other with smooth-shafted spears, and Cúchulainn, finding himself hard-pressed by Garb, finally felt the anger come upon him and tossed his spear from him and seized Garb by the shoulder, wrenching and tearing it until he ripped it from its shoulder bone. Then Garb screamed his defeat.[5]

"Is there anyone alive here?" Laeg asked cautiously.

"I am alive," Cúchulainn snapped. "Hand me my sword."

Laeg handed *Cruadín Catuchend* (Hard-head) to Cúchulainn, who unsheathed it and delivered a stroke to Garb, cutting off his two heads on his single neck and delivering a return-stroke so that they came together upon the ground. He delivered a third blow to him that cut the pieces in two on the ground.

"Well, what kind of fight was it?" Laeg asked.

"So long as I live I think it will be against me," Cúchulainn said, and made the lay:

> "Garb of Glenn was evil in form
> And tried to take me apart by storm
> But many wounds have fallen upon him
> And now his sight on earth is dim.

Fifty wounds he inflicted upon me
On my left side, on my right, we
Can see what he has done!
But on this firm earth there is none
Who can match my spear play.
We came here not to stay
But to make our way, to fight
Only if he came within our sight."

Laeg: I said to you before you entered this glen
You would have to meet the evil Garb of Glenn.

"Put the two heads into the chariot, Laeg," Cúchulainn said. "And whip up the horses to the house of Conall Mac Gleo Glas in Cualngé."

"It shall be so," replied Laeg.

So they rattled down rocky roads until they came to the river near Conall's house called Abann Cholpthai.

"That is a big river," said Cúchulainn. "Hand me a shaft from the chariot, and I'll try to find the ford for the horses."

At that moment, Conall's hound Conbél heard the noise of the water rushing against Cúchulainn's shoulders and opened its maw and bayed loudly. Its mouth was so great that a boat with three banks of oars could pass over it. It leaped forward, and Cúchulainn threw the shaft into its throat, then thrust his hand in after the shaft and seized the dog's liver and twisted it around the dog's head. He broke the bones in its body and threw them from him from Abann Cholpthai in Cualngé to Belut.[6]

On went Cúchulainn to the gate of the city. "Tell them to open the gate, Laeg," he ordered. "But do not say Cúchulainn is here. Say instead that a lad from the city wants in."

Laeg went to the door and shouted, "Open the door!"

"Who asks for this?"

"One of the youths from Emain," answered Laeg.

"One who hasn't come to this banquet already is obviously not a royal youth of Emain," replied the watch. "It is not fitting that we open the door for anyone."

"Don't say that," warned Laeg. "This boy is fierce and without love for his fellow man."

"We pledge our word," the watchman said, "that any youth who has been disgraced from Ulster will not enter until sunrise tomorrow."

Cúchulainn heard the answer and turned to a pillar-stone standing nearby. He lifted it to his shoulder and hurled it into the gate, shattering the posts and killing a hundred and fifty slaves who were waiting upon the Ulster men. No one escaped to boast of that slaughter.

He unsheathed his sword and went in over the hosts. Then a foul-tongued, ill-mannered man named Bricriu Mac Carbad Oll of Ulster saw him and sang:

"Cúchulainn is here, warriors of Ulster!
He holds a sword in his hand to thrust
Into your hides. This is no time for drinking!
Rise up and ready yourselves or fall stinking
With dead flesh to the great earth!"

Conall: Who brings a naked weapon to me
Here in my mead-house? I can see
Where this is someone who kings
Cannot protect from death's dark sting!

Cúchulainn: The hero in whose hand you see
This bold weapon is not one who will flee
From your wandering words! Bricriu,
If you don't stop blathering it's you
Who will feel my sword's bite!

Know all of you here I am under
The safe-guard of Cú na Cerda
From the Red Branch! But I say
That no one here will slay me today
For I know what Bricriu has said
And I can leave him alive or dead!
Or any of you, for that matter.
You can be either wiser or sadder.

"Where are my soldiers?" roared Conchobor. "Senoll the Solitary, Bruchur from Bruachairne, Sescnén Mac Fordub, Mani Roughhand."

"Where are my sons?" said Fergus. "Buinne the Fair and Illann of the many children?"

"Where are Uisnech's sons, Naisi and Ainle and Ardán?"

"Well," said Conall, "where are my brothers? Get up, you clods, and help Cúchulainn!"

Storm and tempest tossed and turned in the house that night, and thunderous battle could be heard for miles away. Then Sencha rose up and shook the Branch of Peace until all fell quiet and the shields were placed back on their pegs and swords sheathed once again. Cúchulainn placed his sword into its sheath. Then he took a wand of white silver and walloped Conchobor on his head. And the blow made his eyes glass and his knees wobble and a hollow sound echoed from his pate.

"If I liked, this could be my sword instead," Cúchulainn said. "And 'tis the sword I'd rather give to you except you don't have anyone to protect you and you are my foster-father and my mother's brother."

Conall Cernach and Fergus hustled up to him and gave Cúchulainn kisses of welcome and led him over to the champion's seat. When Conchobor's eyes cleared, he sent Cúchulainn a goblet of mead on a tray of pure white silver with the message that he should drink with "life and health" from the king.

Laeg came in front of them and sharpened two stakes, placing Goll's head on one and Garb's two heads on the other.

"Well, Laeg," said Conchobor. "What head is that shaggy one?"

"The head of Goll Mac Carbad," answered Laeg. "The son of the king of Germany who fought Cúchulainn at Áth Mór.[7] On the Plain of Murthemne."

Atherne said: "Not Áth Mór but Áth nGuill.[8] That shall be its name from now until Doom."

"And what are those two heads on the other pole?" asked Conchobor.

"Garb of Glenn Rige's two heads," Laeg said.

"Good night!" swore Conchobor. "He killed fifty of my men when we passed through."

"Good job, Cúchulainn," Conall said with irony. "You have 'whitened' your hands this day."

"What evil has he done?" Conchobor asked.

"A hundred fifty slaves who were waiting on your men were killed with one cast of a pillar-stone," Conall said.

"Oh," Laeg said, clearing his throat apologetically to get attention. Conall looked at him. "Didn't you have a good hound?"

"With the exception of Brazier's Hound, there's none like him in all of Erin," Conall said.

"I have one of his pups," ventured Conall Cernach. "Its father was no better. I'll give you that for Cúchulainn's honor."

"And I will give you a hundred fifty slaves," Conchobor said.

And so they stayed there to the end of three fortnights in the house of Conall Mac Gleo Glas. The barren part of their guesting was on the first night, and it was not the last.

Then the Ulster men returned to Emain. That was when Cúchulainn said to Laeg, "Drive a goad into the horses and lay the rod to them and get to the house of Eogan Mac Durthact

and to the men of Farney that we might leave this place for a
year so that no one will see the face of those they have insulted."

"Well, my son," said Conchobor, "that shall not be true.
You take the words of your own mouth as truth."

"I won't accept that," said Cúchulainn. "But I will accept
whatever the judges and poets of the province pronounce."

Ulster's men were brought in separately, and this was their
judgment:

> A scruple for every nose
> An ounce for every seat
> A lively horse for each stud
> A scruple for every cow-shed
> A pig of Mucram for every herd
> A bondmaid for every city.

Cúchulainn gave two-thirds to his foster-father, his lord and
his mother's brother. The other third he gave to the poets of
his own province so that this adventure of his would be remembered with their songs like every adventure that had happened
and that early rising like every early rising.

So far the Violent Death of Goll son of Carbad and the
Violent Death of Garb of Glenn Rige.

The Intoxication of the Ulster Men

Mesca Ulad is found in several sources, including *Lebor Na hUidre* and *The Book of Leinster*. Yet the story in both of these is incomplete, and it becomes rather difficult to follow because names have a tendency to change from manuscript to manuscript. This is a rather wild and humorous story, with both a mythic and a historical subtext. The author apparently gave free rein to his imagination, and some passages are highly lyrical while others are simple declarative statements. Basically, the story hinges upon the mythic subtext of a ritual killing around Samhain, which marked the end of the old year and the beginning of the new. This is a regeneration motif that also concerns the theme of tribal warfare, but it apparently also was linked to a mythological fragment that concerned Cúchulainn and Cúrói. Since Cúrói was associated with the southwest of Ireland, one had to come up with a reason for the Ulster men being in that part of the country. That brings about the drunken party that sends the Ulster warriors reeling from the Great Hall of the Red Branch in a wild chariot race down to Temuir Lúachra (Temuir of the Rushes), and we are treated to a wildly imaginative account of Cúchulainn trying to find his way from Dún Dá Bend to Dún Delgan via Temuir Lúachra, which is similar to going from Dublin to Sligo via Cork, a rather roundabout way of getting from the east to the northwest by going to the southwest. Incidentally, Cúchulainn's boy-name was Sétanta, which translates loosely as "he who knows how" or "he who knows the way." The account here is from both *Lebor Na hUidre* and *The Book of Leinster.*

WHEN MIL ESPÁNE'S SONS reached Erin, their wiliness proved to be too much for the *Tuatha Dé Danann,* and Amergin Glunmar Mac Mil, who was a king-poet and king-judge, was left to divide the land between the sons of Mil and the *Tuatha.* He quickly seized upon the idea of dividing the land in half, giving the *Tuatha* the land belowground while the sons of Mil, his own people, took the land aboveground. Of course, Amergin planned something much different for the *Tuatha,* but the *Tuatha* agreed in all seriousness to this offer and slipped away like mist into the hills and fairy mounds, where they become one with the fairy people, no longer seeming to have form but becoming shadows, nervous twitches at the corners of the eyes where motion appears but is gone when sought.

But not all of the *Tuatha* found their way into the shadowland: five of them stayed behind, knowing full well what the intentions of the Mil sons had been when the arrogant division was made. And so they took dark pleasure in working war plans among those who remained aboveground. Five of them stayed close to Ulster, for these were the *Tuatha* who took the greatest pleasure in battle, often using any excuse, no matter how tiny, to take war into another province. These were Brea Mac Elgan in Dromana-Berg, Redg Rotbel on the slopes of Mag Itha, Tinnel Mac Boclachtna in Sliab Edlicon, Grici in Cruachan

Aigle, and Gray Gulbann Mac Grac in the Ben of Gulban Gort Mac Ungarb.

Oh, the time they had making up quarrels through the subtle hint and jab of playful talk that kept Ulster divided into three parts during the time of Conchobor Mac Fachtna Fathach, who shared control of the province (although, if truth be told, not unwillingly) with Cúchulainn Mac Sualdim and Fintan Mac Niall Niamglonnach from Dunl-da-Benn.

Now, although this division was just a simple slashing of boundaries with a mark on a hide map, it was also a clever division that left each man with a portion to defend separate from the others. Yet all remained close enough, where they could instantly be called upon if a wanton raider strayed into their midst. Cúchulainn held that part from the hills of Usnech of Meath to the middle of Traig Baile, while Conchobor had Traig Baile to Traig Thola and Fintan governed Tráhig Tola to Rind Semni and Latharnai.

For a full year, the province was governed by thirds until Conchobor hosted the Feast of Samhain at Emain Macha. Oh, but a grand time he made of it, too, with a hundred vats of the finest mead—which some of his stewards complained might be a bit too much for the numbers of chieftains who would be attending. Conchobor pondered carefully upon their words, then sent his woman herald Leborcham to Cúchulainn at Dún Delgan and Findchad Fer Benduma Mac Traglethan to Fintan Mac Niall Niamglonnach at Dún Dabenn.

Leborcham arrived at Dún Delgan and found Cúchulainn mulling around among his guests, for he was giving a great banquet for his own people. He stood in the middle of a laughing crowd, a cup of mead clutched in his mighty hand, his eyes saucy-shining from drams taken. But when Leborcham told him that Conchobor wanted him to come to Emain Macha, merry Cúchulainn refused, saying that he had been planning this feast for his people for a long time and hanged he would be if he would step away from them after all the work he had put into feast-making.

Then Emer, Cúchulainn's wife, the daughter of Forgall Monach, the sixth-best woman in all Erin, broke in upon the argument and told Cúchulainn that he owed it to Conchobor to attend him when the king asked and a great shame would come upon Cúchulainn if he did not make his way to see what Conchobor wanted.

"All right," Cúchulainn said sullenly. He looked at the cup in his hand and sadly put it aside, hiccuped, then said, "Laeg, you rascal! Harness the horses and make the chariot ready for a quick trip!"

Laeg, however, had seen Leborcham arrive and knew what her appearance at Dún Delgan meant and had already made ready for travel. "The horses are harnessed—as you would see, if you cast an eye around you other than at the saucy haunches of one of the serving wenches! What are you waiting for? The evil hour to descend and strip you of your valor?" He waved his hand. "When you're ready, jump into it and we'll race away. It's thistles or thorns to me!"

Cúchulainn shook his great mane and seized his war weaponry (although he didn't understand why he should have that along since Ulster's borders had long been at peace) and leaped into the chariot. He took the straightest and shortest roads to Emain Macha, determined to get the biding over with as quickly as possible and return to Dún Delgan. As he rattled through Emain Macha's gates, Sencha Mac Ailill came to welcome him upon the Macha green.

"Welcome, welcome!" he cried, coming forward, arms outstretched. " 'Tis always a great honor to greet the great bringer of prosperity to Ulster! The gem of valor, the warrior content of the Gaels, the dear, many-armed, crimson-fisted son of Deichtine, the—"

"Enough," Cúchulainn interrupted irritably, waving away

THE RED BRANCH TALES 153

the banter. "When a man speaks like that to me, I grab my sword and hold my balls suspiciously. Those are the words of a man looking for a gift, or I have the strength of a woman. Which I haven't. Well, you know what I mean. What is it you want?"

"Well," Sencha said, scratching his stomach through his mantle, "you always were perceptive, Cúchulainn."

"What is it?" Cúchulainn asked wearily.

"I'll tell you, but only after I have the proper propriety placed before me," Sencha said.

"You always were a banderer of words," Cúchulainn said. "Well, what is it? What do you want? And while you're on and about it, give me the names of those who will guarantee you in return for a present from me."

Sencha slyly placed his finger alongside his nose and said, "All right. I can see the niceties of speech are being wasted here." He gulped as a dangerous glint came into Cúchulainn's eyes. "But," he continued hastily, "I have the two Conalls and Lóegure. That is, Conall Anglonnach Mac Irel Glúnmár and Conall Cernach Mac Amorgen and Lóegure Búadach. I presume those meet with your approval?"

"They do," Cúchulainn said.

"So, what security do you want regarding the gift?"

"The three young, noble, valorous gillies Cormac Conloinges Mac Conchobor, Mesdead Mac Amergin, and Eochaid Cenngarb Mac Celtchar."

"Hmm," Sencha said, pretending to think. "You name your men well."

"Get on with it," Cúchulainn said. "The sun's traveling fast and is hot upon my pate. Standing here playing palaver with you is thirsty work."

"All right," Sencha said. "I want you to give your third of Ulster to Conchobor for a year."

Cúchulainn shrugged. "Well, if that's all, certainly—if it's for the good of the country. He's a fountain of rule and a goodly man with words and ideas. 'Tis a stupid man who would try to refute or rebut his word. Besides, he's the son of the kings of Erin and Alba, and within his right to have what he wants. But"—he waggled a finger under Sencha's nose—"if the province doesn't better itself under him, then we'll have a battle of boys and he'll be placed back on his third at the year's end."

"Sounds reasonable," Sencha said, relieved that Cúchulainn had been so agreeable. "Come with me and I'll treat you to a drop of the best mead around."

"I had that back home," Cúchulainn said. "And I could have been drinking it there among my own if you would have gotten off your backside and made the trip down with your request."

Sencha drew himself up. "The sake," he began.

"I know. I know. The proprieties must be observed," Cúchulainn said disgustedly and slapped him on the shoulder, dropping him to his knee, stunned. "Come on, then. This has been thirsty work."

He strode ahead of Sencha into the Great Hall of the Red Branch, leaving the Word Man to struggle to his feet, wincing as he touched the great bruise forming upon his shoulder. "One of these days," he muttered darkly. But there was no one around to see or hear him so his words were safe, and he trailed after Cúchulainn into the Great Hall.

Then Fintan arrived, and the good Druid Cathbad met him and made him welcome.

"Ah, here you are!" Cathbad cried. "Most beautiful and illustrious youth, noble and great warrior of Ulster, against whom neither plunderers nor reavers nor spoilers nor pirates nor raiders nor foreign warriors can stand!"

Fintan shook his head, looking suspiciously at the Druid. "I think those are the words of someone who wants something from someone. Well, what's the favor this time?"

"Not much," Cathbad said modestly, spreading his fingers as if it were nothing at all that he asked. "Just a little something that's well within your power to grant."

"Well then, spit it out," Fintan said.

"I need to have security," Cathbad responded.

"What is it you want?" Fintan asked.

"Celtchar Mac Uthecar, Uma Mac Remanfisech from the Cooley streams, and Ergi Echbel from Bri Ergi."

"This must be some favor you're after," Fintan said, his eyes narrowing.

"What do you want for a guarantee?" Cathbad asked.

"That serious, is it? Well then, I'll take the three sons of valiant Usnech, the three torches of valor: Naisi, Ainle, and Ardán."

Cathbad nodded in agreement, and they went into the house, An Téte Brecc, where Conchobor waited patiently.

"Conchobor is now the ruler of all Ulster," Cathbad said. "That is," he said apologetically, glancing at Fintan, "if Fintan will grant him the third that he holds."

"Yes, why not?" Sencha pressed before the other could speak. "Cúchulainn has already given his third."

Fintan glanced at the great warrior, who belched and waved his hand, bored already with the comings-and-doings of the affair.

"If he agrees," Cúchulainn said, "then let him come and sit and raise a cup with me. That's my request. Conchobor, I mean. Let him come and we'll raise a cup to settle the affair."

"Uh-huh," growled Fintan, looking around him. "It seems to me that this has been decided before we were asked to come here, Cúchulainn."

Cúchulainn lowered his cup slowly and looked around him. "You think so?" he asked quietly.

"This is a put-up job if ever I've been jobbered," Fintan said hotly. "This has been bad bargaining bandied about."

"I warned you," Cúchulainn said, shaking a finger at Sencha. He rose, upsetting the cup of the warrior next to him, splashing the mead over his lap.

"Where are my guarantors?" Fintan roared. "Where are the securities and bonds?"

Then the guarantors came forward savagely, battering and bashing heads. Nine were quickly covered with blood, nine more with wounds, and nine stretched out senseless upon the floor before Sencha seized the silver branch and waved it furiously. The Ulster warriors fell away from fighting one another at the sight of the Peace Branch and the sound of the bells furiously jangling upon it.

"This is disgraceful," Sencha said. "Shame upon all of you for acting like little children here. Conchobor won't be the king for another year, yet for a year to a year was the bond that was asked and one year cannot begin before the old has ended."

"All right," Cúchulainn said. He dropped the man he had been holding at the end of his arm to the floor and stalked to Sencha. "All right, speaker, we'll play it your way. But you don't come between us again at the end of the year. Understand?"

"Understand. Yea, verily," Sencha said nervously, recoiling from the angry glint in the Hound's eye. Madness, he thought. Madness. But he wisely kept this to himself.

Cúchulainn eyed him suspiciously for a moment, then nodded in agreement and went back to his seat, satisfied, and raised his cup. The others returned to their places, and for three days and three nights, the feast continued until the vats were emptied, and then they returned to their own houses and strongholds and fine dwellings.

At the end of the year of Conchobor, it was obvious that prosperity had descended upon Ulster. Not a single residence was wanting, justice had been easily and mercifully administered, and the land brought forth fruit from Rind Semni and Latharnai to Cnocc Úashtair Forcha to Dub and Drobais, and not a single son stood in place of his father or grandfather, and everyone served properly the proper lord.

One day Emer and Cúchulainn lolled about, visiting about the state of the land, and Emer said, "I think that Conchobor is now the *Ard Rí*—the High King—of Ulster."

"Things could be worse," Cúchulainn answered.

"I think this is the time for us to hold a feast for him," Emer said. "That is, if you really think he would be the good king always."

"Why not?" Cúchulainn said.

And so they ordered a huge banquet to be prepared, and since Cúchulainn remembered the shanty time before, he ordered that a hundred vats of every kind of ale and mead and beer be prepared for his feast, for he did not want any Ulster man to go away with a thirst clutching his throat.

At the same time, Fintan decided it was time for him to hold his feast, and he, too, remembered the hundred vats only and ordered that an extra hundred vats of every kind of ale and mead and beer be prepared for his feast as well. And as luck, or ill luck, depending upon one's view, would have it, each decided the same day to ride to Emain Macha and formally deliver the invitation to the feast.

Cúchulainn arrived first at Emain and had just unyoked his horses when Fintan rode in. Cúchulainn nodded and walked into the Great Hall and delivered his invitation as Fintan came through the door.

"What's this?" Fintan asked as his eyes adjusted to the dim light in the Great Hall.

"I'm inviting Conchobor to my house for a feast in his honor," Cúchulainn said, adding graciously, "Come yourself, for you too are invited."

Fintan looked around him and roared angrily, "Where are my guarantors?"

"Here we are," the sons of Usnech said, rising up together.

"So. That is to be the way of it, is it?" Cúchulainn said. "Well, I have my own."

The Ulster warriors ran to retrieve their arms, and this time Sencha decided that discretion was the better part, and he slipped away without raising the Peace Branch between them, for their anger was so great that the very air vibrated from it. Even Conchobor left the Great Hall, knowing that reason had fled for certain from them and they would just have to sort it out themselves.

Now one of his sons followed him, Furbaide, the one who Cúchulainn had fostered, and as he looked upon his son, an idea came to Conchobor.

"My son, if you are willing, you can put a stop to all of this," he said.

"How's that?" asked the lad.

"Go before your foster-father, Cúchulainn, and lay on with weeping and wailing about the uselessness of this whole affair. He's never been in a battle or duel when he would not fix his mind upon you. He would do anything for you."

So Furbaide went back into the Great Hall just as the warriors were pairing off and went up to Cúchulainn, tears as big as goose eggs dripping from his eyes, and said, "Just when peace has come over the whole province, you would spoil it for the petty sake of a feast."

"Ah, now," Cúchulainn said, shaking his head in embarrassment. "I'd do most anything for you—you know that—but a man's word is his honor, and I've given mine, now!"

"And I have," Fintan said squinting at Cúchulainn. "I promised that the Ulster warriors would come with me tonight."

Now Sencha had followed Furbaide in, and as the silence deepened in the Great Hall, he put forth his idea. "Now there's no reason for fists and fighting, for why don't we spend one-half night feasting with Fintan and the second half feasting with

Cúchulainn? That way, the honor of both is resolved and this little lad's tears will stop."

Cúchulainn glared at Fintan and slowly nodded. "Well, I'm for it, if you are."

"Then I agree as well," Fintan said.

With a deep sigh that nearly sucked all of the air out of the Great Hall, the Ulster warriors rose around Conchobor, grateful that a wise ending had prevented the sure blood that would have swamped the floor once the two heroes had their swords in their hands. Conchobor nodded absently and motioned for the messengers to come close and rapidly delivered his message to be taken throughout the province, inviting all to Fintan's feast. Conchobor gathered the warriors of the Red Branch about him and took them to Dún Dáben and the house of Fintan Mac Niall Niamglonnach.

All Ulster was relieved that no fighting had broken out (although there were a few hotheads among them who regretted not being allowed to show their skills with their swords), and not one among them did not show up with his wife or one-year wife or proper mate and each of those with a lady, but Fintan had thought of this and many a servant had been made ready so none were without an attendant—even those who came from the smallest villages that had only an inn and a stable to give them a name. Each person, regardless of his or her rank, had lovely and finely decorated sleeping chambers, richly appointed. The lofty balconies were well-strewn with fresh rushes, and the guards who had led their lords safely to Fintan's house had long and comfortable houses replete with their own cooking houses. A long hostel had been prepared with colors that reflected all clans where the men and women could meet and make merry. As choice as the portions were that were made available to the lords, the same were made equally available (on a smaller standard, of course) to those who stayed there. Four corners and four doors, each richly decorated, were in that hostel, and enough food available for a hundred men came to every nine men.

It was left to Conchobor to assign the lodgings, and he thought carefully before appointing places to those by deeds and families and grades and arts and gentle manners. Servers came promptly to serve and cupbearers to pour, and discrete door-keepers were stationed at each door and corner of the hostel to guard any who might need it from old jealousies that might be recalled in the flood of wine and beer. Musicians played and sang and tales were spun and glories recited and presents of rich jewels and gems were freely handed out so that no one was dissatisfied.

Cúchulainn watched the merrymaking with sharp resolve, and close to the stroke of the hobgoblin hour he sent his charioteer Laeg Ringabra outside, saying, "Check the stars and see if the witching hour has come upon us. I trust you, Laeg," he said, for he had been watching the generous potions that Laeg had been pouring down his gullet, "for you have waited on me and watched me at several feasts and banquets in strange lands and kept me from making a fool of myself. Now do what I bid."

And Laeg went out, hoping that the time had not come, for, truth be told, there was a dark-eyed, dark-haired beauty who had been cooking his senses on low simmer with her burning glances, and if he wasn't mistaken, there had been promise in the last look when she had slowly licked the sweet honey from her lips and—

He sighed and went outside and sat, staring at the moving stars and listening to the faint music that seemed to trickle from the spheres until the softly tinkling sound stretched down at the top of the moon's rising. Laeg sighed and rose and went in to where Cúchulainn stood against the wall of the feasting-house.

" 'Tis midnight now, Cúchulainn," he muttered and looked

around hopefully for the dark-eyed beauty, but she was nowhere to be seen.

Cúchulainn smiled at those words and strode to where Conchobor sat next to the hero's seat that had been left vacant for Cúchulainn and told Conchobor that the time was ripe for the move to his fortress. Conchobor sighed and rose, shrugging off the attentions of the young women who had been pampering him, and reached for his horn. He blew it (sputteringly, but loud enough for all to hear), and the Ulster warriors fell silent. A needle falling from the main beam would have echoed throughout the hall when it struck the floor, so deeply did quiet rule where laughter had been only moments before. The Ulster warriors waited for their king to speak, but he could not speak before his Druids, and finally Cathbad stepped forward, weaving slightly from drink taken, and said, "What—what is it you wish, Conchobor?"

"Well, now," Conchobor said with relish, rubbing his hands together, for what better could have been than for another feast to attend at the end of this fine time? He cleared his throat and said, "Well, Cúchulainn has reminded me that it is time for us to journey to his feast." He glanced at his warriors, then at those of his retinue, who appeared a little the worse for wear after their quick fling at Fintan's party. "Tell me, do you want to earn the thanks of all the Ulster warriors here by leaving the weak and the women behind?"

Cúchulainn had planned for this and said, "Of course. Provided that our champions and warriors and singers and poets and players come with us."

The Ulster warriors rose as one and strode out to the hardworn green.

"Ah, now, Laeg," said Cúchulainn, rubbing his hands with relish, "find an easy ride for the charioteers for those who follow."

Laeg leaped for the chariot, nearly missing the rail, and

took a deep breath, calming himself from his near miss. He was the best among those there—for none but the best could work for Cúchulainn in the great arts of turning around, backing straight, and leaping over ditches and gullies.

"Are you ready?" Cúchulainn asked.

"Of course," Laeg answered slowly, choosing his words with great care. "What a silly thing to say."

"Good," Cúchulainn said with relish. "Raise the horses to their battle run."

Laeg gave him a strange look, then obeyed, and the brave war horses leaped into their battle-charge. The other warriors looked with surprise at the furious start, then bawled at their charioteers to whip up their horses and galloped after them, a thunderous horde.

They rolled easily over the green of Dún Dában, past Cathir Osrin, Li Thúaga, and Dún Rígáin to Ollarba in Mag Machae, past Slíab Fúait and Áth na Forare to Port Nóth Con Culaind, past Mag Muirthemni (they should have turned there) and Crích Saithni, across Dubad, across the rush of the Boyne and into Mag mBreg and Mide, into Senmag Léna in Mucceda, into Cláethar Cell, across the Brosnas of Bladman, with Berna Mera ingine Trega on their left and Slíab nEblinni ingine Gúare on their right, across Findsruth into Machare Már na Muman, through Lát Martini and the territory of the Smertani, with the bright rocks of Loch Gaire on the right, across the rush of the Máig and into Clíu Máil maicc Úgaine into the Crích na Dési Bice, into the land of Cúrói, son of Dáiri.

So rapid was their travel that every hill they roared over was leveled, all flat plains fell quickly behind. Every stream and river they forded went empty for the moment after the horses' knees splashed the water onto the banks, and a passerby would have thought that the streams had been bare-stoned since time began. The iron wheels of the chariots sliced neatly through the roots of trees, leaving a field of fallen forest behind them.

After a while, Conchobor frowned and said, "Where are we? I don't remember taking this route before from Dún Dáben to Dún Delgan."

Bricriu Poison-tongued said, "I don't think we have. But you don't have to yell," he added crossly. "A whisper is as good in this place. I'd say that we've crossed the borders of Ulster a while back."

Sencha Mac Ailill bristled at Bricriu's speech and said, "Little do you know then. I give my word that we haven't."

"As do we," growled Conall, for he had little liking for the poison-tongued one, who had caused so much trouble before.

"Uh-huh," said Conchobor, unconvinced. "Well, where are we? Who will find out?"

All of the charioteers tightened their grip upon the reins and pretended to be busy with the horses under their command.

"Well," Bricriu said crossly, "I'd say that was up to Cúchulainn, wouldn't you? Surely he knows. His boasts alone would say that, for he claims there isn't a territory around where he hasn't slaughtered at least a hundred men."

Now Cúchulainn had heard this and told Laeg to rein in his horses enough that he rode next to Bricriu and said, "I bear the responsibility, Bricriu. I'll ride forward and see what I can find."

Cúchulainn rode forward into Drum Colchailli, now called Ani Cliach, and said, "Well, Laeg, I'd say this is a fine fix we're in. Tell me, do you know where we are?"

"No, I don't," Laeg said. He looked around them nervously.

"Well, I do," Cúchulainn said. "This is south of Cenn Abrat of Sliabh Cain. The mountains of Eblinne are northeast, and that bright lake is Lind Limerick. I would say that we are in Drum Colchailli in the land of the Deise Beg. To the south, we will find Cliu Mail Maic Ugaine in the land of Cúrói Mac Dáire Mac Dedad."

Then, as if by magic, a blanket of snow dropped down deep

to the shoulders of the Ulster warriors, and the shafts of the
chariots disappeared beneath its wet whiteness. The charioteers
marked a defense of the perimeter while the warriors wearily
raised stone columns to shelter the horses, and these *echlasa* still
stand stony tall today.[1]

Cúchulainn and Laeg returned to where the Ulster warriors
huddled miserably against the snow, flakes clinging to their eye-
lashes and long curls.

"Well?" demanded Sencha. "Just where are we?"

"We are in the land of Cúrói Mac Dáire, the Crích na Dési
Bice," replied Cúchulainn.

Bricriu threw up his hands. "Alas! Woe be to us all!"

"Ah, shut up, Bricriu," Cúchulainn said disgustedly. "I'll
show you all how to retrace your steps so that we arrive at our
enemies' doors before daybreak."

"Woe to the Ulster men," said Celtchair Mac Uthechar.
"Was there ever a man born that could give this advice?"

"We have never known you to give us bad advice before,
Cúchulainn," said Fergna Mac Findchóem, a royal hospitaller.
"Until tonight, that is. This seems a counsel of weakness, ti-
midity, and cowardice you are proposing."

"Alas, that the person who gives such counsel should be
allowed to go without becoming a target for our darts and the
edges of our weapons," said Lugaid Lámderg Mac Léti, king
of Dal Araide.

"Well," said Conchobor impatiently, "then ask what you
want."

"Yes," said Cúchulainn. "What is it that you want? Speak,
and don't whine and whimper like a bitch minus one dug for
her litter! And," he added, eyes glinting dangerously, "I'd put
a cap on your tongue if you're thinking about raising your
swords to me. There'll be many a headless one stumbling
around in the snow if that be the case."

"Easy, now!" Conchobor said quickly. He turned to the others. "Well, then? And keep a civil tongue in your heads."

"We want to spend a day and a night in this land so it won't look like we are slipping out along a fox's track with our tails between our legs in valley or wasteland or wooded forest."

"All right, then," Conchobor said. He turned to his champion. "Then tell us, Cúchulainn: where should we make camp for a day and night?"

"Easily answered," Cúchulainn said. "The fair green of Senchlochar is upon us, and this rough winter is not timely for a fair. Now Tara Luachra is on the eastern slopes of Luacha, and there are many houses and dwellings there that will shelter us."

"Then," said Sencha Mac Ailill, "I say we're off to Tara Luachra."

And they harnessed their chariots quickly and followed Cúchulainn, who led them on a straight road to Tara Luachra.

Now Tara Luachra may have been empty once, but not that night, for a son had been born to Ailill and Maeve whose name was Maine Mo Epert. He had been placed in fosterage to Cúrói Mac Dáiri, and Ailill and Maeve had come that night with their chieftains for a feast celebrating their son's first month. All were there along with Eochaid Mac Luchta and the men of his land and Cúrói, of course, with the men of Clan Dedad. Despite the presence of all these warriors, though, the woman-warrior Maeve still moved uneasily among the men. The daughter of Eochaid Fedlech, the High King, was guarded by two Druids and watchers, Crom Deroil and Crom Darail, two foster-sons of the great Druid Cathbad.

Now it happened that they were on the ramparts of Tara Luachra, looking and guarding, when Crom Deroil frowned and stared off hard into the distance, then turned to his friend and said, "Did you see that?"

"What?" asked Crom Darail.

"For a moment, I was certain that I saw a red-sworded army thundering down the eastern slopes."

"I would not think a clot of blood and gore in the mouth of one who said that would be too much," Crom Darail said irritably. " 'Tis only the giant oaks we passed last night on our way here that you are seeing."

"Uh-huh," Crom Deroil said sarcastically. "Then I suppose it is those same oaks who are riding in royal chariots and coming toward us?"

"Ah, that's nothing but the royal houses we passed," said Crom Darail.

"Then why are those all-white shields on them?"

"No shields those," said Crom Darail, "but the columns and posts of the houses."

"If they are columns, what are those red-tipped spears waving above the dark breasts of that mighty host?"

"Off with you, now! Those are only the antlers and horns of the stags and deer running about."

"If they are stags and deer, why is that black sod flying over their heads from the hooves of horses?"

"Ah, those aren't war horses at all but the herds and flocks and cattle of the country springing around after being let out of their sheds. You're mistaking birds for sod."

"If those are birds, why then it isn't a single flock I'm seeing," said Crom Deroil.

"If that is a flock with the color of a flock
Then I'm certain that it isn't the frock
Of one bird. I'm seeing. Many-colored cloaks
With golden pins are around their necks.

If these are flocks from a rugged glen,
They carry bitter spears with them.

And I don't see where they could
Have come from just any wood!

I think we do not see flurries of snow
But stout and warlike men who flow
Across the ground in a threatening band,
Each carrying a hard red shield. Stand

Back, I say, and take a good look.
It's as easy to read them as a book
Is to a Druid. Come! I say, take
A good look for your own mind's sake!

"And don't be telling me that I'm not speaking the truth,"
he added. "For if I'm a liar, why then did they bend beneath
the branches of those towering oaks when they rode beneath
them? Eh? Speak now, or does your tongue stick in your
craw?"

Crom Deroil shook his head and said,

"Crom Darail, what do you think I see?
Shadows coming through the mist? We
Do not see any bloody slaughter ahead
For any here. I say you're drunk on mead.

It isn't right for you to argue with me
On every silly point that you think you see.
You see hunchbacked men in low bushes
But they are not men coming to us in rushes.

Stay and watch and you will hear no
Clarion or valiant war cries although

You make out of them what you will.
See? As bushes they are remaining still.

Even if they were a grove of alder trees
Standing over a woody grave, you see
That they are not running along
A warrior's path to this dún!

Now, take a good look, I say,
And tell me if it's men today
That you see or the branches of trees
Coming toward us. Should we flee

From trees? Shiver and shake
From the bark of trees that you make
Into silver shields of warlike men?
If you think that you see warriors, then

Where is the noise of their horses?
Where is the clamor of swords? Those
Are not cries you are hearing but
The moaning of wind. Don't shut

Your eyes to the obvious! Take
A good look for your honor's sake!
They are not men of flesh and bone
But only trees and red rocks and stones!"

Cúrói Mac Dáire overheard the two Druids arguing on the wall.
"I don't hear much harmony in those words," he growled.

He stepped out onto the wall while the sun slipped over
the horizon and Crom Deroil said with satisfaction, "Now,
you'll be able to see."

He waited a minute as the sun rose high in the air, then
said,

> "On many-hilled Lúchair the bright sun
> Shines on its flanks. Youths whose dún
> Is far away come between the trees
> And the brown moor far from the sea.
>
> If that is a flock of ravens,
> If that is a flock of craven
> Rails, if that is a flock
> Of starlings, a flock
>
> Of herons or barnacle geese,
> Or shrill swans newly released
> From a loch, then they are
> Closer to earth than far
>
> Heaven. Cúrói, son of dear Dáire,
> The man who walks the far
> Ocean streams and fountains,
> Tell us what comes across the mountain."

And Cúrói answered,

> "Ah, my trusty Druids who see
> Far, I know your great perplexity.
> What you see is terrifying
> For those are not cattle roaring
>
> Or hard-skinned rocks from
> Dark, green wood, nor from
> Waves roaring at Muir Miss
> Where nothing is a-miss.

If they are cows, then a man
With a bloody spear rides them.
I see a sword for each cow and
A shield on the left of each hand

And above all else I see the flutter
Of a standard that causes men to shudder.
Great is tremor in this land
That comes from that band."

And as he spoke, the two Druids saw the first full, fierce rush break across the glen. The fury was so great as the chariots roared down upon the fortress that every spear in a rack fell to the floor in the armory of Tara Luachra, every shield on a peg, every sword on the wall. All fell with a fearsome clatter to the floor. Thatch tumbled from roofs like brown flakes, and a quick image of the sea flooding over the walls from the world's hidden corners came to the Druids.

A strange rattle came from inside the fortress, and the Druids realized that it was the teeth of the warriors chattering in fear at what they could not see. The Druids fainted, Crom Darail tumbling over the wall outside while Crom Deroil fell inside, landing in a water trough that brought him sputtering to his feet just as the first wave of warriors washed over the walls.

The warriors landed on the green, and the snow melted to thirty feet from them, such was the fierce madness of the Ulster warriors.

Crom Deroil squawked in fear and rushed into the house where Maeve and Ailill and Cúrói and Eochaid Mac Luchta stood. Maeve looked up, annoyed, and said, "What is that dreadful noise? Is it coming from the air? The western sea? Or eastern Erin?"

"From Erin east across the slopes of Ir Luachair." Crom

Deroil panted. "Woe! Woe!" He wrung his hands. "I saw a barbarous force, but I cannot tell if they are men from our land or foreigners. But if they aren't foreigners, well then, they have to be men from Ulster!"

Maeve frowned and looked at Cúrói. "Well, if they are from Ulster, wouldn't you be able to tell us? You have raided much among them and even gone on raids with them."

"I would know them"—Cúrói shrugged—"if I had a description of them."

"I can describe the first band over the wall," Crom Deroil said.

"Well then, don't bat your jaws like a hungry hatchling," Maeve snapped irritably. "Give it to us, then!"

"I saw a royal and large band, and each man within the band was the equal of a king. Three in front of the band came hard toward the wall, and the middle one was a huge warrior, broad-eyed, like the moon in its fifteenth was his face. His beard was fair and forked and pointed. His bushy, reddish yellow hair was looped to the slope of his hood. Around him he wore a purple-bordered garment with a gold brooch holding it over his white shoulder; next to his white skin was a satin shirt. A purple-brown shield with a yellow-gold rim was over him. He held a gold-hilted sword, highly embossed. A bright purple spear was in his firm right hand along with a forked spear. At his right stood a true warrior, brighter than snow his countenance. At his left side, a little black-browed man, radiantly dressed. A fair, very bright man played the edge feat over them, his sharp, inlaid sword in one hand and his large warrior sword in the other. He would send them up and down past the other so that they brushed the hair of the large man but did not cut it."

"A smart description," Maeve said, pursing her lips.

"That's a band of goodly warriors," Cúrói said.

"Who are they?" Ailill asked.

"Easy to tell from that description," said Cúrói. "The great central hero is Conchobor Mac Fachtna Fathach, the lawful king of Ulster and descendant of the kings of Erin and Alba. On his right side is Fintan Mac Niall Niamglonnach, the man of the third of Ulster with face as white as snow. The little black-browed man is Cúchulainn Mac Sualdim. Ferchertne Mac Corpre Mac Ilia is the fair-beaming man playing warlike feats over them. A king of poets he is and guards well Conchobor's rear when they are in enemy territory. That man must be consulted before anyone can speak to the king."

"Outside and to the east," Crom Deroil said, "I saw three splendid warriors. Two of them were young, almost like children. The third had a forked, purple-brown beard. They moved so lightly and swiftly that the dew was not disturbed on the grass beneath their feet. I don't think even that great host was aware of their travel, yet they moved swiftly across the ground."

"Gentle and light and peaceful is the description," Maeve said.

"And that describes their band," Cúrói said.

"Who are they?" queried Ailill.

Cúrói shook his head. "Those are three noble youths from the *Tuatha Dé Danann*. Delbaeth Mac Ethliu, Angus Oc Mac Dagda, and Cermat of the Honey-mouth. They come at the end of night to excite the army with thoughts of valor and battle. They have mixed themselves throughout the host. The army does not see them, but they see the army."

"Then," said Crom Deroil, "I saw another three distinguished warriors in front of a warlike company. A wrathful brown hero is there and a fair, splendid hero, and a valiant champion who could rival a king with thick, yellow-red hair that is like a honeycomb at the end of harvest. He has a two-forked black beard that is equal to a hero's hand span. His face shines like foxglove or a freshly burning ember. They carry three red-brown shields, three warlike spears, and three heavy swords. They wore purple."

"Now who could these be?" Maeve asked.

"A heroic band indeed," Cúrói said.

"And?" Ailill pressed.

Cúrói sighed, then grinned and said, "They are the two Conalls and Loegaire. Conall Anglonnach Mac Irel Glunmar and Conall Cernach Mac Amergin and Loegaire Buadbach from Rath Immil."

"Then," Crom Deroil said, pausing for effect. "Then, I saw the three hideous men in front of the band. Three linen shirts girded their bodies, over which they had thrown three hairy, dark gray garments with three iron pins holding the garments in folds over their chests. They had coarse dark brown hair and three silver-gray shields with hard bronze bosses, flat-headed spears, and golden-hilted swords. They snorted and bellowed like hounds on the scent of a fox."

Maeve shuddered, her breasts bobbing delightfully, and said, "That is a savage description!"

"That's what they are—savages," said Cúrói grimly.

"Who are they?" Ailill asked.

"The three leaders of battle for the Ulster men: Uma Mac Remanfisech from Fedan of Cooley, Ergi Echbel from Bri Ergi, and Celtchar the Great Mac Uthecar from Rath Celtchar from Dún Da Lethglas. It's beginning to look like we have great trouble here."

"Well," said Crom Deroil grimly, "there's more. I saw a large-eyed, large-thighed, great man with a noble visage, immensely tall with a splendid gray garment around his broad shoulders. He wore seven short black cloaks around him, which were shorter above and longer below. Nine men came at each of his sides. He held a terrible iron staff"—he paused to shudder at the memory—"and he played with the men on either side, killing them with the rough end of the staff, then laying the smooth end on them to bring them back to life. Thud—thud."

"A wonderful description," Maeve said huskily. Her husband shot her a dark look.

"He is a great one," Cúrói said.

"And," Ailill said acidly, "just who is this great one?"

"That," Cúrói said, is the great Dagda Mac Ethliu, the good god of the *Tuatha Dé Danann*. He mingled with that army in the morning to stir up strife and confusion, but no one saw him though he sees everyone. We," he added meaningfully, "are definitely in trouble."

"Then I saw a stout, broad-faced man, brawny and beetle-browed, broad-faced and white-toothed, wearing not a garment and carrying no weapon or blade. He had a dark leather apron that came to his armpits. Each of his arms was the size of a man's waist. The entire Clan Dedad could not lift the stone pillar outside, but he hefted it with ease and performed the apple feat with it, rolling it from one finger to the next. Then he tossed it from him as if it was a thistle wisp, fluffy and light."

"Sturdy and stout is that description," Maeve said.

"A mighty one has been described," Cúrói said.

"Who is it?" Ailill asked.

"Triscatail Trénfer, the strong man of Conchobor's house, who has slain three men with only one angry look."

"Then I saw a young lad, like a child, bound and fettered. Three chains were wrapped around each leg and his neck and a chain around each arm and leg. Seven men held tightly to the chains—*seventy-seven men*—yet he handled them with ease, tossing them around as if they were puffballs. When he smelled the enemy, he struck the head of a man against a stone, and that man would say, "It isn't for valor or glory this trick is performed but for the food and drink within the fort." Then the young man would blush and go meekly with them until another savage wave came over him."

"A terrible description of destruction," Maeve murmured.

"That's who he is," Cúrói said.

"Who?" Ailill asked.

"The son of the three champions I have already told you about," Cúrói said. "They are Uma Mac Remanfissech, Errge Echbél, and Celtchair Mac Uthechar. That many men are required to restrain him when they go to war. His name is Uanchend Arritech, and although he is only eleven years old, he has never consumed a portion of food that he did not offer to everyone in the house."

"Then," continued Crom Deroil, "I saw a rabble with one man among them, baldheaded with stubby black hair and great, bulging eyes—one bright one—and a blue Ethiopian face. He wore a ribbed garment draped in folds with a bronze clasp over his breast. He carried a large bronze wand in his hand and a melodious little bell, which he tinkles to give pleasure to the king."

"An amusing little fool," Maeve said.

"Perhaps," Cúrói said.

"Well," demanded Ailill. "Who is he?"

"That's the royal fool Roimid. Fatigue and sorrow fall away from any Ulster man once he sees Roimid."

"Then I saw an older man in a hooded chariot over tall horses. He wore a large, many-colored cloak with golden threads around him and a gold bracelet on each arm and a gold ring on each finger, and his weapons were rich with gold. Nine chariots went before him and nine behind and nine on a side."

"Regal. Dignified," said Maeve.

"Rightly so," Cúrói answered.

"And he is?" Ailill questioned.

"That is Blaí Briugu Mac Fiachtnae from Temuir na

hArdda, who must have nine chariots with him everywhere he goes. He alone listens to the speech of that host, and they seldom talk to anyone but him."

"Then," said Crom Deroil, "I saw a vast troop of kingly swagger with one man standing before it. He had bristly black hair and a gentle blush in one cheek and a furious red blush in the other. He seemed to be first kindly, then angry in speech. On his shoulders was an openmouthed leopard, and he carried a white shield, a bright sword, and a great warrior's spear the height of his shoulder. When the spear burned brightly, he struck it with his palm and bright sparks flew. Before him was a caldron of blood, a dreadful pool of night made by Druids from dogs and cats and the head of the spear he thrust into the blood when it burned too brightly."

"A terrible description," Maeve said and shuddered.

"A terrible man," Cúrói answered grimly.

"Who is that creature?" Ailill asked.

"That is Dubthach Doeltenga, a man who has never earned thanks from anyone. When the Ulster men go out together, he goes out alone. He has the death-dealing Lúin of Celtchair, and the caldron of blood is needed to quench the fire of that spear before it burns the man who holds it. It burns like that when it senses battle."

"Then I saw a sleek, hoary-headed man with a bright cloak around him and fringes of pure silver. He wore a pure white tunic next to his skin and held a glittering white sword under his cloak and a bronze branch the size of his shoulder. His voice was sweet music, soft and slow."

"That sounds like a judicial man," said Maeve.

"It is," said Cúrói. "That is Sencha Mar Mac Ailill Mac Maelchlod from Carnmag, a good speaker and peacemaker. A man of the world from sun to sun who can make peace with three words."

"Then I saw an ardent and handsome band with a youthful

lad with curly yellow hair who gave judgment when no other could."

"A wise and clever description," said Maeve.

"A wise and clever man," said Cúrói.

"And," Ailill asked.

"That is Cain Cainbrethach Mac Sencha Mac Ailill. When his father cannot judge, he does."

"Then came a dreadful foreign trio with short and bristling, shaggy hair, black clothing, carrying short bronze spears in one hand and iron clubs in the other. No one spoke to them, and they spoke to no one."

"Terrible and foreign is that description," Maeve said.

"That describes the three doorkeepers of Conchobor's royal house: Nem and Dall and Dorcha."

That was the first group to reach the green, and the great Druid could describe no more for Cúrói to identify.

"The Ulster men are here," Maeve exclaimed.

"You do have a way with the obvious," Cúrói said.

"Was this predicated? Did you know anything about it?" she asked.

"I didn't know," Cúrói answered.

"Does anyone in the fort know?" she pressed.

"The ancient one of Clan Dedad Gabalglinde Mac Dedad, who is blind and has been here for thirty years, is in the fort. He might know," answered Cúrói.

"Then go and ask him if this was prophesied and, if so, what was made of it," Maeve said.

"Who should go?" Cúrói asked.

"Let Crom Deroil and Fóenglinde Mac Dedad go," Maeve replied.

The two men hurried as fast as they could to Gabalglinde's apartment and rapped sharply upon the door.

"Who is it?" Gabalglinde asked.

"Crom Deroil and Fóenglinde," they replied. "We have

come to ask you if there is a prophecy or a prediction concerning the men of Ulster and what provision might have been made."

"Oh," the ancient one replied. "There have long been prophecies about that." His voice quavered. "Let's see now, what was the provision? Oh yes. There must be an iron house with two wooden houses around it, and a house of earth beneath it with a very sturdy iron top upon it. All the dead wood and fuel and tinder are to be packed into the house of earth until it is full. The prophecy was that all of the chieftains of Ulster would one night gather in that iron house. At the feet of the bed are seven chains of fresh iron for binding and making fast. Fasten them around the seven pillars on the green outside."

Crom Deroil and Fóenglinde returned to Ailill and Maeve and told them what provision had been made for the Ulster men.

"Let one of my people and one of yours go to meet them, Cúrói," Maeve said.

"Who should go?" he asked.

"The same pair that the Ulster men might be welcomed by in Connacht by me or by you."

"I'll know if they come to fight or in peace by who takes the welcome," Cúrói said grimly. "If Dubthach takes the welcome, there'll be fighting. But if Sencha takes the welcome, we have a chance."

Again, the messengers were sent. They approached Conchobor with great nervousness, bowing and scraping as they addressed him.

"Welcome, welcome, great king of Ulster," said Fóenglinde as the two went out to greet the Ulster men. "Cúrói Mac Dáire and the chieftains of two provinces visiting in the fort make you welcome."

"We accept your welcome, as does our king," said Sencha,

and Crom Deroil heaved a sigh of relief and used the sleeve of his robe to wipe the perspiration from his face.

"We don't come for battle," Sencha said (and his words slurred a bit), "but on a rather"—he hiccuped—"drunken spree from Dún Dáben Clíu Máil Maicc Ugtaine. We thought it would be dishonorable if we didn't spend a night in your lands."

Messengers returned to Maeve and Ailill and Cúrói and Echu and the chieftains of the three provinces and told them what Sencha had said. Poets and minstrels were hastily assembled and sent out to greet the men from Ulster while a house was readied to feast them. The messengers said that the greatest hero among the Ulster men would have the honor of selecting the house for them. A great clamor arose among the Ulster men as they argued about who should be granted this right. A hundred powerful warriors seized their weapons, but Sencha pacified them.

"Let Cúchulainn go," Sencha said. "You came to see the measure of his house, and you shall be under his guarantee until you return to your homes."

So Cúchulainn went and the Ulster men trailed after him, one by one. Cúchulainn quickly found the largest house within the fortress and, as luck would or wouldn't have it, it was the iron house sided by two wooden houses.

The Ulster men crowded inside the strange structure, and attendants came to serve them. Meanwhile, the others secretly stored wood in the earthen house beneath. Much food and drink were served, and as the feasting became merry, the servants slipped away until the last man firmly closed the door behind him and latched it. Seven iron chains were wrapped around the house and fixed to the seven pillars upon the green outside. Then fifty blacksmiths were brought with their bellows to blow the fire, and the fire was lit in the earthen house. Then the heat began to creep into the iron house.

Suddenly Cúrói's men began to shout outside the house, and the merriment inside ceased. Then Bricriu frowned and said, "Why is the floor so hot? My feet feel like they're on fire." He bent and touched the floor with his fingers, then jerked them away and blew on them, yelping, "I see the treachery here! They are roasting us alive!"

The men rushed for the door, but it held fast. Bricriu peeked through a crack and swore as he singed his eyebrows against the hot iron. "They've chained us in here!" he bawled. "Treachery! Treachery!"

"Well, let's find out how sound the door is," Triscatal said. He rose and slammed a huge foot against the door, but it held fast.

"This isn't a good feast, Cúchulainn," Bricriu said mournfully. "I think you have brought us into the enemy's cage."

"I'll get us out," Cúchulainn said grimly. He plunged his sword into the wooden wall, but it rang like a bell when it struck the iron on the outside. "Why, the outside of the house is iron!" he exclaimed.

"Oh no," moaned Bricriu, and he began dancing as his toes became burnt on the floor. . . .

[N.B. The rest of the story from this version is lost. However, there is another version that begins when the Ulster men are arguing about who should go first into the house. Some of the names of the heroes are changed and spelled differently. Should I continue? Yes, I should.]

"Only the best warrior can go to select the house," the messenger said.

"That's me," Triscoth said.

"No," answered the fool. " 'Tis I."

"No, it's me," said Nia.

"Me," said Daeltenga.

"Either of us could go," said Dub and Rodub.

Each man rose, glowering at the others. Sencha sighed.

"You can't even manage that decision?" he said, exasperated. "The one the Ulster men honor the most should go, even if he isn't the best warrior. Not," he added quickly, holding up his hand, "that I'm saying he is or he isn't."

"Which of us is that?" the Ulster men asked.

"Cúchulainn. He should go."

They grumbled about this choice but grudgingly let the youthful warrior go ahead of them into the fort.

"Is this the best that Ulster has to offer?" Fintan asked.

Cúchulainn jumped up until he was on the top of the enclosure, then leaped down upon the bridge, and the weapons rattled in their racks and fell to the floor inside the fortress. The Ulster men were taken to a secure oaken house with a door of yew three feet thick with two iron hooks and a spit through them. The house was sumptuously laid out with plump flock-beds and pillows and bedclothes. Crom Deroil sent their weapons on after them and they sat down. Cúchulainn's weapons were honored by being placed above them.

"Let water for washing be brought for them," ordered Ailill. And servants brought in food and ale and mead and kept the goblets and cups filled until the Ulster men rolled drunkenly around, singing bawdy songs and performing feats of strength.

"Watch this!" Nar demanded and tried to balance a full goblet on his forehead, but it tipped and drenched him. The Ulster men roared with laughter, and Crom Deroil asked quietly if there was anything that they desired.

When they were all drunk and merry, Sencha clapped his hands and said, "Now then, show your manners, men of Ulster, and give this princely fellow the thanks for giving you all this food and ale."

"True, true," Dubthach said, belching. "Upon my word, I swear that no one will take anything from this land except what birds can carry in their claws. But," he said, pausing to drain another cup, "the men of Erin and Alba will take your land and your women and riches and break your children's heads against stones."

During the great raid, Fergus had said of him,

> "That dratted Dubthach of the Chafertongue,
> Look at all the damage he has done!
> Why he is the one who slew those women
> And kept us fighting against their men.
>
> He did a hateful and most hideous act
> By killing Fiacha, Conchobor's son, back
> At Emain Macha before we left. And Maine
> Mac Fedlimid, he killed him all the same.
>
> He cares not a jot to be Ulster's king
> For the only thing he likes is battle-ring
> And if he wants to attack the men
> He'll wait until they're seated, then kill them."

"Well, you may think that's wrong," Dubthach said, "but— say, isn't it getting warm in here?" He went and studied the wall closely. "Look here how the wall is made. Look at its strength and the fastening upon the house. Why, even if you were anxious to leave, you could not. Now, you may think I'm crazy, but there's something wrong here. Where's that so-called hero who brought us here?"

Cúchulainn came forward and made a great somersault upward. He struck the roof of the house, knocking it off, and peered down outside at the men below. They had formed into a band to attack the Ulster men. Ailill placed his back to the door to protect them, and his seven sons joined hands with him at the door.

Cúchulainn dropped down lightly inside the house and

went to the door and gave it a kick. His foot went through it up to the knee.

"If that was a woman you kicked, she'd be in her bed now," Dubthach said.

Cúchulainn kicked the door again and knocked it flat on the ground, pinning Ailill sprawling beneath it.

"May I be saved," Sencha said fervently. He looked at Cúchulainn. "What do you propose to do?"

"Have the men seize their weapons and place their backs against the walls, equal on all sides. Then we'll send one man outside to speak to them. If it comes to that, throw the house off of you."

"Who should speak to them?" asked Sencha.

"I will," said Triscoth. "And any I stare at will die."

Outside, the warriors were also holding counsel.

"Who shall go inside and talk to them?" they asked.

"I will," said Lopan. He went into the house. "Is everything all right, great heroes?" he asked.

"Oh, certainly," they replied.

He glanced at Triscoth, who stared back at him.

"Man for man?" Triscoth asked.

"Certainly," Lopan said uncertainly.

"I am Triscoth, and I speak for the men of Ulster," he said. "They don't have good speakers, but we have lookers." And he gave Lopan such a fierce look that Lopan toppled over in a dead faint.

Fer Caille came into the house with nine men with him. "Is everything all right?" he asked.

"Man for man is how men should speak," Triscoth said and looked fiercely at Fer Caille, who fainted dead away.

Then Manach Anaidgned came into the house with nine men armed with spears. He looked at the men on the floor. "I think you've done them wrongly," he said. "They look quite pale."

Triscoth looked at him, but Manach laughed and said, "Look and see if I die!"

And with that, Triscoth seized him and hurled him against the nine men, killing them all.

Outside, the others gathered to attack the men inside the house, but the Ulster men had had enough of poor hospitality and heaved the house up and over on top of the others. Then they roared out, swinging their swords, and the battle went fiercely until the middle of the next day before the Ulster men were routed as they were fewer in numbers.

Ailill watched the battle from his balcony in the fortress and gloating, said, "The tales of the Ulster warriors were tales worth telling until today. I thought they were heroes among all others in Erin, but now I see that treachery is all they do. A battle isn't a battle unless there's a king in it. Why," he roared to the Ulster men, "if I had been in that battle, I would have settled you. But I don't fight castaways, for it would harm my honor."

With that, Cúchulainn suddenly dashed through the throng and attacked them three times. Furbaide Ferbenn Mac Conchobor attacked them as well, and none of the others would wound him because of his great beauty.

"Why don't you wound this warrior?" one asked. "Not agreeable to me are the deeds he performs. Why, if he had a head of gold, I would take it if he killed my brother."

Furbaide heard his words and threw a spear through him and he died.

Then the Ulster warriors felt the battle urge come upon them and roared back into the fray, and when they had finished, only three of the enemy survived. They plundered the household, sparing only Ailill and his seven sons because they had not entered the battle against them, and from that time on Tara Luachra was uninhabited.

Crimthann Nia Nair escaped from the battle and met with

Richis, a female satirist, west of Laune. "Was my son lost?" she asked.

"Yes," said Crimthann.

"Come with me until you avenge him," she said.

"What revenge?" he asked.

"You must slay Cúchulainn for his sake," she replied.

Crimthann gulped and said, "But how can that be done?"

"Not difficult," she said. "Use only your two hands on him because you will find him unprepared."

Then they turned and rode back toward the Ulster men and found Cúchulainn bathing his face in the waters of a ford in the country of Owney. Richis walked toward him, hips switching, a broad smile on her face, and then she stripped her clothes away, standing naked in front of him, proud nipples rising in the cold air, her flesh pebbling, black triangle like a bramble patch between her leg.

Immediately, Cúchulainn looked away so he would not see her nakedness.

"Attack him now, Crimthann!" she snapped.

"Here comes a man," Laeg, Cúchulainn's charioteer said to him.

"You are mistaken," Cúchulainn said. "Even if you aren't, I can't look up with that woman standing there like that."

Laeg quickly pulled a stone out of the chariot and cast it at her. It struck her across her back, breaking it, and she fell dead to the ground.

Cúchulainn raised his head and saw Crimthann near him.

"Shit," mumbled Crimthann, but he attacked bravely all the same.

Cúchulainn slew him and took away his head and spoils.

Then Cúchulainn and Laeg went after the Ulster men until they all arrived back at Cúchulainn's fortress and the Ulster men tumbled wearily into the beds that had been readied for them. They stayed there forty days and forty nights and consumed the feast that Cúchulainn had prepared for them. Then they departed, leaving their blessing with him.

Ailill came from the south to Ulster and remained as a friend with them. They gave him the width of his face in red gold and silver and seven *cumals*—women slaves—for each of his sons. Then he returned to his own land in peace and harmony with Ulster.

Conchobor never had a threat to his reign from that moment on as long as he lived.

Bricriu's Feast and the Exile of Dóel Dermait's Sons

Fled Bricrenn ocus Loinges mac Nduíl Dermait is found only in *The Yellow Book of Lecan*. It was apparently written by Móir mic Fhir Bhisigh, the scribe of the book, around 1391. The story, however, seems to date to the ninth century. The title is a bit ambiguous; it suggests *Fled Bricrend (Bricriu's Feast)*,[1] but that work, a comic telling of three heroes each trying to be proclaimed champion of Ulster, is the second longest tale in the Ulster Cycle, after *Táin Bó Cuailngé*. The reader will note the change in the spelling of names from those that appear in *The Book of Leinster*.

ONCE A FAMOUS KING OF Ulster, Conchobor Mac Nessa, made a law that each warrior of the Red Branch would host the rest of the warriors for one night of feasting, while the king would repay the warriors with a feast in seven nights or four nights, the minor chiefs would host one night. The chiefs' feasting was very important, for those were the nights attended by the women of Ulster. The host's wife would oversee the feast and would provide the cooking of seven oxen and seven boars and seven sides of bacon and seven unblemished wethers[2] and seven pigs' feet and seven hearts with fish and chicken and vegetables among other dishes. Seven vats of honeyed beer would be available to quench the thirst of the feasting warriors.

On this particular day, the feasting went to Bricriu Nemthenga, and the food was brought for the feast while Conchobor's caldron was filled. This caldron was so large that a ladder was placed inside and out of it so the servants might fill pitchers and carry them around the Feasting Hall to replenish emptied goblets. But Bricriu was known to be a troublemaker, and the warriors refused to come to his feast unless he kept himself away from them in an apartment next to the Feasting Hall. Since it was a great honor to host the king and his warriors, Bricriu agreed to do this, but he still laid plans to disrupt the feasting with a bit of mischief making.[3]

When Conchobor's servers rose to carve the meat, Bricriu rubbed his hands together in great glee and said to his wife, "Ah, but now there'll be a slight for those who would drink the ale and eat the food."

But Conchobor overheard Bricriu's words and picked up his silver wand and struck it against the bronze pillar standing next to his couch. Immediately, all the warriors fell silent, for such was the signal that the king wished to speak. Conchobor looked sternly at Bricriu and said, "What are you trying to do, Bricriu? Why would you want to have a slight cast among the Ulster men? Is it because you want their portion of the feast as well as your own?"

Bricriu looked hurt that such an accusation would be cast his way and said, "But, Conchobor, why would I do that? You can see that I have plenty to eat and drink before me. Besides, I am the host, and it would not be good manners for me to consume the feast that I have had prepared. At great cost, I might add"—which he did immediately—"or"—he smiled slyly—"claim that the feast has been a success."

[N.B. There appears to be a lacuna here; no reason is given for the warriors to take affront at Bricriu's words. The presumption is that they rose to go out to prove themselves champions.]

Twelve Ulster heroes immediately rose and left to slay the people of the provinces. [?] Those were Fergus Mac Róig, Conall Cernac Mac Aimirgin Lóegaire Búadach, Cúchulainn Mac Sualtaim, Eogan Mac Durthacht, Celtchair Mac Uithechair, Blai Brugaid, Dubthac Dóel Ulad, Ailill Miltenga, Conall Anglonnach, Munremar Mac Geircinn, and Cethern Mac Fintain.

Cúchulainn went as one of fifty men into Oln-Ecmacht over the Dub and Drobes to the Dublin in the territory of Ciarraige. Once there, they divided themselves into two groups with twenty-five following the river to the west while twenty-five went east. Along with Cúchulainn went Lugaid Reo nDerg and Laeg Mac Rinagabra, his charioteer.

When they came to Áth Ferthain, they found themselves in a playing field with three hundred around them. It was there that Findchóem, daughter of Eochu Rond, came upon them and said, "A life for a life!"

Lugaid frowned and glanced at the others. "Why," he asked, "would we do that?"

"I am the woman of a man and call upon you for help," she said.

"All right," the others said. "We will support this. Who is it that you seek?"

"Cúchulainn Mac Sualtaim. I have loved him for a long time after hearing the tales of his great deeds," she said.

Lugaid hid his smile beneath his hand and said, "I welcome you on his behalf. You will find him with the rest."

"A life for a life!" she repeated loudly, and when Cúchulainn heard her, he gave a hero's leap to her side. She placed her hands around his neck and kissed him deeply. He pulled away, blushing, as the other warriors laughed.

"What now?" they asked.

"It is enough of a deed that we should place these people under our protection and take the daughter of the king of Uí Maine back with us to Emain Macha."

They left for the north, traveling through the black night until they came to Fid Manach, where they saw three fires in front of them in the forest with nine men to each fire along with the leaders of each. Cúchulainn attacked them quickly and killed three from each fire in addition to the three leaders. Then he went over Áth Moga into Mag nAí toward Ráth Cruachan, where they heard his shout of victory.

A watchman heard the ululating cry and went to see who gave it, then returned to Cruachan, where he told all what he had seen and what they looked like.

Maeve frowned when she heard the watchman's words. "I'm not certain who they could be," she said slowly, "but it could be Cúchulainn and his foster-son Lugaid and Laeg. The woman might be Findchóem, daughter of Eochu Rond, king of Uí Maine, and if she is, then whoever took her is fortunate if he had her father's permission, unlucky if he did not."

A great cry came from without the gate, and Maeve sighed deeply, saying, "Will someone please go out and see who has been killed?"

Maeve's herald hurried to do her bidding and brought back the heads to be identified by Maeve and her husband, Ailill.

"Does anyone here recognize them?" Ailill asked.

"No," came the chorus from the others in the hall.

"I do," Maeve said. "They are the three raiders who have been stealing from us. Put the heads out on the walls so others can see what happens to those who raid the herds of Ailill and Maeve."

When Cúchulainn learned what had happened to the heads

THE RED BRANCH TALES   191

of the men he had killed, he said, "I swear by everything upon which people swear that if those heads are not credited to me, I will put the walls of Cruachan on top of them."

The heads were immediately given to him, and the warriors were taken into the guesthouse of Cruachan and made comfortable, according to the rules of hospitality.

In the morning, Cúchulainn arose before the others and went out, taking his weapons with him. He placed his back against a standing-stone, watching, waiting, for he knew that Findchóem's father would be coming for her.

A noise came from the south as loud as thunder, and the watchman hurried to report to Maeve.

"What do you think caused that?" she asked her warriors. But none could answer her.

"What do *you* think it is?" they asked, none being willing to venture a guess.

"Who knows unless it is the Uí Maine who have come to Cruachan in search of Findchóem," she said. She motioned to the watchman. "Go and have another look and tell us what you see."

Obediantly he left, then came running back almost immediately. "I can see a mist that has filled the plain to the south, but no one can see through that mist."

"I know that," Maeve said. "It is the breath of the horses of the Uí Maine, who are galloping in search of Findchóem. Go and see what else you can see."

The watchman again returned almost immediately, saying, "I see a glitter of fire from Áth Moga to Sliab Badgnai. Can you explain that, Maeve?"

"Not difficult," she said. "That is the shining of the weapons of the Uí Maine and the red anger from their eyes as they search for Findchóem."

This time, Maeve rose with Ailill and went out to see for herself what she could see. The others followed, crowding against each other from the high point of the walls, looking eagerly to the south. They saw the army coming toward them led by a warrior wearing a purple fourfold cloak with its hem edged in gold. He rode a roan horse and carried a shield with eight parts of gold on his back. He wore a silver-striped tunic, and his fair hair flew streamed backward to fall upon the flanks of his horse. The neck-rein was a chain of gold weighing seven ounces. He was Eochu Rond and carried two spears inlaid with gold and a gold-hilted sword on his belt.

When he saw Cúchulainn, he immediately threw a spear at him, but Cúchulainn leaped effortlessly, lightly up and danced upon its deadly point, then turned the spear back toward the Eochu Rond. The spear caught the horse in the neck. Pain-crazed, the horse leaped and threw his rider. Cúchulainn ran forward to where the dazed Eochu Rond lay, gathered him in his arms, and carried him into the fort.

The Uí Maine were angry at that, for they thought Cúchulainn had behaved dishonorably. But Maeve and Ailill did not let either one depart until they made peace with each other. When Cúchulainn went to leave, Eochu, still recovering from his fall, said, "May you not have an easy time sitting or lying down until you discover what happened to the three sons of Dóel Dermait."

Cúchulainn left for Emain Macha, taking the heads with him. There, the heads spoke to him once he had settled himself in the champion's seat and took the goblet handed him. His clothes seemed to burn him, and his feet grew hot from the ground. Frowning, he leaped to his feet and turned to the other warriors, saying, "I think I know what Eochu Rond meant now, when he said his farewell. I must search out what happened to the three sons of Dóel Dermait before I die."

He left the Great Hall of the Red Branch with Laeg, his charioteer, following him with his spears. Lugaid Reo Derg came after him as he approached the door. There he found nine craftsmen waiting, and when they saw him, one said, "It would be a good thing if someone from the king brought us food and drink."

Cúchulainn frowned. "I am not a steward," he said. But he felt the insult of their words and leaped over them and struck their heads from their shoulders.

He left Emain Macha and traveled southeast until he reached Ard Macha, which was a heavily wooded forest at the time. There he found Conchobor's smiths making things for the king. They saw Cúchulainn and his companions coming toward them and said, "It would be good if the king has sent us food and drink."

When Cúchulainn heard their words, he frowned and said, "I am not a steward." He leaped over the nine of them and struck off their heads. Then he continued on toward Tráig in Baile east of Dún Delcan. There the son of the king of Alba had come from the other side with a ship laden with satin and silk and richly engraved drinking horns for Conchobor. They had arranged for Conchobor to meet them, but he had not arrived. When they saw Cúchulainn, they said, "This is weary waiting between wave and stone."

Again, Cúchulainn felt insulted and said, "I am not a steward." Drawing his sword, he attacked them, hewing his way through the ship's crew and warriors until he reached the king's son.

"A life for a life, Cúchulainn," the son said. "I am sorry, but we did not recognize you. The sun was in our eyes and—"

"Do you know what took the three sons of Dóel Dermait out of their country?" Cúchulainn interrupted.

"No," the young man said, adding quickly, "but I have a boat that you may use, if you wish."

Cúchulainn took his small spear, engraved an *ogham* upon

it, and gave it to the king's son. "Take this to Emain Macha," he instructed. "There you will be allowed to sit in my seat until my return."

The son carried his possessions from the boat and placed them on the strand to wait for the promised messenger while Cúchulainn entered the boat and raised the sail to begin his voyage. For a day and night, he sailed until he came to a large, fine, and noble island. A silver rampart girded it below a bronze palisade. He found a house with golden pillars, and within the house a hundred fifty compartments were readied. A *fidchell* board and a *brandub* board and a *timpán* were there. A couple with light gray hair were in the house, each dressed in purple robes with dark red-gold brooches in their cloaks. Three young women sat at looms, weaving cloth with a golden border. The man of the house greeted him, saying, "Welcome, Cúchulainn, for Lugaid's sake. Welcome to Laeg for the sake of his father and mother."

The women repeated the welcome, and Cúchulainn's heart lifted. "This pleases us," he said. "Until today, we haven't received the half of such welcome."

"Today, you will receive it," the man said.

Cúchulainn then said, "Do you know what took the sons of Dóel Dermait out of their country?"

The warrior shook his head. "But I will find out. Their sister and brother-in-law are on the island to the south of us."

Now there were three lumps of iron by the fire. The three women rose and put the lumps into the fire until they were hot, then dumped each into a vat of water so Cúchulainn, Lugaid, and Laeg could bathe. When they were finished, three drinking-horns filled with rich mead were brought to them. A bed was made for them with warm blankets on top and a rug beside the bed. Then, while they were resting, they heard the arrival of a host with horns blaring and jesters shouting rude jests.

They rose and saw fifty warriors approaching the house, and between each pair was a pig and a bullock and a goblet filled with hazel mead.[4] With the fifty warriors were others carrying firewood upon their backs led by another man dressed in a purple cloak fastened around his neck with a gold brooch. He wore a white tunic with a red border and carried large and small spears in one hand and a golden sword in the other. He came in and greeted Cúchulainn.

"Welcome, Cúchulainn, for Lugaid's sake. Welcome to Laeg for the sake of his father and mother."

The fifty warriors echoed his greeting, and the pigs and bullocks were brought forth and slaughtered and placed in a huge caldron until they were cooked. They made a meal for a hundred, and this was brought to Cúchulainn and his companions. The rest of the meat went to the host. Rich mead was brought to them to drink, and much merriment was made. Soon they were drunk, and the time had come for them to go to bed.

"How would you like to spend the night, Cúchulainn?"

"Do I have a choice?" the warrior asked.

"You have a choice," the host said. "Here are Ringabar's three daughters, Eithne and Etan and Étain. Over there are their three brothers, Eochaid and Aed and Oengus. Then there are their mother and father, Rian and Gabar, and Finnabar, the storyteller. There also are the three brothers Lóeg and Id and Sedlang."

Cúchulainn eyed all and said, smiling:

"I do not know with whom
Fair Etan will pass the night,
But I know she will not sleep alone."

Etan smiled and went to bed with Cúchulainn. When morning came, Cúchulainn gave her a gold thumb ring.

The next day, Cúchulainn sailed until he saw the island where Condla Cóel Corbacc and Achtland, the daughter of Dóel Dermait, lived. He rowed toward the island, pulling so hard on the oars that the *currach* rose higher than the highest point on the island. Condla Cóel Corbacc rested on the island with his head against a pillar-stone in the west and his feet against a pillar-stone in the east. A woman combed his hair. When Condla heard the *currach* scrape against the land, he rose and took a deep breath and blew the boat back onto the sea. Then he said, "Though you may be angry, great warrior, we do not fear you. It is not prophesied that this island will be destroyed. So come ashore and be welcomed."

Cúchulainn landed and came ashore. The woman cast a saucy glance at him and winked, but Cúchulainn ignored her and said to the warrior, "Do you know what took the sons of Dóel Dermait from their country?"

"I do," said the woman. Cúchulainn looked at her. "Yes," she repeated, "I do. I will go with you, for it is by you that they are to be saved."

So Cúchulainn and the woman entered the boat. Cúchulainn looked at her and said:

"So, what is the foolish course,
Woman, and what is the source
Of your knowledge? Know that
I truly desire to save Dóel Dermait's
Sons from whatever threat
Is before them or what they've met."

The woman looked lovingly upon Cúchulainn and the others and pointed into the distance, saying, "See that white rampart? That is where Cairpre Cundail lives."

"Ah," Lugaid said. "Their father's brother?"

The woman nodded, and they traveled to the white rampart, where they saw two women cutting rushes.

"What is the name of this land?" Cúchulainn asked.

One of the women rose and said to him:

> "The country to which you have come
> Has a host with horses on the plain. Some
> Seven kings rule this land and
> Each has seven rules for its band.
>
> Seven kingly men rule equally
> And, for each, seven women equally.
> Under the foot of each woman lies
> A kingly man waiting to die.
>
> Seven herds of horses and seven
> Hosts for each man, each has seven
> Victories on this land. As well each
> Has seven sea wins beyond the beach.
>
> "Besides the great plain battle
> Each has won seven battles.
> No weakling or thief may say
> The tale of this country and its way."

Cúchulainn went to the woman and struck her a great blow upon her head so her brain burst out her ears.

"This is an evil thing you have done," the other woman protested. "But it was prophesied that you would commit an evil murder here. A pity that it wasn't me to whom you spoke."

"I'm speaking to you now," Cúchulainn said dangerously. "What are the names of the people here?"

"That's easy:

"Dian son of Lugaid
Leo son of Iachtán
Eogan Whitehorse
Fiachna the Phantom
Cond of the *Sídhe*
Senach Redheel.

All seek to do battle-red
From their chariots red.
Many warriors will find
Their sides pierced by unkind
Warriors who number a host
And are ready for your boast."

After hearing that, Cúchulainn and his companions went toward the fort. Laeg draped a woman's cloak over his back. When they came inside the courtyard, the woman with them went to report how they had been treated at the rushes.

"That is what one could expect if one plays a fool," Cairpre Cundail said.

Then Cairpre rushed out and attacked Cúchulainn. They fought from the morning to the end of the day, but neither one could wound the other more than the other wounded him.

At last, Cúchulainn seized the *gae bulga*. When Cairpre saw this, he stopped his attack and said, "A life for a life, Cúchulainn."

Cairpre threw his weapons away and took Cúchulainn by the hand and led him into the fort. He arranged for Cúchulainn to be bathed, and that night the great warrior slept with the daughter of the king.

The next morning Cúchulainn asked, "What took the sons of Dóel Dermait from their country?"

Cairpre settled himself and began to tell the story from the beginning to the end.

Now Cairpre had been challenged by Eochaid Glas to battle the next day in the glen, and Cúchulainn went with him to the glen.

"Someone is coming into the glen, you sorry warriors," he [sic] said.

"Someone is already here," Cúchulainn said.

"I don't like the sound of that voice," he [sic] said. "It sounds like the warped one from Erin."

Then Eochaid attacked Cúchulainn, but the boy-warrior leaped up and balanced on the edge of Eochaid's shield. Eochaid blew Cúchulainn into the sea with a mighty breath. Again, Cúchulainn leaped up on the edge of the shield and again was blown into the sea. A third time he leaped onto the shield and was hurled again into the sea.

"This is a miserable way to fight!" Cúchulainn exclaimed. He threw his spear high into the air, and it came down hard upon Eochaid's helmet, piercing through it and his crown, and pinning him to the ground. Eochaid tumbled backward, and Cúchulainn leaped upon him, slipping Eochaid's armor off. Then he hacked Eochaid apart with his sword.

The members of the *Sídhe* who had been insulted by Eochaid came into the glen and bathed themselves in his blood to free themselves from his insult. Then the sons of Dóel Dermait went to their land.

Cúchulainn returned with Cairpre to the fort, where he was ladened with rich gifts. He returned to the island where Condla and his wife lived and told them the tale of what had happened. Then he went to the island of Riangabar, slept with a woman, and again told his story. The next day he returned to Ulster.

At Emain Macha, Cúchulainn found his food and mead waiting for him. He made himself comfortable, then told the Red Branch warriors and Conchobor what had happened to him. Then he traveled to Cruachan and told the story to Ailill and Maeve and Fergus.

Eochu Rond was summoned, and when he heard what had happened, he said:

"My daughter Findchóem caused me
To stray after combat across the sea
With Eochaid Glas. I regret the way
Of the marriage on that black day.

I killed many while red with anger:
Nine smiths and nine brewers.
Nine merchants also I slew
One morning before the dew.

When I came to Dóel's land,
I went to the seat of Cairpre Cláen.
There, I heard a great praise
Of my sharp sword. I raised

A sharp battle with Cairpre
Over the far-reaching sea.
Our swords dulled each other
And our shields smashed each other.

But scarce a bramble from a cloak
Was taken by Cairpre. A cloak
Of peaceful sleep came to us
Until we reached Eochaid Glas.

Then my red-rage against hundreds
Turned against me and he sundered
Me with a grievous wound.
That was an inglorious wound!

Findchóem and I were sorry and
After I spoke with the band
Of Dóel Dermait's sons,
I spared Cairpre Cláen."

After hearing this, Cúchulainn made a peace with Eochu, and Findchóem stayed with Cúchulainn when he returned to Emain Macha with great riches.

This is why this story is called *Bricriu's Feast*. Another name, however, is *The Exile of the Sons of Dóel Dermait*.

Finit.

The Battle of the Gathering at Macha

This story is a bit confusing. It is alluded to in *Senchus Sil Ir,* where the Ulster warriors have "gray beards at the battle of Aenach Macha." *Cath Oenaigh Macha* is given in the time of Tigernmas, a mythical ancestor of the Ulaid. To add to the difficulty, there is also a lacuna in the manuscript, and some names have been added in the list of casualties that do not appear anywhere else in the battle. This story can be found in the Royal Irish Academy. Again, the reader's attention is called to the changes in the spelling of names from other stories.

Now it came to pass that a great fleet by Niall Niamglonnach, prince of Asia, and Torc and Tren and Tradar and Ranc and Morc and Black Morglonn and Donn and Dubhan gathered on the Red Sea.

From the Red Sea, they sailed to the North Sea, where they found Daball Dianbuilleach Mac Dub Mac Harold and Mealla

Morglonnach, prince of Scandinavia, and Arm Mac Linndarmand of the Uighe and Eolach Mac Linndarmand of the Belgae
and Rothnuall, prince of Norway, with sixty ships. They came
upon each other at Carb Harbor in Buagh Island near Norway,
which is now called the Orkney Islands.

When Daball saw them he said,

> "I hear the harsh screech of long ships
> Slaughter against the bank. This trip
> Will result in great fury and combat.
> Mealla watches well as does Eolacht
> And Rothnuall until we come to Ruba great
> Where we shall stop and our anchor frets."

When Niall heard this, he said:

> "Oh Turc, Oh Tradair, Oh Tren,
> Oh King, Oh Morc, Oh Morglonn!
> Hold back your powerful acts.
> Keep your wanderers back."

Messengers went from Daball to demand that Niall provide
him with a bond of hostages. Niall, however, said they had no
right to ask this, and so at Carb Harbor the famous battle began.
The asiatci[1] army was reinforced from the east, and then they
decided to go and conquer the Western world. They went to
Scotland, where they took hostages and captured Ruba Rigarb,
the king of Scotland. Then they took hostages from France and
Lodar Laebhcosach, who was the king of Britain. After this,
they sailed to Erin to the City of Heroes now called the Fort
of Two Half-Chains. Cealtchar Mac Uthechar was there, and
they fought a great battle and stayed one night and sailed to
Feile Estuary (there Eochaid Aiream gave his eye to the poet

Fear Ceartne for the sake of his honor² so Fuile Estuary is the name of the Bann in the north) and camped.

They attacked and plundered Cethearn Mac Finntan and Leidhe Mac Fergus Mac Leidhe and raided Blai Wood, Locha, Glen Gabla, and from the Cruibe Falls to the Fort of Two Peaks. Cethearn and Leidhe Leimderg attacked them but could not defeat them, and at last they were forced to send messengers to Conchobor in Emain Macha to warn him that Ulster had been invaded by raiders.

That night, the fleet sailed up from above the Inber Feile shore. In the morning, the warriors rose to make battle and counseled each other, for they had a problem with leaving their ships without anyone to defend them. They really needed to leave a third of their force behind, but this would sorely deplete their numbers. So Daball said, "Let us simply burn our ships and conquer the land."³ They burned their ships and left to march over Blen-corra-crincosaigh, over the Plain of Úmór, over Liath-muine, over the Ancient Plain, to the Great Rath and to Mogh Na nOg (this is where the three Illanns of Emain Macha were slain and the three Aenguses and the three Cobhtachs of Cuib and the three Cairpres of Cualgne and the twelve sons of Fergus Mac Róich and the seven sons of Dubthach) and on to the Excellent Fort now called Genann's Fort. There they rested and camped.

The Ulster warriors went to Neide in Scotland and down to the southern part by Slieb Gullion and up in the north by the Foyle.⁴

Leabarcham was taken to Conchobor, who told her, "Go and summon Clan Rugraide and let the Clan of Aengus Red-mouth come and Eogan and Conall the Rough and Imchad Mac Durrthacht and Laegaire Buadabach and Irgalach Mac Laithem and Black Daire from Cuailngé and Ros and Daire and Im-chadh and Gennann from Feiswswen Fort and Ceathern Mac

Finntan Mac Daire Orgall and let Fiacha the Bloody come and Nert, Tren, and Find, sons of Ros Forgall, and Gearg Mac Feabargel from Glen Derg. Go to the three sons of Aimargen from Dunseverick to Conall to Rodhan to Rochad to Rothan to Sosa to Badhna to Find the Poet, to the three sons of Cathbad, to the Plain of Ith at Indais, to Cethearn Mac Finntan Mac Niall, to Leidhe son of Aengus, and to the lesser Ui Echach.

"Let Connad Mac Murna come, and the sons of Eochaid Yellowheel, and Subaltach Sighe and the Men of the Plain of Murthemne and the Ui Eachach of Siabh Fuad and the Men of the Plain."[5]

Leabarcham parted from Conchobor and went forward to the White Plain to the seven sons of Donn Mac Durrtacht, to the youths of the Conaille, to the Plain of Murthemne to Subaltach, to Suig Eamain, to Comarlinn, to Slibh Fuad, to Slibh Gullion, to Glen Rossa, to the City of Heroes, to Cealtar, to Roth's Fort, to Leide, to Dunseverick, to Aimargen and his sons, Conall and Mes Degadh, and down to Line Plain, to Cliu, to Cuailngé, to Port Palap, to the tomb of Emer Donn, where Saltair of Cashel says Emer fell from the hand of Palap Mac Eremon, to the Fort of Two Peaks, to Sulcar Mountain, to the Great Plain, to Coal Plaine, to the Amazon's Stream, to Genann, to Cathbad's Fort, to the Fort of Loch Sen-tuinne, to the land of the Garbraide, to Erne, to Liath-muine, to the three Sons of Uslenn, to Glais Cro, to the Rath of Murn, to Glen Cadhan, to Carrickfergus, to Fergus Mac Róich, to Laegaire's Rath, to Goll and Irgoll, to Bernas Plain, to the north of the province, to Asal Plain, to the Great Rath in the Erne, where Morn Mac Midhna was slain, to Cathbad, to the Plain of Ith at Indais. She brought Clann Rudraide in a day's ride to Conchobor at Emain Macha, where they discussed whether they should surrender or fight the forces of the princes of Scandinavia and Asia.

The foreign fleet,[6] meanwhile, marched until they came to

Emain and said they would grant no terms but intended to exterminate the Ulster men.[7]

"Alas," moaned Conchobor, "for this meeting. Our army is surrounded both east and west." Then he said,

> "Rise up, people of Emain
> And help defend the Ulster men
> And Garmna and Emain's fort.
> Come, gray army, and let us sort
> Out this difficulty. You must
> Defend the Cruithnig, I trust
> You know why, for Cuailngé
> Stands in the hard path way
> Against these invaders who come
> To steal our land away from
> Us. Do great deeds, I say,
> And bring us victory, I pray."

Then the invaders came, numbering sixty regiments, and Genann Mac Cathbad said, "Don't be afraid, men. Let us fasten gray wool to our chins so you will bring fear and horror to our enemies." All the men who were beardless did this.[8]

Then the armies came hard together and Torc, Tren, and Tradar met Ros, Daire, and Imchad, and the three invaders fell on the assembly ground of Emain Macha, and their three graves are there. Ranc, Morc, and Morglonn met the three sons of Donn Mac Durthach and the foreigners fell in the same place. Then Niall and Armgar and Torhnuall came against Conchobor's regiment and fought with Cetearn Mac Fiachra and with Nert and with Tren until they fell together at the same time, all except Fiacha. The foreigners charged up to Niall's Fort, where Niall Niamglonnach Mac Rugraide fell. Daball Dianbuillach was slain there by Fergus Mac Róich at the Stream of

Ancient Eochaid and all the foreigners around him as well. From there they went to Shield Hill, where they left their shields and turned from there to Glais Cro, where they all were slain by the Red Branch in a bloody battle. Then the Ulster men returned home with great plunder and booty.

These were the casualties from Conochobor's army: Imchad, Nert, Tren, Fiacha, many sons of Umor, Imchad Mac Donn, two sons of Yellow Conaing, brothers of Laegaire, Lugaid, Eogan the Fair, Eochad Redweapon, Ros from Red Rath and Duban from White Rath, Fiacha Mac Fachtna Fathach and Conchobor's brother, and five hundred soldiers of the Ulaid fell. They collected the foreigners' heads and placed them there on the Rock of Heads in the assembly of Emain. That is why it is said,

> "Great was our loss in the glorious battle
> Where seven hundred heard death's rattle
> With the blameless prince of great Erin
> With Fiacha Mac Fachtna Fathach slain.
>
> Seven strong regiments of Asia are lain
> With twenty-seven princes who were slain.
> Great was this tremendous battle-fray
> Against Daball, the prince of Norway."

The Deprivation
of Mongán

This is a humorous tale of a youth who uses his skills to play practical jokes on the then most notable poet. I have a problem with placing this story in the time of the Red Branch because it comes from *The Yellow Book of Lecan*. Although it seems to belong in this category, some of the people mentioned are also mentioned in various annals as living far past the date of the Red Branch.

NOW THIS HAPPENED DURING THE time when Eochu Rígeigeas was the chief poet of all of Erin. Fiachna Mac Boetán invited him to make a verse for Fiachna, who was the king of Ulster at that time, and well, Eochu was an Ulster man as well.

"I really should avoid this," Eochu said. You have a young son, Mongán Mac Fiachna, who is the wisest youth in Erin, and I am certain that he will make up stories and pretend to things that the bad people may use to contradict me. I might be forced to curse him, and if I do, then I am certain that you would quarrel with me."

"Don't worry about that," Fiachna said. "I will speak to Mongán and tell him not to try to play word games with you. I promise he will be most civil toward you."

"Well," said Eochu doubtfully, "you are the king, and the king's word is law. All right. I'll do it. But I shall need a year."

One day while Eochu was teaching, the boys whispered, "Why do you let him get away with this, Mongán? You should challenge this joking jester."

"Hmm, well, perhaps you are right," Mongán said.

Now Fiachna went on a royal visit and took Eochu with him. One day they saw six large pillar-stones and four clerics by the stones.

"What are you doing here?" Fiachna asked.

"We seek knowledge and instruction," they said. "God has brought to us, however, the best poet in Erin, Eochu, to tell us who placed these stones here and why they were arranged in this manner."

"Well," Eochu said doubtfully, scratching his chin. "I can't seem to remember that. But I would think that the Children of Deda set them up to build the City of Cú Rói."

"Well, Eochu," one cleric said. "Some of the others say you are wrong."

"Ah, don't blame him," another joined in hastily. "Perhaps he just doesn't know."

"Well, then," Eochu said. "What is your explanation?"

"Why, these are three stones of a band of champions and three stones of a band of warriors. Conall Cernach placed them, along with Illand Mac Fergus, who slew three rabbits here in his first deed. He couldn't raise the pillars because of his youth, so Conall Cernach helped him, as was the custom of the Red Branch whenever they performed their first valorous act—that is, to raise the pillars, you understand. The number of pillars indicates the number that they slew." The cleric laughed. "Ah, be off with you! You're not as wise as you think!"

"Don't feel badly, Eochu," Fiachna said as they rode away. "Those are wise scholars indeed."

They continued on their way until they found a large, lime-washed fortress in front of them with four purple-clad youths standing before the door. Eochu came up, and Fiachna said, "Well, what is it you youths want?"

"We want Eochu to tell us what this fortress is and who lived in it," they replied.

"A lot of fortresses were built," Eochu said. "So many, in fact, that they do not all fit within my memory."

"Ah, nuts! He doesn't know," said one youth.

"Well, what do you know?" Fiachna asked.

"That isn't hard," the youth replied, shrugging.

> "It was while Eochu was making merry, it seems,
> While drinking mead from a goblet green
> In the garden upon the lawn
> In the time before the dawn.

"And yet, you tell us you do not remember *that?*" The youth snickered.

"You did that well," Eochu said.

They went on and found another fortress in front of them and four youths quarreling before the door.

"I'm right."

"You're wrong."

"Right."

"Wrong."

"Enough," roared Fiachna. "Now what is this all about?"

"We were arguing over the name of this fortress and who built it," the boys said. "But we see that God has sent a wise man to tell us that."

"Don't shame the poor man," one of the boys said. "He won't know."

"Well," Fiachna said, looking at the youth. "Do you?"

"That's not hard," the youth said.

"This was built by the man who dug
Ráth Imgat for the woman with big lugs.
She was the daughter of Buise Mac
Didracht and fond of drinking sack."

The youth squinted slyly at Eochu. "Ráth Imgat is its name, Eochu. I don't know why you didn't know that."

Eochu felt his cheeks flame, and Fiachna placed his hand upon the poet's arm. "Don't pay any attention to them," he said. "I don't feel any the less for you."

They went back home and found Mongán and his friends waiting.

"Well," said Eochu, "I know you did that, Mongán."

Mongán grinned. "You said it."

"It won't make any profit for you, however," Eochu said. "For I curse you: the great sport you made for yourself at my expense means that you will not have any sport for yourself. Your loins will dry, and you will not have any children except horseboys, and you won't leave behind any inheritance or enjoy the fruits of your tree."

And that is why Mongán was deprived of any children. *Finit.*

The Vision
of Ferchertne

Brinna Ferchertne inso tríana codlud is seldom translated because it is a vision that the poet Ferchertne had of Cúchulainn and the Red Branch storming the fortress of Cúrói and
of Cúrói's death. Most of these details are found in *Aided Cúrói*, which is the most popular of the tales about Cúrói's
death. I believe the only copy of this poem is in the Bodleian
codex Laud 610, fols. 117b1–118a2. More detailed versions of
the information within the poem can be found in *The Yellow
Book of Lecan*, pp. 123a–125a. It appears to come from the late
tenth century or early eleventh century, and many of the seg-
ments are corrupt. I have taken a try at translating some of
them but cannot be certain they are correct. A prime example
is the last segment, which is so corrupt that I could only make
a guess at what it might have been. I have provided the original in a note.

I SEE TWO HOUNDS[1] fighting a deadly bout
Between Cúchulainn who boasts of Cúrói's rout.

When the Eraind[2] took Ireland, many of their bands
Settled in places peacefully as far as Uisnech in Meath's land.

Many bloody battles the hardy warriors had to fight
On their Emain Macha raid past Tara where they stayed one
night.

One of Cúrói's greatest feats came when he slew the champion
Fliuchna,
But that began his suffering as well when he drove off the kine[3]
of Iuchna.

After he had outraged Ulster's men—that is a long story to
tell—
He stole Blathnait, wrapped in hide, from Cúchulainn after
feasting well.

For a full year Cúchulainn searched silently throughout the land
Until he found the way to Cúrói's city from a wandering band.

When Cúrói's wife betrayed him, she did an evil deed
That caused her harm and in disgrace, she left the Eraind.

The treachery of Cúrói's wife began the terrible slaughter
In Argat-glenn—this was Blathnait, great Menn's daughter.

She tied Cúrói's hair in ringlets to the bedposts—a cruel
story!—
As Cúrói tried to rise up against them like a champion to glory.

He slew a hundred men upon first rising from being tied
And another hundred fifty and wounded fifty more besides.

But it was Cúchulainn who came hard upon him with his sword
And left him in a litter upon the shoulders of six lords.

They went out upon the mountains and avenged Fliuchna the champion.

Besides carrying off their women and loot they stole Iuchna's kine.

Senfiaccail Setnach was there, worn out, his bones decayed,
But he quickly received support after Mac Dare was destroyed.

As for the herald of the prince, he was found where battle laid
Thickest where he slew fifty armed men before being killed.

Blind Tredornan threw himself quickly against the Ulster host
As hard as a stone where he slew sixty warriors—this is no boast!

The battle of Eochaid Mac Darfind was in the glen where
It's anyone's guess who put the gray flagstones there.

The fight of Eochaid went from the promontory as far as the glen
As he slew a hundred men in fair fight until more fell upon him.

Then Eochaid fell to the numbers, but not in a fair fight
So that his cairn is on Mag Rois where battle is heard at night.

Cairpri Cuanach came upon them and slew a hundred men
As he had boasted to Conchobor he would until a sea drowned him.

Cló unleashed his fury upon them and a hundred men were slain
Until he came upon Cúchulainn and on cold ground was lain.

Russ Mac Deda came bearing arms stoutly but the band
Of Ulster warriors slew him in vengeance at his stand.

Then came Nemthes the Druid who knew full well what lay
In store for him but still he killed a hundred twenty that day.

Forai of the Fian came then—his is a different story
As curly locked Dedorn came and ousted him from glory.

Ferdoman came into the battle and made a terrible slaughter
And even cut off the hand of Fiachaig Mac Conchobor.

Ingeilt Mac Riangabra came into the battle-fray and he
Put Carpre Mac Conchobor under bitter waves of salty sea.

Lugaid and Loegaire flew fiercely harder than two battle ravens
And left his chariot to its hero and the charioteer raving.

Loegaire cried to the host to move forward on the double,
"Do not grant him fair fight if we expect to avenge our trouble."

Fergus then seized hold of his cheek before the host could slay
him
And that forced Ulster's warriors to grant fair fight to him.

For sixty days he stayed on the field and every day one man
was killed
And that was his glory until the Eraind arrived and his bravery
was stilled.

Then came the Eraind following their great king. A huge band
Of seven thousand seven hundred and seven score thousand.

It was upon Mag Enaig where the combat reached that night
Where they were driven against silver rocks in a chariot-fight.

Upon a grave-covered slope the host came together and raised
a shout
And that is the name that is on it from that hardy bout.

Sad truly is the encounter of Blathnaite and Fercertne.
Their graves are in Land Cindbera above the promontory.

I see the three kine of Echda marching through the sloughs
And a noble warrior and stallion horses of every color.

THE RED BRANCH TALES   217

I see coracles along a river and enemies that are seized;
I see a host across a great house and a warrior who is crazed.

I see the coming of the son of Nessa and our strength cannot compare
With the strength of the Red Branch so we should beware.[4]

The Story of Mac Dareo's Hostel

Bruiden Maic Dareo is the story that explains how rule was established in Ireland after the kingships were suppressed by the peasants. Buan and Monach became the eponymous ancestors of the Dál Buain of Ulster, whose ruler, Miliuc Mac Buain, was the master Patrick served when he was a slave. According to the genealogists (who most certainly are not accurate), Buan becomes a remote descendant of Fergus Mac Róich, while Monach becomes a descendant of Cathair Mór. The story here is found in *The Book of Fermoy* in the Royal Irish Academy, with a much abbreviated version in *The Book of Ballymote*.

MANY PEASANTS MUTTERED IMPRECATIONS under their breath in Erin during the time of the three kings, namely Fiacho Findolaidh, Fiac Mac Fidheccach, and Bres Mac Ferb. Fiacho Findolaidh was the High King at the time. Fiac Mac

Fidheccach was the king of Munster, while Bres was king of the Ulster men.

The heavy rent and harsh taxes that were laid upon the peasants by those three kings were vast and measureless. The peasants were spiritually poor as well, as they felt the chains of bondage upon them, which they had to endure for the free races who were pressing upon the land where the peasants lived. The peasants decided to hold a meeting where they could decide what to do.

Now there were three who were their chiefs in council. These were Buan and Monach and cat-headed Cairre, who was the leader. He was of the Luaighni, and because the Luaighni were the strongest among the clans, he became the king.

The peasants decided that they would prepare a banquet at the house of Cairbre, which is at the hostel of Mac Dareó in Breifne, and invite their lords to the dinner and, while they were feasting, slay them and take the kingdom for themselves.

The feast was carefully prepared for the space of three half-years by the peasants. They were generous with their fruits and crops so that the lords would not suspect anything. This was at Magh Cró in Connacht.

Now the men of Erin came from all over for that great entertainment. Nine thousand attended and took part in the feast. They were closely served throughout the feast, given the choicest of every food and the finest liquor by the servants until they were drunk and very merry. Then the peasants rose up in wrath and slew them.

The hostel became hideous and horrible as the red ravenous vulture ran gleefully among the dead, great beak dripping blood and gore. The women wailed [text missing] and seven streams of steaming blood streamed through the seven doors of the hostel so thickly and deeply that half-grown boys could swim in them. [text missing]

This was the end of the free races in Erin, save for the

three man-children who were carried away in their mothers' wombs while their husbands were being slaughtered. The three ladies who stole out of the hostel were Side the Swift, Crube, and Aine. They went across the sea, seeking sanctuary from the servants, for their husbands had allies there, namely the king of Scotland, the king of the Britons, and the king of the Saxons.

Luath Mac Daren, the king of the Picts, was a friend of Fiacho Findolaidh. Báne, daughter of Scál, king of the Fomorians, was Luath's wife. Luath's daughter was given to Fiacno Findolaidh. Side the Swift was her name. [text missing] She was the mother of Feradhach Find Fáil Mac Fiacho Findolaidh.

Fiac mac Fidhecach, the king of Munster, was a friend of Gortniad, the king of the Britons. Crufe was his daughter, and she bore a son to Fiac named Corb Aulom.

Bres Mac Ferb, the king of Ulster, was a friend of Caindial, the king of Saxons. Aine was his daughter's name, and she bore a son to Bress Mac Ferb named Tipraite Tírech.

These three were raised in the land where Cairbre was king because the men of Erin were under the power of the peasants. The boys did not dare to go to Erin for fear that the peasants would slay them.

Then the earth refused the harvest to the peasants after their great murder of their lords, and a twenty-year famine spread across the land so that no grain came from the earth, no fruit hung upon the trees, no fish swam in the rivers, and no cow gave milk. Good weather did not appear and peace did not rise in Erin.

Eventually, Cairpre died, and the men of Erin offered the throne to his son Morann. Morann said he would not take it because it was not right that he should.

"What should we do?" asked the men.

"Well, I'll tell you," Morann answered. "The three heirs who are deserving of the throne are in Alba: Feradhach Find and Corb Ulom and Tipraite Tírech."

"Then we shall send for them and make them kings," they said.

The men of Erin sent for the three and promised to make them kings. They gave them sureties of sea and land and sun and moon and all the elements, promising to serve them well as long as the sea surrounded Erin and their seed and breed stayed in the land.

So the three came from the east, and each went to his own land: Tipraite Tírech to the east of Erin, where he took the throne of Ulster; Cairbre Corb Ulom to Munster in the south; and Feradhach Find to Temhair. The High King became Feradhach Find, and the leader of counsel and judge was given to Morann Mac Maen.[1]

And things went well in Erin at that time, and the land recovered from the peasant rule. From these kings came the three free men of Erin again, Conn, Eogan, and Araide—Conn from Feradhach, Eogan from Corb Ulom, Fiacha Araide from Tipraite Tírech.

Then the historians composed the following:

> The free races of Erin were all slain by one man
> Except the three boys who escaped from Cairpre.
> Childbearing escaped him eastward as the mothers
> Of those boys went to Alba where the boys were born.
> Feradhach the Fair of Fál, Corb Aulom in great Munster,
> And Tipraite Tírech were their full names.
> The blemish-free daughter of the king of Alba, Báne, was the
>   mother
> Of Feradhach. She was the daughter of Luath Mac Dairera.
> Crufe, daughter of bright Gartnia, who ruled the victorious
>   Britons,
> Was the mother of Munster's blameless Corb Ulom.
> The peasants made a great resolve, then, after the land
> Left them without milk, fruit, and crops like corn.

They repented of what they had done and called
The sons back again and raised them to be high kings.
They gave guarantees firmly and promised to obey
The sons if they would come back from Alba.
The guarantees were the sea, heaven, land, moon, pleasant sun,
And promised to obey them from hill to hill as long as the sea
    held around Erin.
Conn, Eogan, and noble Araide were the sons of the three chiefs—
Araide in faultless Emain, Conn of the Hundred Battles in Tara.
Eogan in Cashel of the kings where his seed settled and
Each of the men began the free races again.

Morann was famous as he had "the truth of sovereignty,"
which was Morann's ring. If the ring was placed around the
neck of a guilty one, it would tighten by itself until life choked
out of the man. That was how they came to decide truth and
falsehood. Morann lived during the time of Feradhach Fecht-
nach.

Feradhach took his vengeance upon the peasants, taking
tribute from them and giving them great tasks to perform for
the deed they had done in killing the free races in Erin.

Feradhach was later killed in Tara by Elim Mac Conri, king
of Ulster, and by Eochaid Anchenn, king of Leinster, and by
Sanbh Mac Cet Mac Mágu, king of Connacht, and by Forbré
Mac Fine, king of Munster. By the counsel of the peasants, this
was done again, and Tuathal escaped from them over sea, where
he was raised in the east until twenty years had passed.

The Cattle-Raid
of Cooley

This version of Recension III is taken from Egerton 93 and
H.2.17, which was prepared by Feargal Ó Béarra for the *Son-*
derforschungsberich 321: Mündlichkeit und Schriftlichkeit in der frü-
hen irischen Literatur at the Albert-Ludwigs-Universität, Freiburg
im Breisgau. Because the recension itself is fragmented, it has
received very little attention from scholars, who have spent the
majority of their time with the complete recensions available in
Lebor na hUidre and *The Book of Leinster.* My own translation of
Táin Bó Cuailngé, published as *The Raid,* was taken from both
The Book of the Dun Cow and *The Book of Leinster,* with some
minutiae taken from *The Yellow Book of Lecan* and Rawlinson
B. Rather than duplicate my translation of *The Raid* here, I have
used Recension III in the story of Cúchulainn and his deeds to
provide an account of *Táin Bó Cuailngé.*

A lacuna exists at the beginning of this recension, which
opens in medias res with an account of Cúchulainn's first raid
after assuming his weapons when he slew the sons of Nechta

Scéne—Fannell, Foill, and Tuchell—and took their heads as his trophies. On the way back to Emain Macha, Cúchulainn also captured a flock of birds, which he had tied to his chariot railing.

W E BEGIN:

. . . and bound them to the iron wheels of the wicker chariot.

"They do not cause you any problems."

Ivar rose, his bones snapping and creaking, and gathered the birds, sighing and groaning with the effort, as he tied them to the chariot railings with leather thongs. Then he and the young Hound stepped into the chariot, and Ivar picked up the reins, slapping them on the backs of Conchobor's great blacks. They lunged, then gathered themselves into a ground-gaining lope as the chariot rattled its way back to Emain Macha.

Now it was Leaborcham who happened to be walking along the palisades of Emain Macha and saw the chariot rapidly approaching fortress. She shielded her eyes with her palm and squinted against the sun's rays and gasped as she saw the lone warrior dancing upon the chariot's rail. She ran as fast as she could to Conchobor's house and rushed in unannounced.

"Here, what's this?" Conchobor asked, annoyed. Then he saw how Leaborcham's eyes gaped wide with fear in her head, her tongue panting from the efforts of her run, and an anxiousness spread rapidly through him.

"What is it? Calm yourself, woman! Drink!" He thrust a cup of water into her hand. She gulped it, then gasped. "Now what has you stirring so?"

"A lone warrior approaches in his chariot," Leaborcham said, panting the words out in a rush. "A terrible figure! If something is not done immediately, the Red Branch house will run red with blood that he spills in his fury!"

"Who is this warrior?" demanded Conchobor.

She shook her head. "I don't know. But the chariot and

horses appear to be yours, Conchobor. And the driver seems to be your charioteer."

"Hmm. This could be the small boy who left with a man's weapons earlier today," Conchobor said, frowning and raking his fingers through his red beard. "And *if* that is the boy, and *if* that boy has the battle-fury upon him, then a great slaughter will be seen as he fights for a victory."

He drummed his fingers on the arm of his chair, racking his brain for an answer to the problem coming toward him. That Cúchulainn could be slain was a certainty, but he was fond of the boy and did not want to harm him and, besides, slaying the youth in his battle-frenzy would be very costly to the Red Branch as well, for many warriors would be slain before the youth fell, even if large numbers were sent against him at the same time.

His eyes fell upon the large breasts of Scamhalus. He snapped his fingers, suddenly remembering Cúchulainn's shyness around women in the Great Hall.

"I have it," he said, his eyes gleaming. He gestured at Scamhalus. "Gather your friends and let the young women strip naked and go out to meet this warrior. Behave like wanton women, exposing yourselves fully to him, your breasts and nipples and womanhood. He will not be able to stare at such nakedness and will hide his eyes. When that happens," he continued, turning to his manservant waiting beside him, "have the warriors seize him and plunge him into barrels of cold water until his hot rage goes away."

The servant rushed away to do Conchobor's bidding while Scamhalus, excited at the adventure ahead, gathered her friends—Scannlach, Sciathan, Feidhlim, Deightine Fionchas, Finghle, Fidniamh, and Niamh, the daughter of Celtar Mac Uichechair—to her and rapidly explained their mission. The young women laughed among themselves and stripped their clothes from their white bodies. Boldly they bounced out of the gate, brazenly showing themselves to Cúchulainn as he approached. His eyes took in the flower of Ulster womanhood, and a great embarrassment came over him. He hid his eyes behind his hands, and at that moment, the warriors of Ulster seized him and plunged him into a barrel of cold water.

He gasped and lashed out in fury as the water came to a boil so fast that the oak staves and iron bands around the barrels burst. Cúchulainn started to fight, but again his eyes fell upon the nakedness of the women, and he closed his eyes. The men seized him again and thrust him into the second barrel. Bubbles the size of a warrior's fist rose and burst, and the warriors seized him as he gasped indignantly and plunged him into the third tank.

This time, however, the water rose tepidly, and Cúchulainn came to his senses, blinking wide-eyed at those around him as the battle-frenzy left him. Scamhalus and Sciathan wiggled forward and stood wide-legged and saucy in front of him, and he blushed scarlet at their nudity and again hid his eyes.

"Ah, now," Scamhalus said. "It seems the warrior has become a boy again. Although," she said a bit wistfully, " 'tis a grown man's spear he carries with him."

All laughed at this, and the warriors plucked Cúchulainn from the tub and gave him over to the women, who toweled him dry furiously with much jesting and coarse joking. They combed his hair, fifty blond and platinum locks, and chucked the four dimples in his two cheeks. He had a yellow dimple, a gray dimple, a blue dimple, and a purple dimple, and seven jewels each of his eyes. Seven toes were on each foot and seven fingers on each hand, and those fingers had the paralyzing grip of a griffin's claws in them and the quickness of a hawk's talons.

They dressed him in a purple cloak, held together with a silver brooch over his deep chest. When it sparkled in the sunlight, people had to avert their eyes. Next to his skin, they placed a finely woven tunic bleached white with fringes of gold and silver. A dark purple shield, almost black, was slipped on his arm, and two five-pronged spears were placed in his hand. Around his head they slipped a jeweled circlet with a large amethyst in the center.

This, then, was the young boy who performed the deeds of a seasoned warrior while still a child. What wonder, then, would it be to think that he could now slay one, two, three, or even four men at once or even cut a four-pronged tree with one flashing sweep of his sword? Tonight, on the eve of the great army's crossing of Ulster's border on the famous cattle-raid, the child was a full seventeen years and far more experienced in battle than he was as a child.

The Ulaid were happy and joyful with the savagery in battle displayed by Cúchulainn, but to those warriors who invaded Ulster's borders, only grief and gloom and depression followed by a gut-wrenching fear came when they heard the story of the deeds done in Cúchulainn's boyhood and knew that greater deeds would be performed by a seasoned warrior like that.

It is because of this accounting of the boy-deeds of Cúchulainn that the invaders decided to detour over Dubh instead of marching straight across the land to Cooley, where the great bull waited.

Cúchulainn watched the detour, musing aloud, "Why, I wonder, does this foreign army march away and not take with them the cattle and captives they have gathered so far as plunder from their raid?"

Then a great noise rose, and Cúchulainn laughed and said to his driver, "Gather the horses and yoke the chariot so we can see what is happening now."

He rode toward the noise, and as he neared, he recognized the sound of ax against wood. And then he came upon a single man cutting and hewing trees. He reined in beside the man and stared curiously at him. "What are you doing?" he asked.

The man sighed and ran a forearm across his forehead,

wiping dripping sweat from his eyes. "I am cutting chariot shafts," he said. "If you have a sympathetic bone in your body, you'd step down from your fine chariot and give me a hand so that I can finish this job and get away before the madman Cúchulainn finds me and marries me to the dirt."

"Well," Cúchulainn said mischievously, wrapping the reins around his chariot rail and stepping down. "What would you rather do? Chop and cut or collect and gather?"

"Well," the man said, staring disgruntled at the branches behind him, "frankly, I'd rather collect and gather."

Cúchulainn shrugged and took the ax from the man's hands and began to chop the trees before him. When they fell, he took them in his hands and stripped the branches from the trunks by pulling them through the palm of one hand so that bark and knots flew through the air. When he finished baring them, not a fly could stand on the trunks, so polished and slippery were they.

"That's quite a trick," the man said, eyeing the pile of wood in front of them. " 'Tis no stranger you are to such work. I'm grateful for your help. Tell me, though, what is your name?"

Cúchulainn laughed. "Why, I am the scourge you mentioned. Cúchulainn."

The man blanched, and a great trembling came upon him as his legs shook so hard he could barely stand. "Ah, no! 'Tis dead I am for certain."

Cúchulainn shook his head. "Not at all. It is not my habit to kill charioteers or messengers or any who do not bear arms against me. Be easy now, and tell me your name."

"I am Orlam, the son of Ailill and Maeve." The man gulped. "But I serve another."

"And where is your lord, the man you serve now?" Cúchulainn asked pleasantly.

"Over there," the young man said, pointing. "He's resting against that standing-stone."

"Then I shall go and see him," Cúchulainn said. "Off with you, now."

The man leaped into his own chariot and raced away while Cúchulainn went to where Orlam had pointed and challenged the man there to combat. The battle was over in the flit of a swallow's wing, and Cúchulainn took the man's head and rode to the top of a hill and shook the bloody trophy by its locks at the warriors below him. That is why the place is called Leaca Orlam north of Deisgart Locadh. It is sometimes called Tá-imhleacht because of the mortal blows dealt to the lazy man there by Cúchulainn.

[A narration appears to have been omitted here.]

Now, there is also the place known as the Combat of the Three Sons of Ara. Those were Meas Linne, Meas Láighe, and Meas Leathan. Their charioteers were Luan, Úal, and Muilche. The warriors placed three poles of white hazelwood in the hands of the charioteers so that the six of them could come at once against Cúchulainn. Cúchulainn wounded them, and the eldest son fled, racing away in his chariot. Cúchulainn gave chase and caught up to him at Críoch Chonaill, where the yoke of Leathan's chariot broke. Leathan turned to fight and was sorely wounded by Cúchulainn. It was then that Leathan's char-ioteer, Muilche, challenged Cúchulainn's charioteer, Laeg Mac Ringabra, who quickly killed him. That place is now named Guala Muilche. This was the only heroic battle by Laeg during the raid.

Now on that day, the Brown Bull came to Críoch Mhairge with fifty heifers following him. The Mórrigan, disguised as a battle-raven, landed on the standing-stone above his head and spoke to him, saying, "Well, great Brown Bull, the Connacht men are searching for you. If they catch you, you will be taken like any ordinary bull they have stolen to their camp."

It was at this time that she told him what was in store for him:

"You will be taken back to Cruachan Ai
Where the White Bull reigns. You will see
This long enemy of yours and a battle
Will rage between you with a rattle
Of horns and bellow of anger. You
Will battle over Erin's land until you
Defeat the White Bull. Then you will
Return to Cooley and there you will
Fall from the wounds of your fight
And see the green hills with failing sight."

The Brown Bull recognized the Mórrigan's words and left toward Sliab Cuillin in the north of Ulster with his heifers. Foirgeimhean, the cowherder, followed him.

Now the Brown Bull was no ordinary bull. Fifty heifers were mounted by him each day, and if they didn't calve by the end of nine days, they would die. The Brown Bull was a bull from the Otherworld, and so large that fifty children could ride on his back at one time, each playing *buanfach,* shouting and laughing gleefully with their game. He liked children, and while they played upon his back, he remained patiently still so that he would not spoil their game. When he faced his pasture, a strange music arose from him that caused men in the north and south and east and west to pause in their work and listen wonderingly to what seemed to come to them on gentle winds.

That night, the men camped near Cooley, and Cúchulainn, weary by now from his raids upon their flanks and camps, declared that each time he saw Maeve, he would fling a stone at her. Maeve did not believe this, though, and one evening when she stepped from her tent, her pet squirrel perched upon her shoulder, a stone struck off the squirrel's head, splattering her white face with blood. Another time, she stepped out with her pet bird on her shoulder, and it, too, lost its head. That place is now called Méidhe and Eoin, and Loch Sreoidh is the name of the lake.

One day Ailill and Maeve's handmaiden rose, yawning, and left to gather water for drinking and washing. As she was leaving the tent, her eye fell upon Maeve's golden circlet carelessly tossed aside and, as pure mad prank, she picked it up and slipped it around her head. Forty other maidens rose and saw this and laughed as the handmaiden primped and postured, imitating Maeve's arrogant stand and gestures.

"Your Majesty!" cried one, giving a mocking bow. "Shall we depart for the ablutions?"

"By all means," declared the handmaiden loftily. She stepped from the tent, swaying as Maeve swayed in her walk, the other maidens trailing her, laughing in her wake.

But Cúchulainn thought the handmaiden was Maeve and threw a stone at her. The stone struck the handmaiden in the middle of her forehead, shattering the circlet into three parts and stretching her lifeless upon the plain. This is called Réidh Locha Cuailghne.

Now the Connacht men decided to attack and raid Mag Breag and Mag Midhe and Machaire Chonaill and Cúchulainn's land the next morning. They stated their plans boldly in the presence of Fergus Mac Róich, who warned them:

> "Beware! Cúchulainn will not give you
> A free ride across Ulster and through
> The land held by the Red Branch. Those
> Heroes will soon rise and come close
> Upon your heels. If you go on a raid
> Across Mag Muirtheimhne, you will trade
> Many lives for your arrogance. I think
> That you should know how Nechta Scéne's
> Sons came out of their sturdy beds. I've seen

Their heads mounted upon the beams
Of the Red Branch Hall. It seems
To me that you should take care
That you think before acting. Beware!"

The Connacht men ignored him, however, and early the next morning, they arose and attacked Mag Muirtheimhne and plundered the rest over the lands of Cúchulainn.

Then the streams and rivers of Crioch Chonaill Muirtheimhne flooded redly, and behind them came the flood of Glais Cruinn. A brave warrior tried to cross the waters of Glais Cruinn by taking a heavy rock on his back to help weigh him down against the rush of water. Yet the Glais Cruinn swept him off his feet and he fell flat, the stone weighing him down so he could not rise, and he drowned. The Connacht men brought him up from the depths and buried him there, erecting the fatal stone over his grave. This is called Lia Uallan.

The Glais Colptha came in a great red flood against the Connacht forces and swept away fifty chariots and warriors, carrying them to the sea. This place is now called Cluain na Carbad.

When the Connacht men came to Glais Cholptha, they did not find the Brown Bull, and while they were debating about their next move, Cúchulainn attacked them and killed one hundred armed princes, including Raen and Rí, the two *seanchais* who had come with Ailill and Maeve to record the raid. It was the death of these two that caused the *Táin* to be lost for so many years.

Then the men of Cruite Caínbhile came to the Connacht forces from Dá Eas Ruaidh to support Ailill and Maeve. They held great power and were wise in wizardry. But when they saw the great fort of the men of Erin, a forbidding terror came upon them and they turned into wild deer and fled north to the standing stones at Lia Mór.

The Connacht army them marched between the sea and the mountain, but Maeve did not let the men cross the mountain, but rather dig a pass through to the other side. This is now called Bernus Thána Béalav Ailean. The army moved on and made camp at Béalav Ailean, which became known as Liasa Liag because it became a place for pastures and cattle. It is also called Gleann Dáil because much blood was spilled there.

The army then traveled over Seaghan, which became known as Glais Ghadlaidh as ropes and leads were needed to bring their cattle across the man-made pass. They made camp in Druim Éan in Croch Chonaill Muirthemhne. Cúchulainn camped near them, high in the hills in Fuinche. From there he raided down upon them, trying to drive them south out of Dealga Muirthemhne. He slew one hundred warriors in a night raid that left the Connacht men trembling in fear.

The next day, when Ailill rose and saw the dead warriors sprawled over the ground, he became red with fury and said, "We are not pleased with the thunder feat of Cúchulainn last night. We must go to him and make terms."

"What terms?" Maeve asked suspiciously.

"Leave the cattle alone and the camp of captives alone and cease slinging stones upon us in the dead of night."

"Oh? And what will you give if he gives this?" she asked.

"How do I know? I haven't heard his answer," Ailill said irritably.

"Then who will carry these terms to him?"

"Mac Roth, our messenger, of course," Ailill said. "Who else?"

Mac Roth stood nearby, listening to this exchange, and when he heard that he was to take a message to the Hound, he grew pale. "Ah, I don't know where to find him," he said quickly. "And even if I was to see him, I would not know it was him. I mean, well, I don't have the slightest idea of where to find him and what he looks like."

Ailill furrowed his brow and said, "I wonder if Fergus might know."

Fergus laughed. "I don't know for certain, but if I was to guess, I would say that he is between Ochain and the sea, waiting in the snow for us. He did not sleep last night and will rest between the wind and sun."

Reluctantly, Mac Roth left, making his way to where Laeg Ringabra waited.

"Whose servant are you?" Mac Roth demanded of Laeg.

Laeg pointed. "I serve that warrior," he said.

"Um-hm," Mac Roth said. He went down to where the warrior waited, watching his approach. "And who might you serve?" Mac Roth asked, coming up to him.

"I serve Conchobor Mac Fachtna Fháthaigh mhic Rosa Ruaidh mhic Ruadhraighe—the *Ard Rí*—the High King—of this province."

"I see," Mac Roth said. "And would you happen to know where I might find this fellow Cúchulainn, who is related to him? If one is to believe the wagging tongues of Erin."

"You may say to me everything you would say to him," Cúchulainn said.

"I have come with peace and terms for him," Mac Roth said.

"And?" Cúchulainn asked politely. "What might those be?"

"The dry fold of the cattle to you and the captive camp if you will not sling stones into the Connacht camp at night."

Cúchulainn shook his head. "No, I will not accept that."

Puzzled, Mac Roth scratched his head. "Why not? Seems good to me."

"The Ulaid kill the dry cows when there are no milch cows among them, and give the meat to the satirists and guests and soldiers, and the captive women are brought in to be bed-mates of the Red Branch warriors. If I were to agree to those terms,

I would be insulting all Ulster warriors, who already have those terms and rights."

Mac Roth went back to the camp of Ailill and Maeve, shaking his head in dismay. "Well?" asked Ailill impatiently. "Did you find the man?"

"I found him," Mac Roth said grudgingly.

"And?"

"Well, I *think* I found Cúchulainn. At least I found a man where he was supposed to be. The snow had melted thirty feet on either side of him, and he had twenty-seven mailshirts that he had removed. His charioteer stayed some distance from him, as the battle-fury from the warrior was too hot to approach."

"Then you found Cúchulainn," said Fergus.

"Does he take our terms?" asked Ailill.

"No," Mac Roth said. "He refuses."

"Why?" Ailill asked.

"It seems the Ulster men kill their dry cows and slaughter them for meat for their guests and soldiers and bring the captive women to be bed-mates. Well," Mac Roth said, scratching his head, "that's what he said. Hard to make hide or hair out of it. It's a puzzling way he has about him."

"Then offer him other terms," Ailill said.

"What terms?" Mac Roth asked, heaving a silent sigh at the thought of having to retrace his steps.

"Tell him that we will restore all of his land that has been destroyed and compensate him for our actions, according to what the Ulster men and Fergus in this camp say is fair. In exchange, let Cúchulainn enter my service, for it is better to serve me than a minor king such as Conchobor."

Mac Roth gave him a sharp look, for he recognized the foolishness of these words, which were among the most foolish spoken on that great raid.

"I think," Maeve said tactfully, "that it would be better to offer other terms to him."

"Oh? And what might those be?" Ailill asked, raising his eyebrows irritably.

"Offer him the milk of the cattle and the freeborn of the captives if he holds off his sling and stoning," she said.

"And who should carry this to him?" the others asked simultaneously.

"Who else but Mac Roth, the messenger?" Maeve said, and Mac Roth heaved a great and desperate sigh as he rose and left to make his way to Cúchulainn.

"I have come with other terms for you," he said as he approached the warrior. "I know that you are Cúchulainn now, and can answer for yourself instead of pretending otherwise."

Cúchulainn was amused at this and said, "What might those terms be?"

"The milk of the cattle to you and the captive freeborn. In exchange, you promise to not use your sling and stones upon our camp at night."

"No," Cúchulainn said. "I cannot accept those terms for the same reasons that I told you before."

"Well, is there anything that you *will* accept?" Mac Roth asked irritably. "This coming and going is accomplishing nothing." Except making my stomach ache, he added to himself.

"Yes, there are," Cúchulainn said.

Surprised, Mac Roth said, "What might they be?"

"No, that I will not tell you. You must find that out from someone in your camp," Cúchulainn said.

Mac Roth made his way back to the camp, where Fergus and Ailill waited.

"Did he accept those terms?" Ailill asked.

"No, he did not," Mac Roth answered.

"Why not?"

"I think it's because he has never yet betrayed his mother's brother."

Ailill shook his head, pressing his lips together in a thin line. "Well, is there anything he will accept?"

"Yes, but he says that you have to find the one in the camp who will tell them to you," Mac Roth said.

"And if I cannot find him?"

Mac Roth shook his head. "Then we are not to send anyone to him again."

"Maybe Fergus will know the meaning of this," Ailill mused.

But when he approached Fergus, the great warrior shook his massive head, saying, "Well, I'm not knowing the all of it, but I have an idea about some of it."

"And?" Ailill asked.

"The milk of the cattle and the captive freeborn to him and a man to visit the ford each day to challenge him in single combat. If he slays that man, another man will come to him. If no one is willing to come, then you must break camp and retreat from him. The Ulster men who are wounded and ailing by him must be healed by your doctor. The daughters he might desire must be sent to him and their dowries paid to him by you. And, you must feed and care for him on the rest of the raid."

Ailill sighed. His head began to pound, and he pressed his hands tightly to his temples. "Will he let us off any of those terms?"

"Maybe," Fergus said. "He might accept food and care from you."

"Well, Fergus," Maeve interjected. "I do not know this Cúchulainn at all."

"Fiacha Mac Fir Feabha, take our words to him and ask if he will talk with us in the glen," Fergus directed.

Fiacha made his way to where Cúchulainn waited.

"Welcome," Cúchulainn said.

"Thank you," Fiacha answered. "I trust that welcome well."

"As you should." Cúchulainn laughed. "I offer you tonight's lodging on its strength."

"And I offer you victory and blessing, my foster-son," Fiacha said. "But I do not come for lodging but to ask if you will meet in the glen, where Maeve might talk with you."

And so Cúchulainn went to the glen and Maeve came to offer terms to him.

> "Well, Cúchulainn, I ask that you quit
> Slaying us with your sling when we sit
> Down to our evening meal. Your fame
> Has come to us on this raid and the same
> Terms that have been offered I now pledge.
> I am Maeve of Múr Mac Maghac. My pledge
> Will not be broken for I am not a coward.
> Cooley's cattle will not be driven toward
> Connacht as long as you live. What say you?"

And Cúchulainn answered:

> "As you can see, I protect Ulster's borders
> From your army and raiding disorder.
> I will not accept any of your terms unless
> Every milch cow and Erin woman, dressed
> In all her finery, comes to me. Understand?"

Maeve went back to where Fergus waited for her and said, "Well, Fergus, is that the famous Cúchulainn who has no equal in the land, according to your men?"

"Actually," Fergus said, "there is no one in the world to equal him in combat and contest."

Maeve pouted at these words, then said, "Well, will he let us off any of those terms that you mentioned?"

"As long as you send him food and care," Fergus said.

"Well, then," Maeve said, "go to him and tell him that we agree."

"No, that I will not do," Fergus said.

Mystified, Maeve looked at him and said, "Why not?"

"I don't think you mean to live up to your bargain," Fergus said bluntly. "It's not a warrior's promise I carry, but a fickle woman's word that has as much weight to it as air."

Maeve's eyes narrowed in fury, but she wisely held her tongue and said, "I promise that I will adhere to them."

Fergus nodded with misgivings and asked that his chariot and horses be brought to him. When they were brought to him, Eardchomall Mac Aodha Leithrinne came with them.

"Where do you think you're going?" Fergus asked.

"With you," Eardchomall said. "I want to see this famous Cúchulainn."

"No, I don't think so," Fergus said, climbing in his chariot. He gathered the reins between scarred fingers.

"Why not?" Eardchomall asked petulantly.

"You're too arrogant," Fergus said calmly. "You're young and you have a youth's senseless wildness about you. You also are quick to anger, and when you are angry, you do not think with your noodle. You'll anger Cúchulainn and be slain."

"What if I place myself under your protection?" Eardchomall asked.

"I can care for you," Fergus said, "but I don't think you are willing to listen to me."

"Well then, I won't ask for your help," Eardchomall said arrogantly.

Fergus shrugged. "Well then, let your folly be your guide."

They rode in their chariots to where Cúchulainn rested with his back against the standing stone of Croch Rois while playing *buanfach* with Laeg. Cúchulainn had a good match with

Laeg as they split the games equally among them, but Laeg also kept a keen eye upon the plain, and not one beast crossed that wide expanse without Laeg noticing it.

"A lone chariot-warrior comes toward us," he said to Cúchulainn.

"What kind of chariot is it?" Cúchulainn asked, studying the game before him.

"A beautiful and large chariot," Laeg answered. "It seems as large as a fort to me. The warrior driving is like a high tree over a tall forest, thick-trunked and golden-haired. He has a green cloak folded around him, and a silver brooch shines from his breast. A hooded shirt with red trim is around him, and he carries a white shield with red-gold animals embossed upon it. Two sharp five-pronged spears are in the chariot beside him. The big spear is as large as the rudder of a big boat. And," he added, "another chariot seems to be following him."

"Oh? And what is that chariot?" Cúchulainn asked.

"A young man's chariot," Laeg answered, shrugging in dismissal.

"Hmm. One of the young Connacht warriors, I suspect," Cúchulainn said. "Probably interested in seeing what I look like. Although I am the most loved and the most famous one around here at this time, not all know me."

Then Fergus pulled up, and Cúchulainn made him welcome. "You are welcome, Fergus," said Cúchulainn. "I offer you a night's lodging here."

"I believe you mean that, Cúchulainn," Fergus said.

"You may trust that," Cúchulainn answered. "If a flock of birds lands upon that plain, I will prepare you a full goose for yourself and half of the one I eat. If a fish enters a river, you shall have a whole salmon for yourself and half of mine. And you will have a full serving of watercress and seaweed and a cup of water freshly drawn for yourself. Your bed will be of fresh rushes, and peace will be held around you until you awaken from your own heavy sleep. If one challenges you, I shall answer him, and you shall be under my protection until you return to your camp. This I promise."

Fergus looked fondly upon him. "I wish you victory and give you my blessing, my foster-son. But I did not come for lodging but to put an end to the negotiations begun yesterday."

"Then begin," Cúchulainn said.

"I promise that all you have asked for and all that you have not asked for will be fulfilled," Fergus said.

"Then I will accept," Cúchulainn said, but lifted a hand warningly. "But fair play and single combat must be granted."

After agreeing to this, Fergus left, taking his leave regretfully, for he regarded the Hound favorably, yet he was aware that if he tarried too long the others would think he was betraying them.

But Eardchomall stayed behind, eyeing Cúchulainn boldly. "What are you staring at?" Cúchulainn asked.

"You," Eardchomall said mockingly.

"That shouldn't be difficult," Cúchulainn said quietly. "The eye sees everything that it wants, far and near. So, how do you see me?"

Eardchomall shrugged. "Well enough," he answered carelessly. "You obviously know something about war and fighting. But I wouldn't count you among the nobles or worthy warriors."

Cúchulainn raised an eyebrow. "I see. Well enough said, but if you had not come under the protection of Fergus, you would return to them with shattered joints and bones, dragging behind your horse and chariot."

Eardchomall flushed hotly at this. "I don't take words like that lightly, Cúchulainn. Tomorrow, I shall be the first to meet you in combat at the ford."

"Better think that over," Cúchulainn said. "I don't take a step backward for anyone."

Angry, Eardchomall whipped his horse and rode furiously after Fergus. Coming up behind the grizzled warrior, he spoke with his charioteer, saying, "What do you think? Would it be better for me to fight Cúchulainn in a duel tomorrow at the ford or to fight him now, tonight?"

His charioteer shrugged. "To my way of thinking it would be bad one way and worse the other. Fight tonight and you'll have cuts and bruises to carry tomorrow."

Moodily, Eardchomall pondered these words, then replied, "Turn around and drive toward the ford. Why wait for tomorrow what can be done now?"

Obediently the charioteer swung the chariot in a wide circle and drove back toward Cúchulainn. Laeg saw the chariot returning and said, "That last chariot comes back toward us."

Cúchulainn shrugged. "What of it? That was Eardchomall, who was under the protection of Fergus. I don't want to fight him. But I had better meet him at the ford before he gets there so he will not think I am purposefully avoiding him."

Cúchulainn climbed into his chariot, and Laeg drove down to the ford to meet the rash youth.

"What do you want here, Eardchomall?" Cúchulainn asked.

"To fight you," Eardchomall said.

Cúchulainn shook his head. "That is a foolish thing to want. I don't want to fight with you, for you came to my camp under the protection of Fergus."

"That means nothing." Eardchomall sneered. "I won't leave from here until I have your head tucked under my arm. Or," he finished offhandedly, "if you take mine. Unlikely, though, that."

"Yet there is great truth in your last words," Cúchulainn said. "If we fight, I will have your head as a trophy. Note how easy this would be." And with that, he swung his javelin, neatly shaving the hair from Eardchomall's head without drawing a drop of blood. Eardchomall's proud mane fell to the ground,

leaving him as bald as a stream stone. Wonderingly, Eardchomall rubbed his hand over his naked pate and blushed bright red.

"Note, fool, how easily I could have killed you. Now you
are a laughing matter to your people."

Tears of rage sprang from Eardchomall's eyes. "I won't go
until we fight!" he bawled.

Cúchulainn swung his sword, cutting the sod out from under him. Eardchomall tumbled backward, the block of sod
landing neatly on his chest. "You can't win at this. I warn you
for the last time."

Eardchomall leaped to his feet, drawing his sword and
swinging wildly. "I won't go!"

Cúchulainn leaped lightly up, then dropped down to Eardchomall's shield and severed his head from his shoulder. The
trunk stood for a moment, shocked at missing its head, and
Cúchulainn again swung his sword, cutting the body in half.

Eardchomall's charioteer saw this and turned the chariot
and rode furiously after Fergus. When Fergus found Eardchomall's chariot at his shoulder, he frowned and said, "Where
is your master, boy?"

"Back at the ford," the charioteer said, wide-eyed with fear.
"Cúchulainn slew him by the ford."

"What?" Fergus roared. "Why would this distorted demon
break his pledge to me? That man was under my protection.
Turn," he commanded his charioteer. "Drive back."

Cúchulainn watched as the chariot pulled up at the ford
and Fergus leaped out. "Why did you break my word, you
whelp? That man came under my protection, and you guar-
anteed it!"

"Which would you prefer, then?" Cúchulainn demanded.
"I am the only one who stands between the Connacht men and
Ulster. Would you have me let Eardchomall kill me or I kill
him? He left me little choice in the matter. I warned him three
times."

Fergus sighed. "I would prefer that what was done be done," he answered. "A blessing upon the hand that dropped that foolish one! It was his own words that brought about his death."

Cúchulainn nodded. "You may ask his charioteer which of us was the guilty one with the rash words."

And that ended that. Eardchomall was tied to the back of his chariot and dragged back to camp, the two halves of his body rolling around behind the chariot and his lungs and kidneys wrapping themselves around stumps and trees.

When they entered the Connacht camp, Maeve came out and saw the torn and sundered body of the youth and said in a loud and terrible voice, "You may have been a foolish youth, but this is a man's pain you bear."

Fergus shook his head and sighed. "Aye, that it is. I don't know what drove that lad crazy to go fighting and word-playing with the battle-hound like that. No one can play that game alone against Cúchulainn, whether he be a seasoned warrior or a rash youth."

And so ended the Combat of Eardchomall upon the raid.

Then the Connacht warriors gathered to discuss who should go and meet Cúchulainn at the ford on the early morning. All agreed that Nadrandain should be the man, and so he was summoned to Ailill and Maeve's tent. He entered and stared suspiciously around him.

"Why have you brought me here?" he demanded.

"I want you to challenge Cúchulainn to single combat tomorrow morning at the ford," Maeve answered.

Nadrandain shrugged and left, spending the night making himself ready. The next morning, he rose and left to challenge Cúchulainn, taking his arms with him. When he saw Cúchulainn, Nadrandain took one of his twenty-seven darts of tempered holly wood and threw it at him. Cúchulainn leaped lightly upon its point, and when Nadrandain saw this, he rapidly threw the second at him, then the third, then the fourth, and each time Cúchulainn danced lightly upon the dart-points, as if he was stepping lightly on spring bubbles.

[a lacuna exists here]

So it was the next morning that Fiacha went to Nadrandain and told him that he must go to the ford to meet in single combat against Cúchulainn. When Nadrandain attacked Cúchulainn, the great Hound swung his sword and severed Nadrandain's shield in twain, then swung his gray sword, stricking Nadrandain's head from his shoulders. Then Cúchulainn gathered the head and chanted,

"See how Nadrandain has died
Despite how boldly he had cried
About being able to defeat the Hound!
Look well! His reasoning was not sound!"

When Maeve heard this, she took a third of the Connacht army and went to Slí Mhór Mhidlkuachra. Cúchulainn followed her, and when she saw the Hound waiting for her men, Maeve went into Leath Ghuife, with Cúchulainn following grimly along. Maeve refused to fight there and went on into Oirthear Leargan and was followed by Cúchulainn. Maeve then went to Carn Mac Buachalla and again was followed by Cúchulainn. But after that, Cúchulainn turned back, because he wanted to stay in his own land, for that and its people were most important to him. While he was returning to his own land, he slew the six sons of Mac Buachalla and Guife.

Along the way, he also killed the six men of Crannacha and others as well. Two of them were called Artúr, two sons of Léighe who were called Beochroidhe, two named Dúrchoidhe but known as Drúcht and Ealt, and Taidhean Tedhe, Tualann and Trasgur, and Tulghlaise. Twenty Fochaird also fell and ten Findchadh.

While he was coming from the north, he stumbled across
Buidhe Mac Báin-Bhlaí and eight others who belonged to the
guard of Ailill and Maeve. Each of them wore a blue cloak and
drove the Brown Bull in front of them.

"Where did you get those cattle?" Cúchulainn asked.

"From that mountain," Buidhe said carelessly, pointing.

"And where is the Brown Bull's herder?"

"The same place where you are going," Buidhe said. "Speak
to him there."

That place was named Foirgeimhean, for that was the name
of the Brown Bull's herder, and the valley from which the
Brown Bull was taken was named for him as well.

"I see," Cúchulainn said. "And how are you called?"

"I am Buidhe Mac Báin-Bhlaí," the man said, "and I have
no fear of you."

"Then let us go down to the ford and decide upon the better
man," Cúchulainn said.

They went down to the ford, but Buidhe swung his sword
only once before his head bobbed alone in the water. The ford
was named after him. But while the two were exchanging those
two great blows, the eight others drove the Brown Bull away
into the middle of the Connacht camp.

While this was happening, Maeve came down from the
north with a vengeance, attacking and looting Cruithne and
Cuailngé and the land of Conall Mac Aimhirghin at Dún Sob-
hairche. There, Findhór, the wife of Ce003altar Mac Uithechair,
was taken captive along with fifty of her women warriors.
Maeve tortured and killed them, and that is why Más Na
Ríoghna is so named.

A fortnight later, the army formed from the four great
provinces gathered at the camp of Ailill and Maeve along with
the eight who had brought the Brown Bull down across the
land. They discussed what to do about the combat promised to
Cúchulainn and how to keep him away from the ford. Cúr Mac

Dallaith was brought to Ailill and Maeve's tent.

"Why am I brought here?" he asked.

"We want you to challenge Cúchulainn tomorrow and try to keep him away from the ford," Maeve said.

The next day Cúr, who was known as a vain and arrogant man who treated all others rudely, left to challenge Cúchulainn. The Connacht men welcomed his departure, for they had decided that if he slew Cúchulainn they were well off and just as well off if Cúchulainn slew Cúr.

"Beware the man who comes," Laeg said to Cúchulainn as he noticed Cúr's approach.

And Cúchulainn heeded the words of Laeg and shattered the head of Cúr so that his brains leaked out into the water. The ford was named for him after that.

"Well, that's one man who fell," Fergus mused. He belched and looked around him at the sour faces. "I suppose it's time to pick another to go to the ford."

"No," Maeve said crossly. "Let us return to where we camped last night."

The four provinces moved their camp to Druim Éan, where Cúr Mac Dallaith and Loth Mac Da Bran and Bran Mac Dathe Mheanaich and Fraech Mac Teora nAighneach fell after each had challenged Cúchulainn. And after they had died, the Connacht men decided that the next one to challenge the Hound should be his foster-brother and friend who had trained well with Cúchulainn and was regarded as his equal in skill and art.

So Ferbeath Mac Fhir Bheand was brought to the tent of Ailill and Maeve, and when he entered and saw the great expectation upon their faces, he said, "Why have you brought me here?"

"It would give us pleasure if you would go to the ford tomorrow and challenge Cúchulainn to combat," Maeve said. And she gave him great inducements to make him go to the ford.

"I will go and renounce my friendship with Cúchulainn," Ferbeath said. And so he went to Glenn Na Coig.

"This is not fitting, Ferbeath," Cúchulainn said when he saw Ferbeath.

Ferbeath shrugged. "That does not matter. I renounce your friendship here."

"So be it," Cúchulainn replied angrily, and left. But as he was going, Ferbeath threw a holly shaft at him, and it pierced Cúchulainn's foot. Cúchulainn wrenched it out and threw it back at Ferbeath. The shaft shattered his head, and he fell lifeless to the ground at the mouth of the valley called since Glenn Ferbeath.

Cúchulainn then said to Laeg, "Go to the Connacht camp and ask Lugaid Mac Nóis if word of my holly cast has come to the camp, and if it has, which warrior will be sent to challenge me at the ford tomorrow."

So Laeg went to the camp and to the tent of Lugaid.

"Welcome to my tent," Lugaid said.

"I trust that welcome," Laeg replied.

"As well you should," Lugaid answered. "I offer you a night's lodging here."

"And I offer you victory and blessing," Laeg said. "But I didn't come to you for lodging. I come on the behalf of your friend and foster-brother, who sends warm greetings to you and wonders if his cast to Ferbeath has returned to the camp and, if so, which warrior will be sent to him at the ford tomorrow."

"I don't know," Lugaid confessed. "But no one has made any overtures to me. I wouldn't accept the challenge or request anyway. But I have a vain and foolish brother, Láirin Mac Nóis ó Blathmhic, who will go to the ford. Please return to Cúchulainn and ask him to meet me at Glenn Ferbeath so I may visit with him about this."

Laeg returned to Cúchulainn and told him about Lugaid's request, and Cúchulainn went to the glen to meet Lugaid. After they made warm welcomes to each other, Lugaid appealed to Cúchulainn.

"No one has made an offer to me to fight you," Lugaid said. "But I have an arrogant and foolish brother who has taken up the challenge and will come to meet you in combat at the ford tomorrow. I ask that you not kill him, but I will not take it harshly if you give him a good thumping that may knock some sense into him and drive foolishness away."

"I shall try," Cúchulainn said. "I will not kill him by choice, but I will give him a beating that he will remember until the Day of Judgment."

Satisfied, Lugaid left Cúchulainn so that others would not think that he was betraying them by carrying secrets to the Hound.

While this was happening, Maeve pointed out Láirin to Ailill and said, "That is the man to whom I refer."

"And?" Ailill asked.

"Notice how he is always fawning around our daughter Findabair. I say that we promise her white thighs to him if he should take up the challenge with the Hound."

And goblets of heady wine were pressed into Láirin's hands, and it was Findabair herself who carried drink to Láirin and kissed him wantonly before each sip.

The next day Láirin arose and gathered his weapons to him and left for the ford. Fifty young women rose to follow him, for Láirin was a handsome youth and vain of his looks, and young women thought highly of him.

When he came to the ford, he saw Cúchulainn waiting for him and made a rush at him without warning. But Cúchulainn easily stripped the weapons from his hands and struck him to the ground. He gathered dirt in his hands and scrubbed it across Láirin's face, then rose and stood back. When Láirin tried to attack him bare-handed, Cúchulainn seized each of his sides in his hands and squeezed mightily. Láirin screamed in agony as his insides were wrung dry and shit splattered into the stream, turning the clear water brown. Cúchulainn then seized the pain-racked youth by the scruff of the neck and groin and threw him in front of his brother's tent. Láirin was never without three pains in his belly from that time on, and always the shit ran from him like water. But he was the only one who challenged Cúchulainn upon the raid who did not die.

Then the Connacht men again met to discuss what should be done about Cúchulainn. They summoned the royal warrior of gMuimhnight, Lóch Mór Mac Nafeibhis, to the tent of Ailill and Maeve.

"Why am I brought here?" Lóch asked.

"To challenge Cúchulainn tomorrow at the ford," Maeve answered.

"No," Lóch said. "This isn't right. I cannot fight a beardless youth. There is no honor in that. And Cúchulainn does not have any hair upon his face. But my brother, Loing, does not have a beard, either, and it would be fitting for him to fight Cúchulainn."

So Loing was brought to the tent and told by Maeve that he should fight Cúchulainn the next morning and try to drive him away from the ford.

But the next morning, after Loing rose and went to the ford, he was slain by Cúchulainn, who threw his lifeless body in front of his brother's tent. Then Lóch raised a great lament and cried that he would avenge his brother if the man who slew him had a beard.

Maeve heard this and gathered fifty of her beautiful women, all dressed alluringly so their breasts and selves were open to view, to Cúchulainn, telling him that if he wanted to fight a true champion, he needed to wear a false beard. They spent the night with the Hound and, upon returning to Maeve's camp in the morning, they were told that Cúchulainn would do as they had suggested.

Cúchulainn made a magic beard and pasted it around his chin and showed himself to the Connacht army in the valley. Maeve saw this and said to Lóch, "Note the bearded warrior there. It is fitting for someone to fight him."

"And that I will," Lóch said, "but not until seven days have passed."

"Seven days!" Maeve exclaimed. "It isn't fitting to leave that man seven days without challenging him." She thought a moment, then added, "So let us trouble him every night with a small band and see if we can catch him by surprise."

So it was that every night a small band would stalk Cúchulainn and try and creep up on him, but he slew all of them effortlessly. Those who died at Ath Greancha were seven named Conall, seven named Aengus, seven named Uarges, seven named Cebre, eight named Fiach, ten named Ailill, ten named Dealbath, ten named Tasach.

Maeve then sought advice about what should be done with Cúchulainn, for she was losing too many people to his hungry sword. The men advised her to ask that he meet her, and she should dress seductively so that his eyes were not upon anything but her. They would then send a group of the best warriors to attack him.

So Maeve sent word to Cúchulainn that she wanted to make a peace with him and that he should come unarmed as a gesture of good faith. She sent her messenger Traightean Mac Traighleathain to Cúchulainn with the message, and the Hound promised that he would meet with Maeve at the appointed time and place.

"How will you meet with Maeve?" Laeg asked him.

"As she asked," Cúchulainn said.

Laeg shook his head. "Ah, but that woman is known for her treachery. I would be cautious tomorrow."

"Then how should I meet her?" Cúchulainn asked.

"Wear your sword at your waist," Laeg responded. "That

way, you will be armed if treachery is planned. A warrior is not entitled to his honor-price if he appears without arms. That is the law of cowardice."

"Then let it be so," Cúchulainn said.

And so it was that the next morning Cúchulainn went to Ard Aighneach to meet with Maeve. Maeve, however, had hidden fourteen of her best men to wait for Cúchulainn. These were two named Las Sinna, the sons of Buicridh; two named Ardan, the sons of Lic; two named Oghma, the sons of Crund; Drúcht and Dealt and Dathean, Téa and Tasgure, Tualangt and Taur and Gléise.

As soon as Cúchulainn appeared, the men, anxious to finish their task, attacked him, throwing fourteen spears at once. Cúchulainn, however, easily avoided them and, drawing his sword, attacked and killed them. Then he spoke, saying,

> "Great is this, my warrior-deed
> For I slew man, the bright seed
> Of a huge army. I wage battle
> Against those who come to steal cattle
> From Ulster and Cooley. Many die,
> Brave warriors who wish to lie
> In Maeve's white arms in exchange
> For treachery plotted upon this range."

This place was called Focherd from that time, for *fó* means well-done and *cerd* refers to the great feat of arms Cúchulainn performed there.

Then Cúchulainn rose up in rage against the deceit planned for him and went into the Connacht camp, slaying two named Daighre and two named Ainle and four named Dunghas Imligh.

Now Maeve began gently to tease Lóch, saying, "Ah, now, isn't this a great insult? The man who slew your brother continues to kill more warriors while you sit around, safe in camp, talking boastfully of what you plan to do. 'Tis a brave warrior you are, one who learned well the art of fighting from his foster-mother."

Angry at this teasing, Lóch went to Cúchulainn to avenge his brother's death. When Cúchulainn appeared, wearing his false beard, Lóch said, "Come, Cúchulainn, let us find somewhere besides this foul earth on which to fight." He said this because he regarded the place where his brother was slain to be evil and unclean.

So the two of them traveled to the upper ford between Méidhe and Géidhe at the head of Tír Mór, and there they fought for a long time, each practicing rare and difficult feats of strength and arms.

Then the Mórrigan, the daughter of Aodh Earnmhais, came to their battle, for she had promised Cúchulainn that she would come to hinder him when he was sorely pressed. She came in three disguises. First, as a shaggy green she-wolf and bit off Cúchulainn's toes. Cúchulainn struck her a fierce blow with his mace that shattered one of her eyes. And while he was fighting off the she-wolf, Lóch managed to wound him in the buttocks.

Again, she returned, this time as an eel, and wrapped herself around his feet as he stood in the ford, tripping him. Before he could rise, Lóch stabbed him through his liver.

"This is bad," Fergus said, shaking his head. He turned to the other exiles, who were watching the battle with him. "One of you give Cúchulainn some encouragement, so if he dies, he dies as a warrior."

Bricriu Bitter-tongue started to lash Cúchulainn with words. "And what kind of a strong warrior is this who falls when a small salmon runs between his toes? What kind of a hero acts like this in front of a strong warrior? For shame!"

A great rage roiled through Cúchulainn, and he smacked the eel with his left heel and broke her cheek.

Yet she returned again, this time as a white heifer with red ears, and fifty heifers followed her as they raced through the water toward Cúchulainn, trying to put a *geis* upon him. But he used a spear feat and broke her legs, and then he performed the thunder feat nine and three hundred fifty times upon his shield to frighten the herd, and they raced away to the east, trampling the tents of the Connacht army on their way to Ard Na Puball.

Lóch struck Cúchulainn with a sword thrust that severed his liver. This so weakened Cúchulainn that he called to Laeg to send down his *gae bulga,* and Laeg sent it floating down to him. Cúchulainn seized it and thrust it up into Lóch so that it pierced his heart.

"Enough!" cried Lóch. "You have slain me. Now slay me so that I do not fall upon my back so that the Connacht men will say I died a hero's death."

"That you shall have," Cúchulainn said, and struck him again so that Lóch died facing forward, and in this manner, his spirit sailed from him.

Now Cúchulainn was sorely wounded and fell into a deep, healing sleep. And after sleeping, he rose, refreshed, saying, "Go to Emain Macha, Laeg, and tell the Ulster warriors that they must come and help me protect their cattle, for I can no longer do this by myself. Tell them that I am not receiving fair play and combat, and the Mórrigan has helped another wound me sorely."

And then he recited this poem:

"Rise, Laeg, and go to the Ulster men
Languishing at Emain Macha and tell them
That a great weariness has come upon me
And that I am sorely wounded and bloody

From defending their land and property.
Blood leaks from wounds on both my

Right side and left and none were given
By the hand of a woman. I've been shriven

By the hands of many warriors and my
Weapons have drawn much blood. Try
To make them understand that they
Must come and help to keep at bay

The mighty army from Connacht. Maeve
Is relentless in her quest and gave
Many commands to her men to slay
Me in ways without honor. By day

They come and creep upon me by night,
Using darkness to clothe them from sight.
This is not the way a warrior should fight,
But it is the way dishonorable men fight

Who cannot win any other way. A tree
Is not easily cut down, but if we
Trim its branches one by one, it falls
Eventually when its sap has run. All

Know this and it is time that Ulster's men
Come to battle those Connacht men
Who have driven off their cattle. Let
Maeve's men hear the sword-rattle. Get

The Red Branch into their chariots and
Bring them here. Lóch has mangled
My hips with the help of the she-wolf
Who distracted me with her bite. The wolf

Was followed by a gnawing eel that
Tripped me for Lóch's blow, but
I defeated the eel and then the cow
That followed. I slew Lóch with a blow

That left him lifeless in the stream
And then I feel into a sleep. I dream
Of vultures in the camp of Maeve. I
Hear the mourning cries lifted to the sky

By wailing warriors over Muirtheimhne's plain.
But I no longer can carry the fight the same
Way I did before. I am wounded and bloody
And Conchobor must come to aid me."

As Laeg was readying himself for leaving, he noticed a lone
warrior making his way across the plain toward their camp. He
shaded his eyes, trying to make out the warrior's features, but
could not and said, "Cúchulainn, I see a lone warrior coming
toward us."

Cúchulainn groaned and levered himself up on his elbows.
His very being shrieked in protest. "What manner of man is
he?" he asked wearily.

"He is fair and tall, his hair cut square across his shoulders.
He wears a green cloak fastened with a gold brooch and a
purple tunic embroidered with red-gold thread. He carries a
huge sword and a black shield with a silver boss. In one hand
he has a five-pronged spear and a double javelin. But"—he
hesitated, frowning—"he walks past others who do not appear
to see him."

"Ah." Cúchulainn sighed, lying back down. "It must be one
of my friends from the *Sídhe,* for they surely know by now
about my difficulties as I stand alone against the four great
provinces of Erin. And why shouldn't they? Surely a man who

stands against a champion at the ford every day and slays fifty who come to him at night would come to the attention of those who think fair play should be granted a man in combat."

The warrior strode up to where Cúchulainn lay and said, "I salute you, Cúchulainn, and have come to aid you."

But Cúchulainn said, "No one aids me."

"Nevertheless, I have come to help you," the warrior answered.

"Who are you?"

"I am your father from the Otherworld," the warrior responded. "I am Lugh Mac Eathleand. Now sleep for a little while. Your heavy slumber in Learga will heal you. For three days and nights I will take your place and fight with the Connacht army."

And with that, Lugh sang a low, sweet lullaby that soothed Cúchulainn. Slowly, his eyelids grew heavy, and he fell into a deep sleep. While he slept, his wounds came together and healed themselves, and after they had healed, Lugh said the *Éile Logha*:

"Arise, mighty son of Ulster!
Your wounds are healed. Muster
Your strength and help will come
From the fairy mound. Some
Others will aid you, but for now
I will stand for you and show
Your image to Connacht. You
Have no strength left and to
Try to wreak your anger upon
Maeve and her warriors when
You are ill will accomplish nothing.
But now, you are healed. Evil things
Have healed. Rise, Cúchulainn!"

For three days and nights, though, Cúchulainn slept the healing sleep that equaled the sleep he would have from the Luan to Samhain to the Cétdaín after Imbolg. During that time, Cúchulainn slept little, catching a nap now and then while leaning against his spear. But when he was awake, he struck down all warriors from the four provinces who came against him. Lugh applied healing herbs to his wounds while he slept and healed the cuts and joints, and Cúchulainn did not feel any pain of healing during this time.

Now while Cúchulainn slept, the boy-troop came south from Emain Macha to aid their hero. These boys were not affected by Macha's curse, for no beard grew upon their chins. They were training to be warriors under Conchobor but had yet to take arms. One hundred fifty boys came south to fight, but all were slain except Fallamhain, who vowed that he would not return to Emain Macha until he had taken Ailill's head and his diadem. But this was not easy, for Ailill's diadem was kept by the two sons of Beith Mac Bháin. They sorely wounded Fallamhain, and finally, he fell dead.

Then it was that Cúchulainn rose refreshed from his sleep. A great crimson blush of health came across his body as he stretched and yawned and asked Lugh, "How long have I slept?"

"You have slept three days and nights," Lugh replied.

Cúchulainn's face fell. "Ah, but that is sad news to hear."

"Why?"

"Because the Connacht men have not been attacked for that long," he answered.

"No, they were attacked," Lugh said.

Cúchulainn frowned. "By whom?"

"The boy-troop came down from the north. All hundred and fifty of them following Fallamhain Mac Conchobor. They waged three battles against the Connacht army, but all save

Fallamhain were slain then. Fallamhain vowed not to return
without Ailill's head and diadem, but that was kept on a pillar-
stone between the two sons of Beith Mac Bháin, who slew him
when he tried to take it."

Cúchulainn was angered by these words, and when five
men came to challenge him the next day, he slew them ruthlessly. These were five men of Ceann Cuirseach, two called
Cruadh, two named Caladh, and one Dearothar.

Then six men came to fight with him, and he slew the six,
named Traigh and Dorn and Dearna and Gol and Meabhol and
Earn.

Then a hundred armed men came to fight him, and he
slew all hundred.

The hill where this happened is called Cuilleann Chinn
Duine, and it was here that Maeve and Ailill camped. Ath
Chinn Chuille was the name of the ford and Glais Chró the
name of the stream. It is called Glais Chró because it ran with
blood and gore from those Cúchulainn had slain.

Cúchulainn tried to drive the Connacht army from the
south and out of Muirtheimhne that night, killing over a hundred of their warriors until morning light streaked across the
plain. Then a great weariness came upon him and a great ache.
As he rested, bleary-eyed, he saw a knock-kneed hag driving a
yellow milch cow with three teats toward him. Cúchulainn
asked her for a drink, and she milked the cow's third teat for
him. Cúchulainn drained it and said, "May that make me whole
again, hag. And may the gods' blessing come upon you for
helping me." One of the hag's eyes was instantly healed.

Cúchulainn asked for another drink, and the hag milked
the second teat. Cúchulainn drank the dram and said, "May
that make me whole as well, and may the gods' blessings fall
upon you." And her cheek healed immediately.

Then Cúchulainn requested a third drink, and she milked

the cow's teat and gave it to him, and he drank and said, "May the one who gave me that be whole and fine again, and the blessing of the gods come upon you."

He stretched, feeling refreshed, and said, "The help you have given cannot be compared."

"Well, Cúchulainn," said the Mórrigan, who had been disguised as the hag. "You foretold that I would not get help from you, but here it is that you have healed me."

Cúchulainn grew angry at this and said, "If I had known that it was you who was helping me, you would not have received my blessings."

But the Mórrigan smiled and changed into a crow and flew over the bush into Greallach Dolair in Muirtheimhne. This is referred to now as *Sgé na hEinche ar Muirtheimhne*.

The Connacht men camped that night at Ath Aladh in Muirtheimhne and sent their spoils south into Cliothar Bó Uladh. Cúchulainn settled into a camp with his charioteer at the mound in Learga. When his campfire lit the night, he saw the glitter of golden arms in the sky and the Great Lights over the four provinces of Erin. Then he rose and brandished his weapons and a great fury descended over him and his hero's yell rolled from his throat. So terrifying was this shout that it seemed as if all the goblins and sprites and glen-ghosts and demons from the air echoed his fury, and this became the Némain that terrified the Connacht army in its camp and a hundred brave warriors fell dead from fright at the shout.

"Alas," Cúchulainn mourned, "had I been in good health, the youth of Emain Macha would not have perished."

Lugh said, "This is not a disgrace upon you. No one can question your valor."

"Then come with me and help me to avenge the death of the youth," Cúchulainn said.

Lugh shook his head. "I cannot go with you."

"Why?" Cúchulainn asked.

"If I go and fight with you, then your battle will not receive the glory and honor that it should," Lugh said. "This battle was meant for you to fight and for you alone."

Then Lugh disappeared.

"Well, Laeg," Cúchulainn said. "It appears that it is up to us to avenge the deaths of the boy-troop."

"I'll go with you," the valiant charioteer said.

"Then yoke the scythed chariot," said Cúchulainn. "I trust that you have all its equipment with you?"

"Aye, that I do," Laeg said. He left to ready the terrible chariot for battle and then dressed himself in his charioteer's garb, a smooth tunic of skins, supple and fine and made from fawnskin, which did not hinder his movements. Over that he draped a black cloak that had been given by Simón Draoi to Nér, the Roman king, and by Nér to Conchobor, who gave it to Cúchulainn, who gave it to Laeg. Then he placed his four-cornered hood upon his head. This hood had every color within it. Around it he placed his red-gold headband that was the mark of a charioteer. He took his long goad to prod the horses and then dressed the horses in their armor plate so they would not be harmed by the enemy.

Then Cúchulainn rose, dressing himself in his twenty-eight tunics made from skins that had been waxed until they were like supple boards, binding them around him tightly with leather thongs to help him remember himself if the battle-rage came upon him. Over that he put his girdle of hard leather that had been made from the ox-hides of seven heifers. This would keep spears and javelins from harming him. Then he put on his apron of light silk that had been edged in white gold, and over that a brown-leather apron.

He gathered his weapons to him, the eight little swords with his ivory-hilted killing sword, his eight little spears and five-pronged spear; his eight javelins with an ivory-handled javelin, and eight darts. He took his eight shields and his main shield, a dark red, curved shield with a silver boss all covered with iron rims. His main shield, however, had a sharp edge that allowed him to use it to slice his enemies when needed. Then he covered his head with his crested war helmet that had four great gems upon it, and gave his warrior's shout, which made it seem as if a hundred bloodthirsty warriors were descending upon his enemies. Last, he put over him a special cloak given to him by Manannán Mac Lir when he visited the Tír Tairngire. When he drew the red-lined hood over his face, he could see all his enemies in front of him but none could see him.

Then a great distortion came over him and he went through his warp-spasm, so he appeared horrible and misshapen to any who might have seen him. His flesh quivered like a tree against the flood of a stream, and every joint and every part of him went through a wild contortion. His feet and shins and knees went to his back, and the large calf muscles came to the front. The muscles of his neck rose until they draped over his head, and his jaws became immense. One eye dropped inside his head as if inside a red hollow, while the other bulged out and lay over his cheek, and this eye was as big as a five-fist caldron. His lungs and liver flapped at the front of his mouth, and the beating of his heart was like the sound of a mastiff baying with the wind. Badb's candle blazed in his eye, and fiery sparks seemed to fly from his hair, which stood out from his head like nails that would impale any apple that dropped upon them. His hero's halo gathered itself like a red cloud and shot to the top of his head like a gout of dark blood rising up the mast of a ship, dissolving into the dark like the sun into the winter night.

He leaped into his scythed chariot with its sickles and hooks and sharp blades spinning around each wheel that would slice men's legs from under them, their heads from their shoulders, drag their entrails from their bodies. He performed the thunder feat of a hundred and two hundred, then three and four hundred, and drove down upon his enemies so furiously that the

iron wheels of his chariot plowed up the earth like dikes made
to halt the flow of water. He rode hard around the Connacht
camp, ringing them in so that they would not be able to flee
when he fell upon them. Then he came down upon them, a
terrible demon that drove terror into the hearts of all, piling
their bodies high so that they fell sole of foot to a headless neck.

No one could count the many who fell in that great battle,
for kings and warrior-chieftains and warriors and mercenaries
and minor lords, all who came before him were slain. Among
them were those named after others who had fallen before and
others that would fall after and a hundred and ninety kings.
Every third man was slain or sorely wounded by his charge.

Yet Cúchulainn was not harmed. His charioteer and horses
as well were unharmed. And that is *An Cartbad Searrdha* so
far.—Amen—*Finit.*

The next morning, Cúchulainn, dressed in his finery, went
on top of a hill to show himself to the women and womenfolk
and to warriors and maidens and poets so that they would know
him from the dark horror who had visited them the night before. So beautiful was he that the women all ached and yearned
for him.

Three colors of hair fell over his shoulders: brown, red
granite, and golden, with a golden circlet holding it back from
his forehead. A necklace of many gems encircled his throat. He
had four dimples in each cheek—yellow, green, blue, and purple—and seven gems in each eye and seven toes on each foot
and seven fingers on each hand, each with the strength of a
griffin's grip.

He wore a purple cloak over his shoulders, five-folded and
fringed. A tunic of silk was next to his skin and covered with
gold and silver fringe. He carried a dark purple shield and a
gold-hilted sword. Five-pronged spears with iron heads were in
the chariot beside him, and in each hand he carried nine heads
he had taken the night before.

The women begged the warriors to lift them up on the warriors' shields, the better to see Cúchulainn, and when Dubthach heard the women exclaim over Cúchulainn's beauty, a great jealousy came upon him and he said:

"What manner of man is this
That draws the admiration of witless
Women? Why exclaim over his beauty
When he kills so many? What a pity!

Many graves will rise from his slaughter
Of men who will be moaned by daughters
And sons who will not know them. Only
Death will come from this. Wait and see!"

When Fergus heard this, he turned and put a mammoth foot up Dubthach's backside, booting him into the rear ranks of the army, saying,

"What words are these but words
Of one who cannot match the Hound's sword?
See where Dubthach retreats to the rear
Of an army he seems to hold so dear!

Although the exiles may not like
His slaying of their friends like
A scythe cutting through wheat,
He has fought fairly with each feat.

Dubthach's words are foully given
As Dubthach is jealously driven
And cannot match the Hound's deeds
Or his honor match the Hound's creed."

Then the men of Connacht met again to decide who would do combat against Cúchulainn, but everyone who was chosen said, "No, not me! Sooner cut my throat, I would. Might as well do that as go up against Cúchulainn."

Maeve then approached Fergus and asked him to go against Cúchulainn, but Fergus refused, saying, "It is not fitting for me to fight against my own foster-son or the champion of Conchobor and the Red Branch."

He had his chariot and horses brought up, however, and went to the ford and met with Cúchulainn.

"Welcome is your coming, Fergus," Cúchulainn said.

"I trust you mean that," Fergus said.

"I do. And I offer you a night's lodging," Cúchulainn said.

"And I offer you blessing and victory," Fergus answered. "But I must tell you that I have come to challenge you in combat."

"That is a shameful thing for you to do without your sword in its sheath," Cúchulainn said gently.

"I don't care an apple-seed about that," Fergus said. He rubbed his eyes sheepishly. "Aye, but even if there was a sword in that sheath, I could not draw it against you, lad, truth be told. Yet my honor is at stake. So, if you will retreat from me now, then I will return the favor later when you most need it."

And such was Cúchulainn's admiration for Fergus that he stepped into his chariot and rode away from the ford. And when Maeve saw this, she gloated, saying, "See how Cúchulainn runs away from you, Fergus, my lover? Why don't you chase him?"

"That would not be seemingly," Fergus said roughly.

And the Connacht men then decided that Cúchulainn was no braver than any other man and if he was separated from his wonderful weapon [the *gae bulga*] then he would be vulnerable. So Maeve sent for a special Druid who was gifted with satire to come and demand the weapon from Cúchulainn, but Cúchulainn slew the Druid instead.

Then Maeve sent for a warrior who had terrorized Connacht's borders, one Fearchú Loingseach from Loch Cé, and this warrior came, saying that he would slay Cúchulainn and in this manner earn the obligation of Ailill.

So Fearchú went with thirteen of his men to kill Cúchulainn. They threw their spears at him, but Cúchulainn caught the spears on his shield. Then he drew his sword and attacked them, hewing the weapons from their hands. He squeezed their heads and offered a raging, bloody battle to Fearchú, who accepted, then fell when Cúchulainn cut his head from his shoulders. Cúchulainn said,

"Fearchú was not a weak man,
Nor were his men, yet I've slain
All of them who came to the ford
To combat with me on the greensward."

And that was the Death of Fearchú, and the Fight with Cailitin and his children followed next with the Fight with Ferdiad to follow. . . .

The Battle of Rosnaree

This story serves as a sequel to *Táin Bó Cuailngé*. It is the story of Conchobor Mac Nessa's retaliatory raid against Maeve and Ailill in Connacht after the famous *Táin Bó Cuailngé* (*Cattle-Raid of Cooley*). About two miles below Slane, the Boyne River was fordable, and on its southwest bank was Rosnaree, where Dathi's mother had her home, Cormac Mac Art was buried, Conn of the Hundred Battles was slain, the saints Fintan and Finnian first established cells, and Columcille discovered the skull of Cormac, which he reverently put back into the grave. *Cath Ruis na Ríg* is taken from *The Book of Leinster.*

ONCE UPON A TIME (as all good stories begin), Conchobor was in bright green Emain Macha after the last battle of the *Táin,* but he was not happy. Food did not sit well upon his stomach, and he could not sleep well, tossing and turning throughout the night. Although many wondered what it was

that made the king of the Red Branch so uneasy, none ventured
to ask him. So for three fortnights, the good king brooded and
grew sullen and taciturn as time passed until few were willing
to come close to him. Then the Ulster warriors were told that
Conchobor was in a great decline and a long-sickness had come
upon him.

A great gathering was made at bright green Emain Macha,
and the warriors discussed and argued over who should be the
one to approach Conchobor and question him about his illness.
They wanted to know what had brought him so close to death
and made him as pale as fresh-fallen snow, and about why food,
even his former favorite dishes, no longer had any taste other
than bark and sand to him. Finally, they decided the task should
fall to Cathbad the Druid, who had raised Conchobor.[1]

Cathbad went to Conchobor, and when he saw the weakness of the king, he wept floodlike tears of red blood and his
breast and bosom quickly became wet. Conchobor saw the state
of his Druid and took great pity upon him. Rousing himself,
he said, "Good Cathbad, faithful servant, what is it that has
made you so sad, sorrowful, dispirited?"

"I have a good reason for this." Cathbad snuffled. He used
the sleeve of his robe to mop the tears from his face and beard
and blew his nose on the sleeve edge. "I don't know what
wound has struck you, what evil sickness has made you nearly
a walking-dead and left you as pale as the ghost you almost are
for three fortnights."

Conchobor sighed heavily and weakly waved his hand. "I
have a good enough reason," he said. "Four great provinces of
Erin have come to me, and with them they brought their men
of music and amusement and of eulogy. I have listened to the
stories of the ravages and devastations, about how our fine fortresses and houses were burnt until they were little more than
outhouses. But the worst tale I heard was the one about Ailill

and Maeve, who came against me and took the calf of my own
cow out of its pasture."

Then he said,

"To my mind has come a cause of grief,
Cathbad, that has left me bereft
Of feeling for happiness fled
When I heard those brave deeds

Done for the sake of one bull
That a woman wanted. A full
Army was assembled by
Maeve of the Thunder Thighs

To carry off our silver and gold
And all things precious. It is told
Many times now in song and story
About how Maeve reached her glory.

She raided easily through our land
Into Dáire's fortress, and then her band
Went to Dún Sescind and left little there
And then to Sobairge which they left bare.

As far as I can tell, that horny bitch
Of the twitching thighs which
Make men mad left no wall standing
In Ulster. Now I sit here bandying

Words while my bull and the brown
Bull of Dáire that has caused many to frown
Have gone. That wicked witch slew
Too many of the Red Branch's heroes."

He shrugged. "Well, there 'tis, Cathbad. So, good man, what do you suggest we should do?

> "Tell me your counsel, Cathbad.
> How can we change our sad
> State of affairs? Maeve escaped
> That famous battle. Escaped!
>
> It is this that has destroyed me.
> She should not have brought her army
> Across our plains to get my bull.
> Even if upon its head that bull
>
> Had golden horns she should
> Have stayed home. Oh, I could
> Have done much to help her
> If she would have asked. There
>
> Is a reason, you know, why
> That bull of hers didn't stay by
> Her herd. No bull wants a woman
> To lead him any more than a man
>
> Does. And tell me, wise Cathbad:
> Was it for white thighs and butt
> That so many men had to die?
> I have heard many men still sigh
>
> After her like mongrel dogs sail
> After a rambling bitch's tail.
> I think maybe the time is ripe
> For us to revenge our gripes!"

Cathbad: If I remember correctly, Conchobor,
You have already gained your revenge. For
Didn't the Red Branch win that battle
Over the four provinces raiding our cattle?

Conchobor: What is a battle where no king
Falls to feel Black Death's deadly sting?
It is the lack of this that makes me feel
The way I do. Unless Maeve and Ailill

Should fall before my sword, I think
My heart will break. Not food or drink
Has passed my lips since our return
Without our bull to our Emain.

He shook his head. "Come, Cathbad, give us the counsel that
we need."

"I advise you to stay where you are for the present," Cathbad said promptly. "The rough winds and dirty roads are hard
to travel. Besides, our warriors are busy trying to rebuild those
fortifications that were destroyed in the war. Right now, they
are raiding to reclaim our lands that were taken into the territories of strangers, and once those are rewon, why, they'll have
to build strongholds there to keep a tight grip on Ulster's lands.
I say that you wait patiently until the summer weather blows
balmy bright and every grassy sod becomes a soft pillow and
our old horses again find their spirit. Let our newborn colts
grow frisky strong and our men heal from the wounds and
hurts they received after the raiding battle. Wait until the nights
grow short.

"Spring is not the time to begin
An invasion. Why it's almost a sin
To leave when every gap is cold

Through which we must march boldly.
Many know that you have good
Cause to go after Maeve stood
So handily against you. But weak
Animals stagger in March. Seek
Out the April animals if you
Want to have strong animals to
Use in your Connacht invasion.
Spring is not the time for invasion."

Cathbad scratched his chest through his robe and peered from under bushy eyebrows through the gloomy room at Conchobor. "So I say we stay here awhile and gain our strength. There is no disgrace to your honor for not rushing harum-scarum after Maeve's white thighs. She's gone away from you on the back of a horse. Now is not the time for vengeance, I say. She will be dealt with measure for measure. But in time, Conchobor, in time. Meanwhile, start by rebuilding your forces. Send tidings and messages out to Conall the stern, the triumphant, the exultant, the victorious, the red-sworded, to where he is currently living in the land of Léodus and raising taxes for tribute. Send to your friends in the islands of Cadd and Orc and in the territories of Scythia and Dacia and Gothia and Northmannia. Send captains on voyages across the Ictian Sea and the Tyrrhenian Sea to plunder the Saxon roads. Send tidings to your absent friends in the Gallic lands and the foreign lands. I'm thinking of Amlaib or Olaib, the grandson of Inscoa, the king of Norway, and to Findmór Mac Rofher, the king of the seventh part of Norway; to Báre of the Scigger,[2] to the fortress of the Piscarcarla, to Brodor Roth and to Brodor Fiúit, and to Siugraid Soga, the king of Súdiam.[3] Send messages to Sortabud Sort, the king of the Orkney Islands, and to the seven sons of Romra, to Il, to Ile, to Mael, to Muile, to Abram Mac Romra, to Cet Mac Romra, to Celg Mac Romra, to Mod Mac

Herling, to Conchobor, the victorious son of Artur, son of Bruide, son of Dungal, to the son of the king of Scotland, and Clothra, daughter of Conchobor, who was his mother."

Conchobor gave a deep sigh and passed his hand over his eyes, pressing the pads of his thumb and forefinger hard against the bridge of his nose. "Well, who should I send on that embassy?" he asked.

"Who else should go but Findchad Mac Conchobor and Aed the Handsome, the son of Conall Cernach, and Oengus Mac Oenlám Gába, and Cano the Foreigner, to teach the path of the ocean and seas to them," Cathbad said. He waved his hand across in front of him, putting an end to the moment.

These were the ones who were sent to travel across the seas and ocean to where Conall Cernach raided in the territory of Leodús. They explained the purpose of their visit, giving him the glad tidings that Conchobor had directed that they deliver in his place.

Conall received them gladly, placing his hands around the neck of Findchad and giving him the three kisses of welcome. They told him the tale of the raid and how the Donn Cuailngé had been lost. When he heard the story of Cúchulainn, his lips grew thin and the hard plains of his face ridged with fury. The firm heart of Conall boomed like the roaring of surf against earth.[4] "If I had been in Ulster when that happened, no spoil would have been taken from its land," he growled. "I would have given those Connacht men blow for blow."

Then Conall's ardor cooled, and he gave them a feast such as he was used to having, with a great amount of drink readied and meat portions roasted. And as the Ulster nobles rested, Conall sent messengers to his absent friends in the Gallic lands and to the foreign lands of the foreigners, asking them to gather at his fortress after securing their galleys and ships.

Then Conall sent wise men and messengers to the lads of Ulster to set the Ulster minds at ease so they would know that he was coming with what force he could gather. When Conchobor heard that, he held a great counsel and sent word out to the border kings, telling them about the plans he was making.

When Cúchulainn heard the word, he said, "I'll hold a feast while we wait for Conchobor at the fortress of Delgan."

"I will make another splendid banquet," said Celtchair Mac Uthechar, "while we wait for Conall Cernach at the rock of Murbolg."

"And I will make a monstrous banquet," boasted Loegaire, "at Inber Seimne in the north."

Now the great armada made ready for sail under Conall Cernach Mac Amairgin and Findchad Mac Conchobor and Aed Mac Conall Cernach and the nobles of Norway.

As they came out onto the great current of the Mull of Cantire, a great sea rose up for them. Seals and walruses and crane-heads and monsters of the deep, huge whales of the sea rose up for them, too. Such was the strength of the raging storm that the fleet was divided into thirds. A third followed Conall Cernach to the rock of Murbolg. Another third went under Alaib, grandson of Inscoa, king of Norway, and under Find Mór, son of Rafher, king of the seventh part of Norway, and under Báire of the Færoe Islands from the fortress of the Piscarcarla and these went to the strand of Báile Mac Buain at the mouth of Luachann.

Then Conchobor led nine hundred and sixty-five warriors to the mouth of Luachann, and a house of drinking and great merriment was made by him in bright Dún Delgan.[5] Conchobor was not there long before he saw the tall spars of the ships approaching under full sail. Bright scarlet banners flew easily in the wind, and the great arms of battle and bright blue spearheads shone in the sun.

"Good men, wise men, give me sureties and bonds and guarantees," Conchobor said.

Sencha Mac Ailill gave him a quizzical look and said, "Why do you want it, my lord?"

"The burden of your charge to me is great," Conall said. "I am ready to bestow much land and wealth and jewels upon you. It is only right that I should ask for obedience if I deliver these favors to you. No evil should come to me from the end of one year to the next while we prepare for war."

"But why do you ask this?" Sencha persisted.

"Because," Conchobor said patiently, pointing at the proud ships. "I do not know if they are Galían of Lagin, or the Munster men of great Muman or the province of Ólnecmacht who have arrived here. Look: those ships fill the harbor."

Sencha shrugged. "All right," he said. "I give my word that there is not a soldier there who is not known to me. If they are truly men of Erin, then I will ask a truce of battle from them until a fortnight has passed. But if they are the foreigners we are expecting, then they will be welcome indeed."

"If they are the foreigners, then your honor-price will be less," Conchobor said.

Sencha went down to where the great armada had gathered and said, "Who goes here?"

They told him that they were the foreign friends who had come in answer to Conchobor's call, and Sencha took the glad news back to Conchobor.

"Good news, Conchobor," he said. "They are the ones you sent for from the foreign lands."

Conchobor should have been glad, and perhaps he was; still, a small clot of blood broke free from his heart, and he spat it on the ground, feeling the pain of what was to come at the same time. He looked over to where his great champion, the Hound of Ulster, waited patiently.

"Well, Cúchulainn," Conchobor said. "Let the horses upon the plain of Murthemne be caught and four-wheeled chariots harnessed to them. Bring the nobles of Norway in chariots and four-wheeled carts to Dún Delgan, where a house of drinking and feasting has been prepared."

The horses of the plain of Murthemne were caught and yoked and the chariots and carts taken out to greet the Norway nobles. The nobles were taken to Dún Delgan, where the great house had been readied for them by Conchobor. When the nobles entered, carvers rose to carve for them and servants came forward to pour drinks for them. The merriment began, and soon the nobles were drunk and carefree. When one of them was taken with too much drink, he was put into his sleeping rooms. Tunes and amusing songs and stories were sung and told to the visitors, and they tarried there comfortably until the morrow's sun rose.

Conchobor was the first to rise early that morning and asked that Cúchulainn be brought to him. When the young champion appeared, Conchobor said, "This has gone well, Cúchulainn. Give the nobles of Norway the rest of the banquet today so that they are well-satisfied, then send messengers throughout Ulster to gather the other warriors. I will go to the mouth of Luachann and make camp there. Make certain that the hundred and fifty elders and old champions retired under Irgalach Mac Macclách Mac Congal Mac Rudraige lay aside their exercising of arms and weapons and join me on this campaign. I need their war counsel."

"This is a good idea. I will be certain to convey your wishes to them," Cúchulainn said.

When Cúchulainn brought the elders to Luachann, they entered upon a great feast. Then Conchobor went into the great royal house where the veterans and old champions had gathered. They lifted their heads, bleary-eyed, from their couches and saw the radiant king standing before them. Great happiness spread among them, and they leaped from their couches. Conchobor smiled to see their great eagerness.

"Good king," they said, "what has brought you to us to-day?"

Conchobor expressed surprise and said, "Haven't you heard? The four provinces of Erin came against us in a great raid, bringing their music men and jesters and storytellers with them so that the ravages they brought down upon Ulster might be made even greater through song and story. They burnt our fortresses and fine dwellings until they remained little more than outhouses, crappers for children. I propose a raid of vengeance against them now, and have come for your counsel so the journey will be profitable."

"Ah!" cried the old ones. "Let our war horses be brought and our old chariots yoked. We shall go on this raid with you."

The old ones' chariots were brought and yoked, and they went on to the mouth of Luachann that night, their blood singing from the thought of the battles to come.

News of the gathering quickly spread through the four provinces of Erin. The Three Waves of Erin reverberated at that: the Wave of Clidna, the Wave of Rudraige, and the Wave of Tuag Inbir. Eochu Mac Luchta went on with the clans of Recartaig Dedad to Temair Luachra in the northwest. Ailill and Maeve went to Cruachan Ai in Connacht. Find Mac Ros, king of the Galíans, went with the Derg clans to Dinn Ríg.[6] Cairpre Nia Fer went with the Luagni of Temair to their place.

A resolution came to be drawn by Eochu and the Clan Dedad: "Every living thing for payment and every payment for its living thing and reparation of his territory and this land will be made over to Conchobor Mac Fachtna Fathach. A palisade in the place of every palisade, a summer house in the place of every summer house, a cow in the place of every cow, a bull in the place of every bull, and the Donn Cuailngé over and above,[7] red gold to equal the width of Conchobor's face—all this will be given to the Red Branch to ensure that no hostility will be brought against the men of Erin."

Messengers were sent to Ailill and Maeve, informing them of this resolution. When she heard it, Maeve grew furious and said, "This man has played us false, Ailill. I say as long as there is a man to handle a shield-strap this message will not be delivered to Conchobor!"

"That's not for you to decide, woman," Ailill said sternly. "What have we to lose? Our share of that payment is not greater than that of any other person in Erin who went with us on that raid. Sometimes discretion and tact are needed instead of sword and spear."

"Humph!" Maeve exclaimed. " 'Tis easy to see where you side! Men!" She flounced out of the room, breasts heaving in anger, and brave men stepped hastily away from the flaming-haired woman who stormed through the halls of Cruachan Ai that day.

"Let her ramble," Ailill said, shaking his head. "Women need their moments." He turned to look at the messengers. "Well, who should we send with this proposal?"

His words echoed down the Great Hall, and Maeve heard them and came back, eyes brittle with blue fire. "Who else?" she said sarcastically. "Dorn Ibair, grandson of Cepp Goba and Fadb Darach, grandson of Omna?"

A roar of laughter came from Fergus. Ailill turned to him, frowning. "What is it that you find so funny?" he demanded.

"The man that is the greatest enemy to the Ulster men is being sent by Maeve to them! Even if the only thing he had done was to mortally wound Mend Mac Salcholcu on the Boyne, it would be wrong for him to go," Fergus said, laughing. "But the men of Ulster have a sense of humor. They won't harm him; let him go."

So Find Mac Ros, king of the red-handed province of Lagin, went with the clans of Derg to Temair north to where his brother Cairpre Nia Fer was. The offers were made known to them there, and they debated what to do with the message.

They decided that they should send Fidach Ferggach of Fid Gaile, for he was wise, modest, and a most tactful man. Together, the group went to where Conchobor had made his camp with his army.

When they arrived, they said, "Every living thing for its payment and every payment for every living thing. Reparation of the territory and land to you, Conchobor, and a wall in the place of every wall that was destroyed, a summer house in the place of every summer house, a cow in the place of every cow, a bull in the place of every bull, and equal over and above the Donn Cuailngé, the width of your face in red gold, all this in exchange for no raid upon the men of Erin."

Conchobor looked at them and said,

> "Why have all of you come this far?
> Are you paying homage to me? Far
> Be it for me to expect that you
> Have come to bring peace! True?"

> Envoys: We have come from great Cruachan,
> Which has no little fame, to ask you, stern
> Conchobor, to restrain your plans to raid
> Our lands. We do not mean to upbraid
> You. This also comes from Maeve and Ailill,
> Those who led the great raid upon you until
> You rose from your weakness
> And brought down upon us great stress.

> Conchobor: Hmm. I see what you're about.
> Well, let me hear your request. But
> Know this: that although your band
> Appears great, there are others in this land
> Who feel anger at what was done
> For the sake of a red-haired wench's fun!

"But," Conchobor said, holding up his hand as they made ready to speak, "know this well: I will not listen to your terms until a place has been made for me in every province where they have set up huts and tents and booths."[8]

"Very well, Conchobor," they said. "And where will you make camp tonight?"

"In Rosnaree above the clear, bright Boyne," Conchobor replied. He never bothered to conceal his movements from his enemies, so secure was he in the power of the Red Branch warriors.

The messengers went south to Tara, where Cairpre Nia Fer and Find Mac Ros waited to hear what Conchobor had had to say. When his terms were given, Cairpre said, "Good. If Conchobor and the Ulster men turn their faces to us, then let Ailill and Maeve come to our aid. If they go past us into Connacht, then we shall go and help there."

The messengers went to Ailill and Maeve, and Maeve asked them for what word they had. When they told her, her face grew crimson and she said,

> "If the king of Macha comes,
> His army will be overcome.
> We will make certain that he loses
> For the war-path he chooses."

> Envoy: If our armies arrive in time,
> We will raise a battle in kind
> Against the Ulster foe who raids
> Connacht lands unafraid.

Meanwhile, Conchobor came with his great army to Acall Breg and to Slige Breg. There Ailill, a landowner, met him.

"Well, Conchobor," Ailill said. "What is that large army for? Where is it your pleasure takes you?"

"To Rosnaree above the clear, bright Boyne," Conchobor said.

"Hmm. Well, you're too late," Ailill said. "That place already is secured by the armies of the Galían and Luaigne of Temair, who got there first."

Conchobor shook his head. "I have no intention of going around them. I don't care about their numbers.⁹ Let our tents be pitched here and camp readied. Begin dinner, and let our tunes and merriment carry across the land."

The men scurried to establish camp, and soon cook fires were readied and meat sizzled on spits and drink poured into drinking-horns. Baths were readied for the men and their hair neatly combed, and great merriment was made by all.

"All right, brave Ulster men," Conchobor said. "Will one of you go out and scout the enemy so we know what we face?"

"I'll go," Féic Mac Follomon Mac Fachtna Fathach said quickly. He gathered a horse and galloped away into the hills above the Boyne. There he began to count the foe. Soon, however, he grew restless and said to himself, "I could go now and let the men of Ulster think that those men down there have driven me away. They will then come down hard upon the enemy from the north. The battle will be no less honorable for them than for me. But now that I think about it, why should I wait?"

He mounted his horse and forded the Boyne, then gave the grind of a left-hand mill on them.¹⁰ He rode down hard upon them from the flank, and the great army shouted in confusion around him. Then Féic rode away from them, back toward the Boyne. He forced his horse into a great leap, but a wave rushed high toward him and took him under and he drowned. That place is now named Féic's Pool.

Conchobor waited impatiently for Féic to return. At last he went back to the Ulster men and said, "Is there another among you who will go and scout the enemy for us?"

"I'll go," said Daigi Mac Daig. He went forward to the same hill and began counting the soldiers. But then his spirit grew stronger, and he said, "I'll go north and tell the Ulster warriors that the army is chasing me and the warriors will come down hard upon the enemy. But I would receive no honor greater than that which every man will earn. So I'll take the battle to them right now."

He put his horse to the river and rushed rashly down upon the army. But this time the army was ready for him, and many lances came flashing out and wounded him, and he fell to the ground, dead.

Again Conchobor waited, longer this time, chafing at the passing time. At last he said, "Good Irgalach Mac Macclach Mac Congal Mac Rudraige, who is the right one to send to spy upon the enemy?"

"Who else but Irel, the son of Conall, great at arms and great-kneed. But he is like Conall for wreaking havoc and has the skill of Cúchulainn at war feats. He is as wise as the Druid Cathbad and four counsels and as smooth-talking as Sencha. He is as brave as Celtchair and as kingly as yourself. Who else?" Irgalach said, shrugging.

"I'll go," Irel said, when he heard the praises.

He rode over the same hill and crossed the Boyne at the same place as the others. He began counting the forces, but unlike the others, his sense of bravery and honor did not get in the way of his job. Soon he brought the numbers back to Conchobor.

"How many did you see?" Conchobor asked eagerly.

Irel shook his head. "A vast number. I don't think there's a ford on the river or stone on the hill nor any road in Breg or Mide that isn't full of their chariots. Their apparel and gear and garments look like a blaze of royal colors on the plain."

Conchobor: Is it true, what the men declare,
Great white-kneed Irel. Tell me truly, swear

If there are three battalions on the left
Waiting to come down the road as swift
As eagles? Is this a prize deceit
Made from Ailill and Maeve's seat?

Irel: It's true; they wait in ambush for you
There in the wood where the Boyne runs through.
There wait three battalions of Clan
Derg who blaze like fire upon the plain.
The others that you sent to spy
On them will not be returning. Why
They chose to charge that army
Is a firm mystery to me.

And Conchobor rose up and said, "Men of Ulster! You have heard the report. What is your advice to us about the coming battle?"

"Our advice," said the old veterans, "is to wait until our strong men and our leaders and commanders and supporters arrive."

Although Conchobor chaffed at the delay, he took their advice.

They did not have long to wait. Soon they saw three chariot-warriors leading a band of twelve hundred each. These were Cathbad the Druid, Aitherni the Importunate, and Amargin the physician. Conchobor waited until they came up to him, then said, "Good Ulster warriors, what is your advice?"

"We advise that you wait for the others to appear," they said. They didn't have long to wait before they saw three other riders coming toward them and a band of thirteen hundred along with each rider. The riders were Eogan Mac Daurthacht and Gáine Mac Daurthacht and Carpre Mac Daurthacht.

"What do you advise?" Conchobor asked, when they came up to him.

"Wait until our strong men and battle leaders arrive," they said.

Soon three other chariot-fighters came over the hill, and each fighter led a band of fourteen hundred. These were Connad Buide Mac Iliach, Loegaire Buadbach, and Cairell the Wild One.

"What do you advise?" Conchobor asked.

"To wait until the rest of our people come," they said.

"Well," Conchobor said, scratching his head, "I'll be honest. We aren't prepared for you. A third of the Ulster army is here and there is only a third of the Erin army over there," he said, turning and pointing. "Why shouldn't we give battle now?"

Conchobor rose, calling for his war gear, and a third of the army of Ulster made ready to go with him. They went over the Boyne and charged down upon the Erin camp, hacking and whacking, slicing and dicing, slashing and dashing. But the Ulster warriors could not seem to gain the upper hand, and soon the center of the Ulster army stood like an old oak surrounded by young oaks that were soon cut off and the sturdy oaks left standing. Only the champions and heroes were left.

Then *Ocháin,* Conchobor's shield, was battered and roared.[11] The Three Waves of Erin answered: the Wave of Clidna, the Wave of Rudraige, and the Wave of Tuag. Then all of the Ulster shields answered the roaring, and the warriors fought to stand beside Conchobor.

At that moment, Conall came over the hill at the head of his army. Although the other horses tried to pass Conall to come to the king's aid, no horse was swifter than grim Conall's horses, which came down hard upon the foe. Foam-flecked mouths and wild-eyed, the horses were as fearful as their master, and the young fighters still standing among the Ulster men watched in awe as terrible Conall came, his face enraged, and the young men knew there would be no flight from that man. They went into the oak grove and came out with thick branches in their hands and followed along behind Conall into the battle.

Conchobor had begun to retreat from the battle when he saw Conall approaching. He called out to him, "Good, Conall! Help us with this battle!"

Conall shook his head. "It's easier to go into battle than try to stop a retreat," he said.

"The countercharge will surprise the foe
And turn the tide of battle although
The enemy is fierce and fights hard.
This is how songs are sung by bards!
Let the youths who have gained their
Arms come with me to fight. Bear
Well to your left as you go to fight.
There is no surrender in sight."

Then Conall drew his long and terrible sword from its sheath and charged down upon the army, the music of his sword singing loudly in the battle-din. The ring of Conall's sword upon shield was heard throughout the battalions at that moment. The music made hearts quake in fear, and eyes fluttered and faces grew white with terror as they drew back from the battle.

Conall glanced behind him and saw Mes Dead Mac Amargin approaching. "Come forward, Mes Dead, and bring the battle with you."

"Doing that would be like breasting a great flood," Mes Dead said. He looked behind him and saw Anruth the Tall approaching. "The battle of your favor, Anruth. Bring your protection."

"It would be like an arrow against a rock," Anruth said. He looked behind him and saw Feithen the Tall coming. "Feithen, the battle of your favor. Bring your protection to my rear while I charge our enemies."

Feithen looked behind and saw Feithen the Small approaching. "Small Feithen, hold the rear while I unleash my fury on the armies."

"Like striking a head against a cliff," replied the other. He looked behind him and saw Aithern coming. "Hold the rear, Aithern, until I release the force of my anger on the armies below."

"That is my right over the right of any others," Aithern said. But then he glanced back and saw Cúchulainn coming. "Cúchulainn, we need your help! The men are trying to retreat!"

"That will be the day," Cúchulainn said grimly. "Not a man of Ulster will look on my face and try to go past!" With that, he raised his goad and laid about him to the left and the right, and the retreat stalled as the men of Ulster milled in confusion. Then they righted themselves and turned again into battle.

Conall came down hard upon the enemy, his sword sounding a musical din until ten hundred had fallen by his good right arm. Cairpre heard the music of Conall Cernach's sword and came hard against Conall until his shield crashed against the shield of Conall. They fought stubbornly against each other until Conall's sword smashed through Cairpre's shield.

The three royal poets of the king of Temair came to help him—Eochaid the Learned, Diarmait the Songful, and Forgal the Just—and they brought fight to Conall. The brave Ulster warrior looked at them and said, "I give you my true word that if you were not poets and doctors, I would have killed you long ago. But since you have nosed your way into this battle, there's nothing to hold me back now." With that, he delivered a swift hard blow that severed the heads from the bodies of each.

Then a band of fifteen hundred of the Lúaigni of Temair came up between Conall and Cairpre and carried Cairpre away to safety in their midst. Conall went mad and smashed furious blows upon the army, slicing them in two, and the army wavered, then panicked from Conall's fury and broke apart, and he slew them in small bands and ten hundred fell.

The king of Temair heard that and could not bear to listen any more to the singing of Conall's sword. He came hard into the battle, swinging his own war-sword, and eight hundred heroes fell by him. Suddenly he came face-to-face and shield-to-shield against Conchobor. When his shield struck *Ochain,* it moaned, and all of the shields of the Ulster men moaned as well. The warriors fought down toward him, and Conchobor said, "Good men of Ulster, I did not know today who was the braver: the Galían of Lagin or you, but none can stand against you this day."

Then Loegaire Buadbach came with his band of three hundred warriors and fought down against Cairpre. Fintan came with a band of a hundred against Cairpre. But still, thirty hundred of the Galían and the Lúaigni came to carry Cairpre away from the battle.

That was the moment for Cúchulainn, who roared through the army until he came face-to-face and shield-to-shield with Cairpre. Cairpre clasped his two hands on his weapons and threw a spear over the battalions of the Galían. But Cúchulainn went through them without a scratch upon him. Laeg Mac Riangabair met him with Cúchulainn's arms, namely the *Cruadín*[12] and the terrifying *Duaibsech,* his dangerous spear. Cúchulainn took the spear and threw it toward Cairpre, and the spear sped through Cairpre's chest and pierced his heart and cut his back in half.[13] But before his body could fall to the ground, Cúchulainn leaped forward and lopped off his head. He raised Cairpre's head toward the enemy and shook it, giving his battle-cry. The enemy froze in their tracks, staring with fear upon the horrible sight.

Then Sencha rose and shook the Branch of Peace, and the Ulster army stood still. The Galían went under Find Mac Ros and laid their shields across the track behind them. Irel Mac Conall Cernach went after them, cutting them down as he came

murderously forward. Then Fidach the Wrathful of the Wood
of Gaible turned and met him at the ford and battle raged.

"Long is the arm that the Ulster men are making toward
us," said the men of Lagin. That is why that place is now called
Ríg Lagen.

The men of Ulster went on to Temair that night and stayed
there a full week. At the end of the week, they heard the sound
of chariot wheels coming to them and the noise of a full army
in march. Erc Mac Cairpre Mac Feidelm[14] Noi-chruthach came
and placed his hand upon his grandfather's breast and asked
that his father's land be granted him.

"All right," said Conchobor. "Take it and my blessing with
you.

> "Take my blessing, but obey me.
> Do not raise your sword against me.
> If you try to bring your army
> Against mine, I am sure we
> Will slay you. Do not fight the Hound
> Either, for you are not sound
> Enough in strength to defeat him
> Who is well-versed in battle-din.
> Do not be like your father and
> Bring against us your battle band.
> The three sons of Ros Ruad the king
> Held these lands hoping to bring
> Us to defeat. Find in Alend and Ailill
> In Cruachan, Cairpre in the north, still
> They were not enough for this deed
> Although together they sowed the seed
> Of battle. They were three pillars of gold
> But now their army is gone. The bold
> Men have all been slain in battle
> That began with their raid for cattle."

From this battle came the beginnings of battles yet to come: the Battle of Findchora and the great sea voyage around the Connacht men and the Battle of the Youths. But those are other stories. This one is finished.

The Story of
Fergus Mac Léti

I must confess that I have a problem with including *Echtra Fergusa maic Léti* within the Ulster Cycle because this appears to be a story that was made by the eleventh-century law schools to give depth to commentaries upon the law. Fergus Mac Léti seems to have been created as a doppelgänger to Fergus Mac Róich, but the placement of the story doesn't lend credence to Fergus Mac Léti having been a contemporary of Fergus Mac Róich. This tale is actually found in two legal manuscripts, H.3.18, pp. 363b–365a, and Harl. 432, fol. 5.

A̅T THE TIME, THERE WERE three races in Erin: the Féni, the Ulaid, and the Gáilni. Three royal chiefs contended for the throne of the Féni, Conn Cétchathach[1] and Conn Cétchorach[2] and Eochu Bélbuide[3] Mac Tuathal Techtmar. It was Eochu who went into exile with Fergus Mac Léti, the king of the Ulster men, seeking allies after having sorely wounded Conn. He re-

294 RANDY LEE EICKHOFF

mained quite some time with Fergus before returning to his own clan, where he was slain by Asal Mac Conn Cétchathach and the four sons of Buide Mac Ainmirech—Eochu Oiresach, Énda Aigenbras, Ailill Antuarad, and Tipraite Traiglethan—and a son that had been born to Dorn Ní Buide.

Of this was said: "The son of Dorn is a foe to us, and I say that he should be put to death if caught or else his mother should assume the responsibility for his deeds. No one should help her or support her. If she does assume the responsibility, then she may go into bondage and serve others for the rest of her life. Otherwise, she should be placed in a boat and set adrift as far as three *muirchrecha*[4] out to sea for her offense."

The protection of Fergus was violated with the slaying of Eochu and the killing of those who followed him. Fergus came with armies to avenge the killings and stayed until his terms were met: twenty-one *cumals,* of which seven were in gold and silver, and land, that land that once was Conn Cétchorach. This is that area called Níth because of the many dissensions that rose about it. Fergus was also given a bondwoman to serve him, this being Dorn Ní Buide, a sister of Buide's sons who had violated Fergus's protection or as pledge for the surrender of a captive. Seven *cumals* had to be pledged for every hand that had slain Eochu. From this, the penalty for breaching a king's protection has been fixed at a captive for every five persons concerned. Conn gave the land in atonement for the liability of Asal, his son.

In consideration of this, Fergus agreed that peace would reign and went to his own land, taking with him the bondmaid. When he reached his land, he went on to the sea with his charioteer, Muena. There they fell asleep on the beach, and sprites came to the king and took him away after removing his sword.[5] They carried him to the sea, where he awoke when his feet touched the water. He caught three of them, one in each hand and the third upon his breast, and the leader of the sprites said, "Life for a life."

"Let me have three wishes, then," Fergus said.

"You may have anything within our power to grant," said the sprite.

Fergus then asked for a charm to allow him to pass under seas and pools and lakes.

"You may have that except for Loch Rudraige, which is within your own land."

The sprite then gave him herbs for his ears, which he could use to travel underwater.

Some, however, say that the sprite was a dwarf and that the dwarf gave him his cloak, which Fergus wound around his head to pass underwater and that this was the dwarf who [word unrecognizable] the breast of Fergus and pinched his cheek while asking quarter from him.

"Why did you do that?" Fergus asked.

"That is a point of fair play with us," the dwarf responded.

And this is why one grasps the breast and cheeks of another while seeking quarter and appealing to his sense of honor.

One day Fergus tried to pass under Loch Rudraige while leaving his charioteer and chariot on the bank. When he dove under the lake, he saw a *muirdris,* a fierce monster, that kept inflating and contracting itself like the bellows of a smith. When Fergus saw it, his mouth wrenched back to his throat, and he raced onto land in terror. He asked his charioteer, "How do I look to you?"

"Bad," said the charioteer. "But sleep will cure you."

The charioteer then made a pallet upon the ground for Fergus, and he lay down and fell asleep.

While he slept, the charioteer went to the wise men of Ulster, who had assembled in Emain Macha, and told them about the king's adventures and his current condition. He asked them what person should be king, since they could not have one with a blemish. The wise men decided that the king should go to his house alone so no one, neither fool nor half-wit, could throw his blemish back into his face, and that he should always have his head washed while he lay upon his back so that he would not see the blemish upon his face. For seven years, he was guarded like this.

Then one day came when he told his bondmaid to wash his head. He thought she was moving too slowly and gave her a blow with his whip, whereupon she taunted him by describing the blemish upon his face. He gave her another blow with his sword and sliced her in half.

Stung by the thought that he carried the mark of a coward upon his face, he went back to Loch Rudraige and dove again under the waves, and for a whole day and night the waters roiled from the battle between him and the *muirdris*. At last, Fergus emerged from the waters with the head of the monster. The Ulster men saw him, and he said to them, "I am the survivor." Then he fell dead, and for a whole month the waters remained red from the battle.

Of this, a song was made,

> Great Fergus, the son of Léte, once went
> Into the waters of Rudraige and there sent
> A great monster to its death for giving him
> The great blemish that became his disfigurement then.

Finit.

The Strong Man's Bargain

This version of *Cennach Ind Rúnao* is from the Edinburgh manuscript. It appears that this story is incomplete and is taken from the end of *Fled Bricrend,* which I translated as *The Feast.* In that story Cúchulainn is the only hero to play out the beheading game with the ogre who challenges the entire Red Branch. The ogre was Cúroi, who came to determine which of the heroes was entitled to call himself the champion of the Red Branch.

ONE EVENING AFTER TIRING OF games and play, Conchobor and Fergus and other warriors came and sat down in the Great Hall of the Red Branch. Neither Cúchulainn nor Conall Cernach nor Lóigaire Buadabach, was there that night. But all the other heroes were there. At the hour of evening, at the end of the day, they saw a tall and very strong man coming toward them in the house. It seemed to them that no one in Ulster could come to half his size. He was terrible and hideous. He wore an old, smelly hide next to his skin and a black cloak over his shoulders. He carried a large tree-club the size of a winter shed in which thirty calves could fit. His eyes were yellow in his head, and each was the size of a caldron for a large ox. Stouter than the arm of any hero there were the fingers of each hand. In his left hand, he carried a block which would be a heavy carry for thirty oxen, and in his right hand an ax which had been forged with a hundred and fifty charges of glowing metal. The handle was the size of a plow yoke.

He went and stood at the bottom of the fork that was before the fire.

"Is the house too small for you?" said Dubthach Chafertongue to him. "Cannot you find any other place to stand but at the bottom? Maybe you want to outshine the lighting in the house? Sooner, though, we would have the house on fire."

"I have what I have," said the man. "And it will be judged so that the whole household will enjoy its light."

The Cattle-Raid of Flidais

The *Táin Bó Flidais* exists in two versions—one long and detailed, the other much abbreviated. The latter is to be found in *Lebor na hUidre, The Book of Leinster,* and Egerton, 1782. Three copies of the longer recension are known: one in the Glenmasan manuscript, a sixteenth-century vellum in the Advocates' Library in Edinburgh; one, incomplete, in *The Yellow Book of Lecan;* and a third in a paper manuscript of the seventeenth century in the Royal Irish Academy, B.IV.I, fols. 127ff. This is a strange tale, as the reader will discover, for it appears to leap about indiscriminately, yet the manuscript does not show a lacuna.

AFTER THE CHILDREN OF UISNECH had been slain while under the safeguard of Fergus Mac Róich, he came to Emain Macha and heard how Conchobor had ordered their deaths.[1] He did not come upon Conchobor in Emain Macha then, but the place was empty and bare before him, and he found no

deeds or triumphs which he deemed the better,[2] and he came
and stood over the graves of the Children of Uisnech and
grieved greatly for them.

Fergus had left these as guarantors: Cormac Conloinges
Mac Conchobor, Buinne Borbruadh Mac Fergus, Illann Finn
Mac Fergus, Dubhthach Mac Carbaidh, Aengus Mac Aonlámh
Gáibhe, Biordherg Mac Ruadh, Dubhthach the Chafer of Ulster,
Ailill the Honey-tongued, Édar Mac Édghaoth, Fiacha Mac Fer
Ebha, Goibhnenn Mac Lurgnech, Suanach Mac Sálghobha, Lu-
haidh Redhand Mac Dedha, Síthar Mac Edghaoth, and others
who are not given here.[3]

After his grief, Fergus plundered and slaughtered throughout the country and assumed lordship over the land for more
than a year.[4] Some say that Fergus was the king of Ulster at
this time for seven years and for that time the sun did not rise
over the edge of Emain's rampart so this time is called the black
reign of Fergus.[5] During this time, Conchobor was banished.
But the Ulster army was great in numbers, and the numbers
fell to arguing amongst themselves, and this led to much dis-
order and destruction, for Fergus governed carelessly.[6]

Then the men of Ulster assembled, namely the Children of
Amergin, the Children of Iliach, the Children of Durthacht,
and the wise men of Ulster, and Amergin and Cathbad spoke,
saying, "It is not right, Fergus, that the sun should stay eclipsed
during your reign. We have finally understood why the sun does
not rise anymore. You hold the smallest amount of land in all
of Erin. You deserve much more than this; you would not have
enough land if you held all of Erin under your rule. It is not
fitting that you should have a disgraceful reign. You are entitled
to take a larger share of the province than this. We say you
should take the *eric*[7] of the sons of Uisneach, and much of the
gold and silver and hereditary treasures that belong to the king
of Emain Macha for your own. You should have the apartment
of your choice, gilded and elegant with hangings and furniture

and well-carved pillars, and apple trees to shade the apartment and space within the apartment for fifty warriors and poets and wise men and youths and a third of the Great Hall of the Red Branch for yourself and those who follow you. Neither friend nor foe should touch it in your absence, even if you are kept long from it. The hero's portion should be kept for you, and you should share in the tribute to Emain forever. This share should be: seven vats of beer, seven deer, seven boars, one beast of every kind of wild game, and Conchobor's drinking horn."

Then he recited a verse,

"By having Eochu's share [text missing]"

Now Bricne set out westward from Cruachan Ai, and he and his companions traveled by keeping Ráh Fionnchaoimhe on their left, that which is now called Crích Airtigh; across Sliab Na Fairgsiona, now called Lugho; across the western part of Crích Lughna mic Fir Tri, now called Corann; over Colbha Criche Cein, now Crích Ghaileang, over Sál Srotha Deirg, now called the swift stream of Moy; along by Loch Con and Loch Cuillinn; and up to the fort of Ath [word unintelligible] now called Caorthannán, that is, to the fort of Oilill Finn Mac Domhnall Dualbhuidhe, the fierce king of the Gamanrighe.

Now in all the world, there was not a better ruler than Fergus in hiring people, for he gave them three thousand horses, three thousand chariots, three thousand swords, three thousand various-colored clothes, three thousand shields, three thousand golden helmets, three thousand long spears, and three thousand mantles of various colors to the three thousand kings, cattle-lords, champions, soldiers, warriors, and heroes of the Red Branch who swore allegiance to him. To these, he also gave three thousand spindles of red-gold thread to trim their tunics and cloaks.

Fergus had many great deeds to his name in regards to the

strength he had shown in battle and combat. He was equal to seven hundred soldiers, and when he was at Emain Macha, he fed Conchobor's household every seventh night and the women, youths, and poet-singers of Ulster. We know this from the poet's verse:

> "Conchobor's household and the Ulster men
> Did not go hungry in the household. Then
> Fergus fed them every seventh night;
> All the ones who came within his sight."

And Fergus was known for his stamina in bed, for seven women were needed to satisfy his lust until he went to Cruachan and had his great affair with Maeve, who needed thirty men a night to satisfy her or one Fergus. For the seven he had, however, he needed seven bushels of water to bathe his fair head when washing; enough to feed seven to feed him once; and enough beer to drink for nine for him once.

He became famous for the following battles: the Battle of Inbher Tuaidhe, in which fell Niall Niamhghlunnach Mac Rudhraighe; the Battle of Carrag Eóluirg, in which fell Red Ruirech, the soldier; another Battle of Carrag Eóluirg, where Eólorg Mac Sdarn, the High King of the Lochlanns, fell; the Battle of Inbher Uaithne against the Bregians, where Fionn Mac Inneónach, king of Temhair fell; another Battle of Carrag Eóluirg, where fell Echtach, the Woman-Warrior;[8] the Battle of Maistiu over the tribe of Ros; the Battle of Mullach Dubh Rosa; the Battle of Macha over Conchobor; the Battle of Cepda over Durthacht's tribe; the Battle of Luachair over Dedha's people; the Battle of Dún Dá Bhenn; the Battle of Boirche; and many others not recorded here.

When Ailill Finn saw that, his household and his great council were summoned. After much debate, they came up with a plan to send messengers to the Gamanrighe and appoint a day to assemble the army. Two chief horsemen were brought, Engán from the Dún and Édar from Glen Édair. Ailill sent Édar to the north to assemble the Gamanrighe from the Erne by the sea and then to Irrus Domhnann. Engán went the other way to Inbher Dá Égonn. This was the muster for the raid on the cattle of Flidais: to the two sons of Cornán Cosdubh, Aengus and Aodh, to the youths of Mag Eine, to the soldiers of Mag Ceinne, to the seven Breslenns of Bréfne, with their three hundred champions between the mountain and sea now called Dartrighe, to Cornán Cosdeubh, to the ridges of Sligech, to Darta of the Brigandage with his sons, the two Reds, to Échtach Mac Édarbha, to Dúnadh Cinn Chunga, to Dáil and Anainn, the two daughters of Goll of Oilech, to the yeomen of the Plain of Oilech, to the officers of Ailill Finn with their seven hundred champions, to Gaman of Síthghal, to the fortress of Cenn Slébe, with its three hundred Gaman, to Dubán Mac Cúghamhna, to Dún Droighin, to the seven Fosghamhain of Irrus, to Dún Dá Os, to the seven Eochaidhs, to Mag Imrinn, to Dún Gaman Ruadh Na Rée, to Dún an Aoinfir, to Fer Caogad, to the seven war-hounds of Ailill Finn, to Dún Inbhir Dá Os, to Édarha Mac Uathach, to his fort, to Ilar Uathach Mac Édarba, to his glen.

They came in battalions and regiments in a huge army to Ailill Finn, for those were his mercenaries he kept on retainer for war when he was beset.

He sent Engán, the chief herald, back on another journey south to fetch the rest of the Gamanrighe to come to Ailill Finn's aid: to Aodh Mac Échtach, to Dún Coirrslébhe, to Cairbre the Contest, son of Dubhthach, to Dún Croimghlinne, to Muiredhach Menn Mac Ailill Finn, to the fortress of Sliab Mór, called Mag Sliab, to Red-head Fidhach, to Dún Leitrech, to Mancha, to Mag Linne, to Aengus Mac Échtach, to Ara, to Ros Mac Romain, to Boirenn, to Ugha Échtach Mac Finn, to Rod Mac Ros, to Sliabh Rod, to Mongach, to Dún Inbhir, to Aengus

Mac Ailill Finn, to Dún Thonn, to Ro Nár, to Fraoch Mac Fidhach, to Port Cachais, to Dún Cláire, to the seven sons of Iobhar Caoin, to Glen Easa, to Failbhe, to Ros Mac Dubh Dá Thonn, to Ros Nár, to Dún Cinn Chunga, to Ebha daughter of Édarbha, to Glen Cuidbhech, to Beg from Boirinn, to Illann Mac Échtach, to Leiter Finnchuill, to Genann Mac Faobhar, to Leitir Genainn, to Runaree, to Dún Osra, to Cobhthach of Cenn Sáile, to Dún Airthir, to Conn Cimidh, to Mugh Miodhísiol Mac Dubh, to Caoinbhrethach Mac Finn, to Dún Maghrois, to Uamnach daughter of Ibhar, to Dún Inbhir Dá Thonn, to the seven sons of Ibhar, to Acaill, to Goll of Ecaill, to the seven Dubháns, to eastern Inis Caoin, to the seven war-hounds of Ailill Finn from the island of Mag Maoin, to the seven war hounds of Inis in Sgáil, to the seven Finns from Inis Finnáin, to Eithne Oigdherg, to Dún Trethain, to Tuadh, to Leiter Bealaigh, to Fiacha Finn Mac Faobhar, to Dún Fiachach, to the three Fosghamlain, to Dún Mór, to Fer Derg Mac Dolar, to Dún in Derg, to Dubthach Dubhgha, to Dún An Aoinfir, to Domhnall Dualbhuidhe, to the king of the Gamanrighe, to Dún Tuaidhe, to Ferdiad Mac Damhán, to Dún na Céd, to Guas and to Gossa, to the two sons of Ferdiad, to Flann the Tall Mac Rfidhach, to Cathair of Cruinnsliabh, to Muinchenn, to Dún ós Loch, to Dáire Derg, to Dún Dáire, to Gobha Glas, to Finnchadh na Fert, to Darta of the Brigandage.

Satisfied with his efforts, Ailill Finn went back through the host and was not wounded. He proceeded on his way by means of his skill and valor to Cenn Trágha Tursgair, now called Trágh Cinn Chertáin, and found Certán Cerda there with his ship in the large harbor. When Ailill saw that, his courage grew, and he went and asked for the ship to be sent to him.

"Absolutely not," said Certán Cerda. "I have a great grievance against you, and now that you are in trouble, I will have my vengeance."

Puzzled, Ailill Finn shook his head and said, "All right. Tell me what's wrong."

Certán spat and said, "My wife is in your company instead of mine."

"I have never committed that deed. I give you my word," Ailill protested. "But if you truly believe yourself to have been wronged, I will pay the *eric* even though I am innocent. I will give you a hundred bowls, a hundred cups, a hundred horns, a hundred swords, a hundred helmets, a hundred shields, a hundred spears, a hundred tunics, a hundred hauberks, a hundred fast horses with different bridles, a hundred milch cows with their calves, a hundred mares bearing, a hundred sows and litters, a hundred broad-backed oxen, a hundred fleshy wethers, and besides that, a hundred bars of red gold and my own friendship."

"I won't accept that." Certán grunted. "My ship leaves without you."

"That is wrong," Ailill said. "It isn't right to leave one such as myself to his enemies."

But Certán did not listen to Ailill and took his ship away from the harbor and left Ailill upon the strand. When Ailill saw Certán doing that, he placed a stone in his sling and heaved it at the ship. The stone struck Certán in the neck and tore his head from his body. That is why that place is named the Strand of Cretán's Head today.

Then Fergus came upon Ailill Finn, and Ailill became enraged and came hard against Erin's men, and the books tell us that it is impossible to calculate the number of men Ailill slew that day and no thanks to Cretán for not taking Ailill away.

Let my curse and the curse of Ailill fall equally upon him for that. *Finit.*

The Colloquy of the Two Sages

This story is taken from *The Book of Leinster*. Adnae's name appears to have come from *adnál,* which means "very shameful." Ferchertne is the son of Cairbre and the chief poet of Conchobor.

ADNAE, SON OF UTHIDER, of the tribes of Connacht, was the teacher of Erin in science and poetry. He had a son, Néde, who went to Alba to learn science with Eochu Echbél. Néde stayed with Eochu until he had learned all he could in science.

One day Néde walked to the brink of the sea, for he had heard the poets sing of the edge of water as the place where science would reveal itself to one who was patient. While he sat there, he heard a sound within a wave, a wailing chant filled with sadness that seemed strange to him. At last, unable to understand it, he cast a spell upon the wave that it might tell him the problem. The wave roared forth the news that it was mourning the father whose robe had been given to the poet

Ferchertne, who had taken the place of Néde's father.[1]

Then the young man went to his house and explained to his tutor what he had discovered. And Eochu said, "It is time for you to go home. There is no room for two sciences in one place, and your studies show that you have great knowledge in science and are worthy of wearing your father's robe."

Néde left with his three brothers: Lugaid, Cairbre, and Cruttíne. While they traveled, a puffball bounced to greet them on the path. One of them asked, "Why are you called a puff-ball?"

But it did not answer, and because it did not answer, and they did not know why it was called a puffball, they returned to Eochu, and they stayed a month with him, studying the ways of the puffball.

Again they ventured forth, and a rush chanced to meet them, and since they did not know why it was called a rush, they returned again to Eochu, where again they studied the ways of the rushes.

At the end of that month, they set out again and came upon a thistle, and since they did not know why it was a thistle, they returned again to their tutor for another month of study.

Now, though, since their questions had been answered, they went on to Cantire and then to Rind Snóc and passed over the sea until they came to Rind Roisc. Then they traveled to Smne and over Latharna, over Mag line, over Ollarba, over Tulach Roisc and Ard Slébe to Craeb Selcha and over Mag Ercaite to the river Boyne and then up over Glenn Rige and Húi Bresail to Ard Sailech (now called Armagh) to the elf mound of Emain Macha.[2]

The young boy carried a silver branch with him, which placed him above the others who carried a branch of gold, and above the poets who carried a branch of copper.

Then they went to Emain Macha, where Bricriu met them

on the green. Bricriu said that if Néde would give him his purple robe, he would advise Néde how to become the wisest in all Erin. So Néde gave him his purple robe, with its adornment of gold and silver, and Bricriu told him to go and sit in the place of the wise man in the Great Hall of the Red Branch. He also said that Ferchertne was dead, but here Bricriu lied, for Ferchertne was in the north, teaching his students.

And then Bricriu slyly added: "No beardless man receives the Place of the Wise in Emain Macha."

Now Néde had skin as smooth as a woman's skin, and no beard would ever grow upon it. So Néde took a handful of grass and cast a spell upon it and held it to his chin so others would think a beard had grown thickly upon his chin. He went and sat on the wise man's chair and wrapped his robe about him. Three colors were in that robe: a covering of bright bird's feathers in the middle, raindrops of silver on the lower half outside, and gold bands on the upper half.

Then Bricriu went to Ferchertne and said, " 'Tis sad, indeed, Ferchertne, that you should have to step away from the chair of the wise today. A young man has taken that chair now in Emain Macha."

When he heard that, a great anger came over Ferchertne, and he stormed into the Great Hall and stood on the floor with his hand on the column of wisdom and said, "Who is the one who claims to be the poet here?"

This was in the time of Conchobor Mac Nessa and was written by Néde Mac Adnae, who was of the *Tuatha Dé Danann*. This is what he said: "I am the son of Dán Mac Osmenad, who brought the words of the poet to man."

So Ferchertne entered the house and said on seeing Néde:

"Who is this poet, a poet who wears the splendid robe and chants poetry? I think he can be only a pupil, for his great beard is nothing but grass. He appears to be a poet of argument instead of chanting poetry as a poet should. Never have I heard of Adnae's son having the secret of ready knowledge. That seat is not Néde's seat."

To which Néde said: "Well said, ancient one, my senior, for every sage is one who should be willing to correct the mistakes of every ignorant person. But before he releases his anger upon someone, he should see what evil is within that person that justifies such anger. He must remember:

"Welcome is even the piercing sense of wisdom.
Slight is the blemish of a young man, but seldom
Can his art be rightly questioned. So step lightly
Along the path you would tread. You behave badly
By saying that I do not have the food of wisdom
Yet I say that I have drunk deeply of the milk of wisdom."

And Ferchertne said: "A question, lad, who would instruct his elders: From where have you come?"

And Néde said: "That's not hard to answer: from the heel of a sage, from a confluence of wisdom, from perfections of goodness, from brightness of sunrise, from the hazels of poetic art, from splendid places out of which truth is measured according to quality and righteousness is taught before falsehood is allowed to set, where colors are seen as they are and where poems come alive again.

"And you, my senior one, from where have you come?"

And Ferchertne answered: "I come along the columns of age, from the streams of Leinster, along the *Sídhe* of Nechtan's wife, along the forearm of Nuada's wife, along the land of the sun and the dwelling of the moon, along the young one's birth cord.

"Now, young lad, what is your name?"

And Néde answered: "That's easy: very-small, very-great, very-bright, very-hard. Anger of fire and fire of speech, a loud knowledge, and well of wealth, sword song, a good art from the fire.

"And you, my senior, what is *your* name?"

And Ferchertne answered: "Easy to say: nearest in omens, good in declaration, wise questioner in science, skilled in art, a vessel of poetry, rich from the sea.

"A question, lad, what art do you practice?"

And Néde answered: "A blush upon the face, piercing flesh, a tinge of shyness, a throwing away of shame, an offering of poetry to search for fame, a care for science, art for all to speak, a giver of knowledge, a stripper of speech in a little room, the maker of a sage's cattle, a stream of science, great teaching, the giver of easy tales to delight kings.

"And you, senior one, what art do you practice?"

And Ferchertne answered: "I hunt for support, establish peace, arrange armies, and gratify young men who celebrate art. I make a bed for kings [text missing], bring the shield of Athirne, and share the new wisdom learned from the stream of science, a fury of inspiration, the structure of the mind, the art of small poems in clear arrangement, tales that follow a wise road, a pearl that makes sciences after a poem."

"And you, young teacher, what do you try?"

And Néde answered: "I go into the plain of age, into the mountain of youth, into the hunting of age, onto the road of a king's death, into an abode of clay, the place between candle and fire, between battle and horror, among the mighty Tuatha men, among the stations of wisdom and the streams of knowledge.

"And you, wise sage, what do you try?"

And Ferchertne answered: "To travel upon the mountain of rank and into the communion of sciences, into the lands where wise men live, into the teeming river and the fair of the king's boar, into the little respect of new men and the slopes of death, where there is great honor for he who would pluck it.

"A question, teaching lad, what is the path you have traveled?"

And Néde answered: "The white plain of knowledge, and onto a king's beard, on an aged wood, on the back of an ox, on the light of a summer moon, on mast and fruit, on corn and milk, on little corn, across a ford of fear and on the thighs of a good horse.

"And you, senior one, what path have you traveled?"

And Ferchertne answered: "On Lugh's *bod* (penis), upon on the breasts of soft women, on the hair of wood, the head of a spear, a silver gown, a wheelless chariot, a wheel without a chariot, on the three ignorances of Mac Ind Óc.

"And you, teaching boy, what art has birthed you?"

And Néde answered: "I am son of Poetry, Poetry son of Scrutiny, Scrutiny son of Meditation, Meditation son of Lore, Lore son of Inquiry, Inquiry son of Investigation, Investigation son of Great-Knowledge, Great-Knowledge son of Great-Sense, Great-Sense son of Understanding, Understanding son of Wisdom, Wisdom son of the three gods of Poetry.

"And you, my senior, whose son are you?"

And Ferchertne answered: "I am the son of the man who has been and was not born and has been buried in his mother's womb; he has been baptized after death, and in his first life death engaged him, the first cry of every living one, the cry of every dead one, lofty A[3] is his name.

"Now, lad, what word do you have?"

And Néde answered: "Good tidings: a fruitful sea, a strand overrun, a smiling wood, fleeing blades, flourishing fruit trees, growing grain fields, swarming bees, a radiant world, happy peace, a kind summer, armies well-paid, sunny kings, wondrous wisdom, a fleeing battle, everyone to practice his own art, valorous men, needlework for women, laughing treasures, every art complete, glad tidings.

"And you, master, have you a word?"

And Ferchertne answered: "I have indeed: terrible tidings of evil during the time which will always be when chiefs will be many and honors will be few and the living will stamp out fair judgments. The cattle of the world will be barren and men will cast off modesty and the champions will disappear. Men will be bad and wise kings few as many usurpers will reign. Disgraces will fall upon man and every man will be blemished. Chariots will wreak upon the race and foes will consume Niall's plains. Truth will fall away and sentries will fight while every art will become a fool's art and every lie will be seen as truth. Everyone will die through pride and arrogance, and neither rank nor age nor honor nor dignity nor art nor teaching will be served. Skillful people will become artless and every king a pauper and every noble will fall as every lowly born will rise and neither God nor man will be worshiped. Rightful princes will become victims of usurpers who carry the black spears. Belief will disappear and floors will fall and cells will be undermined. Temples will be burnt and storerooms become wastelands. Flowers will rot and bad judgments will destroy the fruit of trust, hounds will rove the earth and people will fall into darkness and become victims of misers. At the end of the world, poverty will triumph as artists go to quarreling, and satires will be delivered on command, limits will be placed upon people, everyone will slay his neighbor, brother will betray brother, neither truth nor honor nor soul will survive in the storms of darkness. Sages will be despised and music will turn to sour notes. Champions will fall and wisdom will become false judgments. Temples[4] will come against the law and only adultery will reign. All good poems will become dark and skill in embroidery will pass to harlots and whores. Kings will judge falsely and anger will become the bylaw of everyone and no one will serve where he is expected to serve. Everyone will turn his art into false teaching and false intelligence, to seek to surpass his teacher; so that the junior may like to be seated while his senior remains standing. No shame will be found in gluttony and the farmer will close his house against the artist, who will be forced to sell his soul and honor for a cloak and food. Greed will fill every human being and the proud man will sell his soul and honor for the price of one scruple. Modesty will be cast off and lords will be destroyed and ranks despised. Poets will disappear and righteousness will fall while false judgments will be seen as right. Every territory will be overpopulated and every forest will become a plain and every plain a forest and everyone will be enslaved along with his family. Pestilence will reign and terrible tempest. Leaves will sprout in winter and fall in summer. Autumn will find no crops and spring no flowers. Famine will reign as wheat fields fail. Liars will reign and a death of three days and three nights will come upon two-thirds of the people. Plague will come upon the beasts of the sea and forest. Then will come seven years of sorrow and wailing and flowers will rot and in every house there will be cries of sadness. Foreigners will seize the plain of Erin, those who hesitate will fall and daughters will conceive to their fathers. A desolation will come around the meadows and the sea will break over the Land of Promise. For seven years, Erin will be left without judgment and mournful slaughters will come. Then shall come the signs of the Antichrist's birth and in every clan monsters will be born, streams will run against streams, dung will become gold, water will turn to wine, and mountains to plains, bogs will become clover, and bee swarms will be burnt on the upland plains, while seven dark years spread rapidly across the earth to hide the lamps of heaven. That will be the Judgment, my son. Great tidings, awful tidings, an evil time!

"Tell me, my son, little in age and great in wisdom, who is above you?"

And Néde answered: "My creative God, my wise prophets, my hazel of poetry. I know my mighty God. I know that Ferchertne is a great poet and prophet."

Then he knelt to Ferchertne and took off his robe and handed it to him and rose out of the poet's seat to sit under Ferchertne's feet.

Then Ferchertne said: "Stay, little in age and great in wisdom. Stay and be magnified and glorified! May you be famous and loved in man's and God's way. May you become a repository of poetry and a king's arm. May you become a rock of wisdom and the glory of Emain Macha. May you rise higher than everyone."

And Néde said: "May you be the same as a tree with the same stump and a kind man filled with poetry, the wisdom of the perfect folk, the father by the son and the son by the father. May you be the three fathers of age, flesh, and teaching. You are my father in age, and I acknowledge your wisdom."

Finit. Amen.

The Trouble of
the Ulster Men

This untitled account of the periodic debilitating affliction of the Ulster men is found in MS. Harleian 5280 of the British Museum. It is traditionally called *Ces Ulad,* a name given it by Vernon Hull. It is very difficult to translate this piece because many of the words have yet to be defined.

ONE DAY CÚCHULAINN AND HIS charioteer, Láeg Mac Ríangabra, went on a short raid for riches along the Boyne River.[1] Cúchulainn carried a *fidchell* board and a *búanbach* game as well.[2] In a bag around his waist, he had several smooth and deadly stones for his sling, and in his hand he held a spear that he would use to catch fish. He had a leather cord tied around his wrist so he could retrieve the spear once he had cast it.

Fedelm Foltchaín and her husband, Elcmaire, came down the other side of the river Boyne and saw Cúchulainn across from them. Elcmaire said to his wife, "See! A most unwelcome intruder, Fedelm!"[3]

Fedelm said, "Stay here and guard me while I see if the man in the front seat and his companion are able to race after dressing their horses with such fancy and carrying such things as *fidchell, búanbach,* and the birds which he seems to have gathered at every plain."

Then Cúchulainn caught a speckled salmon on the point of his spear from the Boyne.[4] Elcmaire went into the ford and pulled out a four-sided pillar so that the chariot took great fright. Cúchulainn then cut off Elcmaire's thumbs and his big toes.[5]

Fedelm promised to stay a year with Cúchulainn and strip herself naked to the Ulster men upon their arrival in Emain Macha. On that day a year later, she stripped and showed herself, and it is this that has caused the great sickness to come upon the men of Ulster.[6]

The Wooing of Luaine

This story is found in two manuscripts dating from around 1390, *The Yellow Book of Lecan* and the *Book of Ballymote*. Although it is called *Tochmarc Luaine*, it is not considered one of the official "courtships." This would seem to follow directly after *The Exile of the Sons of Uisnech* because Conchobor is mourning the loss of Deirdre. (See my translation of *The Sorrows*.) As his mourning takes on more tragic overtones, his men decide that they must find a wife who can make him forget his grief. But tragedy begets tragedy, as we shall see.

Conchobor Mac Nessa sat beneath the great oak tree, staring at the smoke-blackened ruins of what had been the Great Hall of the Red Branch.[1] Workers and warriors passed by, carefully keeping their faces averted for fear that the king's eye might catch their own. They did not want to share the great grief and the sorrow and dejection that seemed to have cloaked their king in darkness since the death of Deirdre.[2] Nothing seemed to lift the cloak away from his shoulders. Music had no charm for him, and the enjoyment that he took in beauty and the brightness of the day seemed to slip past him. Beautiful women stayed a short distance away from him, dressed in their finery, but he gave them no more than a casual look and then heaved a great sigh and moved back into his own dark thoughts.

Many of the landowners would come to him and sit with him and speak in low voices, advising him to begin a search of Erin's kingdoms for another king's daughter or a lord's daughter who might distract him from the grief he felt, but still he sat until one bright day when he heaved a great sigh at the song of a wren in the branches above him. This was the day when the builders had nearly finished erecting the great beams of the new Great Hall. His long, pale face frowned for a moment, then he raised his head and called for his messengers to come to him.

Leborcham, daughter of Ae and Adarc, and Leborcham Rannach, daughter of Uangamain, both hideously ugly, made their way to where he sat, knowing full well that they were safe from his fury. They listened as he instructed them to search the length and breadth of Erin, through the towns and fortresses, and see if they could find a maiden that might help Conchobor forget his grief.

The two hags left to do his bidding, but their search was in vain, for they could find no daughter of Erin who did not have a blemish to detract from her beauty. They did not bother with these women, for they knew only the most beautiful could ever win a place against the ghost of Deirdre in the king's memory.

One day, weary from her travels across the land, Leborcham, the daughter of Ae and Adarc, came upon the dwelling of Domanchenn Mac Dega and discovered a maiden so lovely, with pale skin and curly red hair, that she nearly eclipsed the sun with the brightness shining from her innocence. Her name was Luaine Ní Domanchenn.

Leborcham motioned for Domanchenn to come with her outside the common cottage where they lived and there, in the cool shade of a beech tree, told Domanchenn that she had been sent by Conchobor to find such a one as his daughter, for she was the only young girl in all of Erin who could come close to Deirdre's beauty and wisdom. Domanchenn clapped his hands in delight and, after a brief haggling, agreed to a proper bride-price.

Leborcham returned gratefully to Conchobor's house and related everything she had learned about the girl she had found. At first, Conchobor listened listlessly, then as Leborcham continued to elaborate upon Luaine's charms, his interest quickened and love began to fill him until at last he decided to go himself to see this wondrous woman Leborcham had found. And when he saw her, the glow of love built into a burning flame and he asked that she be his wife. He agreed to pay the bride-price (and, indeed, it was more than fair for one such as Conchobor) and then returned to Emain Macha to hurry the builders along and make his home ready for his new bride.

Now at this time, Manannán Mac Athgno, the king of Inis Gall,[3] came to the shores of Ulster, to raid and burn the province for revenge over what had happened to the sons of Uisneach. He had been a great friend of Deirdre and Naisi and had even fostered their children: their son Gaiar and daughter Aíbgréne.

Now there were four Manannáns, but none of them lived at the same time. Manannán Mac Allot lived during the time of the *Túatha Dé Danann* and had been a splendid wizard of that race. He was properly known as Orbsen and lived in Erin, and Emain Ablach was named after him. He was slain in the battle of Cillen by Uillen Abradruad[4] Mac Caither, Mac Nuadu Airgedlám,[5] while he was fighting for the throne of Connacht.

While they were digging the grave, they uncovered a great spring that burst from the earth and flooded the ground around, and they named it Loch Oirbsen after him.

The second was Manannán Mac Cerp, who lived in the time of Conaire Mór Mac Etirscél. It was he who wooed Tuag Ní (daughter of) Conall Collamair, who was Conaire's foster-son. Tuag Inber is named after her.

Manannán Mac Lir was a wizard and the best sailor ever to sail to Erin. By simply testing the air, he could tell whether there would be fair weather or a storm, which helped him on his trade routes between Erin and Alba and the Isle of Man.

Manannán Mac Athgno was the fourth Manannán. This one came with the great fleet to avenge the sons of Uisneach, who had lived in Alba for sixteen years under Manannán's grace. While there, they had conquered that land from Sliab Manann to the north of Alba and expelled the three sons of Gathal Mac Morgann—Iatach, Triatach, and Mani Lámarb—from that land that had once been ruled by their father, who had been slain by the sons of Uisneach. The three sons went in exile to Conchobor, and there they killed the sons of Uisneach.

Manannán's vengeance was brutal. He stormed over the shores of Ulster, raiding and burning, and taking great riches from the land until the Ulster men finally managed to assemble in the passes of the north and offered him a battle.

By this time, however, Manannán's anger had settled a bit, and he agreed to a peace treaty that was negotiated by his friend the poet Bobarán, the foster-father of Gaiar Mac Naisi. Gaiar received compensation for the death of his father, who had been betrayed by the Ulster warriors. Naisi's two brothers, Annle and Ardan,[6] were left against Conchobor's honor. All of Liathmaine was given to Gaiar after being taken from the lands of Dub-thach Bitter-tongue, who had gone into exile from Ulster with Fergus Mac Róich after they burned the Great Hall of the Red Branch. But peace was made, and Manannán left the lands of

Ulster and remained friends with Conchobor from then on.

Now when Athirne Ailgesach[7] and his two sons, Cuindesach and Apartach, heard about Luaine's betrothal to Conchobor, they went to her father to ask for favors. Yet when they saw her, the three of them immediately fell in love with her.

"Ah," Athirne growled one day. "Certain I am that I'll fair burst if I can't have her loveliness in my bed."

"I feel the same," Cuindesach said and was promptly echoed by Apartach.

They went to her, begging her to go away with them. "We'll fair die if you don't come with us," they whined.

But Luaine was aghast at their begging. "I'm going to be Conchobor's wife. How dare you make such suggestions to me?"

"Ah, lass, we can't go on living unless we can go into you," they whined in reply.

"Away with you, now," she said angrily. "Roses will grow on haw trees before I sleep with the likes of you."

Angered now, they put their heads together and helped each other write three satires upon her, leaving the stains of Black Shame, Red Blemish, and White Disgrace upon her face. When she looked into the bronze mirror in her room and saw the ugliness that had come over her face, her heart broke and she died. Afraid of Conchobor's wrath and what the Ulster warriors would do to them for what they had done, Athirne and his sons fled to Benn Athirni above the Boyne.

When Conchobor, who had long been without a wife to warm his bed, returned to the house of Domanchenn Mac Dega—his relations and lands were with the Tuatha—he was accompanied by the Ulster warriors Conall Cernach, Cúchulainn, Celtchar, Blai Briuga, Eogan Mac Durthacht, and Cathbad the Druid and Sencha the Poet. There they found the maiden dead and her people in black mourning. A great silence came hard over Conchobor at that time, and he felt the pain of grief that he had not felt since the death of Deirdre.

"Now," he cried out, "what vengeance would be just for this evil?"

The warriors looked at each other and whispered among themselves, but Conall Cernach spoke up, saying, "What better than that they give their lives for this? It would be good for the world to be rid of them, too, for 'tis many times we've been forced into battle because of Athirne's wagging tongue and rages."

Then Luaine's mother, Béguba, came before Conchobor and the Ulster warriors, wailing with sadness and sorrow. "Ah, Conchobor," she said. "This evil will have long effects, for 'tis not just the death of one that will come from their dirty deed, but both her father and myself will die of grief as has been prophesied by a Druid. I ask that you take vengeance where we cannot."

Cathbad shook his head and said, "Be careful what you do, Conchobor. Athirne has a sharp tongue about him that's been dipped in snake venom. He will bring down the birds of prey against you:

> Satire and Disgrace and Shame;
> Curse and Fire and Bitter Word;
> And the six sons of Dishonor will flame:
> Miserliness and Refusal as a sword
> And Harness and Denial,
> Rigor and Rapacity, all
> Will become warriors at his call."

It was then that Domanchenn came forward and said, "Are there such cowards among the Ulster warriors as this? What greatness is there in fearing a man with words to banter?"

"A good question," said Conchobor, eyeing the flushing faces of his warriors. "How will you act, men of Ulster?"

As one, the warriors gathered in council. Cúchulainn advised the destruction of Athirne. Combative and righteous, Conall agreed and looked on. Celtchar the Wounding remained silent, conspiring. Munremar the Famous made the plans. Cúscraid the Custodian decided. They returned their decision to their king: the heroic, haughty, severe, two-edged youths of Ulster had determined to go and destroy Athirne's dwelling.

A mighty sorrow was raised around Luaine's body, and the death-chant and funeral-games were performed, and the headstone carefully planted. The grief of her mother and father was dreadful, and it was sad indeed to be in the presence of the wailing they made.

Conchobor: On the plain is this grave of Luaine, daughter of Red
    Domanchenn.
Never came to golden Banba a woman that was harder to
    maintain.

Celtchar: Will you tell us how that is, Conchobor my king?
Which loss has caused the most grief-sting:
Luaine the Fair or Deirdre of the Sorrows?

Conchobor: I will tell you which, Celtchar, and you may borrow
My words on this: Luaine was better for she never uttered
Any lie to harm another. But there was no rivalry started
Between either. The prophesy that has carried her off is sad
And worse is that which has taken her now to bad
Death. Here, her barrow has been dug and her grave
Stands as a reminder to Béguba and Dega's grave
Son and Luaine. Black death has cut the lives of each
And in such time that they all have now reached
The same end in the same barrow. I say Athirne must
Receive the evil for the evil he's done. And I trust
That each of his four children will in turn

Man, sons, wives, all deeply burn
In Death's arms in vengeance for this grave affair
Regardless how Athirne and the others may despair.

Conchobor led the grieving for Luaine, and then took to the road with his Ulster warriors against Athirne. They followed Athirne to Benn Athirni, and walled him in with his sons and all his household, and killed his two daughters, Mór and Midseng, and burned his fortress with him inside.

That deed seemed evil to the poets of Ulster. Amergin said:

"Athirne's tomb here, let it not be dug by you poets with your
   songs.
Woe to him that wrought the man's destruction, woe to him
   whose wrongs
Caused his slaughter! He had a hard spear whose shining
   brightness
Was like that which Cridenbél the satirist used to make. Its
   likeness
Would slay a king if we let it. Now here, I will make his
   lamentation
And we'll plant him in his grave and over him build his new
   station
In the earth, and that should be enough for any mortal man
Who thinks evil has been done by the Red Branch band."

And so it was done.
Finit.

The Hostel of
Da Choca

Togail Bruidne Da Choca was apparently recorded sometime around the eighth century in the now lost manuscript *The Book of Druim Snechta*. It appears to be a close parallel to *Togail Bruidne Da Derga* and probably derived from that story, one of the oldest in the Ulster Cycle. Da Choca's hostel, considered one of the five great hostels of Ireland, was in Meath.[1] This account was taken from the fragments in the sixteenth-century manuscript H.3.18 and the seventeenth-century H.1.17. Although the tale appears to be incomplete, the story is continued in "The Battle of Airtech," which follows.

AFTER CONCHOBOR'S DEATH, THE MEN of Ulster held a council to determine who would be the next king. Some argued that Fergus Mac Róich would be the best among them to be king, but others claimed they had suffered much while he was in exile and declared that they would not have him as their king. Others said that it rightly should be Cormac Conloinges Mac Conchobor who should reign over them. Conall Cernach was trying to get his fosterling, Cuscraid the Dumb of Macha, another son of Conchobor, to be the king. The Ulster warriors were ready to go to battle on account of this, but Cuscraid refused to give battle for fear that the clans of the Red Branch would all be destroyed. Conall Cernach was not there and later reproached his foster-son for refusing to do battle.

Then Genann Mac Cathbad said, "Now I know the makings of a king in Erin. Cormac Conloinges Mac Conchobor is a noble child of Erin and endowed with the great gifts: the gift of shape and of valor and of hospitality and of truth and so forth. 'Tis to him, moreover, that Conchobor, when he thought to die, commanded that the kingship be given to Cormac, the eldest of his sons and the foster-son of Fergus, who never plundered us when he was with Cormac."

The Ulster men agreed with what Genann had to say.

Then they sent messengers to Cormac in Connacht to bring him back to be crowned—Genann Mac Cathbad, Amergin the Poet, Imbrinn Mac Cathbad, and Uathechtach Mac Feradach were charged with this. So the troop of charioteers went forth until they came to Cruachan Ai. Ailill and Maeve and Fergus were there, and they made the messengers welcome. Maeve asked news from them, and that is when they announced that they had come for Cormac so that he would be named king in place of his father.

A messenger was sent to fetch Cormac, who was hunting at Síd Nenta across the water. Cormac came to Cruachan, and Maeve of the Friendly Thighs and White Breast welcomed him, saying, "It would be good of you to show your gratitude for the way that we have hosted you here. You cannot accuse us for not having made you welcome."

Her eyes looked knowingly into his, and he grinned and

said, "I will always be grateful to you. Ask of me anything and you will not be refused."

Genann told Cormac the news that he had been charged with delivering, and a messenger was dispatched by Cormac to his people, who lived nearby in Connacht. They came quickly from Irrus Domnann and the outlying districts, all of the Ulster men, women, and children who had been living in exile.

Now Cormac had many *gessa*, and these were he was forbidden to listen to Craiphtine's hole-headed lute; to pursue the birds of Mag Dá Cheo; to drive his horses over an ash yoke; to swim with the birds of Loch Ló; to make love with a woman on Senáth Mór; to hunt the beasts on the slope of Mag Sainb; to go with dry feet over the Shannon; and to visit the hostel of Da Choca.

These were all forbidden to him by Cathbad the Druid on the night he was born.

The next day Cormac left Cruachan to make his way to Emain Macha. Three hundred warriors went with him besides the women and boys and hounds and servants.

When they left Cruachan, Cormac formed his people into three groups. The first group wore blue forked mantles with silver brooches and over them short capes with kilts to the knees. Each man carried a mighty spear, and the shields were fringed and speckled. Their swords had pointed hilts.

The second band had ribbed shirts over their skin. They wore beautiful speckled mantles with white bronze brooches. Their hair was combed backward over their heads, and they carried bright shields and five-barbed javelins. Their swords were shiny with ivory hilts.

The third band wore hooded shirts and satin tunics. They carried huge brown shields. Golden-hilted swords were on their belts, and each man carried an eight-edged javelin. Their mantles were purple and five-folded with silver and gold brooches.

Cormac was in the middle of this group, and a fine figure of a
warrior he was with long blond hair and a mighty arm.

Now there were many wizards who predicted evil things
would happen to Cormac while on this journey, which they
claimed omens had told them would not be easy or fast. And
by chance it was on that very day that some things forbidden
to Cormac happened. His hounds hunted on Mag Sainb—
where he was chasing the birds of Mag Dá Cheo, which is called
the Lough of the Birds today.

And if this was not enough, Craiphtine the Harper went
to him and deliberately played his hole-headed lute to him to
ruin his reign and his life, for it was Craiphtine's wife, Scenb,
the daughter of Scethern, the wizard of Connacht, who had
become Cormac's lover. This Scenb was red-haired and high-
breasted and loved to wrap her long white legs around Cormac's
waist. They had made love in three places at Athlone. That is
where she planted the Trees of Athlone that were called Sadness
and Dark and Hard Dumb: Olur and Meith and Miscais. She
said:

> "The names of the woods around us
> Are Dark and Hard Dumb and Sadness.
> Dark for that is where we make
> Love away from others' eyes and take
> Our pleasure where silence reigns. We
> Feel sadness there for I know we
> Cannot sleep together forever.
> Around this great plain ever
> Running are Olar, Meith, and Miscais."[2]

When they went into the wood to get away from the jealous
eyes of Craiphtine, the yoke of Cormac's chariot broke, and this
is why the wood is now called the Wood of the Yoke, and a
yoke made from ash was placed under his chariot.

Then they traveled over the lands of Maine Fer Dá Giall[3] until they reached Lough Ló. There they made love on the grassy bank, and later Cormac went into the water and swam with the lake-birds with Scenb, and they laughed and made merry, dunking each other under the water and swimming between the legs of each other.

It was here that Craipthtine learned they were swimming with the birds, and he sang a hundred and fifty youths into the shape of birds and placed a poisoned spell under their wings and sent them to shake their wings on the waters. The birds then fell asleep on the bank, and Scenb, who recognized the magic of her husband in the birds, changed herself into a hawk and went among them, killing all save one.

From there Cormac and Scenb went to Druim Airthir, which is now called the Garman, on the brink of Athlone. As they unyoked their chariot, they saw a red woman washing her chariot and its cushions and its harness. When she lowered her hand into the water, the river ran red with blood, but when she raised her hand from the water, not a drop remained in the river among the stones. That is how Cormac and Scenb stayed dry-footed when they crossed over.

"It is horrible what that woman is doing!" Cormac exclaimed, shuddering. "Let one of you go and ask what she is doing."

So one of Cormac's party went over and asked her what she was doing and she chanted, saying,

> "I wash the harness of a king
> Who will soon feel Death's sting."

The messenger returned to Cormac and told him the evil prophecy that Badb had just made for him.

"It would seem that a great evil is about to happen," Cormac said. Then he shook his head and motioned for his party to wait while he went to the river to speak with her and ask her whose harness she was washing. He spoke the lay:

> "Woman! Speak truthfully now! Whose
> Harness are you washing now? Whose?"

> The Badb: You recognize its shape, don't you,
> Cormac? It is yours and that of the men you
> Have brought with you and who you trust.
> Soon, most of you will become dust.

Cormac shook his head at this and said, "Evil words you chant grimly to us. These are dark omens indeed!"

He turned to go, when suddenly he saw a beautiful woman coming toward him. She wore a light green mantle around her, and in the mantle a precious brooch was pinned over her shapely breasts. She wore a bright-hooded dress with gold thread next to her, and two white bronze sandals had been strapped around her dainty feet. She wore an ornamented band around her forehead, holding her red hair back from her high, white forehead. She smiled seductively at Cormac and dropped down lightly upon the grass beside him.

Cormac swallowed, not knowing what to say, and foolishly said, "Are you coming on the trip with us?"

"No." The woman laughed. "And I don't think it would be a good idea for you to go any farther yourself. This was a grim gray day when Craiphtine the Harper played his lute for you. That may have ruined your life. He did this deliberately, you know, so that you would violate the bans that have been placed upon you and shorten your life. We might never have come together but for this, for I know that if you go on, we will never again meet." Then she said:

"If it is to be your death,
Cormac, it will come by stealth.
Be watchful, but be bold
Or stories about you will be told
That will not do you honor.
Death is death, Cormac, but honor
Must always be held dear.
Do not make death your fear!"

Then she rose and shook her dress free of the leaves and took her leave, chanting as she went:

"Bad *gessa* will come to me
If you follow me. Please see
That there is nothing to be done
This day under this sun,
For much evil has been placed
In motion for this time-space."

Cormac sighed and lay down in the grass at the end of the ford and closed his eyes, sleeping. And an awful vision was given him while he lay there, and when he awoke, he found himself coated with perspiration.

It was at this time that a group of Connacht men made camp in Mag Derg after wrecking and raiding a party in Ulster's land. Those who were there were Sanb Mac Cet Mac Maga and Bairenn Brecc Mac Cet and Dub and Coibden Cuindsclech, two sons of Lámfota and brothers of Lon Fiach, and Maine Athremail, the son of Ailill and Maeve, and Garman Gablec, the son of Daman, and Buidech, daughter of Forgement, the She-Warrior, and Eochaid Becc Mac Eochaid Ronn, the king of Fir Craibe, along with a great host of other warriors.

The Ulster men said to Cormac, "It is not right that women

of Ulster and their treasure should be held prisoners close to us without our fighting to free them."

"We shouldn't," Cormac answered. "We should not make war on Maeve or her people, for we weren't attacked by those men."

"Is this, then, the type of man who will be king over us?" demanded Dubthach derisively. "What king would stand by and watch his people be slaughtered and enslaved without helping them? Besides, are not the people of Connacht our enemies?"

"Attack," said the evil men and destroyers. "Stay here if you will, but we will attack whether Cormac goes with us or not."

With that, the Ulster warriors lifted up their war banners and came down upon Mag Deirg against the wreckers to the Plain of Derg, named after Derg Dolair of the Fomorians, who fell there during the battle with the *Tuatha Dé Danann* at the Battle of Mag Tuired. Those with Cormac were Illan the Fair and Fiachra the One-eyed, two sons of Fergus; Amirgin the Poet; Uathechtach Mac Feradach; three sons of Traiglethan: Siduath, Cuirrech, and Carman; nine sons of Scél: three Flanns, three Finds, three Conns; three Faeláns; three sons of Niall; three Collas; three sons of Sithgal, Luan and Iliach and Eochaid; two sons of Suamach, the son of Samguba, two of Cormac's foster-brothers. Nine comrades of Cormac were there: three Dunguses, three Doelguses, three Donnguses, and Dubthach the Chafer-tongue of Ulster and his two sons the two Ons. And nine sons of Ler Mac Etirscél. Find, Eochaid, Illann, the three pipers. Two Aeds and two Fergnes, the four horn players. Drec and Drobel and Athairne, the three wizards. Find and Eruath and Faithemain, the three spencers. Three *úchletchs* ("breastplates" signifying "guardians"?), Uait and Muit and Aislinge. Aed and Eochaid, two sons of Bricriu. And Ilgablach. And Caindlech, daughter of Gaimgelta, Cormac's foster-mother. And

Caindlech, daughter of Sarba, Dubthach's wife. Cacht the Bloody, son of Ilguine.

They marched with dry feet over Luan's Ford and went east toward the others. There the two armies came together, raising a loud battle-din that echoed over the land, hacking and mangling and striking each other, foe upon foe, until at last the Ulster warriors defeated the men of Connacht.

There fell by Dubthach and by Illann Mac Fergus, Dub and Coibden Cuindsclech, two sons of Lámfota; two brothers of Lonfiach at Cruach Duib now called Duib-thír and Tír Coibden. Bairenn Brecc Mac Cet was slain by Fiacha Mac Fer Febe on Mag Bairenn. Then Garman Gaiblech Mac Daman, Maeve and Ailill's servant, was slain by Cormac Conloinges on the angle of the ford which is now called Garman's Angle. Druim Airthir had been its name before. Then Ercail Mac Condair was slain by the older Flann upon the road now called Slige Ercail, and Flann died on Tulach Flainn. Uathechtach Mac Feradach was slain with a counterstroke by Sanb Mac Cet Mac Maga and by Maine Athremail, the son of Ailill and Maeve. That was upon the plain now called Mag Uatha, which was called Mag Deirg from the Battle of Mag Tuired from the time of the *Tuatha Dá Danann* from this battle down to the time of Columcille. Mag Úra was its name when Columcille scattered the ashes of St. Ciarán Mac in Tsáir there to drive the demons away. Caindlech, the daughter of Gaimgelta the She-Warrior, fell at Caindlech's Brake, slain by Maine, son of Ailill and Maeve. Luan Mac Suanach was slain at Athlone so that it is from him the ford is named. Buidech, the daughter of Forgemen, slew Luan. The twins Camall, daughter of Maga, bore to Eochaid Ronn, Illann the Fair and Illann the Brown, were killed at the ford. That is why the river is called Na Emain.

After that the men of Ulster gathered, and Lámfota said, "You are evil for your deeds done against Ailill and Maeve. Killing their people will bring them down against you, now!"

"What's this?" Dubthach said sharply. "A slave is now threatening us?"

He jabbed his spear at him, and Lonfiach saw that and went away angrily to Ailill and Maeve to report what had been done to their people.

The Ulster men savored their victory for a moment, then continued on their journey toward their own country. Some of them were sorely wounded, and all were tired from their battle and needed a place to stay and rest.

"Let us stay at the hostel of Da Choca," they said. "You know, the house of the smith and of his wife, Luath, daughter of Lumm Lond, at Sliab Malonn."

"We will *not* stay there!" Amirgin snapped. "What foolishness this would be to stay so close to the land of our enemies after slaughtering some of their people. The lands of Da Choca are in the province ruled by Ailill and Maeve. I say we avoid Fir Malonn and go on to our own lands. What do we care if it is night or day? Maeve's deeds are not slight enough that we should ignore all that she has done."

Dubthach laughed loudly. "Walk away from the arms of a woman? What is this foolishness? Besides, why should we worry? Fergus is in the west with her and—" He made a lewd gesture with his arm. "We all know how well-armed he is."

"I don't know." Illann Mac Fergus frowned. "The man isn't as watchful now as he used to be. Getting fat and sassy. But we need food and shelter and sleep, so we should mount a guard, I say, and stay where we can."

So they went on to settle in at Da Choca's house. Now this place was one of the six hostels of Erin: Bruiden Da Choca on Sliab Malonn. Each of those hostels was at a place where four roads came together. Whoever came to stay was allowed to stab his fork once into the great caldron and eat whatever he could pull out, but he could do this only once. Every hostel, however, was also an asylum for the "red hand."[4]

Da Choca waited until Cormac and his men went into the house, then came in with fifty servants and his wife, Luath, the daughter of Lumm Lond. They made their visitors welcome, and all took a seat.

Now as soon as they were seated, they saw coming toward the hostel a big-mouthed, swarthy, swift, sooty woman, lame and squinting with her left eye. She wore a threadbare mantle that was very dirty. She was as dark as the back of a stag-beetle from crown to ground, and her gray hair hung in raglets over her shoulder. She leaned against the doorjamb, eyed evilly those who were there, then said:

> "Sad will be all here in this hostel today
> For much blood will be spilled on this day.
> Heads will be severed from bodies, I say,
> And blood will be spattered on walls this day."

Then the Badb spat and wiped her ugly mouth and went away.

Messengers came from Ulster in the north, sent by those people who thought that Cormac was long overdue in Emain Macha. So they sent a large band southward to Cruachan to meet them and urge Cormac to press on strongly so he could be made king. The land had been long enough without a ruler. These messengers were told that Cormac and his people had gone to Senáth Mór. They followed them at full speed and found the field of battle.

"This is true," they said. One pointed at a deep mark on the green. "Here is the mark of Cormac's swordpoint."

They shook their heads and hurried on toward the hostel.

They arrived shortly after the Badb's grim prophecy and just in time to hear the gloomy, tearful, and mournful words of Genann speaking, saying, "I see warriors riding hard over Mag Deirg from the west. I think they are all from Ulster."

Their spirits lifted and Cormac went to see for himself what heroes had come down to meet him from Ulster.

They entered the hostel and took their places upon the couches that had been made ready for them. Amirgin sat on the champion's seat to the right of Cormac. Cacht sat down at the doorpost across from him on the other side. Fiacha Mac Feraba sat on the champion's seat by the king's left. Fiacha Caech Mac Fergus sat across from him. Illand the Fair, son of Fergus, was near Cormac's right hand, while Dubthach was near his left. Every man sat where he was entitled to sit according to his father or grandfather's place.

Meanwhile, Lofiach had made his way to Ailill and Maeve and told them what the Ulster warriors had done. Immediately they called a council of the Connacht warriors.

"We must be careful," cautioned one of the elders. "Fergus is still here, and we all know what a mighty warrior he can be. The rest of the Ulster men will follow his lead in everything."

"Leave Fergus to me," Maeve declared. "I will keep him occupied while you pursue Cormac and storm the house where they are sleeping."

She dressed in her thinnest gown and went to Fergus, her breasts nearly bare, red hair shining. Later, while they were lying naked in each other's arms, Maeve said, "You know, Fergus, this isn't right what Cormac has done. And have you given thought to him? Isn't he the son of the man who exiled you from your own country? I have it on good authority that it was he who sired Cormac on Nessa, and to think that he will wear that crown that was once yours!"[5]

Fergus stirred himself and studied Maeve's nakedness. He looked down at the heavy scars on his own body, then sighed, stretched until his bones cracked, and said, "Well, then, I think something needs doing, isn't there?"

And he rose, dressed, gathered his arms, and set off after Cormac.

Those who went with him were the sons of Maga, including Cet, and Aille Ard-agach, and Eochaid Becc, son of Eochaid Ronn; and Maine Intogaid, son of Maine Mórgor; and Maine, son of Cet; and Mog Corb, son of Conor Redbrow, son of Find Mac Rosa. Their army numbered a thousand. Lonfiach went along to guide them, and not one among them was without a shield or spear or sword.

Then Suamach Mac Samguba, the *seanachie* and fosterer of Cormac Conloinges, sang, prophesying to all what would happen, for he had great knowledge in these things.

"Woe who trusts after Cormac
After Loinfiach Mac Lámfota [text missing]"

They made their way to the hostel and halted, hiding as they sent out Mog Corb and Corb Gaille to spy at the hostel. When they returned, they reported on what they saw.

Mog Corb said, "We reached a huge palace filled with angry and furious folk inside dressed in wondrous costumes with beautiful foreign buckles and armor and sharp javelins. Some of the men had their hair combed backward, while others were closely shorn and on others their hair stood high upon their heads."

"Those belong to the household of the king and his soldiers. Woe be to whoever attacks them!" said Lonfiach. "They will slay many to defend their king."

"Then we went to another house on top of the hill, where we saw women with bright limbs and hyacinthine eyes wearing dresses colored red and blue and green. Gentle boys were there and hounds upon leashes and musicians and minstrels and jesters. But we saw no warriors or soldiers there."

"I know those," said Lonfiach. "Those are the womanfolk of the king and of the queen, Ném, the daughter of Celtchar Mac Uthechar. They will be closely defended as well."

"We reached another house," said Mog Corb, "below it on the slope of the hill. Inside were many lords and mighty men and kings' sons and great princes. Although the royal torches were not giving a great amount of light, we saw enough of the various robes and ornamented brooches and gilded shields and swords all inlaid with gold. I could not recognize Cormac, unless he was the one at the midbeam of the house: a tall man with a noble face, even teeth, gleaming eyes, and fair, long, golden, flaxen hair upon him. He has a long, two-forked spear and wears a purple gown with a silver brooch. He has a great sword by his side."

"That is Cormac," said Loinfiach. "You have done well."

The destroyers sat down to wait for the end of the night to wreck the hostel.

While the people inside the hostel were drinking, Amirgin slept. And while he slept, he dreamed of Connacht men rushing the hostel, and on each side there was great slaughter around it. He awoke in horror and rushed to tell Cormac.

"What did you hear?" Cormac asked. But the others were shouting and laughing, and he could not hear Amirgin.

"Be quiet!" he roared. The din slowly settled as the others turned to look wonderingly at him. "Now," he said. "Again. What is it?"

And Amirgin said, "All of you need to ready yourselves, for I fear the Connacht men are coming down upon us even as I speak."

At that moment the Connacht men circled the house three times, raising their battle-cry.

"I was afraid of this," moaned Amirgin.

"Not to worry," Cormac said confidently. "There are enough warriors here to give them a good battle."

Then Suamach Mac Samguba went east to warn Cormac and reached the Hill of Tears, those tears which the Dagda had shed upon hearing about the death of his own son. Now when

Suamach saw the flame of the wrecking inflicted, his heart broke, and that place is now called Druim Suamig.

The Connacht men fired the house, and when Lonfiach saw this, he repented having brought the Connacht warriors to the hostel and went inside to stand beside Cormac. But he found Dubthach instead, and the Black Chafer-tongued man swung his huge sword and cut off his head and Lonfiach became the first to fall.

Then fires were kindled at every point of the hostel. Fergna Mac Finnchonna rushed out and killed fifty of the men and put out the fires and drove the Connacht warriors back over the hills. Then he came back into the hostel.

But the Connacht army came back and relit the fires. This time Fiacha Mac Feraba rose, went out and put out the fires, and slew a hundred warriors as he drove the rest away from the hostel.

Again the Connacht men returned and lit four vast fires in the hostel at each corner. This time Dubthach went out and killed a hundred in merciless battle and put out the fires and went back into the hostel.

At five points, this time, the Connacht men built fires. Then Illann the Fair Mac Fergus roared out of the house and put out the fires and killed a hundred of the Connacht army, driving them back over the hills.

But Lugaid Redhand came with a great battle-stone on his shoulder and hurled it at Illann Mac Fergus and stretched him lifeless on the ground. Fiacha Mac Fer Feibe took the stone onto his own shoulder, and Amirgin said, "That is the stone of a hero and great shame will come to them from it!" Fiacha hurled the stone at Lugaid and killed him. Then Cet retrieved the stone and threw it into the hostel, killing a man, only to see it seized by Fiachra Caech Mac Fergus, who hurled it back outside, killing another with it.

Seven outside and seven inside were killed with that stone.

Then Dubthach hurled it out and over the hostel, so that it is the one stone that is now in the well of Cell Lasra, for no royal house was ever far from water.

Amirgin sang:

"Fiachra hurled the stone and seven
Men were slain and sent to heaven.
This is the stone at the bottom of the well
That left many men lifeless. It will
Remain there for many years until
It is needed again and then it will
Be drawn from the well like water."

It was then that Cormac said, "Enough of this! I say we take the slaughter to them instead of staying in this hostel and being destroyed!"

The others shouted their willingness to follow him, and they roared out of the hostel and formed themselves into battle groups. Then they charged into the middle of the Connacht men, and great slaughter was found on both sides.

Cormac found a stone under his foot and cast it at Mog Corb, shattering his shield and knocking him to the ground. This is the stone that is in the well in the middle of the hostel. He didn't get to his feet before Cormac and Cacht Mac Ilguine rushed up to kill him. The battle rolled back and forth, with first one champion gaining an advantage and then the other.

Out of the battle went Eochaid Becc Mac Eochaid Ronn, king of Fir Craibe, and Maine Antacaid Mac Maine Mórgor, who fell tiredly beside Cacht Mac Ilguine and by Cormac Conloinges. Many graves are on that hill, now called Becc's Hill from Eoch and Becc Mac Eochaid Ronn.

Then they returned victoriously to the hostel, but few were left alive after the great destruction on the hostel green. The two Ons, Dubthach's two sons, were at the ford, and each of them had slain nine men in the massacre. That is why it is now called the Ford of the Ons east of the hostel. Clartha Cloen was slain by Cet Mac Maga in Clartha, and that hill is named after him. Boccán was slain by Amargin, and from him Ard Boccáin in Crích Malonn takes its name. Len fell in Loch Lein in Bodamir. Crech Soindimm and Crech Doindim fell on the Height of the Crechs, and Dubthach slew Cliaach Cetroeach on the ridge that bears his name. Én Mac Maga fell at Én's Ford by the sword of Fiachu Mac Fer Febe. Fidach Mac Én fell at the Ford of Fidach's Recess. Caindlech, the daughter of Uarb, Dubthach's wife, was slain at Caindlech, while Buidech fell at Buidech's Lawn.

Then a battle came with Cormac Conloinges and Dubthach and Amargin and Cacht Mac Ilguine on one side and Cet and Ailill Ardágach, his brother, and Maine Mac Cet and Buanann Mac Damán on the other. Buanann was slain by Dubthach. Maine fell by Amargin. Together, Cacht Mac Ilguine and Ailill Ardágach fell in a duel. Corb Gaillne, came to Cormac Conloinges and slew Cormac. This is what *The Book of Druim Snechta*, declares that Corb beheaded Cormac and that Anlón Mac Doiche Mac Maga took the head to Athlone.

Others declare that Amirgin forbade the beheading and hunted Cet from Cormac and three times wounded Cet. However, the other version is in the books.

Then Da Choca was slain in the hostel, but his wife, Luath, the daughter of Lumm Lond, went to Luath's Lough, and a great burst of blood broke in her heart so from her Loch Luatha is named.

Yet out of the thousand Connacht men there, only five escaped. Of the three hundred Ulster men, only three escaped—Amirgin the Poet, Dubthach, and Fiacha Mac Fer Febe. Imrind Mac Cathbad had fled the night before the destruction.

Amirgin made Cormac's grave and mound and sang over the grave:

"Great is the grief of Ulster tonight
After the destruction of Cormac in unfair fight.
Much blood has been splattered upon the ground
And battle-cries still ring in the night's dark sound.
Again, Ulster is without its king
Who has fallen to Death's dark sting."

Of these tragic deaths at the hostel, this is sung:

"Cormac was in the hostel slain
And upon the ground Illan is lain.
Many champions died in battle
But not for the sake of any cattle."

As to Fergus, this is here set forth.

While he was staying in Cruachan, his servant Ergarb went to him and told him about the march of the Maines and of the sons of Maga after Cormac and his people and that they had been charged to slay them at the house where they slept. Fergus quickly gathered his chariot and went forth to stop the destruction.

But when he arrived at the hostel, he found only Amirgin and Dubthach and Fiacha still alive, although all three were red with blood from their wounds.

Then Fergus made a great sorrow above the grave of his fosterling and beat his palms together loud like a thunderclap, and tears of blood streaked from his eyes to fall upon the ground. He made a swift circuit of the battlefield and found the bodies of his household and friends, and a great grief rose within him. But he felt the greatest grief at the death of Cormac and not his own sons.

Then he went back to the three living and soothed them and praised them for their great deeds.

Fergus: Ah! My heart is a prison of gore
My strength and fire have perished sorely
From what has happened here tonight.
Great is the sorrow we'll feel at first light.

Amargin: Cacht and I fought a mighty battle
After these Connacht men came like cattle
To this hostel's bloody slaughter.
Tonight there's many a daughter
Singing her woes about the men she's lost
Whose carcasses have now become dust.

And so this is sung about the great deeds done at Da
Choca's hostel, and thus ends the tale.
Finis.

The Battle
of Airtech

Cath Airtig is preserved in *The Yellow Book of Lecan* and H.3.18 T.C.D. It appears to be the story that immediately follows *Bruiden Dá Choca* because it is prefaced with a reference to Cormac's death at the hostel. The Battle of Airtech is recorded in the *Annals of Tigernach* in the handwriting of Interpolator H, the same one involved with *Lebor Na hUidre: Cath Artig for coiced Ol nEcmacht la Cuscraid mac Conchobair. Cuscraid obit la Mac Cecht. Mac Cecht do thutim fo chetóir la Conall Cernach ic Cranaig Maic Cecht. Glasni mac Conchobair .ix. annis regnauit.* This translation was taken from *The Yellow Book of Lecan.*

AFTER CORMAC FELL AT Da Choca's hostel, a meeting was held at Ulster, and the warriors placed the kingdom under the control of Conall Cernach and offered him the throne.

"No," said Conall, "I won't take it. Give it to my foster-son, Cuscraid the Stammerer of Macha. I am getting on in years and don't have the skill to govern or the strength in my good right hand that I once had. You need someone who will go with you into whatever trouble comes, and for that you need someone like Cuscraid, who would make a good battle-chief." He grinned sourly. "I've got a hunch that bad things are still ahead for Ulster."

They took his advice and made Cuscraid king, and he bound them to him with pledges. Then Conall spoke these words in lamentation of Conchobor and by way of giving instruction to Cuscraid:

> "Great sorrow has racked me,
> A great misty grief wastes me,
> For I feel the loss of my king
> Whose judgment would always bring
> Fair meaning to all. I speak now
> Of comely Conchobor and how
> He was the famous king of Emain.
> My words are not good enough to bring
> Wisdom here; they are a woman's words.
> I am useless now, after my great sword
> Brought great deeds to Emain's glory.
> The veins in my body aren't the story
> That once they were. Then my deeds
> Rang from the rafters! Great deeds!
> But that is long gone, now
> And I have nothing to show how
> I came to have the honor on my name.
> Listen, my friends, if it is all the same
> To you, I would rather my death-rattle
> Come loud in some great battle,
> Surrounded by my comrades and not
> Raw striplings from whose noses snot

Still drips. I am sickly, wounded,
Yet I am still to Ulster bound.

So I say to you, rise up, Cuscraid,
And follow the path that stayed
Your father. Let your meetings
Be frequent and your seatings
Be fair upon your lords' rights
To their borders. Keep in sight
Always the law of hospitality
And bestow upon guests carefully
The horses, jewels, and cows
To which they're entitled. Follow
The law carefully and keep your word
For there's nothing worse than false words.
Keep your rule always consolidated
So your people's fruits aren't dated
By neglect and become very skilled
In every tongue like fields tilled
By wise men. Be just, be righteous,
And let all speak the same. Thus,
You will always be admired well.
In mead court do not let others kill
Others. Reward the good and
Punish the evil. Destroy criminal bands
And always support your lands
From roving foreign bands."

Now Cuscraid the Stammerer of Macha Mac Conchobor divided his land among the children of the Red Branch and the rest of Conchobor's children in this manner:

To Conall Cernach, all from the strand of Inber Colpa to Coba, that is Caille Conaill Cernaigh its name hereafter

To Furbaide Fer Bend, the two Teffas, that is northern
Teffa and southern Teffa
To Glaisne Mac Conchobor, Fir Maland and Fianclair
na Bredcha
To Irial Glunmar, Goll and Irgoll, that is, the land of
Gerg Mac Faeburdel
To Follamain Mac Conchobor, Farney
To Maine Mac Conchobor, Loch Erne
To Lama Mac Conchobor, Lamraige
To Benda Mac Conchobor, Corcu Oche
To Conain Mac Conchobor, the Mugdorna
To Fiacha Mac Conchobor, Ailechthir.

The land of Dubthach Doeltengthach and his two sons,
namely Corc and Conroi, he gave Tir Liath Maini and the place
where Loch Neagh is today.

In this way, he distributed a fifth of Ulster to the clan of
Conchobor as was fitting.

The nobles of Ulster said that it would be a good thing if
Fergus Mac Róich would be allowed to come back from his
exile and peace be made with him. That, they said, would make
the Red Branch far stronger against their enemies, for although
there was frost in Fergus's hair, he still had a mighty arm.
Besides, they knew that Ulster's enemies were plotting against
them and their borders were already being raided on all sides.

Fergus heard about this and came back to Ulster and made
peace with them, joining a covenant with Cuscraid.

Maeve, however, tried to stop Fergus from going back to
Ulster and offered to pay him the honor-price of his sons who
fell at Da Choca's Hostel, namely Illand the Fair and Fiachna
One-eyed. Besides, Maeve had become very fond of the old
stallion when he trotted in her bed.

Fergus went east toward Ulster with a great retinue and
his wife, Flidais.[1] The land Fergus asked for was the land that

once belonged to Sualdam Mac Roch and Cúchulainn. This was Crich Cuailngé Mag Murthemne and Crich Rois and Brug Malcmairi. There was no problem with this, and the land was given to him, and he lived happily there until Flidais died on the Strand of Baile Mac Buain.[2] Then Fergus went back to Ailill and Maeve, for he no longer liked it in Ulster. There he met his death, through the one act of jealousy of Ailill Mac Mata.

Now a great dispute arose between Ailill and Maeve and Conchobor's province in regards to Crich Maland, which had been given to Conchobor in reparation for those slain around him on the great cattle-raid of Cooley. Maeve said that she had given the land only to Conchobor, but the Ulster warriors refused to give it up unless she could wrench it from them in battle.

And this is why the terrible and bloody war was waged between them. Many hard battles came and many gigantic deeds were performed and many swift-slaying heroes fell in that war. Because of that war, many Ulster warriors fell around Cuscraid and Conall Cernach and Amergin Mac Ecetsalach the Smith and around Follamain and Furbaide, two sons of Conchobor. This war brought about the death of Cet Mac Magu and Doiche and Mug Corb and Scannal and Ailill, the sons of Magu, and Ailill Mac Cet and Cet himself and Belchu of Breifne along with all his sons.

And that brought about the raising of the great army by Ulster in the fifth of Ol Egmacht, and with that army they raged the land before them until they came to the land of Airtech Uchtlethan[3] Mac Tomanten Mac Fer Choga of the Fir Domnann.

The three Connachts—Fir Domnann, Fir Craibe, and Tuatha Taiden—came together. Now these were the war lords of the Fir Ol Egmacht: Mac Cecht and huge Cet Mac Magu and Maine Aithremail and Sanb Mac Cet and Maine Maithremail and Ailill of Breifne and Loingsech of Loch Ri and Aengus, king of the Fir Bolg, and Fer Deiched Mac Ferdiad, Daman's son, and Aengus Mac Ailill Find and Mata Mac Goll Eilech and Troga and Flaithri, two sons of Fraech, Fidach's son, and Imchad Mac Lugaid.

The war lords of Ulster were Conall Cernach Mac Amirgin and Amirgin the Poet and the sons of Conchobor and Fiac Mac Fergus and Fergus Mac Eirrge Echbel and Sothach Mac Sencha, Ailill's son, and Fiachu Mac Laidgen, king of the Fir Bolg, and Guala Mac Gerg Mac Faeburdel.

The Fir Ol Egnacht refused to allow Ailill and Maeve to go into battle with them. They formed large battalions and went forward, meeting the enemy with a loud crashing of shields, and hard hacking hardily followed in the harsh havoc between Fir Ol Egnacht and the Ulster warriors. A loud uproar came between them, and men bawled savagely; groans and lamentations followed the clashing and clatter of swords, the whiz and whir of spears and arrows; the roar and rage of large stones stunning shields of war hounds and veterans. Never have there been heroes like that with such strength and skill and bravery. The earth shook under their stamping feet as every man fought in that battle.

Conall Cernach slew Ailill Ardagach and Scannal, the sons of Magu, and Ailill of Breifne and Loingsech of Loch Ri. Cruscraid Mac Conchobor slew Aengus, king of the Fer Bolg, and Fer Teiched Mac Ferdiad. Amirgin Mac Ec Et Salach the Smith slew Aengus Mac Ailill Find. Irial Clunmer Mac Conall Cernach slew Mata Mac Goll Eilech.

Troga and Flaithri, two sons of Fraech, Fidach's son, were slain by Glaisne Mac Conchobor, while Guala Mac Gerg killed Imchad Mac Lugaid.

But many Ulster heroes also fell in that battle. Fiachu and Conain were slain by Cet, and Mac Cecht Corc Mac Dubthach Doeltengthach[4] fell by Sanb Mac Cet. Grala Mac Gorg was slain by Maine Aithremail. Two fell by each other's hands: Benna

Mac Conchobor and Cet, the son of Ailill and Maeve.

But the battle went against the Fir Ol Egmacht from the force of the charge of the Ulster warriors. Amirgin chased the two Eithiars, sons of Fergus Mac Róich, until they fell by each other at Imlech Ai. After that, the Fir Ol Egmach raised a red wall in front of the Ulster warriors, who were forbidden to go over a red wall.

In the Battle of Airtech, the Fir Domnann were finally destroyed. Then the Ulster warriors returned home with great spoil.

Finit.

Fragments

the spoils

IT WAS A CUSTOM with the Ulster warriors that after the gathering of trophies they would meet in the Great Hall of the Red Branch. The point of the tongue of every man they had slain would be brought in a pouch with them. Sometimes, they would bring the tongues of the cattle to multiply the trophies there, and everyone would produce his trophy, but only in turn. And this is how they would do it: with their swords they had used to make their trophies upon their thighs, for if they had made a false collection, then their own swords would turn against them. This was so as sometimes devilkins would speak against them from their arms so their arms became their safe-guards.

Lebor na hUidre, p. 43a

ımbas ꝼoꞆosnaı

THEN THEY [THE DRUIDS] would make a bull-feast so that they might know to whom the kingdom should be given.

They made the bull-feast by killing a white bull, and one man was selected to eat of the bull's flesh and to drink of his blood. Then he would be sung to sleep while his belly was full, and four Druids would chant the *imbas forosnai* over him, which would cause him to see in a vision that man who would be king and what his shape and description were and the kind of work the man was doing at the time of the vision.

And then the man would awake from his dream and explain to the others waiting patiently upon his words to whom the crown should be given. This man would be a young champion, noble, strong, with two red girdles over him, and he stood above the pillow upon which a man lay sick in Emain Macha.

Lebor na hUidre, p. 46, the *Imbas forosnai,* Cormac's glossary

on doomsday

NOW THE UNIVERSAL RESURRECTION that shall be there on Doomsday is not the same as the resurrection called in the authority *praestigia,* that is a phantasmal resurrection like pythonishm. Nor is it the same as the resurrection called *revolutio,* which is the transmutation of the soul into various bodies after the example of the transmuted ones. Nor the resurrection called *metafomatio* nor the transformation according to the example of the werewolves. Nor is it the same as the resurrection called *subductio* as those who die prematurely. Nor the resurrection called *suscitatio* nor the revival of dead persons through a miracle after the example of Lazarus.

Lebor na hUidre, p. 36b

on werewolves

THE DESCENDANTS OF THE WOLF are in Ossory. They have a wonderful ability to transform themselves into wolves and travel thusly as wolves. If they happen to be killed with flesh in their mouths, it is the same condition that the bodies out of which they have come will be found; and they command their families never to remove their bodies, because if they are moved, they could never again return to them.

The Book of Glenn-dá-locha (lost),
cited in *The Book of Ballimote,* 140b,
and printed in the *Irish Nennius,* p. 204

the exile of fergus mac róich

This text is found only in *The Book of Leinster,* and we have only the beginning. It appears, however, that it is a tale similar to others where the men at a banquet are challenged to a grotesque game by a supernatural power. I suggest that the parts lost probably emulated the appearance of Lugh to the *Tuatha Dé Danann* in one of the three sorrows of storytelling, *The Exile of the Sons of Tuirenn,* and Cúrói in *Fled Bricrend.* This does not include the reason generally given for Fergus being in exile, which is found in the story of Deirdre and is known as another sorrow: *The Exile of the Sons of Uisneach.*

Here follows the cause of the exile of Fergus Mac Róich:

THE ULSTER MEN WERE FEASTING at Emain Macha at one of the three fairest feasts that were held in the land: the feast of Tara, the feast of Macha, and the feast in the west of Connacht. Sixty various arts were to be used in each of them.[1]

One day while the Ulster men were feasting—with the notable absence of Fergus and Dubthach Doel[2]—a pair of youthful warriors entered. They appeared to be two champions, each with jet black hair that stood like a stubble field from their heads. If someone threw apples at the head of each, the apples would have been impaled upon the stalks of the wiry hairs. Their two eyes were as large as baskets that would hold a dozen eggs. Their faces were shaped like eggs, but they were jet black, with knees as broad as a calf caldron. Each of their shinbones could have provided enough salt for a sack, and it would have taken half an oxhide to shoe each of their feet. Around them they wore hairy garments closed with white clasps and each hair on those garments would have impaled a child of seven. Around the neck of each they carried a shield as broad as a vat bottom. The shield-boss could have been used as a sheep kettle. In the hand of each was an engraved war javelin. They seemed to have lived many years in smoke as their faces were as black as a caldron's bottom and their teeth were as white as snow and as large as a camel's teeth.[3] Their swords looked as big as weaver's beams. They carried a stench with them as if they had spent many years under the earth. The nose of each was a one-edged knife and as broad as three fists. When they left, the rushes would be white again.[4]

When they came to Emain Macha, the porter rushed to greet them. "How should I announce you?" he asked.

"As we are," they said.

"No one comes to Emain Macha without expertise in some art," said the porter. "Which have you?"

"Not a single art," they said.

"Tell me something," the porter said.

"First, we are able to fight with any man. We are good at the trencher board. We can never miss with the cast of a stone or fork and always find firewood."[5]

"I shall go and relate this," said the porter.

He went into the Great Hall and announced them along with a description of their form and appearance and art.

"Let them be admitted" [text missing].

Findglais

The following is taken from the *Rennes Dindsenchas*:

Bláthnat, daughter of Menn, king of the Men of Falga, wife of Cúroi Mac Dáre, was Cúchulainn's lover. 'Tis she who promised that Cúchulainn should come to her on All-Hallows Eve and take vengeance for Eochaid Horsemouth's cows and for the caldron and for the shaving of Cúchulainn by Cúroi's sword and after when Cúroi smeared Cúchulainn's head with cow shit. And she told Cúroi to gather the clans of Deda to build his fortress in a single day and to do this they should bring every pillar-stone in the land. So Cúroi was left all alone. That was the plan that Bláthnat and Cúchulainn had made between them. They would let the milking of the cows flow with the current so that the stream as it came toward Cúchulainn and his Ulster warriors would be white. Hence, Findglais[6] is its name. And after that, they killed Cúroi and wrecked the town and carried Bláthnat off with them to Emain Macha.

Loch Léin

Lén Línfiaclach Mac Bolgac Mac Bannach Mac Glammac Mac Gomer was the craftsman of Sídhe Buidb.[7] He lived in the lake and made bright vessels for Fand, the daughter of Flidais. Every night, after quitting work, he would throw his anvil east away to Indeóin na nDese[8] as far as the grave mound, and three showers it used to cast upon the holy grave: a shower of water, a shower of fire, and a shower of purple gems. The same thing Nemannach practiced when beating out the cup of Conchobor Mac Nessa in the north. Whence Loch Léin is named.

carn furbaidi and ethne

Ethne, daughter of Eochaid Feidlech, wife of Conchobor Mac Nessa, was Furbaide's mother. Now her wizard had told Clothru, another daughter of Eochaid Feidlech's, that her sister's son would kill her. So Ethne (who was then carrying Furbaide) went from the east to Cruachan to give birth. Then Lugaid of the Red Stripes—he was a son of Conchobor—went ahead of Ethne and drowned her in the river that bears her name. And after she had drowned, he cut Furbaide Fer-benn[9] out of her womb. Furbaide was seventeen years old at the Driving of the Kine of Cuailngé. Then Furbaide went to avenge his mother, and Clothru fell by his hands. So Lugaid went in pursuit of Furbaide and killed him on the top of Sliab Uillenn, and there was built his cairn of a stone for each man who accompanied Lugaid. Carn Furbaidi and Ethne are therefore named. Sliab Uillenn, however, is named from Uillenn Red-edge, son of Find Hua Baiscni, who was killed there.

crac lethdeirg

Lethdeirg[10] was the daughter of Conchobor Mac Nessa and the wife of Tromdae Mac Calatrom, who gave love in a dream to Fothad Cananne. So he and three men, Fethlenn Mac Fidrue and Lurga Mac Luath and Eirisnech Mac Inmaisech, came to her. Fothad was the fourth, but it was after the slaying of Ailill Mac Eogan. Briccen Mac Tuinde[11] gave them a boat. So Tromda was killed, and his wife was taken from him to the crag. That is how Carrac Lethdeirg was named.

ard macha

ᗰACHA, THE WIFE OF Nemed Mac Agnoman, died there and was buried, and it is the twelfth plain that was cleared by Nemed, who bestowed it upon his wife so that it might bear her name. That is how Mag Macha got its name.

Macha, the daughter of Aed the Red, Mac Badburn—'tis by her Emain was marked out—was buried there when Rechtaid of the Red Forearm killed her. To lament her, Oenach Macha[12] was made. That is how Mag Macha got its name.

Macha, the wife of Crund [sic] Mac Agnoman, went to race against Conchobor's horses, for her husband had said that his wife was faster than the horses. She was big with child and asked for time until her womb fell [sic], but this was not granted to her. So then the race was run and she was the fastest. And she said that the Ulster men would suffer feebleness of childbed whenever need should come to them. That is why the Ulster men suffered feebleness for the space of a *nomad* (an obscure length of time) from the reign of Conchobor to the reign of Mál Mac Rochraide.[13] And men say that she was Grían Banchure,[14] who was the daughter of Mider of Brí Léith. And after this she died, and her tomb was raised on Ard Macha and a great lamentation was made. Her headstone was planted there, and that is how Ard Macha[15] got its name.

Lech oenfir aife

Oenfer Aife Mac Cúchulainn was sent by his mother from Scotland and came over sea to Baile's Strand or to Littlefrd in Conailli Murthemni. There he met with his father, and his father asked him who he was. He would not declare his name. He had completed nine years. So father and son attacked each other, and the son fell. Then the son said, " 'Tis hard that I should speak what is or what turns." Then Cúchulainn said, "Aife's only man, though 'twas meet for him to be hidden in his patrimony during my time I shall ever remember my fight with Aife's only man."

Cúchulainn took him away and buried him at Oenach Airbi Rofir, and sang his dirge. Hence Lect Oenfir Aife.[16]

carn máil

The Lord's Cairn in Mag Ulad or Lugaid's Cairn, how did they come to be called? Not hard to say. Lord Lugaid with the crews of seven ships was exiled from Erin to Alba. But he returned with a fleet of Scottish boats, and they gave battle to the Ulster warriors and routed them. The cairn was made up of a stone for every man who came with Lugaid, and it was upon this that Lugaid stood when he gave battle.

sliab callann

Callann was the hound who guarded the herd of Buide Mac Becan Mac Forgamain. When the Donn Cuailngé started to bull the dry cows around him before it was time, he and the hound contended for the cows, and by the bull the hound was slain. Or it may be that the hound fought at the taking of the drove, whereupon a mighty death blow was inflicted upon him by every one or by the Donn Cuailngé at the mountain. That is why Sliab Callann has its name.

Now this is the true account of that hound. He was a pup of Celtchar's hound Dael. He was found in the skull of Conganchnes, for there were three hounds in that skull: the hound that Culan the Craftsman had, the hound that Celtchar had, and the hound that Mac Dá Thó had. Speckled and black and gray were their colors.

ınbeR cıchmaını

LICHMAINE ANDOE, THE SEVENTH SON of Ailill and Maeve, was slain by Fergna Mac Findcháime over a boat on the strand.

Or it was Cichmuine Mac Ailill Find who was killed by fishermen casting their nets on the inver. This is how Inber Cichmaini was named.

móın cıRe náıR

NÁR MAC FINDCHAD MAC CONALL CERNACH was slain there by Etsine the Championess after he had killed her two birds at Snám dá Én on the Shannon. This is how Snám dá Én[17] got its name and Móin Tire Náir was named.

fích mbuana

BUAN, THE DAUGHTER OF SAMAERA, gave her heart to Cúchulainn when the champions, even Loeguire the Gifted, Conall Cernach, and Cúchulainn, went to contend for the champion's portion. For the award they traveled to Emain Macha and were sent to Ailill and Maeve. Ailill refused to choose and sent them on to Asaroe, to Samaera, and he judged that the portion should be given to Cúchulainn.

Then Conall and his charioteer Rathen went over Snám Rathin, and there Rathen was drowned. This is why Snám Rathin[18] got its name. Then Buan followed Cúchulainn on his chariot's trail as far as yon rock (Fích mBuana), and she leaped an awful leap after him and struck her head against a rock and died. This is why Fích mBuana[19] is named.

mag lena

LENA MAC ROED, THE SON of Mes Roeda, was the one who raised his grandfather Mac Dá Thó's pig, which he found in Daire Bainb in the eastern part of Bladma. It grew up with him until the end of seven years, when seven inches of fat were around its snout. When the Ulster men and the Connacht men went to Mac Dá Thó's feast, Maine Athrai, the wife of Mac Dá Thó, sent to Lena to ask for the pig to help his hospitality and offered fifty choice hogs in payment. Lena did not take them. Now one night, shortly before he delivered the pig to Mac Dá Thó, Lena took it to Dublais.[20] There he fell asleep, and the pig rooted a trench over him without his feeling it and he was smothered. Then he [*sic*] attacked the pig and the point of his sword killed it. Mac Dá Thó's swineherd came and took the pig to the feast, and there on the plain he set Lena's grave and headstone. That is why Mag Lena is named.

ʒáirech

From the *gáir*[21] which the youths of Emain Macha made around their foster-brother Cúchulainn as he lay in his bloody bed [fragment literal]. Chariots and horses and weapons and the stones of the mires answered it on this side and that around the ford so that they became like red-hot metal. Whence Gáirech is named.

ınber ðicni

Bicne, Conall Cernach's servant, died there while driving the cattle of Fráech Mac Idath that were brought out of Scotland after the great *murrain* that came in the time of Bres-al Bó-dibad Mac Rudraige or in the time of Bresal Brecc. There died Bicne Mac Loegaire smothered in a quicksand while driving them ashore, and it is there that the cattle shed their horns in grief for him. This is how Beenchor Ulad[22] is named and Inber Bicni[23] is named.

druim suamaich

Suamach Mac Samguba was the storyteller and foster-father of Cormac Conloinges Mac Conchobor, and Cormac's foster-mother was Caindlech, the daughter of Geim Gelta Mac Rodba Mac Tuach Tuile of the clan of Conall Hornskin. When

Cormac went eastward from Cruachan Ai to seize the crown of Ulster, his foster-father stayed behind him because he knew that his fosterling would fall and never be king of Ulster. Suamach followed his fosterling, forbidding him to go on that journey. When he came to the Hill of the Tears—that is, the tears of the Dagda lamenting his son Cermait—there he saw the blaze of the wrecking of Da Choca's hostel. Suamach died forthwith, and Caindlech died on Ard Caindlech. This is how they were named.

SRUB ÓRAIN

LÚCHULAINN PURSUED THE RAVEN FLOCK from Dundalk, and in every border he crossed, he killed one of the birds down to the last raven. That one was destroyed by him at Redg, and at Ramann he cut off its head from it and bathed his hands in its blood and said, when putting the head on the crag, "A raven's stream there."

A hundred fifty was their number, and seven hand-lengths were in each bird's bill and seven cubits around their necks. They had thick bodies and thick feet, which they used to swim the sea. Of whom Srub Brain is said.

Instructions to Princes

According to tradition, the *Tecosca Senbriathra Fithail* was spoken by Cúchulainn while he was lying upon his bed, suffering from the "wasting sickness." This advice was reportedly given to Lugaid. Following the words of Cúchulainn are the proverbs given by other individuals.

part 1

THE BEGINNING OF STRIFE is quarreling.
The beginning of refusal is lending.
The beginning of slander is reproaching.
The beginning of knowledge is inquiry.
The beginning of nobility is honor-price.
The beginning of wisdom is humility.
The beginning of prosperity is prudence.
The beginning of hospitality is plenty.

The beginning of devotion is imitation.
The beginning of wisdom is gentleness.
The beginning of evil is proud works.
The beginning of peace is well-speaking.
The beginning of wretchedness is a bad bed.
The beginning of withering is sickness.
The beginning of wretchedness is melancholy.
The beginning of sickness is laziness.
The beginning of a downfall is a lying.
The beginning of fortune is a good wife.
The beginning of misfortune is a bad wife.
The beginning of evil counsel is irresolution.
The beginning of good is moderation.
Liberality begets eating.
Goodwill begets giving.
Intelligence begets good looks.
Folly begets violence.
Violence begets greater violence.
Hate begets reproach.
Adultery begets contempt.
Laziness begets prophesying.
Humility begets great satisfaction.
Overbearing begets displeasure.
Ale begets reputation.
A wrathful person begets offending.
Beer begets bragging.
Thievery begets uneasiness.
Desire begets perseverance.
Wisdom begets respect.
Folly begets battles.
Abundance begets eating.
Force begets strife.
An evil tongue begets judgment.
A sweet tongue begets judgment.

Joy begets speech.
Poverty begets distress.
Sorrow begets quarrelsomeness.
A battle begets keening.
A famous person begets good treatment.
Wrangling begets misery.
Abundance begets content.
Want begets industry.
Freedom begets aggressiveness.
Slavery begets distress.
A violent person begets activity.
Be cautious that you may not be encumbered with debts.
Be prudent that you may not be raided.
Be compliant that you may be well-loved.
Be liberal that you may be illustrious.
Be generous that you may be honorable.
Be grateful that you may be bountiful.
Be humble that you may be exalted.
Art is better than a heritage.
The whip is better than lying.
Badly armed is better than unarmed.
A conference is better than strife.
A bog is better than living in the same house.
It is better to be a slave than to slave.
A plain is better than a great mountain.
Being heirless is better than great fertility.
A people is better than a dowry.
Flight is better than standing still.
Self-importance is better than self-depreciation.
Certainty is better than promises.
Good fortune is better than wisdom.
An old debt is better than old enmity.
Peace is better than easy warfare.
A good wife is better than good children.

Sleep is better than bitterness.
A heart is better than jaws.
A friend is better than ale.
Intelligence is better than good looks.
Death is better than grief.
A gift is better than the usual.
Recompense is better than refusal.
Due consideration is better than desire.
Confirming is better than seeing.
Wealth is better than servitude.
Confirming is better than uncertainty.
A part is better than destroying.
Graciousness is better than obedience.
A period of time is better than securities.
Generosity is better than great wisdom.
Reproaching is better than assaulting.
Generosity is better than blistering cheeks.
To act is better than to know how.
Wisdom is better than weapons.
Maintenance is better than plenty.
A grip is better than a breaking.
Speed is better than haste.
Work is better than play.
Industry is better than handwork.
A cow is better than a year.
Strength is better than battles.
Death is better than an everlasting blemish.
Gratitude is better than taking away.
A little is better than a refusal.
Lastingness is better than pleasure.
A bad trade is better than idleness.
Prowess at arms is better than a reputation.
True love is better than a hereditary right.
Prosperity is better than a victory.

Work is better than sullenness.

To have an eye is better than to have one put out.

Wisdom merits respect.

Righteousness merits help.

Falsehood merits rebuking.

Perversity merits chastisement.

Quarreling merits separating.

Wages merit service.

A tutor merits his following.

A contract merits security.

Wages merit being protected.

Testimony merits favorable judgment.

A tenant merits his returns.

Good merits increase.

Refusal merits reproof.

A blind person merits protection.

A meeting merits proclaiming.

A young man merits training.

Fosterage merits annulling.

A master merits good maintenance.

An absconder merits proclaiming.

A transaction merits settlement.

A father merits good maintenance.

A mother merits tenderness.

A madman merits instruction.

A sick person merits attention.

A wrong merits time.

Developing merits possession in perpetuity.

A contract merits settlement.

Seventeen signs of good pleading: coloring of narratives, confusion of words, garment of eloquence, intelligent retaliation, steadfast speech, renouncing of ignorance, reflecting upon knowledge, knowledge of sharpness, keen pleading.

Seventeen signs of bad pleading: contending against knowledge, pleading in bad language, much reviling, contending without proofs, slowness of speech, praise of oneself, welcome to a case of pleading, judging against high persons, mumbling speech, making free with wisdom, uncertain proofs, despising books, turning against legal precedents, loudness of voice, unsteadiness of pleading, angry pleading, provoking the multitude, contending with everybody.

part II

From Cormac and Cairbre:

I T IS A REQUEST of mine that I should know how I should behave:
among the wise and the foolish
among the known and the unknown
among the old and the young
among the learned and the ignorant.
Be not too wise, be not too foolish.
Be not too proud, be not too modest.
Be not too haughty, be not too humble.
Be not too talkative, be not too silent.
Be not too hard, be not too easy.
If you are too wise, too much will be expected of you.
If you are too foolish, you will be deceived.
If you are too proud, you will be shown no thanks.
If you are too humble, you will be without honor.
If you are too talkative, you will be unnoticed.
If you are too silent, you will not be seen.
If you are too hard, you will be broken.
If you are too easy, you will be broken.
Be wise against wisdom, lest someone deceive you in wisdom.
Be proud against pride, lest land be taken from you.

Be humble against humility, when your will is being done.
Be eloquent against eloquence when a legal battle is undertaken.
Be hard against hardness, lest someone neglect you.
Be gentle against gentleness, lest everyone deceive you.
Everyone is wise until he sells his heritage.
Everyone is foolish until he buys land.
Everyone is a landholder until it comes to debts.
Everyone is a law giver until it comes to children.
Everyone is too ferocious until it comes to piety.
Everyone is fair-famed until he is satirized.
Everyone is a hospitaller until he refuses to entertain.
Everyone is a roving champion until he comes to husbandry.
Everyone is a hireling until he settles in a dwelling.
Everyone is sane until he is drunk.
Everyone is reasonable until he is angry.
Everyone is decorous until he is cold.
Everyone is calm until he undertakes fosterage.
Everyone is a counselor until he begins to quarrel.
Everyone is joyful until he becomes unfortunate.
Everyone is bold until he meets with refusal.
Everyone is a freeman until he is robbed.
Everyone is a pedestrian until he becomes a charioteer.
Every fortunate person is fair.
Every unfortunate person is ugly.
The sweetest part of every meal is its first part.
The sweetest of all music is the music of slaughter.
The sweetest part of all ale is its first draft.

part iii

WHAT SHALL I FOUND my husbandry on? said his son
to Fithal.
Not hard to say, said Fithal. On a keystone.
What is the keystone of husbandry? said the son.

374 RANDY LEE EICKHOFF

Not hard to say, said Fithal, a good wife.

How shall I recognize a good woman?

Not hard to say: from her figure and from her good behavior.

Do not marry the slender short one with curling hair.

Do not marry the fat short one.

Do not marry the fair tall one.

Do not marry the dark-limbed unmanageable one.

Do not marry the dun-colored yellow one.

Do not marry the black swarthy one.

Do not marry the white-faced boisterous one.

Do not marry the slender prolific one who is lewd and jealous.

Do not marry the evil-counseling evil-speaking one, whatever one you do marry.

A question: What woman shall I marry? said the son.

Not hard to say, said Fithal, if you can obtain them:

the tall, fair, very slender ones,

the pale, white, black-headed ones.

What is the best of women?

Not hard to say: a woman whom men have not known before you unless you are seen;

after that she is not given to them according to her nature and is not hidden from you upon having need of her.

What shall I do with them?

Take them in spite of their defects, whatever their form may be, said Fithal,

for no choice is made at all among them, if they are not taken in spite of their defects.

What is the worst of women?

Not hard to say: a prostitute.

What is worse than that?

Not hard to say: the man who takes her into the ale-house with his family.

What is worse than both of these?

Not hard to say: the son who is born between them.

Skillful women are honey-mouthed, bad women are given to trysting; ill-met are their sons: woe to him who has them!
He is not deserving, he does not uplift, he does not exalt.
For he will not be without guile and without dishonor.
Fifteen characteristics of good women: discretion, prudence, modesty, humility, beauty, gentleness, wealth, nobility, good Gaelic or well-spokenness, delicacy, mildness, honesty, wisdom, purity, integrity.
Fifteen characteristics of bad women: wretchedness, stinginess, vanity, talkativeness, laziness, indolence, noisiness, hatefulness, avarice, visiting, thievery, keeping trysts, lustfuness, folly, treachery.

pARC IV

Here are the words of Flann Fína Mac Oswy:
Forsaking begets accusation.
Love begets words.
A poet gets rewards.
Refusal begets reproof.
Stinginess begets avarice.
Wisdom begets honor.
Humility begets gentleness.
Giving in charge begets strife.
The greedy person begets treasures.
Complacency begets dispossession.
Strife begets a criminal.
A fair tongue begets mediation.
Nobility begets wisdom.
Righteousness begets aid.
Good begets its praise.
Being lazy as a cow begets destruction.
Husbandry begets produce.

A wrathful person begets a disturbance.
A quarrelsome person begets a beating.
Pottage begets lasting strength.
Opposition begets rebellion.
A land begets a champion.
Reading begets books.
A high-spirited person begets hatred.
Happiness begets generosity.
An accomplished person begets nobility.
A base person begets refusal.
A cow begets its fodder.
Life begets sorrows.
A bad woman begets refusal.
A humble person begets dignity.
An arrogant person begets violence.
A blow begets violence.
A good deed begets virtue.
A poor man gets his food.
A hospitaller begets service.
Wisdom vanquishes valor.
Arrogance merits forgetting.
A foster-father merits respect.
A lunatic merits protection.
A disloyal person merits being put in chains.
Cotenancy merits exchanging.
A herald merits proclaiming.
A rich man merits nobility.
Perhaps merits a promise.
Maybe merits a denial upon oath.

parc v

From the mouth of Cormac, *Agallam Cormaic 7 Cairpre,* in *The Book of Uí Maine.*

A SIGN OF SLEEPING is lying down.
A sign of an old law is an old song.
A sign of thirst is a drink.
A sign of anger is hatred.
A sign of a home-thrust is a killing.
A sign of death is fear.
A sign of lust is boldness.
A sign of discretion is silence.
A sign of indiscretion is much talking.
A sign of right is custom.
A sign of hardness is niggardliness.
A sign of chastity is unadornedness.
A sign of folly is the conversation of women. [*Descaid báisi banchobra.*]
A sign of madness is loud laughter.
A sign of greed is watchfulness.
A sign of love is long-looking.
A sign of treachery is whispering.
A sign of strife is quarreling.
A sign of happiness is health.
A sign of sorrow is constant affliction.
A sign of ill-breeding is churlishness.
A sign of ignorance is quarreling.
A sign of shamelessness is ignorance.
A sign of evil is pride.
Fithel dixit

The beginning of misfortune is tipsiness.
The beginning of fortune is soberness.
It is better to be healthy than to be glutted.
Happiness is better than riches.
A blessing is better than vengeance.
Dignity is better than gluttony.
Truth is better than virtues.
Knowledge is better than many things.
Many things are better than contract-binding.
Welcome is better than reproach.
Wealth is better than great learning.
Lastingness is better than riches.
Sufficiency is better than a multitude.
Prosperity is better than a wife.
Hosting is better than settling down.
A following is better than cattle.
Supremacy is better than violence.
Hospitality is better than cattle.
Cattle are better than a promise.
A small family is better than much fostering.
Forethought is better than afterthought.
Wisdom is better than enemies [weapons].
Land is better than heritage.
A heritage is better than land.
A chariot is better than haste.
Haste is better than unsteadiness.
Uncertainty is better than misfortune.
Life is better than victories.
Victory is better than warfare.
Man is better than the creatures.
A bad workman is better than good materials.
Property rights are better than exile.
A prince is better than possessions.
Fair increase is better than crimes.

Activity is better than sickness.

Play is better than roughness.

Better an insult than blistering it.

Fame is better than deeds.

Security is better than bad contracts.

A company following is better than idleness.

Honor is better than food.

Prepared is better than unequipped.

Toward the warlike man peace is observed, that is a proverb that cannot be undone.

A fair reputation is better than oppression.

Precious treasures are better than [cucilche].

Prosperity is better than superfluity.

Respect is better than wealth.

Sloth is better than sickness.

A half is better than complete refusal.

The heath is better than a heritage.

It is better to be willing than to be obliged.

A cow cooked is better than a cow in milk.

A ham is better than a morsel for a dog.

Patience is better than quarreling.

Wealth is better than poverty.

Graciousness is better than regulation.

Good manners are better than awkwardness.

christian addendum

A good gift is knowledge.

It makes a king of a poor man.

It makes a landowner of a landless man.

It makes a good family of a bad family.

It makes a wise man of a fool.

Good its beginning, better its end.

Venerable in this world, precious in the other world.
It is not despairing concerning the end.
A bad gift is secularism.
Not renowned and despised is bad.
Active and transitory its good.
Its living are transfixed, its dead are hell-bound.
The father has not bade a gift of his son.
Woe to him who has the gift of secularism if great repentance
does not come.

Notes

the beginning of emain macha

1. The Red Man's Waterfall.

2. This appears to be a reference to one of the old stories in which Macha had red hair. The suggestion also seems to reflect Maeve of Cruachan, who likewise appears to have had red hair. Each becomes associated with fertility symbols.

3. The Brehon Laws were quite specific that a woman could not be the ruler over men. In fact, there were no provisions for queens as such, although some kings, most notably Ailill of Connacht, granted equal rights of command to their wives. Consequently, Maeve is often referred to as Queen Maeve although technically she did not have any right to the title.

4. Although this detail appears at first to be only a reference point, its importance cannot be ignored. Corann is in County Sligo, and it was on the banks of the river Unius that the Mórrígan (Macha becomes a part of the Mórrígan, the trium war goddess along with Mórrígan and Badb) met the Dagda (king of the gods) where she was washing herself with one foot on the south bank of the Unius and the other on the north. They mated over water, this being part of an ancient fertility ritual. After making love, the Mórrígan told the Dagda about the second battle of Mag Tuired. She ordered him to bring the skilled men to meet her at the river. The Dagda did this, and the Mórrígan killed Indech, a Fomorian who had opposed the *Tuatha Dé Danann*, and gave handfuls of his blood to the warriors. Then she went into battle with Badb and Macha, and together they brought down "a cloud of mist and a furious rain of fire and red blood onto the heads of the warriors." It was after this battle that she prophesied the end of the world:

> No more will I see a world more dear
> To me than this one now here.
> Summer will come but without
> Flowers, and kinsmen will clout
> Kinsmen for lack of milk.
> Wanton women wearing silk
> Dresses will bare their breasts
> To any who ask. Men contest
> Others without valor

> And will be led by dour
> Men who are not kings.
> An evil time rings!
>
> *Cath Dédenach Maige Tuired*

This seems to suggest that the beginning of the end is seen with the death of Díthorba. As this event marks the end of the second seventh rule, it appears that Macha, by establishing the full Ulster rule, inevitably marks the beginning of its end as well. In each beginning we will find the end of each.

5. Here we have another reference to the theme of the old hag found throughout Early Irish literature. This seems to be the source of the famous "washer at the ford," in which a warrior who sees an old hag washing clothes at the ford of a river knows he is marked to die in battle. The most famous example of this theme is when Cúchulainn rides forth to meet Maeve's host in battle when she again threatens the borders of Ulster after losing in *Táin Bó Cuailnge*. This account can be found in *Aided Chon-Chulainn* or *Brislech Mór Maige Muirtheimne*. I have suggested before that this theme seems to be a foreshadowing of the figure offered in the great poem *Caillech Bérri (The Old Woman of Beare)*.

6. This old Anglo-Saxon word wouldn't have been used, but I use it here to express the drunken state into which the five sons have fallen. *Comhriachtain*: sexual intercourse; the suggestion is vulgar.

7. *Eó*: brooch; *muin*: neck; *eó-muin*: Emain Macha (the neck brooch of Macha).

the pangs of the ulaid

1. The mountains are not named in the story, but tradition places them as the Mountains of Mourne.

2. Turning right was the socially correct way to approach him. Had she turned left, it would have been construed as an insult.

3. Although the name of the king does not appear in this story, he is referred to as Conchobor in other tales that suggest an assōciation with Conchobor Mac Nessa.

4. The name means "Strange Son of Ocean." By this declaration, Macha has informed all there that they are dealing with a fate that is completely beyond their control.

the birth of conchobor the king

1. This is a strange request, but it does show the wisdom of Cathbad, who was quick to ensure that Nessa would be friends with him in addition to sharing his bed. This request also is in conflict with another story in which Nessa ensures that Conchobor will become king by talking Fergus Mac Róich into giving up his throne for a year to live with her as her husband. Cathbad was not dead at the time.

2. This is a strange comment for Nessa to make since her weapon is obviously there. The suggestion, I believe, is that she has lost her manly attributes and now must rely upon womanly cunning to get her way. It might be a reference to losing her virginity, which could suggest the sudden awareness of herself as a woman and not a man.

the tidings of conchobor mac nessa

1. The text reads "Muman," but a penciled side note by Whitely Stokes indicates it should be Ulad. There is a difficulty here in that Munster apparently is indicated later in the story by the same "Muman" reference. It would seem that there is a discrepancy in the manuscript, although no lacuna is evident. I suggest that "Ulster" should be read for this reference and that Nessa's tutoring was actually held in Munster instead, which would give some credence to the development of the story line.

2. There is a bit of discrepancy here in that not twenty-four individuals but only twelve are meant. The foster-father would also be responsible for tutoring his charge. The custom of fostering was highly favored during this period; having more than one father gave strength by uniting two houses or, in some instances, clans. Having twelve foster-fathers, Nessa could call upon the men of all twelve houses if she needed. Likewise each of these houses could call upon her—or Eochaid, in this instance—for help if they became victims of raids. Cattle raiding was customary throughout Ireland at this time since cattle were the mark of wealth. There seems to be a certain resemblance between how cattle were regarded in Ireland and how they were regarded in the Mithraic religious practice.

3. Women during this time had a degree of equality that was harshly subjugated when the missionaries or priests gained control of the land. The Brehon Laws did grant women certain rights against which the early church took a rigid stance, such as having a wife contract for a year and then being allowed to step away from the marriage without scandal. In addition, women usually received training similar to that of the men warriors, and it was not unknown for the early Gaels to have women in

their armies, as we can see from Caesar's *Commentaries* when he comments on how afraid his men were of the woman warrior known as Boadacia.

4. Munster was subdivided at this time. Two kings ruled under a third.

5. I interpret this word as "battalions."

6. This seems to be another error in the manuscript, for why would Nessa have started raiding into her father's territory? Perhaps it is simply a reference to a part of Ulster.

7. This statement is contradicted by *Aided Conchobuir*, where Conchobor was a much older man than Christ. Upon hearing how Christ was killed by crucifixion, Conchobor flew into a rage and was killed when his brain banged against the brain ball that had been lodged there in a battle. He had lived for five years after that incident and, given the time frame of the rest of the Ulster Cycle, it seems inconceivable that all of this could have occurred in thirty-six years. The genealogies also give Conchobor a much longer life span.

8. This is a contradiction of version two of the birth of Conchobor, in which Cathbad makes Nessa promise to love him always and always be his wife. It is also, however, an implied contradiction of this story, in which we have seen Nessa give birth to Conchobor and his name be given, at that time, as Conchobor Mac Cathbad—Conchobor the son of Cathbad. I can only suggest that this was one of those times when Nessa invoked her rights under the Brehon Laws to leave her husband. In later stories Cathbad is named not as a wizard but as a Druid or holy man of sorts, an adviser to Conchobor when Conchobor becomes the king of the Red Branch. This would be a natural association, similar to that in the Arthurian Tales when Merlin, the cousin of Arthur, becomes the adviser to Arthur when Arthur becomes the king. Mary Stewart suggests this in her Arthurian Tetralogy, where Merlin is the bastard son of Ambrosius, the older brother of Uther Pendragon. Upon the death of Ambrosius, Uther becomes king and impregnates Igraine, the mother of Arthur.

9. The suggestion here is that of a "wifely contract for a year." A wise man might look at this arrangement with a certain wariness, but we must remember that, despite the references to Christ in the text, these were pre-Christian times.

10. *bod*: Penis.

11. *Ard Ri,* also textual *ardrige*: High King. This seems odd, given the Anglo-Saxon understanding of a king and his rule, but kings in Ireland during this time were more or less elected by the dominant clan and the other clans who owed it allegiance.

12. This was an ancient practice among the Celts. The purpose did, of course, unite the king with all of the landowners (land barons, lords) through a rather pagan observance of matrimony and marriage, but as the king was regarded as a direct link between earth and the gods, such sexual behavior suggested that the woman, "the newly plowed field," would be fertile and bring forth children to her husband. This practice nearly causes the wreckage of the Red Branch when the warriors insist that Cúchulainn's wife, Emer, spend the first night of their marriage in Conchobor's bed and Cúchulainn nearly goes berserk at the thought of his wife having sexual congress with the king. As Cúchulainn has claimed he will marry only a woman who has never slept with a man, a tactful compromise has to be made whereby another will sleep between the two, assuring Cúchulainn that his wife will remain virginal yet the superstitions of the warriors will be satisfied. Cúchulainn's insistence upon a virginal wife, separate from the customs of men, suggests again his link to the Otherworld.

13. A "fist" amounted to six inches, so forty-two inches were between Fergus's eyes.

14. This was the guesthouse where visitors would be put up for the night. It was one of the busiest houses in Emain Macha because Conochobor had visitors, petitioners, and guests throughout the year.

15. This was the armory, a storeroom where the warriors would place their weapons before entering the Great Hall for a feast. An armed guard was usually posted outside the storeroom to keep angry warriors from reaching their weapons after they had been drinking, when insults flew back and forth and old hurts suddenly were remembered with a vengeance. In stories concerning the warriors of this period, drink appears to have been the norm, but rage seemed to follow closely upon drinking, as in the *bacchanae* of Ancient Greece.

16. *Craeb-ruad* actually means "Red Branch." I believe this was Conchobor's private residence, and the Great Hall where the feasting was held was in the other "Red Branch."

17. The *In Caladbolg* becomes Excalibur in the Arthurian legends. In the Welsh language, Excalibur is *Caladvwlch*. The word apparently derives from *calad* (hard) and *bolg,* one definition of which is "lightning." In the Arthurian legend, Excalibur shines with the light of thirty torches and blinds Arthur's enemies.

18. The Ancient Irish believed that the soul was in the human head, not in the heart, where the soul was located by the Christians centuries later. The sacral nature of the head has been discussed in several tracts, such as Geoffrey Keating's *History of Ireland*:

It was the custom of that time that when any champion should battle another champion of great fame, he took the brain out of his head [sic] and mixed it with lime, so that he had it in the shape of a hard round ball to show at meetings and assemblies as a trophy of valour.

Diodorus Siculus records:

They [the Ancient Irish] cut off the heads of enemies slain in battle and attach them to the necks of their horses. The blood-stained spoils they hand over to their attendants and carry off as booty, while striking up a paean and singing a song of victory; and they nail these fruits upon their houses, just as do those who lay low wild animals in certain kinds of hunting.

They embalm in cedar oil the heads of the most distinguished enemies, and preserve them carefully in a chest, and display them with pride to strangers, saying that for this head one of their ancestors, or his father, or the man himself refused the offer of a large sum of money. They say that some of them boast that they refused the weight of the head in gold; thus displaying what is only a barbarous kind of magnanimity, for it is not a sign of nobility to refrain from selling the proofs of one's valour.

Livy records how a chieftain's head was placed in a temple by Bgoii in 216 B.C.

It appears that the Irish believed an enemy's head would give the taker protection from the magical powers possessed by the slain. In some legends the heads of enemies can talk, sing, and offer a prophecy. If a head was placed in a well, the water had a special magic. Perhaps the most famous story about a head is in the legend of Bran, where his head presides over feasts in the Otherworld.

19. This is a pun on the fighting skills of Cúchulainn and the rage into which he would fly, which left him unable to distinguish friend from foe. The most classic example is on the day he first takes arms and comes back to Emain Macha; the fury is so strong upon him that Conchobor sends out all the women of Emain Macha naked to greet him. When Cúchulainn hides his face in embarrassment, the men seize him and plunge him into three vats of cold water to bring him out of his rage.

20. Although "fold" is the literal interpretation of the word used, I believe what is meant is the triumphant death of a champion.

21. I believe this to be a reference to Cúchulainn's *gae bulga*, a magical spear given him by Scáthach. The spear never missed its mark and, when it struck, released darts into the body of its victim.

22. This is a difficult word to interpret, but I believe the modern *bailé,* for ballet, would be an excellent definition.

23. Perhaps this is a reference to the skill needed to slip past the guard of one holding a spear.

24. See my translation of *Fled Bricrend (The Feast).*

the tale of the pig-keepers
1. Their names mean "Bristle" and "Grunt" respectively.

2. The names mean "white-horned" and "brown" or "black" respectively.

3. Talon and Wing.

4. Whale and Shark.

5. Point and Edge.

6. Shadow and Shield.

7. Miser and Hoarder.

athirne and amergin
1. Ritual fasting was provided for in the Brehon Laws, by which one could compel justice from another by sitting in front of his gate or door and refusing food until the owner of the house paid for whatever fine had been levied against him. It appears, however, that Athirne fasted for payment as a way of extorting money.

2. This is gobbledygook.

3. "Red blackberries" suggests a surreal atmosphere or magic found in the Otherworld or fairy mound.

4. I suggest these are hazelnuts. The hazel tree was sacred to Druids, and from it magic wands were cut.

the questing of athirne
1. Ailgessach, "the Importunate," was an Ulster poet.

the battle of etair
1. I think the line should read "My eye is truly gone." The text could be a scribal error.

2. Red-eyed.

3. This is apparently an emendation by the scribe.

4. *geis:* Taboo.

5. Of the Crooked Neck.

6. Goll means "one-eyed." Cúchulainn was sometimes referred to this way when he went into a warp-spasm and one of his eyes would shrink deep into his head and the other bulge so far out that he looked as if he had one eye.

7. The One Who Stammers.

the battle of cumar

1. In other words, the countryside was apparently safe to travel in, yet unescorted ladies doing so would suggest that they were of "loose morals." The word used here is "women," which suggests that the idea of their virtue may have been tenuous.

2. The text refers to the land with the anonymous "her," suggesting the Ancient Irish anthropomorphized belief that the land was feminine. This personification is familiar in many cultures. The goddess most associated with Ireland is Ériu, who is represented as a queen in the sacred ritual marriage of *fled bainsi*, or the selection of the king. We have the story of Ériu's selection in the *Lebor Gabála (Book of Invasions)*. Erin is the anglicized form of the word.

Keating's *History of Ireland* gives a list of names that are both descriptive and eponymous for the land and indicates that more than one goddess had been identified with it. In addition to Ériu, Fódla and Banba were once associated with Ireland. Later Ireland was also referred to as Scotia, after the mother of the Milesians, the last invaders of the land.

The land was mystically at one with a goddess and was not seen as an inert object.

3. This could be an allusion to Tiberius. The other adopted son was Drusus.

4. There is a discrepancy in the date here; one source gives it as 3 B.C., while another dates it around 50 B.C.

5. This appears to be an intrusion by the scribe, suggesting that the story is much older than its principals. The reference to Conaire shows a certain corruption of the text as Conaire, the son of Mes Buccallah, does not play an important role here, although he does in *The Destruction of the Inn*, which is one of the oldest texts. This is one of the ambiguities in the story.

Although the Christian God is referenced here, we note that He does not make another appearance in the story, instead, a Druid attends to the business of the men.

6. In Sligo.

7. This is a vague reference, but I believe it is intended to be Eochaid.

8. In *The Yellow Book of Lecan* she is named Crofind, daughter of Artech U, the wife of Eochaid, mother of the three Finna of Emain and of Clothrand. In one birth the four were born. Onga, another daughter of Artech, was mother of Mumain and Ethne.

9. Men of Ulster.

10. *Ard-Rí:* High King.

11. The uncle of Conall Cernach and one of his chief enemies in the *Táin* Cycle.

12. *Fidchell:* A game similar to chess.

13. There really were no queens at this time although some kings did bestow like powers upon their wives. I use the word here only to designate her standing among others.

14. Mes Buachalla belongs in the Etain and Conaire Mór stories, most notably *Tochmaire Etaine* and *Bruidne Da Derga,* which I translated as *The Destruction of the Inn.*

15. The conversation here becomes extremely crude and sexual.

16. The Ridge of the Women's Sobbing.

17. The making of hazel beds suggests that this was an Otherworld place and brings the story from the world of reality to the shadowy world of the *Sídhe.*

18. The Hill of Og.

19. This would make them brother and sister, and the curse of a forbidden union now has fallen on Bres. Incest was not taken lightly in Ancient Ireland, and the Brehon Laws had strict bans against it. The curious question not answered here is Why didn't Bres know her before? One answer can be that he had lost a sense of what she was like as a result of his fostering or that she was born after he had been sent away. Still, the usticaion for this is rather vague.

20. Lugaid Redstripe is frequently mentioned as a contemporary of Cúchulainn, which again draws a question as to the dating of this piece.

21. Another contemporary of Cúchulainn.

22. This suggests the stone at Scone, where a man who would be king must place his feet in depressions that resemble a footprint of a large man.

the tale of mac da thó's pig

1. His name means "Son of the Two Mutes," satirical touch.

2. Another satirical touch given that Cúchulainn's name means "Hound of Culann" and he is frequently referred to as the Hound of Ulster.

3. Although Maeve was Ailill's wife, she was not, technically, a queen of Connacht although Ailill had given her certain powers. She had married Ailill because he was not the jealous type—a good thing as she was also known as Maeve of the Thirty Men a Night because she needed thirty men a night to satisfy her sexually. This, I believe, is a euhumeristic reference to her as a fertility goddess. The reader must remember, however, that Connacht and Ulster were enemies, and to gather such a hound for oneself would be to deprive the other kingdom of a chance to own it. Leinster apparently was regarded as a neutral ground in this story, although in the *Táin* it sides with the Connacht army in Maeve's attempt to steal the Brown Bull of Cooley.

4. Although he is not named at this point in the story, I suspect this is Mac Roth, who was Maeve's messenger in the *Táin*.

5. I have often wondered about this passage because we learn elsewhere that Conchobor and Maeve lived together as man and wife before she left and married Ailill. The tension here should have been extreme, what with Maeve's intense sexuality. Although the descriptives usually accompanying the mention of her name are conspicuously absent here, one cannot help but remember that she is often referred to as Maeve of the White Shoulders, Maeve of the Welcome Thighs, and Maeve of the Thirty Men a Night.

6. I don't think this is to be taken in a literal sense but rather as "poke his nose into the other's business." It is to be a bragging contest in which each warrior is to explain his feats at arms and whoever proves to have done the greatest will be given the warrior's portion. At such feasts the tenderloin, the best part of an animal, went to the greatest warrior. Usually a king would select one man as such, but in this instance there must be an accounting because two kings are present and for one to rule over the other would be intolerable.

7. His name means "Mournful Cry of the Hand," a colorful way of saying that a hand was lost.

8. Although Eogan is referred to as "king," he is not a king of the rank of Conchobor or Ailill. If a man owned a section of land, he was the king or landowner, what might be referred to as a "land baron" in other countries.

9. The phrase means "the yew-tree of the hound's head."

the violent deaths of goll and garb

1. This seems to indicate that they were either going over a pass or upon a mountain or large hill. The text reads *Athis Murthemni*, but there is no apparent place for this on the map.

2. Goll suggests "one-eye."

3. This would be Emer, Cúchulainn's wife.

4. Garb suggests "rough."

5. This seems to reflect the story of Beowulf and his encounter with Grendel.

6. This appears to be borrowed from the story of how Cúchulainn received his name.

7. Big Ford.

8. Goll's Ford.

the intoxication of the ulster men

1. These are the "stables for the horses of the Ulaid," still standing in a haphazard manner that suggests they could have been walls at one time.

bricriu's feast and the exile of dóel dermait's sons

1. I translated this as *The Feast*.

2. The reference here is to castrated rams who were raised for food. But the ram was a symbol for light as well.

3. Something seems to be missing at this point, for the narrative does not explain the insult or slight Bricriu has planned. From *Fled Bricrend,* however, we know that Bricriu planned to set Conall Cernach's wife at odds with the wives of Cúchulainn and Lóegaire Búadbach, by saying that each should have precedent over the other Ulster wives because her husband was the best warrior among the Red Branch. He told the husbands as well that each was certainly the one who should be given the "champion's portion" as his right. The resulting argument forced Conchobor to select one as the champion, but Conchobor recognized that to do so would cause ill

feeling among the others. Consequently, he sent the three to others to select the champion with hilarious results.

4. The hazel tree is used for magic wands; this type of mead suggests that it too has magical properties. But we must remember that all alcoholic beverages have "magic" if taken in large quantities.

the battle of the gathering at macha

1. I believe this indicates that the army that came from the Red Sea area had taken in Asian or what we would term "Asian," recruits, mercenaries, in fact.

2. The suggestion is that a satire was made against him and to keep the satire from striking him and being permanent, the cost was one eye. This is similar to one of the Norse tales when Odin goes to drink from the Well of Knowledge. The Keeper of the Well tells him he must pay an awful price for All-Knowledge. Odin says he is willing to do so, and the Keeper says that Odin must give the Keeper his left eye. Odin plucks it out and places it in the outstretched hand of the Keeper, who then says, "The secret to All-Knowledge is to watch with both eyes!"

3. This is a common enough story in all cultures. To keep men, warriors, or soldiers from falling back upon the knowledge that they could escape difficulty by simply getting to the coast and sailing away, commanders would burn their ships, thus committing their men to a "conquer or die" philosophy.

4. I believe a part of the story is missing here, for I can find no reason for this "detour" when the alien army has already landed in Ulster. Although there is no evidence of a lacuna in the manuscript at this point, the scribe may have neglected to include the reason because he did not know it, simply forgot it, or there is some obscure explanation for its deletion. This could, however, also be a mnemonic exercise by which the information would be given for memorization and the bard or poet-singer required to embellish the account. Strangely enough, we can see this practice as well in parts of Greek texts where the singer adds in the information that would be pertinent to a particular place.

5. The listing of these warriors indicates that Conchobor is calling all his border guards in to help repel the foreign army. That he obviously has so many upon whom he may call suggests that he is a powerful individual who would be close to an *Ard-Rí* (High King). A High King would rule all the provinces, but not to the extent that he would destroy the authority of the province king. The five provinces had agreed earlier that the High King would be elected from each of the five provinces in rotation. If the

High King was from Muman (Munster), then upon his death the next province would supply the new *Ard-Rí*. At this time, however, there was no *Ard-Rí* sitting.

6. I presume that "army" is meant here, because the fleet had already been destroyed.

7. This appears to be a reference to the Milisians, who came to Ireland centuries before when the *Tuatha Dé Danann* were in power. The Milisians planned to conquer the land, but the *Tuatha* suggested that the land was big enough for all to live upon it. They suggested that the land be divided in half and each tribe (clan) would live on the half apportioned to them. The Milisians agreed and said that they would take everything aboveground and the *Tuatha* could have everything belowground. The metaphorical suggestion is that the Milisians planned extermination, but the *Tuatha* agreed to the proposal and "melted" into the ground, where they joined forces with the fairies and sprites. In essence, they became a part of the land and what came to be known as the Otherworld.

8. By appearing to be older, they would suggest that the invading army was attacking war veterans. The deceit would give the Ulster forces an edge by making the invaders a bit cautious. This is a psychological approach to warfare.

the vision of ferchertne

1. The two hounds would be Cúchulainn (Hound of Culann) and Cúrói (Hound of the Battlefield or Hound of Kings).

2. The clan to which Cúrói belonged.

3. Kine: Cattle.

4. This is highly corrupt. The original reads:

atchī gin hūi nessa   cessa fri fiansa forbair
diasnad hériu ergair,   acciu 'sa hi *corgail*   atchiu.

the story of mac dareo's hostel

1. Note that previously he was the son of Cairbre.

the battle of rosnaree

1. This is understood because some stories name Cathbad as Conchobor's father.

2. These are identified with the Færoe Islands.

3. Sweden.

4. Although this sounds as if Conall Cernach was not involved in the great raid, he was there. This is an inconsistency within the text.

5. This is Cúchulainn's fortress.

6. Dinn Ríg was a hostel associated with the Otherworld.

7. The Brown Bull of Cooley was dead by this time, but the south Munster men did not know this.

8. This is Conchobor's refusal of the bribes being offered to him and the Ulster men if they would forget about conducting war.

9. This is a bit of bragging to offset Ailill, for Conchobor was a careful general and always was aware of the numbers on the field against him. He waited prudently until all of his force arrived.

10. He went the wrong way or else went mad in battle.

11. Whenever Conchobor was in great difficulty in battle, his shield would roar for help. Any Ulster man who heard that call was bound to go to his aid.

12. Hard-Head.

13. This seems to have been the *gae bulga,* although it appears from this passage that Cúchulainn had another magic spear.

14. The daughter of Conchobor.

the story of fergus mac léti

1. Of the Hundred Battles.

2. Of the Hundred Treaties.

3. Of the Yellow Lips.

4. As near as I can tell, one *muirchrech* is the maximum distance that a white shield can still be discerned onshore. This is the distance envoys might travel and still be under the protection of a king. Three *muirchrecha* would place her well out of responsibility for protection and leave her at the mercy of whoever came along. In effect, she is being cast outside the law and cannot come to the courts for protection or justice.

5. This appears to be a parallel to the story in the *Táin* where the sword of Fergus is stolen while he is making love to Maeve. The water imagery is a parallel to his death; he is slain while making love to Maeve in the water.

the cattle-raid of flidais

1. This story, *The Exile of the Sons of Uisneach*, is in my book *The Sorrows*. It is one of the "three sorrows of storytelling." A bit of uncertainty here suggests Fergus did not know if Conchobor had personally taken the lives of the sons of Uisnech or if he had simply ordered their deaths or they had been accidentally slain when he gave an order to seize them. This is a textual ambiguity among the three manuscripts.

2. The reference here is that Fergus found no honorable reason for the deaths of the sons of Uisneach. The line suggests that he believed their deaths had been brought about by Conchobor's dishonorable action. See *The Exile of the Sons of Uisneach* in my book *The Sorrows*.

3. Note that there are quite a few more individuals mentioned here than in *The Exile of the Sons of Uisneach*, where only three are listed.

4. Fergus is raiding Ulster. "Country" is not meant to reflect all of Ireland.

5. This line could well be translated "the black rage of Fergus," which would suggest a different concept: that Fergus's rule was so bad that Ulster began to miss the competent reign of Conchobor, or that Fergus's rage was so terrible that the province suffered greatly as he made it "pay" for its support of Conchobor in his deceit of the sons of Uisneach. There is a discrepancy as well in the text that has Conchobor being exiled for one year, but we have no way of knowing how or why this happened. We must remember that the kings of Ulster were voted on by the ruling clan and that Conchobor held the title of king through this election. This passage may indicate that Fergus, through his brutal rage, may have assumed the throne through force rather than through parliamentary procedure.

6. Fergus's inability to govern is seen in the story concerning Fergus and Nessa when Nessa volunteers to be a "year-wife" with Fergus if he will step aside so that Conchobor might rule for a year and thus gain the right of kings for himself and his descendants. Fergus, who needs seven women a night to satisfy him sexually, is well aware of Nessa's skill in the art of love, and he readily agrees. But when the year is up, the Ulster warriors, who have enjoyed unprecedented prosperity under Conchobor's rule, refuse to let him back on the throne. One of the reasons given is that Fergus was so poor a ruler that he was willing to sacrifice the land and its people to satisfy his lust. Fergus, who has a strange set of personal rules governing behavior, places honor above most things, but it is an honor that is strictly limited to his own perception.

7. *eric*: The honor-price or the pledge demanded.

8. This appears to be Eachtach, the daughter of Diarmait Ua Duibne in lays from *Duanaire Finn*. After Finn Mac Cumhaill refuses to help Diarmait when he has been gored by the boar, Eachtach rallies her brothers for revenge and wounds Finn seriously in battle. This, however, would place the story in the Finn Cycle and not the Red Branch or Ulster Cycle. The woman could, however, be the wife of Lug Lámfhota.

the colloquy of the two sages

1. The suggestion here is that by assuming the robe of the main bard or poet, another would be held in the same rank.

2. It is important to remember that the travelers went to the elf mound at Emain Macha, which suggests that they were seeking knowledge past what is given to man to know. The danger to mortal man is not in becoming educated but in seeking wisdom that he cannot use wisely. Although one would think that this would involve aesthetics and metaphysics, knowledge of the world beyond the mortal dimension is to be found in fairy mounds.

3. I believe this is a reference to *ailm* in the ogham alphabet. *Ailm* means "pine."

4. This could be translated as "churches," which would suggest that the transcriber had intruded upon the text by adding Christian references to the apocalypse.

the trouble of the ulster men

1. Although "raid" is used here, it clearly is meant to indicate that Cúchulainn is hunting.

2. These are games traditionally regarded as being similar to, but not exactly like, chess. *Fidchell* seems to have been more popular as it appears more often in other stories.

3. I suggest that this refers to the Otherworld. In *Táin Bó Cuailngé*, Maeve encounters a Fedelm when she returns from asking her Druid when will be the most propitious time for her to lead her army on the infamous Cattle-Raid of Cooley. Fedelm gives the prophecy that she "sees red," which Maeve promptly (and wrongly, as it turns out) interprets as meaning the Connacht men will emerge triumphant.

4. The speckled salmon indicates that it is a particular salmon, possibly the salmon of knowledge.

5. No lacuna is evident in the text. I suspect that this is an outline for the poet or bard to flesh out while telling the tale.

6. This is a strange reference to the debility of the Ulster men, which is regarded as having been caused by Macha when she is forced to run a race against the king's horses although she is nine months pregnant. It is interesting that this is one of the two stories that accounts for the name being given to the stronghold of the Red Branch: Emain Macha. The other story concerning Macha is that she lays out the boundaries of the fort by drawing them with her brooch. We seem to have a couple of contradictions here. As the dating of the stories is a bit tenuous at this time, one could make a case that these tales of laying out the boundaries of the Red Branch fortress were the originals and later joined to form the one generally referred to as *The Debility of the Ulster Men.*

the wooing of Luaine

1. The Great Hall of the Red Branch had been burned by Fergus, who reacted violently to Conchobor's betrayal of him. Conchobor had promised Fergus that if he traveled to Alba to tell Deirdre and Naisi and his brothers that Conchobor had forgiven them for running away (Conchobor had planned on marrying Deirdre, but she chose instead Naisi), Conchobor would not go back on his word. Fergus believed him, but Conchobor plotted to have Fergus invited to an ale-feast (which he could not refuse because of a *geis*), and during Fergus's absence Conchobor had Naisi and his brothers slain and took Deirdre for his wife. Many warriors of the Red Branch objected to this betrayal and left with Fergus for Connacht, where they went into the service of Maeve and Ailill.

2. Deirdre killed herself after Conchobor, enraged that she would not accept him as her husband after the death of Naisi, told her that she would have to serve as wife to himself and another. She threw herself from Conchobor's chariot and over a cliff in defiance.

3. These would be the Islands of Foreigners. The Isle of Man is included as well.

4. Of the Red Eyebrows.

5. Silver-Hand.

6. This seems to be a discrepancy if we remember that Naisi's brothers were slain with him at Emain Macha. See *The Exile of the Sons of Uisneach* in my book *The Sorrows.*

7. The Urgent.

the hostel of da choca

1. The other hostels were those of Forgal Manach and Mac Da Reo in Bréifne, Mac Da Thó's in Leinster, and Da Derga's hostel in Cúala. See my translation of *The Destruction of the Inn.*

2. The three names given here mean Oiliness, Fat, and Hatred.

3. A Man of Two Hostages.

4. This suggests a murderer or one who has shed blood. It also suggests, however, a place of slaughter.

A literal translation from MS.H.I.17 fols. 7b, 8a gives additional information about these hostels, which were in the Otherworld:

> Erin's six hostels without delay, which existed at the same time
> They refused not angry companies and were harmonious and hospitable to all.
> The famous Hostel of DáBerga in the triumphant District of Cuala, where Conaire fell by savage Aingcél
> The Hostel of Mac Dá Thó—strong noise, whither came the men of Erin: together they consumed the swine and carried off the hound Ailbe.
> The renowned Hostel of Da Choca, which was captured from the Ulster men and was a great hostel until Cormac Conloinges fell.
> The Hostel of Mac Cecht of the two high hands—there was no snake in Connacht, west was the house where there was no better hospitality.
> Blai Brugaid's Hostel of melodious fame, where dwelt fair-haired Celtchar's wife,
> wherein fell Blai Brugaidh by the hand of Celtchar of the Yellow Hair.
> The Hostel of great Forgall Manach, Lusk full justly;
> no one was unthankful to him, Emer's handsome father.
> In every Hostel was the custom that there was always a caldron that couldn't be moved
> which used to deliver at once the proper food to the person.
> The caldron would boil that food in its cheek
> that was enough for just that party.
> On a way of four sound roads every praised Hostel stood
> with four doors out from it where everyone could come thankfully.
> All Erin's men, even if they were very quarrelsome,
> would be at peace if they reached the six Hostels.

5. Fergus had given up the crown in order to have Nessa as his wife. Her son Conchobor was made king in his place. But it was also Conchobor who was the father of Cormac with his mother, Nessa, or so Maeve is suggesting here. This would be very scandalous indeed.

the battle of airtech

1. This is a bit confusing, because Fergus's wife is usually given as Nessa, Conchobor's mother, who talked Fergus into giving up the throne for a year, using herself as a barter. Flidais was a woodland goddess of venery and wild things. Her chariot was pulled by a brace of stags. Consequently, she is usually compared with Artemis, although she did not share that Greek goddess's chastity. The epithet *foltchain* [beautiful hair] is often used in reference to her. She had a magical cow whose milk could feed seven hundred. She is often referred to as the mother of the witch Bé Chuille and the lusty Bé Téite and sometimes, though rarely, of Fand, the wife of the sea-god Manannan Mac Lir. We do not know, however, her husband, although Adammair is sometimes given as her spouse. She is known, for the lusty affair she had with Fergus. According to stories, only she and Maeve were able to satisfy the sexual drive of Fergus, who usually needed seven women a night to sate him.

2. According to legend, Fergus suspected that she was about to betray him and drowned her.

3. Broad-Chested.

4. Chafer-tongue. This is the warrior who had a spear so eager for blood that it had to be stored in a vat of water.

fragments

1. The "arts" referred to were the rules for feasting that one could find among the Brehon Laws, which also stipulated what food and drink would be provided for each of the feasts. Such rigidity seems odd to us today, but we must remember that great value was placed upon honor and station. Where a person sat during a feast indicated his rank and the honor he had earned. The king's champion, for example, always sat next to the king.

2. I believe this is a corruption of Dubthach the Chafer-tongue, who was a hero but also a poet whose tongue was as murderous a weapon as was his famous spear. The absence of Fergus and Dubthach appears to parallel the story of the testing of the heroes in *Fled Bricrend*, in which the champions Laeogaire, Conall, and Cúchulainn are absent when the *bachlach* (similar to an ogre) makes his appearance at a feast to play the Beheading Game.

3. This is an odd comparison. I can only speculate that "camel" here suggests a reference to something larger than anything known in Ireland. This foreign comparison would invoke a feeling of mysteriousness and awe in the mind of the listener.

4. In fact, rushes are not white but green when used, and as they change color they are replaced. The reference is not to color so much as it is to the image of cleanliness. The Irish, at this time, were extremely hospitable and clean, fanatical about maintaining a respectable appearance. Whenever possible, they would bathe twice a day: upon rising they would wash hands and face, and in the evening before the final meal they would bathe completely in a "bath-house." See *On the Manners and Customs of the Ancient Irish,* a series of lectures by Eugene O'Curry, vol. II and III (1873).

5. When Lugh first appears at the court of the *Tuatha Dé Danann,* he announces himself in a similar but far more elaborate manner to the porter or gatekeeper. The suggestion is that these individuals are experts not in one thing but in all things.

6. White Stream.

7. Bodb's Fairy Mound.

8. The Anvil of the Decies.

9. Two Horns. The child was born with two horns on his temples.

10. Red-Side.

11. Son of Wave.

12. Macha's Fair.

13. Great Heart.

14. The Sun of Womanfolk.

15. Macha's Height.

16. The Monument of Aife's Only-Man.

17. The Swimming Place of Two Birds.

18. Rathen's Swimming Place.

19. Buan's Farm.

20. Black Trench.

21. *gáir*: Outcry.

22. A Horn-Casting of Ulster.

23. Bicne's Estuary.